MATH GIRLS²

FERMAT'S LAST THEOREM

$$a^{\heartsuit} + b^{\heartsuit} = c^{\heartsuit}$$

HIROSHI YUKI

TRANSLATED BY TONY GONZALEZ

BENTO BOOKS

http://bentobooks.com

MATH GIRLS 2: FERMAT'S LAST THEOREM by Hiroshi Yuki.
Copyright © 2008 Hiroshi Yuki.
All rights reserved. Originally published in Japan by
Softbank Creative Corp., Tokyo.
English translation © 2012 Bento Books, Inc.
Translated by Tony Gonzalez with Joseph Reeder.
Additional editing by Alexander O. Smith and M. D. Hendon.

Published by

Bento Books, Inc.
217 Tierra Grande Court
Austin, TX 78732-2458
USA

bentobooks.com

ISBN 978-0-9839513-3-9 (hardcover)
ISBN 978-0-9839513-2-2 (trade paperback)
Library of Congress Control Number: 2012918353

Printed in the U.S.A.
First edition, December 2012

Math Girls^2:
Fermat's Last Theorem

Contents

1 Infinity in Your Hand   **5**
- 1.1   The Milky Way   5
- 1.2   Discoveries   6
- 1.3   Odd One Out   7
- 1.4   Clock Math   9
- 1.5   Conditions for a Complete Cycle   15
- 1.6   Going Cycling   16
- 1.7   Beyond Human Limits   20
- 1.8   What Things Really Are   22

2 Pythagorean Triples   **25**
- 2.1   Rooftop Lunch   25
- 2.2   Rational Points   28
- 2.3   Yuri   30
- 2.4   The Pythagorean Juicer   31
- 2.5   Primitive Pythagorean Triples Revisited   32
  - 2.5.1   Checking Parity   33
  - 2.5.2   Trying Equations   34
  - 2.5.3   As a Product   36
  - 2.5.4   Relatively Prime   37
  - 2.5.5   Prime Factorization   40
- 2.6   Finding the Trail   45
- 2.7   Squeaky   47
- 2.8   Rational Points on the Unit Circle   48

3 Relatively Prime   53
3.1 Hidden Depths   53
3.2 Fractions   54
3.3 GCDs and LCMs   56
3.4 Making Sure   60
3.5 The Pop-In   61
3.6 Sequences of Prime Exponents   62
      3.6.1 An Example   62
      3.6.2 Taking It Up a Notch   64
      3.6.3 Multiplication   65
      3.6.4 Greatest Common Divisors   66
      3.6.5 On to Infinite Dimensions   67
3.7 In Awe of Miruka   68

4 Proof by Contradiction   69
4.1 Writing Proofs   69
      4.1.1 The Definition   69
      4.1.2 The Proposition   72
      4.1.3 The Equation   73
      4.1.4 Proofs are Eternal   79
4.2 Another Approach   81
      4.2.1 Parity   81
      4.2.2 Contradictions   84

5 Broken Primes   87
5.1 Imagining Numbers   87
      5.1.1 A Quiz for Tetra   87
      5.1.2 Defining Numbers   89
      5.1.3 On to Quadratics   90
5.2 Sums and Products of Complex Numbers   92
      5.2.1 Adding Complex Numbers   92
      5.2.2 Multiplying Complex Numbers   93
      5.2.3 $\pm i$ in the Complex Plane   97
5.3 Five Lattice Points   100
      5.3.1 A New Card   100
      5.3.2 Pigeonholing   102
5.4 Breakable Primes   106

6 Abelian Groups 119

6.1 The Accident 119

6.2 Day One 121

    6.2.1 Introducing Operations into Sets 121

    6.2.2 Operations 122

    6.2.3 Associativity 124

    6.2.4 The Identity Element 125

    6.2.5 The Inverse Element 126

    6.2.6 Defining Groups 127

    6.2.7 Example Groups 127

    6.2.8 The Smallest Group of All 130

    6.2.9 A Group with Two Elements 131

    6.2.10 Isomorphism 133

6.3 Day Two 134

    6.3.1 The Commutative Property 134

    6.3.2 Regular Polygons 136

    6.3.3 Interpreting Mathematical Statements 139

    6.3.4 Braided Axioms 140

6.4 True Forms 140

    6.4.1 Essence and Abstraction 140

    6.4.2 The Essence of a Heart 142

7 Modular Arithmetic 145

7.1 Clocks 145

    7.1.1 Defining Remainders 145

    7.1.2 What Clocks Really Tell Us 148

7.2 Congruence 149

    7.2.1 Remainders of the Day 149

    7.2.2 Congruence Relations 151

    7.2.3 Different Congruences? 154

    7.2.4 More or Less Equivalent 154

    7.2.5 Equalities and Congruences 155

    7.2.6 The Exception 156

    7.2.7 Crutches 159

7.3 The Nature of Division 160

    7.3.1 Math and Hot Chocolate 160

    7.3.2 Studying the Operation Table 161

| | 7.3.3 | The Proof | 166 |

    7.4   Groups, Rings, and Fields   167
            7.4.1   Reduced Residue Class Groups   167
            7.4.2   From Groups to Rings   170
            7.4.3   From Rings to Fields   174
    7.5   Mod Hairstyles   179

8   Infinite Descent   181
    8.1   FLT   181
    8.2   Tetra's Triangles   185
            8.2.1   In the Zone   185
            8.2.2   A Hint from Tetra   190
    8.3   The Journey   191
            8.3.1   Setting Out   191
            8.3.2   Atoms and Elementary Particles   195
            8.3.3   Into the Particles   196
            8.3.4   The Shores of Quantum Foam   199
    8.4   Yuri's Awakening   201
            8.4.1   Math, Interrupted   201
            8.4.2   The Playground   202
             8.4.3   Drinks with Pythagoras   203
    8.5   Miruka's Proof   209
            8.5.1   Wax On, Wax Off   209
            8.5.2   An Elementary Proof   210
            8.5.3   Final Pieces   214

9   Euler's Identity   217
    9.1   The Most Beautiful Equation   217
            9.1.1   Components of the Identity   217
            9.1.2   Euler's Formula   219
            9.1.3   Exponent Rules   222
            9.1.4   Negative and Rational Exponents   226
            9.1.5   The Exponential Function   228
            9.1.6   Staying True to the Equations   231
            9.1.7   A Bridge to Trig   233
    9.2   Party Preparations   238
            9.2.1   Solve M for Mystery   238
            9.2.2   Mom   239

10 Fermat's Last Theorem   241

10.1 The Seminar   241

10.2 Some History   243

    10.2.1 The Problem   243

    10.2.2 The Era of Elementary Number Theory   244

    10.2.3 The Era of Algebraic Number Theory   244

    10.2.4 The Era of Arithmetic Geometry   245

10.3 How It Was Done   246

    10.3.1 Back in Time   246

    10.3.2 Getting to the Problem   248

    10.3.3 Semistable Elliptic Curves   250

    10.3.4 Whetting Our Appetite   251

10.4 The World of Elliptic Curves   252

    10.4.1 Elliptic Curves 101   252

    10.4.2 Rational Number Fields to Finite Fields   253

    10.4.3 The Finite Field $\mathbb{F}_2$ 255

    10.4.4 The Finite Field $\mathbb{F}_3$ 257

    10.4.5 The Finite Field $\mathbb{F}_5$ 259

    10.4.6 How Many Points?   261

    10.4.7 Prisms   261

10.5 Automorphic Forms   262

    10.5.1 Staying True to Form   262

    10.5.2 q-Expansions   264

    10.5.3 From $F(q)$ to $a(k)$ 265

10.6 The Modularity Theorem   268

    10.6.1 Two Worlds   268

    10.6.2 Frey Curves and Semistability   270

10.7 Math Party   272

    10.7.1 Everyone Arrives   272

    10.7.2 A Zeta Variation   273

    10.7.3 The Fruits of Solitude   275

    10.7.4 Yuri's Realization   276

    10.7.5 No Coincidence   280

    10.7.6 Silent Night   281

10.8 They're Doing Math in Andromeda   281

Index   301

To my readers

This book contains math problems covering a wide range of difficulty. Some will be approachable by middle school students, while others may prove challenging even at the college level.

The characters often use words and diagrams to express their thoughts, but in some places equations tell the tale. If you find yourself faced with math you don't understand, feel free to skip over it and continue on with the story. Tetra and Yuri will be there to keep you company.

If you have some skill at mathematics, then please follow not only the story, but also the math. You might be surprised at what you discover. You may even learn something about the wonderful tale that you yourself are living.

—Hiroshi Yuki

Prologue

We count in a world of integers. We count birds, stars, the number of days until the weekend. When we're children, we count to see how long we can hold our breath.

We draw in a world of figures. We use compasses to draw arcs, rulers to draw lines, and we are amazed at the constructions that result. We run through the schoolyard dragging an umbrella, and turn to see a long, winding line stretching toward the horizon.

We live in a world of mathematics. God made the integers, Kronecker said. But Pythagoras and Diophantus bound the integers in right triangles. And then came Fermat... Ah, Fermat, and his silly little note. A problem that anyone could understand, but no one could solve. History's greatest puzzle—if it's fair to call a problem that took mathematicians three centuries to solve a mere "puzzle."

But true forms are hidden. Things once lost are found again. That which has vanished reappears. Loss and rediscovery, death and rebirth. The joy of life and the burden of time.

Consider the meaning of growth.

Question the meaning of solitude.

Know the meaning of words.

Memories are ghosts lost in the mist. I recall only fragments: the silver Milky Way, a warm hand, a trembling voice, chestnut hair.

So that's where I'll begin, on a Saturday afternoon—

CHAPTER 1

Infinity in Your Hand

Gauss's path was the way of
mathematics, a road paved by
induction. "From the specific to the
general!" was his slogan.

TEIJI TAKAGI
*Historical Tales from Modern
Mathematics*

1.1 THE MILKY WAY

"It's beautiful!" Yuri said.

"Yeah, more like jewels than stars."

I was in the eleventh grade. Yuri was in eighth. She's my cousin
on my mother's side, but she hung around my house often enough
that people mistook her for my sister. We'd been playmates since we
were little, and her house was just down the street.

On days when we didn't have school, it wasn't unusual to find
her lounging in my room with her nose buried in one of my books.
Today, it was a coffee table book of astronomy.

Vega, Altair, Deneb...

Procyon, Sirius, Betelgeuse...

At one level, a field of stars is nothing but a collection of points
of light, but there was something about the fleeting patterns that
enthralled us both.

"I heard somewhere that there are two kinds of people," Yuri said. "Those who look up at the night sky and try to count the stars, and those who look for shapes in them. Which are you?"

"The counting kind," I replied. "Definitely the counting kind."

1.2 DISCOVERIES

"So what's high school like?" Yuri asked, her chestnut ponytail bouncing as she replaced the book on my shelf. "Hard?"

"Nah, not really," I said, cleaning my glasses.

"These books sure *look* hard."

"Those aren't my school books. Those are for fun."

"Wait, the *hard* books are the ones you read for *fun*?"

"Learning isn't fun if you don't test your limits."

Her eyes ran along the shelf. "So many math books." She stood on her toes to read the spines of some of the ones higher up.

"Not a math fan?" I asked.

Yuri glanced back at me.

"I don't hate it, but...I definitely don't like it as much as you."

"Marathon math sessions in the library after school aren't for everybody."

"The library? Really?"

"Don't hate on the library. It's cool in the summer, warm in the winter. Plenty to read. Stick me in a library with a math book, a notebook, and a pencil, and I'm pretty much set."

"Let me get this straight. You do math. For fun. And it's not even, like, extra credit or anything?"

"I don't really need extra credit in math."

"And you do...what? Solve for x?"

"Sometimes. When there's an x to solve for. I also mess with equations, draw graphs, you name it."

"Do I dare ask why?"

"I dunno. The beauty of it, I guess."

"Beauty. In *math*." Yuri raised an eyebrow.

"You'd be surprised."

"Okay," she said. "Surprise me."

1.3 ODD ONE OUT

I pulled out my notebook and waved Yuri over to my desk. She dragged a chair up beside mine and took a pair of plastic glasses from her shirt pocket before peering down at the open page.

"You write like a girl," she said.

"That's not my handwriting. It's a quiz a friend wrote for me."

"Fine, your friend writes like a girl."

"I'll be sure to tell her."

Which number doesn't belong?		
101	321	681
991	450	811

"Doesn't look like any quiz I've ever taken," Yuri said.

"It's more like a game. Just figure out which number is different from the others."

"No sweat. 450, right?"

"Good. And why is that the odd one out?"

"Because it's the *even* one out. It ends with 0. All the others end in 1."

"Exactly. Okay, how about this one?"

Which number doesn't belong?		
11	31	41
51	61	71

"Huh. All of them end in 1 this time."

"You're looking for something else here. This one's still on the easy side, by the way."

"Says you." Yuri crossed her arms. "I give up."

"The answer is 51."

"What's so special about 51?"

"It's the only one that isn't a prime number. You can write 51 as $51 = 3 \times 17$, so it's a composite. You can't do that to the others."

"Somehow I don't feel bad for not knowing that."

"Give the next one a shot:"

Which number doesn't belong?		
100	225	121
256	288	361

"256," Yuri said, "because it doesn't have a pair. See how 100 has that 00, and 225 has a 22, and 288 has an 88?"

"What about 121?"

"Still has a pair. Two 1s."

"Okay, then how do you explain away 361?"

"That's the exception that proves the rule?"

"Nice try. The answer's actually 288."

"How come?"

"It's the only one that isn't the square of an integer:"

$$100 = 10^2 \quad 225 = 15^2 \qquad 121 = 11^2$$
$$256 = 16^2 \quad 288 = 17^2 - 1 \quad 361 = 19^2$$

"Again, not knowing proves I'm normal."

"How about a real challenge? This one took me a whole day:"

Which number doesn't belong?		
239	251	257
263	271	283

"Much more interesting than this problem is the fact that you could spend a whole day thinking about it."

My mother entered the room with two cups of hot chocolate.
Yuri beamed. "Thanks!"

"How's your foot?" Mom asked.

"It's fine."

"You hurt your foot?" I asked.

"Nothing big," Yuri shrugged. "Sometimes I get these pains in my heel."

"Growing pains, maybe?" my mother suggested.

"Dunno. I'm going to the doctor next week to get it looked at."

"Well, I hope it's nothing serious," she said, scanning my bookshelf. "You're over here so much, you should bring some of your own books. Something more...interesting."

"Oh, I love the books here!" Yuri said. "*And* the hot chocolate!"

"You staying for dinner?"

"Sure! If you don't mind."

"You're always welcome, you know that. Anything in particular you kids want?" She looked back and forth between us.

"Something healthy," Yuri said.

"But tasty," I added.

"And exotic!"

"But...with a Japanese flair."

"Why can't you ask for macaroni and cheese like normal kids," Mother sighed, heading back downstairs. "I'll see what I can whip up."

1.4 CLOCK MATH

"I was promised beauty," Yuri said. "These quizzes aren't cutting it."

"Okay, how about some clock math?"

"Clock math," she repeated, brimming with unenthusiasm.

"Draw a circle." I pushed the notebook and pencil toward her. She sat, staring at it. "You do know what a circle is, right?"

"Gee, I think so." Yuri rolled her eyes and drew.

"Okay, now pretending that's a clock, start from the 12 o'clock position and draw a straight line to the 2 o'clock position, then to 4 o'clock, 6 o'clock, and so on, skipping every other number. Make sense?"

"Sure."

"What happens when you do that?"

Yuri drew the lines.

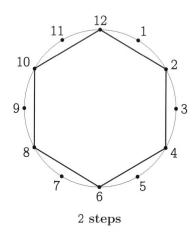

2 steps

"I got a sixagon, and I ended up back at 12 o'clock."

"A hexagon—you hit 2, 4, 6, 8, 10, and 12, and skip 1, 3, 5, 7, 9, and 11."

"Yeah," Yuri nodded, "hit all the evens, skip all the odds."

"Good," I said, "you know about evens and odds."

Yuri punched my shoulder. "Just because I'm not a math geek doesn't mean I'm an idiot."

"The jury's still out on that one."

Yuri wound up to throw another punch, so I put jokes aside and returned to the math.

"Okay, let's start a new clock. This time, try connecting every third number, 3, 6, 9, and 12."

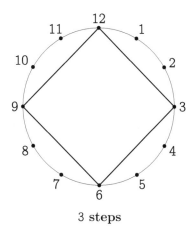

3 steps

"I got a diamond."

"Bravo. Next we're going to make the number of steps 4."

"The number of steps?"

"When we connect every fourth number, I'm going to call that setting the number of steps to 4. So what happens?"

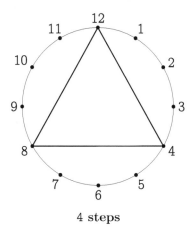

4 steps

"I connected 4, 8, and 12, and got a triangle."

"Okay, here's where it gets good. Next, try connecting every fifth number. In other words—"

"—in other words, the number of steps is 5. I get it, I get it."

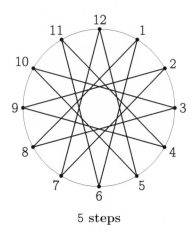

5 steps

"Oh, wow. Totally did not see that coming. I hit all of them."

"Right. You completely cycled through the numbers."

"After a few times around the loop, yeah. You miss the 12 a couple times, which lets you hit all the numbers before you get back where you started."

"Let's call doing that 'making a complete cycle.' So moving around the clock when the number of steps is 5 makes a complete cycle."

"Okay."

"So what happens with 6 steps?"

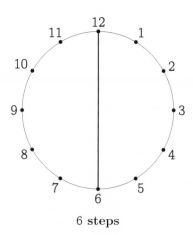

6 steps

"Boringest. Drawing. Ever."

"Maybe we'll hit pay dirt with lucky 7."

"Let's see... 12, then 7, then 2, 9, 4... Looking good."

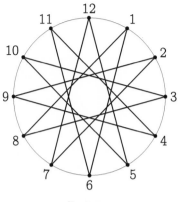

7 steps

"A complete cycle!" Yuri practically squealed.

"Have you noticed something?"

"Like what?"

"Like anything."

Yuri stared at the graph. She pushed her glasses back and tugged on her ponytail.

"What am I not seeing here?"

"Compare it with the 5-step clock. Trace your finger along the lines."

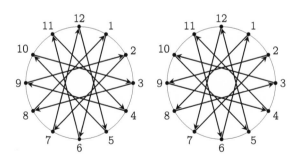

5 and 7 steps

"Hey, they're reversed. Going 7 steps is just like going 5, but backwards."

"Let's see how 8 steps turns out..." I said, reaching for the pencil. Yuri batted me away.

"Hands off."

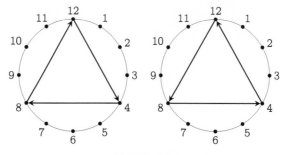

4 and 8 steps

"Cool," Yuri said. "8 is the reverse of 4."

Yuri hurried through a couple more graphs.

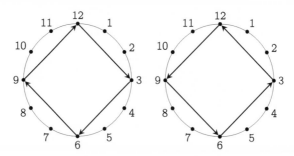

3 and 9 steps

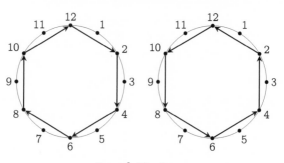

2 and 10 steps

"Y'know, this is kinda neat."

"Don't forget 1 and 11."

"1 step? Oh, you just don't skip anything. That's a complete cycle, too, I guess."

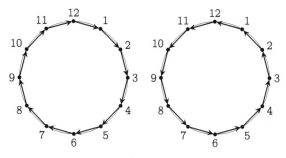

1 and 11 steps

"Poor 6 gets paired with itself."

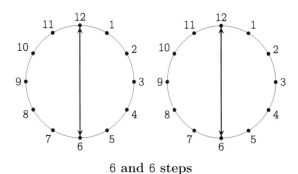

6 and 6 steps

"And that's all of them," Yuri said. "Huh. Who knew you could learn so much just drawing clocks?"

1.5 Conditions for a Complete Cycle

"So this is what you do in the library?" Yuri asked.

"I do all kinds of things. I was about your age when I first played around with this. I filled a whole notebook with clocks."

"Well then there's got to be more to it than just drawing lines."

"Sure there is. Like, when do you get a complete cycle?"

"We already know that. With $1, 5, 7$, or 11 steps."

"Yeah, but why *those* numbers? Let's write down what we know so far: "

Steps and complete cycles

$1, 5, 7$, and 11 steps result in a complete cycle.
$2, 3, 4, 6, 8, 9$, and 10 steps do not result in a complete cycle.

"I just said that."

"Sometimes it helps to write down everything you know. We want to look at these steps and see if we can't find a pattern. Using what you know to find a general rule is called induction. So what do you think determines if you'll get a complete cycle?"

I wrote a problem out in the notebook:

Problem 1-1 (Requirements for a complete cycle)

What property must a number of steps have to result in a complete cycle?

"I have no idea, but this is still kinda cool." She leaned in to whisper, "It's almost like I'm doing real math!"

1.6 GOING CYCLING

"Let's make a table and list the numbers we cycled through for each number of steps," I said. "We don't care what order we hit them, though: "

1	1	2	3	4	5	6	7	8	9	10	11	12
2	2	4	6	8	10	12						
3	3	6	9	12								
4	4	8	12									
5	1	2	3	4	5	6	7	8	9	10	11	12
6	6	12										
7	1	2	3	4	5	6	7	8	9	10	11	12
8	4	8	12									
9	3	6	9	12								
10	2	4	6	8	10	12						
11	1	2	3	4	5	6	7	8	9	10	11	12

"How do you read this?" Yuri asked.

"The column on the left is the number of steps. Everything on the right is the numbers you cycle through, smallest to largest." I pointed at the third row. "So this row says that with 3 steps, we make four stops, at $3, 6, 9,$ and 12."

"Okay."

"Does the table tell you anything?"

"Something about multiples?"

"What about them?"

"Mmm, never mind."

"No, go ahead. What did you notice?"

"Well, it looks like every row is a list of multiples of the first number in the row."

"For example?"

"Like, in the second row. $2, 4, 6, 8, 10,$ and 12 are all multiples of 2. And in the row you just talked about, $3, 6, 9,$ and 12 are all multiples of 3. So that means to hit all the numbers—to make a complete cycle—the smallest number has to be 1, like for step numbers $1, 5, 7,$

and 11. Because 1 is the only number that's a factor of all the numbers!"

"You're absolutely right," I said. "The rows for the number of steps that make a complete cycle start with 1, and *only* those rows do."

"So I solved the problem?"

"Not quite. The problem asks what properties those numbers of steps have. So you have to figure out what kind of steps will have a 1 in the list of numbers that they cycle through."

"Not sure I get it."

"Okay, let's call 'the smallest number you cycle through' the 'minimum cycle number.' You just said a step will give a complete cycle if its minimum cycle number's 1, right?"

"Right."

"So we want to know if there's some way to use the number of steps to figure out the minimum cycle number. Here, I'll write a list of the steps and the minimum cycle numbers you found:"

Steps	$\longrightarrow$	Minimum cycle number
1	$\longrightarrow$	1
2	$\longrightarrow$	2
3	$\longrightarrow$	3
4	$\longrightarrow$	4
5	$\longrightarrow$	1
6	$\longrightarrow$	6
7	$\longrightarrow$	1
8	$\longrightarrow$	4
9	$\longrightarrow$	3
10	$\longrightarrow$	2
11	$\longrightarrow$	1

"Do you see a way to go from one to the other?"

"Not really. It starts off nice—$1, 2, 3, 4$—but then it jumps back down to 1."

"Here's a hint. There are twelve positions on the clock, 1 through 12, right? Let's add that to the list:"

Number of values and steps	$\longrightarrow$	Minimum cycle number
12 and 1	$\longrightarrow$	1
12 and 2	$\longrightarrow$	2
12 and 3	$\longrightarrow$	3
12 and 4	$\longrightarrow$	4
12 and 5	$\longrightarrow$	1
12 and 6	$\longrightarrow$	6
12 and 7	$\longrightarrow$	1
12 and 8	$\longrightarrow$	4
12 and 9	$\longrightarrow$	3
12 and 10	$\longrightarrow$	2
12 and 11	$\longrightarrow$	1

Yuri coiled her ponytail around her finger while she thought.

"Multiples again? The numbers on the left are all multiples of the number on the right. Like, the fourth one from the bottom. There's a 12 and an 8 on the left, and a 4 on the right. 12 and 8 are both multiples of 4."

"And what does that tell you?"

"I've seen this at school... It's a common multiple! No, wait—the other one—a common divisor! The minimum cycle number on the right is a divisor of the two numbers on the left. Since it's a divisor of both of them, it's a *common* divisor, right? The minimum cycle number is a common divisor of the number of values and the steps!"

"Nice! But you left out one important detail."

"What detail? Oh, wait." She held out a hand to stop me from saying the answer. "I get it. It's not just a common divisor, it's the *greatest* common divisor."

"So when will you get a complete cycle?"

"When the greatest common divisor is 1."

"And *there's* the answer to the problem."

"Woo!"

Answer 1-1 (Requirements for a complete cycle)

A complete cycle occurs when the greatest common divisor (GCD) of the number of values and the steps is 1.

"In other words," I said, "when they're relatively prime."

"What's that mean?"

"What you just said—that their greatest common divisor is 1. Here's a formal definition:"

Relatively prime (coprime)

Two positive integers a and b are called "relatively prime" (or "coprime") if their greatest common divisor (GCD) is 1.

"So 12 and 7 are relatively prime," I said, "since their greatest common divisor is 1, but 12 and 8 aren't, because theirs is 4. So here's another way to answer the problem:"

Answer 1-1a (Requirements for a complete cycle)

A complete cycle occurs when the number of values and the steps are relatively prime.

"You learn something every day," Yuri said.

"Good for you, keeping up like that. Making me explain how to read the table and all. It's important to be sure you understand every step in a problem."

"Nah, I'm just dumb, so I have to ask a lot of questions."

"There's nothing dumb about asking questions. What's dumb is *not* asking them when you don't understand something."

Yuri grinned. "I think that's the first time I've been complimented for not understanding something."

1.7 BEYOND HUMAN LIMITS

"So, all this clock stuff... Is this really math?" Yuri asked.

"Why wouldn't it be?"

"Well, jumping around on clock faces, making tables... It feels more like a game. More than anything I've ever done in class, at least. I mean, just what *is* math?"

"Tough question. I guess math is a lot of things, but investigating the properties of numbers is a big part of it. That branch of mathematics is called 'number theory.' Drawing pictures, making tables, guessing how numbers will behave—it might seem like playing around, but this is really important stuff. Big truths usually aren't easy to see at first, so using tools like induction to go from the specific to the general is key."

"Interesting, maybe. But important? I've gotten by fine without it so far."

"Look at it this way: A normal clock only has twelve positions, so we were able to test all the possible steps ourselves. But what if you wanted to know what happens on a clock with a hundred positions? And if you were patient enough to figure that out by hand, what about one with a thousand? Or a million?"

"Your hand'd probably fall off."

"If you drew them all, sure. But therein lies the true power of mathematics—once you notice that the greatest common divisor of the number of values and the steps tells you everything you need, you don't have to draw anything. Just find the hidden pattern, and you can ride it to places you'd never get to on your own.

"Mathematics is a gateway. It lets you travel though time in a heartbeat. It lets you fold up infinities and hold them in the palm of your hand. That's what's so amazing about it."

"Not as amazing as how worked up you get talking about this stuff. You make my math teacher look like she's allergic to algebra."

Yuri laughed. "Speaking of which, you'd make a good math teacher. Bet I'd get better grades in *your* class."

"You'll probably already be graduated by the time I'm old enough to be your teacher... Probably."

"Hey!"

1.8 What Things Really Are

"So I never got the answer to that problem that took you all day," Yuri said. She turned back to the page in my notebook:

Which number doesn't belong?		
239	251	257
263	271	283

"Oh, that. It's actually pretty simple, once you hear the answer. All these numbers are primes, which means they're all odd numbers, since 2 is the only even prime. Do you see how dividing an odd number by 2 will always leave a remainder of 1?"

"Yeah, sure."

"The trick here is to divide by 4, not 2. I'll write it out:"

$$239 = 4 \times 59 + 3 \quad 251 = 4 \times 62 + 3 \quad 257 = 4 \times 64 + 1$$

$$263 = 4 \times 65 + 3 \quad 271 = 4 \times 67 + 3 \quad 283 = 4 \times 70 + 3$$

"Um...so what's the answer?"

"When you divide 257 by 4, you get a remainder of 1. For all the others, you get a remainder of 3."

"Okaaay... And why did you try dividing them by 4, exactly?"

"Well, when you're playing with integers, dividing them by 2 is a pretty common trick to check if they're even or odd, since the remainder tells you. Dividing by 4 does something similar, because it leaves a remainder of 1 or 3 for an odd number. Took me a whole day to think of that, though. I was crushed."

"Who wouldn't be," Yuri deadpanned. "Y'know, as nerdy as you can be, you're fun. I enjoyed that clock stuff. Let's do this again sometime." She paused in thought for a moment. "Hey, I have an idea. Why don't you teach me math? So I don't have to drop out of junior high and wait for you to become a real teacher."

"I don't mind teaching you, but only if you promise to think hard for yourself, too. Don't just assume you know things, make *sure* you know them."

"Ha! You sound just like the cat teacher."

"Sorry? Cat teacher?"

"It's this old cartoon movie my dad has. What was it he said... Something like, 'can any of you tell me what that fuzzy white streak *really* is?'"

"Now you're really losing me."

"He was talking about the Milky Way. About how some people used to think it was a river, but really it's millions of tiny stars. The cat teacher asks this kid about it, but the kid doesn't know. Turns out the cat teacher doesn't know either, not really. The kid rides on the Milky Way Railroad, and finds out the truth."

"Oh, 'Night on the Galactic Railroad.' I've heard of that."

"That's the one!"

"'Can you tell me what it *really* is,' huh? I like that," I said. "Always a good thing to ask."

My mother called from the kitchen. "Dinnertime! Come on down for some healthy, tasty, exotic, Japanese eggplant curry!"

Chapter 2

Pythagorean Triples

Then along comes the Taniyama-
Shimura conjecture, the grand surmise
that there's a bridge between these two
completely different worlds.
Mathematicians love to build bridges.

Simon Singh
Fermat's Enigma

2.1 Rooftop Lunch

"You okay?" Tetra asked.

"Wait...what?" I blinked, my eyes regaining their focus.

"Sorry," Tetra grinned. "Didn't mean to wake you."

Tetra and I had gone to the roof to eat lunch. There was a bite to the wind, but it felt good to be out under blue skies. Tetra was working at a bento box with a pair of chopsticks, while I picked at a muffin.

"Guess I kinda zoned there."

She smiled. "You had me worried for a minute."

Tetra was in her first year of high school, one year behind me. She was a small girl with short hair, big eyes, and a smile that rarely left her face. She was one of my "math friends." *I* was supposed to be tutoring *her*, but her unique take on things often meant our roles were reversed.

"Hey, did you get a card from Mr. Muraki?" I asked.

Mr. Muraki was our math teacher. He had taken a liking to us, and would regularly slip us index cards with all sorts of interesting math problems. They rarely had anything to do with our classwork, which made for a refreshing change of pace. We always looked forward to what he would come up with next.

"Oh, yeah! Completely forgot!" Tetra took out a small card and handed it to me. I read it at a glance; it was just a single line:

Problem 2-1

Are there infinitely many primitive Pythagorean triples?

"That's it?"

"Guess so," Tetra mumbled around a mouthful of fried egg.

"So you know about Pythagorean triples."

"Well, duh! Who doesn't?" Tetra traced a right triangle in the air with her chopsticks. " 'The square of the hypotenuse is equal to the sum of the squares of the sides,' right?"

I sighed.

"Er, *not* right?"

"That's the Pythagorean *theorem*." I picked up Tetra's notebook and wrote the full statement:

The Pythagorean theorem

In any right triangle, the square of the length of the hypotenuse c is equal to the sum of the squares of the lengths of the legs a, b.

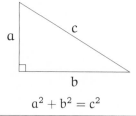

$$a^2 + b^2 = c^2$$

"So...they're different."

"Yeah, but now that you mention it, I guess you could think of a Pythagorean triple as the lengths of the sides of a right triangle, only where each length is an integer. Like this:"

Pythagorean triple

Three positive integers a, b, and c are called a "Pythagorean triple" if $a^2 + b^2 = c^2$.

"The definition of a *primitive* Pythagorean triple is just a little bit different:"

Primitive Pythagorean triple

Three *relatively prime* positive integers a, b, and c are called a "primitive Pythagorean triple" if $a^2 + b^2 = c^2$.

"So if you have a right triangle where the length of each side is an integer, then those three lengths form a Pythagorean triple. If the lengths are also relatively prime, then they form a *primitive* Pythagorean triple. Your card is asking if there are an infinite number of those."

"Okay... No, not okay. What does 'relatively prime' mean?"

"That their greatest common divisor is 1."

Tetra raised her eyebrows.

"Here, let me give you an example. $(3, 4, 5)$ is a Pythagorean triple. See?" I wrote in her notebook:

$$3^2 + 4^2 = 5^2$$

$$9 + 16 = 25$$

"$(3, 4, 5)$ is also a *primitive* Pythagorean triple, because the biggest number that evenly divides these numbers—their greatest common divisor—is 1."

"Okay, I'm with you so far. Can you show me a Pythagorean triple that isn't primitive?"

"Sure, just double these three and see what happens."

"So $(6, 8, 10)$? Well, 6^2 is 36, 8^2 is 64, and 10^2 is 100, and $36 + 64 = 100$, so yeah, this has to be a Pythagorean triple." Tetra paused and rested her chopsticks on her lips. "Oh, but 2 is a factor of 6, 8, and 10, so 1 can't be the greatest common divisor, which means this isn't a *primitive* Pythagorean triple."

"See, that wasn't so bad."

"I'm still missing something, though. Since $a^2 + b^2 = c^2$ will work for any right triangle, and you can just change the lengths of the sides to make an infinite number of right triangles, why *wouldn't* there be an infinite number of primitive Pythagorean triples?"

"You're right. You are missing something. Go back and look at the conditions in the definition."

Tetra stared at the definition. "Ah ha!" She jabbed the notebook with a chopstick. "Here's what I forgot. They all have to be integers. It's easy to set up a right triangle so that *two* of the sides have an integer length, but that doesn't mean the *third* side will."

"Exactly! The way to start working on this problem is to search for other Pythagorean triples like $(3, 4, 5)$, and see if you notice anything. Remember—"

"—'Examples are the key to understanding,' right?" She poked me in the chest with a chopstick. "I wondered how long it'd take to get to that."

2.2 RATIONAL POINTS

Miruka pounced as soon as I walked into homeroom.

"And just where have you been?" she demanded.

Miruka was smart in general, but pure genius when it came to math. Her hair was long and black, and she shunned contacts in favor of a simple pair of metal frame glasses. She was tall, and beautiful, and I felt an almost electric charge in the air just being around her.

"Um...on the roof?"

"Lunch?"

"Yeah. Lunch."

She leaned in, peering into my eyes to see what truths might be hiding there. I detected a hint of citrus in the air.

"And you didn't invite me?"

"Yeah. Uh, no. I mean, you weren't around. I figured you were off with Ay-Ay or something..."

How did I end up on the defensive here?

"I was in the teachers' office, handing in a report to Muraki. I guess he was expecting me; he already had a new problem waiting." Miruka handed me her card. "Weird one this time."

Problem 2-2

Are there infinitely many rational points on the unit circle?

"I guess a rational point is one where the x- and y-coordinates are both rational numbers? Numbers that can be represented as a ratio of integers, like $\frac{1}{2}$ or $-\frac{2}{5}$?"

Miruka nodded. "Obviously there are at least *some* rational points on the unit circle—$(1, 0)$ and $(0, -1)$, for example."

"Sure, the intersections with the x- and y-axes. That makes sense."

"But I'm not sure there are an infinite number of them."

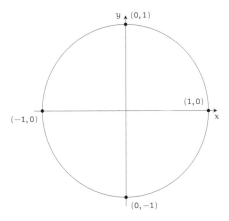

The unit circle and four obvious rational points

"You'd think there'd be an infinite number of others, though," I said, half to myself.

"What makes you say that?"

"Well, there are an awful lot of rational points lying around. Seems like it would be hard to draw a circle that missed them all."

" 'Seems like' won't cut it in math," Miruka declared. "Never trust your intuition when you have the tools to be precise."

"Fine," I rolled my eyes, "let's do this the right way then. Take integers a, b, c, d and represent a point as $(\frac{a}{b}, \frac{c}{d})$, establish the condition that the point has to be on the unit circle, and start crunching away."

"Hmm. That's one way to do it." Miruka turned back to the circle on the chalkboard. "Prime factorization reveals the integers. Ratios of integers reveal the rationals." There was a music in her voice now. "I wonder if there isn't some way to set up a correlation between rational points on the unit circle and an infinite number of *somethings...*"

The corners of her mouth turned up in a mischievous smile.

"But what I'm really wondering is..." she began.

"Is what?"

"Is who you were having lunch with."

"Oh." *Just when I thought I was safe.* "Tetra."

Miruka stared at me for a moment, her expression impenetrable. Finally she straightened, taking a step away from my desk. "For your honesty and bravery, sir knight, I bestow upon you this sword," Miruka said, brandishing a Kit Kat. I took it from her just as the bell rang for class.

Rational points, I could handle. *Girls, I will never understand.*

2.3 YURI

The next day after school I took a bus straight downtown to the hospital, Tetra in tow. The doctors had found something wrong when they checked out Yuri's foot.

We arrived to find Yuri sitting up in bed reading a book, her hair tied back with a yellow ribbon.

"Oh, you didn't have to come visit," she said, but her smile made it plain how happy she was to see me.

"How you feeling?"

"I'm fine. I don't know why everyone is making such a fuss." Her smile faded when she noticed Tetra. "Who's that?"

"A friend from school," I said.

Tetra held out a small bouquet of flowers she'd bought on the way to the hospital. "I'm Tetra. Nice to meet you." Yuri accepted the flowers without a word.

I sat down in the chair beside Yuri's bed. Tetra found another chair and busied herself looking around the room.

"Thanks again for showing me that clock math the other day," Yuri said. "It was really cool how you could make it around all the numbers if everything was relatively prime."

"He's a great teacher, isn't he?" Tetra said. "He's showing me—"

"And that curry!" Yuri interrupted. "It was *sooo* spicy. I drank way too much water. Oh, and that stuff about Fermat's last theorem you told me about after dinner—that was way cool, too."

Tetra shifted in her seat.

Yuri's mother appeared in the doorway, breaking the uncomfortable silence. "Look how handsome you are in your uniform. That was sweet, coming straight from school. And this must be your *girlfriend!*" The conversation only went downhill from there, and after a few minutes that felt like hours, Tetra and I politely excused ourselves. We were almost to the elevator when Yuri's mother caught up with us.

"You don't mind if I borrow your girlfriend for a minute, do you? Yuri wants to tell her something."

2.4 THE PYTHAGOREAN JUICER

We took the bus back to the train station and decided to drop into Beans before heading home.

"You were pretty quiet on the ride back," I said. "What did Yuri want?"

"Nothing major," Tetra replied, before spotting the perfect conversation changer. "Oh, cool! Look!"

Beans had installed a fruit juicer. Wire rails supporting a neat queue of oranges spiraled from its mouth. The barrista hit a button and the next condemned fruit dropped into the machine, where it was guillotined and squeezed, its juices streaming into the glass waiting below.

"Oh, I have *got* to have one of those," Tetra said, squealing with glee as another orange plummeted to its doom.

* * *

"*So* good," Tetra said, setting down her glass. She flipped her notebook open and slid it across the table. "Look what I brought—more Pythagorean triples!"

$$(3,\ 4,\ 5) \qquad 3^2 + 4^2 = 5^2$$

$$(5, 12, 13) \qquad 5^2 + 12^2 = 13^2$$

$$(7, 24, 25) \qquad 7^2 + 24^2 = 25^2$$

$$(8, 15, 17) \qquad 8^2 + 15^2 = 17^2$$

$$(9, 40, 41) \qquad 9^2 + 40^2 = 41^2$$

"How'd you find these?"

"Well, I started with $a^2 + b^2 = c^2$, and increased a one at a time. Then I just played around with b and c, setting them to whatever. I noticed something interesting—in four of the triples I found, c is just one more than b. Doesn't that look like some kind of clue?"

"That probably has a lot to do with how you're searching. When a is small, you're going to have a triangle with one short side, right? Like with $(9, 40, 41)$ there, you get this long, thin triangle. That means the length of the hypotenuse is going to be close to the length of the third side."

"Oh yeah, I guess you're right." Tetra cocked her head. "Too bad we don't have a machine that spits them out for us. A Pythagorean juicer! Just dump a bunch of triangles in, and wait for it to squeeze out a bucket full of primitive Pythagorean triples!"

I rested my face in my hands. "That would make this problem easier, no doubt."

2.5 Primitive Pythagorean Triples Revisited

I loved nighttime. With my family in bed and the world asleep, there were no distractions, no interruptions. I was free to sit at my desk, thinking about math. This was *my* time.

Class can provide some interesting insights, and there's much to be learned from books, but without some quality time putting pencil to paper, it's never enough.

That night, Tetra's problem kept bouncing around in my head: *Are* there an infinite number of primitive Pythagorean triples?

2.5.1 Checking Parity

I started with the list Tetra had made:

a	b	c
3	4	5
5	12	13
7	24	25
8	15	17
9	40	41

I noticed c was odd every time. Intrigued, I circled the odd numbers in the table:

a	b	c
③	4	⑤
⑤	12	⑬
⑦	24	㉕
8	⑮	⑰
⑨	40	㊶

Interesting. Exactly one of a or b is odd in every case. Coincidence? Or something deeper...?

I jotted down a self-posed problem:

Problem 2-3

Does there exist a primitive Pythagorean triple (a, b, c) where a and b are both even?

The answer came surprisingly quickly.

Nope, not gonna happen.

Since (a, b, c) was a Pythagorean triple, I knew that $a^2 + b^2 = c^2$. If a and b were both even, that meant a^2 and b^2 would be even too. Their sum, $a^2 + b^2$, would also be even, as would c^2, since the two were equal. But only even numbers can be squared to produce another even number, which meant c also had to be even.

So if you start with an even a and b, you'll always get an even c. But (a, b, c) is a primitive Pythagorean triple, which means those numbers are relatively prime. And if all three are even, their greatest common divisor will be at least 2—a contradiction! It was impossible for a and b to both be even.

I wasn't sure if that would help with Tetra's problem, but it was an interesting find nonetheless. Whenever I wandered through the forest of mathematics and stumbled across something like this, I made a point of writing it down on a ribbon and tying it to a nearby branch. When you get lost, it's good to have a way to retrace your steps.

Answer 2-3

There does not exist a primitive Pythagorean triple (a, b, c) such that a and b are both even.

2.5.2 Trying Equations

Now I knew a and b in a primitive Pythagorean triple couldn't both be even. But could they both be *odd*?

Problem 2-4

Does there exist a primitive Pythagorean triple (a, b, c) where a and b are both odd?

I decided to try the same approach as before, assuming a and b were odd and seeing what fell out.

If a was odd, then a^2 would be odd, too. Same with b and b^2. Then $a^2 + b^2$ would be a sum of two odd numbers, which would be even, meaning c^2 had to be even since $a^2 + b^2 = c^2$. If c^2 is even then c must be even, meaning it's a multiple of 2. Since c^2 was the product of two multiples of two, it in turn must be a multiple of 4.

I sat back and stared at what I'd scribbled down, wondering if this was getting me anywhere. Not seeing any obvious next steps, I decided to try building some equations and see where that led.

My premise was that a and b were both odd. That meant I could use two new positive integer variables J and K, and write a and b like this:

$$\begin{cases} a &= 2J - 1 \\ b &= 2K - 1 \end{cases}$$

I also knew these variables had to work with the definition of Pythagorean triples, which gave me my starting point:

$$a^2 + b^2 = c^2 \quad \text{definition of a Pythagorean triple}$$
$$(2J - 1)^2 + (2K - 1)^2 = c^2 \quad \text{from } a = 2J - 1, b = 2K - 1$$
$$(4J^2 - 4J + 1) + (4K^2 - 4K + 1) = c^2 \quad \text{expand}$$
$$4J^2 - 4J + 4K^2 - 4K + 2 = c^2 \quad \text{clean up}$$
$$4(J^2 - J + K^2 - K) + 2 = c^2 \quad \text{factor out a 4}$$

The $+2$ dangling at the end of the left side of the equation put a smile on my face—that was a remainder when dividing by 4, meaning the left side wasn't a multiple of 4. But I'd just found that c^2 *had* to be a multiple of 4. And that meant...*Contradiction.*

So my premise that a and b are both odd must be false, proving they could *not* both be odd.

Answer 2-4

There does not exist a primitive Pythagorean triple (a, b, c) such that a and b are both odd.

Combining this with my previous proof, I'd shown that one of a or b had to be even. In other words, a and b had to have different parity.

That meant there were two possible cases: either a was odd and b was even, or a was even and b was odd. I decided to let a be the odd one, and b the even one. Anything I proved under that assumption could always be proved for the other case, just by swapping the letters.

My stomach growled as my pencil headed back towards my notebook.

2.5.3 As a Product

I pulled the Kit Kat from Miruka out of my bag, recalling something she had said that day. "Prime factorization reveals the integers..."

I definitely wanted to get a deeper look into $a^2 + b^2 = c^2$, but how to apply prime factorization to it? Even if I couldn't manage a product of primes, *some* kind of product might be helpful:

$$
\begin{aligned}
a^2 + b^2 &= c^2 &&\text{definition of a Pythagorean triple} \\
b^2 &= c^2 - a^2 &&\text{move } a^2 \text{ to create a difference of squares} \\
b^2 &= (c + a)(c - a) &&\text{a difference of squares is the product} \\
&&&\text{of a sum and a difference}
\end{aligned}
$$

I had my product now, but it wasn't doing me any good. I couldn't claim that $c + a$ and $c - a$ are primes, so I was a long way from revealing anything.

Then I realized I was having a Tetra moment—I had forgotten the conditions of the problem, despite all that time I spent figuring out the parity of a and b. Since I said a is odd and b is even, c must be odd. And if c and a are both odd, that means $c + a$ and $c - a$ must be even:

$$
\begin{aligned}
\text{odd} + \text{odd} &= \text{even} \\
\text{odd} - \text{odd} &= \text{even}
\end{aligned}
$$

Since c and a were both odd, I had this:

$$
\begin{aligned}
c + a &= \text{even} \\
c - a &= \text{even}
\end{aligned}
$$

I introduced three new positive integers A, B, and C, and used
them to set up equations for $c + a$, $c - a$, and b, the things that I
now knew were even:

$$\begin{cases} c - a & = 2A \\ b & = 2B \\ c + a & = 2C \end{cases}$$

I worried A might end up a negative number, but soon realized
that couldn't happen, since a, b, and c were the lengths of sides of a
right triangle, with c the hypotenuse. A hypotenuse would always
be the longest side, guaranteeing that $c > a$, and thus that $2A > 0$.
Okay, let's play around with A, B, and C then.

$a^2 + b^2 = c^2$	definition of a Pythagorean triple
$b^2 = c^2 - a^2$	move a^2 to create a difference of squares
$b^2 = (c + a)(c - a)$	a difference of squares is the product
	of a sum and a difference
$(2B)^2 = (2C)(2A)$	substitute $A, B,$ and C
$4B^2 = 4AC$	multiply
$B^2 = AC$	divide both sides by 4

Now I had the definition of Pythagorean triples converted into a
product, with a little help from the positive integers A, B, and C.

I'd gotten a lot of mileage out of investigating the parity of a,
b, and c, but I was still wandering in the woods without a path in
sight.

*A square on the left, a product on the right. Which way to
head next?*

2.5.4 Relatively Prime

I stared at $B^2 = AC$, wondering what it was trying to tell me. Finally
I stood up and started walking in circles to clear my head.

On my fifth trip past the bookshelf, I recalled something I had
told Yuri when she was browsing my books.

Sometimes it's good to summarize what you know.

I went back to my desk and wrote down a list:

- $c - a = 2A$ $b = 2B$

- $c + a = 2C$

- $B^2 = AC$

- a and c are relatively prime

The last item gave me pause. *Do I really know that?*

I had included it because the definition of primitive Pythagorean triples says that a, b, and c are relatively prime. But just because the greatest common divisor of *all three* numbers is 1, that doesn't necessarily mean it would be the case for any *two* of them. For example, 1 is the greatest common divisor of 3, 6, and 7, but if you just looked at 3 and 6, the GCD would be 3.

After some thought I convinced myself I was safe in the case of a primitive Pythagorean triple, thanks to the equation $a^2 + b^2 = c^2$. Here's how I proved it:

> For a primitive Pythagorean triple (a, b, c), assume that the GCD of a and c is some number g greater than 1. Then there exist positive integers J, K such that $a = gJ, c = gK$. Then b^2 is a multiple of g^2, as follows:
>
> $$a^2 + b^2 = c^2$$
> $$b^2 = c^2 - a^2$$
> $$b^2 = (gK)^2 - (gJ)^2$$
> $$b^2 = g^2(K^2 - J^2)$$
>
> b is therefore a multiple of g, as are a and c. However this contradicts the definition of a primitive Pythagorean triple, which states that a, b, and c are relatively prime. The assumption that the GCD of a and c is greater than 1 must therefore be false, meaning their GCD must be 1, and thus that a and c are relatively prime. A similar argument can be used to show that (a, b) and (b, c) are likewise relatively prime.

Working that out was a relief, but then I started wondering about A and C. Could they be relatively prime too?

Problem 2-5

For relatively prime a and c where $c - a = 2A, c + a = 2C$, are A and C relatively prime?

My gut told me they were, but as Miruka would no doubt be happy to remind me, that wasn't good enough. I had to prove it.

Proof by contradiction had brought me this far, so I decided to stick with it. In this case, the statement I wanted to prove was "A and C are relatively prime," so I would start from the assumption that they *aren't*. That meant their greatest common divisor was greater than 1. I decided to again call the greatest common divisor 'g.'

I knew that $g \geqslant 2$, and since g was the greatest common divisor of A and C it was a divisor of each. Looked at another way, A and C were multiples of g. That meant there existed positive integers A' and C' that satisfied this:

$$\begin{cases} A = gA' \\ C = gC' \end{cases}$$

From the problem, I had this:

$$\begin{cases} c - a = 2A \\ c + a = 2C \end{cases}$$

I tried writing a and c in terms of A' and C', starting with c:

$$(c + a) + (c - a) = 2C + 2A \qquad \text{add the equations}$$
$$2c = 2(C + A) \qquad \text{clean up both sides}$$
$$c = C + A \qquad \text{divide both sides by 2}$$
$$c = gC' + gA' \qquad A, C \text{ in terms of } A', C'$$
$$c = g(C' + A') \qquad \text{factor out } g$$

The last line told me that c was a multiple of g.

Next, I tried finding an expression for a:

$$(c + a) - (c - a) = 2C - 2A \qquad \text{subtract the equations}$$
$$2a = 2(C - A) \qquad \text{clean up both sides}$$
$$a = C - A \qquad \text{divide both sides by 2}$$
$$a = gC' - dA' \qquad A, C \text{ in terms of } A', C'$$
$$a = g(C' - A') \qquad \text{factor out } g$$

From this I learned that a was a multiple of g, too. So my $g \geqslant 2$ was a common divisor of both a and c. But I'd started out saying a and c were relatively prime, which meant their greatest common divisor had to be 1. The contradiction had to be a result of my premise that A and C were *not* relatively prime, so using proof by contradiction I'd shown that they are.

> **Answer 2-5**
>
> For relatively prime a and c where $c - a = 2A, c + a = 2C$, A and C are relatively prime.

So now I had established that A and C are relatively prime. Another ribbon, though I still wasn't sure if it would be useful. I sat back and took a deep breath. My eyelids were getting a little heavy, but the forest beckoned.

2.5.5 Prime Factorization

Looking back through my notes, the equation $B^2 = AC$ caught my eye as a square that was also the product of two relatively prime numbers.

Interesting...

> ### Problem 2-6
>
> · A, B, C are positive integers.
>
> · $B^2 = AC$.
>
> · A and C are relatively prime.
>
> Find something interesting.

Not my finest problem statement.

Ah, well. It's late.

I realized I'd left the a, b, c of my original problem behind, and was now only dealing with A, B, C. It took me a second to even remember the original problem: Are there an infinite number of primitive Pythagorean triples? I hoped I wasn't going too far astray.

Miruka's unusual comment kept popping into my head. "Prime factorization reveals the integers."

I wondered what a prime factorization of A, B, and C would look like.

Something like this, I guess:

$$A = a_1 a_2 \cdots a_s \qquad a_1 \text{ through } a_s \text{ are prime}$$
$$B = b_1 b_2 \cdots b_t \qquad b_1 \text{ through } b_t \text{ are prime}$$
$$C = c_1 c_2 \cdots c_u \qquad c_1 \text{ through } c_u \text{ are prime}$$

I tried combining that with $B^2 = AC$ to see what would happen:

$$B^2 = AC \qquad\qquad\qquad \text{given}$$
$$(b_1 b_2 \cdots b_t)^2 = (a_1 a_2 \cdots a_s)(c_1 c_2 \cdots c_u) \quad \text{prime factorization}$$
$$b_1^2 b_2^2 \cdots b_t^2 = (a_1 a_2 \cdots a_s)(c_1 c_2 \cdots c_u) \quad \text{expand the left side}$$

Hmmm...

Writing out a prime factorization of B^2 puts it in a form where every prime factor b_k gets squared, meaning there would be an even number of each factor. Using 18^2 as an example, you end up with $18^2 = (2 \times 3 \times 3)^2 = 2^2 \times 3^4$, two 2s and four 3s.

From the uniqueness of prime factorization, which says there's only one way to do the prime factorization of any integer, I knew the factors on the left and right sides of this equation would have to match perfectly; every factor that showed up on the left side would have to be on the right side somewhere, and vice versa.

Out of the corner of my eye, I caught a glimpse of my second ribbon, the one that said A and C are relatively prime, fluttering in a chance breeze.

That's it! A and C can't have any prime factors in common!

A prime factor b_k of B couldn't be a factor of both A and C. Using $2^2 \times 3^4$ as an example again, I thought about how that number could be represented as a product of positive integers A and C.

If there's even one 2 in the prime factorization of A, then all of 2^2 had to be there. And if there's even one 3 in the prime factorization of A, then all of 3^4 had to be there. There would never be a case where a prime factor of B^2 was split up between A and C. That meant the factorization of $2^2 \times 3^4$ could only be one of the following four cases:

A	C
1	$2^2 \times 3^4$
2^2	3^4
3^4	2^2
$2^2 \times 3^4$	1

Since there had to be an even number of each prime factor, A and C *both have to be square numbers!*

Answer 2-6

If

· A, B, C are positive integers,

· $B^2 = AC$, and

· A and C are relatively prime,

then A and C are square numbers.

Alright, now that's just cool.

Since A and C are squares, I could represent them in terms of positive integers m and n:

$$\begin{cases} C &= m^2 \\ A &= n^2 \end{cases}$$

Introducing more variables made me cringe, but I was pretty sure I'd glimpsed a path out of this thicket, so I forged ahead. If I got lost, I could just follow the trail back through my notes.

Since A and C don't have any prime factors in common, m and n are of course relatively prime. So now I should be able to write a, b, c in terms of relatively prime numbers m, n.

Starting with $a = C - A$, I could say this:

$$a = C - A = m^2 - n^2$$

Since $a > 0$, I knew that $m > n$. I'd also said a is odd, which meant m and n had to have different parity.

Next, because $c = C + A$, I knew this had to be true:

$$c = C + A = m^2 + n^2$$

The last piece in the puzzle was $b = 2B$.
This one will take a little fiddling.

$$
\begin{aligned}
B^2 &= AC \\
B^2 &= (n^2)(m^2) \quad &&\text{from } A = n^2, C = m^2 \\
B^2 &= (mn)^2 \quad &&\text{cleaning up} \\
B &= mn \quad &&\text{safe to take root, because } B > 0, mn > 0
\end{aligned}
$$

From this, I got:
$$b = 2B = 2mn$$

Finally, I could write a, b, c in terms of relatively prime numbers m, n:

$$(a, b, c) = (m^2 - n^2,\ 2mn,\ m^2 + n^2)$$

I could also go the other way, starting with m and n and using this to create a primitive Pythagorean triple. I tried it out, just for kicks:

$$
\begin{aligned}
a^2 + b^2 &= \left(m^2 - n^2\right)^2 + b^2 & &\text{from } a = m^2 - n^2 \\
&= \left(m^2 - n^2\right)^2 + \left(2mn\right)^2 & &\text{from } b = 2mn \\
&= m^4 - 2m^2n^2 + n^4 + 4m^2n^2 & &\text{expand} \\
&= m^4 + 2m^2n^2 + n^4 & &\text{combine the } m^2n^2 \text{ terms} \\
&= (m^2 + n^2)^2 & &\text{factor} \\
&= c^2 & &\text{use } c = m^2 + n^2
\end{aligned}
$$

Some simple calculations would also be enough to show that a, b, c were relatively prime.

Examining parity, paying attention to conditions of relative primeness, and prime factorization had yielded a wonderful treasure—a general form for primitive Pythagorean triples. It had taken some doing to find them, but find them I had.

A general form for primitive Pythagorean triples

All relatively prime positive integers (a, b, c) such that $a^2 + b^2 = c^2$ can be written in the following form (note that a and b can be interchanged):

$$
\begin{cases}
a = m^2 - n^2 \\
b = 2mn \\
c = m^2 + n^2
\end{cases}
$$

where

- m, n are relatively prime,

- $m > n$, and

- one of m, n is even, the other odd.

From here, Tetra's problem practically solved itself. Since different primes would of course be relatively prime, you could just use an array of them to generate an infinite number of primitive Pythagorean triples. For example, using $n = 2$ and $m = 3$ as a starting point, just advance m through $3, 5, 7, 11, 13, \cdots$, and each distinct pair of m, n would give you a new (a, b, c).

I was exhausted, but that night I fell asleep with a smile on my face.

Answer 2-1

There are infinitely many primitive Pythagorean triples.

2.6   FINDING THE TRAIL

I met Tetra in the library the next day and showed her my solution—a Pythagorean juicer that would spit out a primitive triple every time you dropped in an m and an n.

"Oh, come on!" She practically shouted. "He expected me to do *that*?"

"Shhh!"

"Sorry, sorry." She lowered her voice. "Look, this is cool and all, but it's way over me. I'm never going to be able to sit down and come up with something like this off the top of my head."

"Nobody can. You just have to trudge along until you stumble across what you're looking for. Tell you what, how about I walk you through it, show you why I did what I did."

"Sure, I guess."

I squared my shoulders. "First off," I said, "the fact that we're working with integers, not real numbers, is a big deal here. Well only positive integers, strictly speaking. But anyway, the important thing is that there's no smooth continuity like with the reals. The integers are discrete. Lumpy.

"When you're dealing with integers, thinking about parity—whether a number is even or odd—can tell you a lot. It *only* helps with integers, though, since the reals don't have evenness or oddness."

I grabbed Tetra's notebook and wrote "parity" in it.

"When you have an equation in the form ⟨integer⟩ = ⟨integer⟩, you know both sides of the equation will have the same parity. It's also helpful to remember that adding two odd numbers gives an even number, and so does multiplying any number by an even number."

I added "prime factorization" to the burgeoning list in Tetra's notebook.

"You can also learn a lot from prime factorization. Factoring an integer into primes pulls it apart so you can see what it's built from. Also, if you have an equation in the form ⟨integer⟩ = ⟨integer⟩, the uniqueness of prime factorization tells you the factorization of both sides will be the same. That can be useful too."

"How do I do that?"

"Start by putting things in multiplicative form. The numbers that make up the product are called factors. Like in the AC product we were talking about, the A and the C are factors."

"Okay. How does having the factors help?"

"Well, you see how a single prime can't be split across multiple factors, right, because a prime can't be broken down any further. So if you have a product of two factors, a single prime factor will have to be completely contained in one of them. That's why I used the 'product of a sum and a difference is the square of a difference' rule to write this here as a product of two integers."

I pointed to the step in my notebook.

"Knowing how to write words as mathematical symbols is important, too. Like writing 'even number' as $2k$, or 'odd number' as $2k - 1$, or 'square number' as k^2. It takes some getting used to, but it's not hard. Remember how you compared writing math to writing an essay? Well, you can think of $2k - 1$ representing an odd number as a common mathematical shorthand."

"Oh, I like that," Tetra said, adding "mathematical shorthand" to the list herself. Beneath that, I wrote "relative primeness."

"Relative primeness is another important concept. If you know two numbers are relatively prime, you know they don't share any prime factors, which was key to solving this problem."

"At the end here, right? Gotcha."

"So you just chip away at the problem with a bunch of different tools. You keep looking until you find the trail leading out of the forest."

Tetra let out a long sigh.

"It's a lot to take in," I said.

"Yeah, but I'm getting there. One thing, though. You know how you kept making new variables, like an 'odd number' variable and a 'square number' variable and all? I'm *really* not good at that. Too afraid it's just going to make the problem harder, I guess."

"I know what you mean. Things can get messy if you don't, though."

"If you say so..." Tetra skimmed back over what I'd written. "So when I'm dealing with integers, I should check parity, try prime factorization, put them in multiplicative form, divide numbers by their greatest common divisor to make them relatively prime..."

"Well, those are all things to try, but no guarantee they'll lead to anything."

"I know, they're just ways to look for the trail."

"Right. And if you get lost, you can always backtrack and look for something else."

2.7 SQUEAKY

"This was a really interesting problem," I said. "Feels like there's still more to be found, deeper in. Something about the nature of numbers..."

"I know I've said this before," Tetra said, her voice somber, "but I want to thank you."

"For what?" I said.

"Showing me things. I worked hard on this problem. I really did! But you've shown me things that would have taken me forever to find, if I ever found them at all. The parity and prime factorization stuff is part of it, but it's more than that. I'm starting to get a feel for what it's like doing math with integers. They're kinda, I don't know, *squeaky*."

We both laughed.

"But seriously, I think I underestimated them. For some reason I thought they'd be easier to deal with than real numbers. But they aren't. They're just...different."

Tetra's cheeks flushed.

"When I'm talking with you, I always learn something different than what I get from class, or books. I thought I already knew all this stuff. Pythagorean theorem? Got it! Integers? No problem! But it turns out I hardly knew the first thing..." She shook her head. "No giving up now! I might still be deep in the forest, but I've got a good guide."

2.8   RATIONAL POINTS ON THE UNIT CIRCLE

The next day, Miruka and I were hanging out in our classroom after school. She had promised me a fun proof that there are an infinite number of rational points on the unit circle.

"It all depended on finding an infinite number of *somethings*," she said. "Everything falls into place after that."

She went to the board and picked up a piece of chalk. My eyes followed her hand as it traced out a large circle with uncanny precision.

"First, let's review the problem," she said. "We begin with a point (x, y) and a circle with radius 1, centered at the origin—the unit circle, which is defined as $x^2 + y^2 = 1$. The problem asks if there are an infinite number of rational points on the circle. In other words, if there are an infinite number of rational solutions to $x^2 + y^2 = 1$.

"Start off drawing a line ℓ passing though point $P(-1, 0)$ with slope t:"

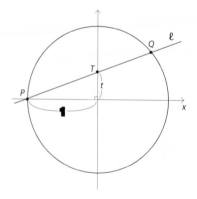

"Since ℓ's slope is t, it passes through $T(0, t)$, and its equation is:"

$$y = tx + t$$

"If we ignore the case where ℓ is tangent to the circle at P, we know it has to intersect the circle at some point other than P. Let's call that point Q. We can figure out Q's coordinates in terms of t by solving this system of equations, since the solution is their intersection:"

$$\begin{cases} x^2 + y^2 = 1 & \text{equation for the circle} \\ y = tx + t & \text{equation for } \ell \end{cases}$$

"Okay, let's solve it:"

$$\begin{aligned} x^2 + y^2 &= 1 & &\text{equation for the circle} \\ x^2 + (tx + t)^2 &= 1 & &\text{substituted } y = tx + t \\ x^2 + t^2x^2 + 2t^2x + t^2 &= 1 & &\text{expanded} \\ x^2 + t^2x^2 + 2t^2x + t^2 - 1 &= 0 & &\text{moved the 1} \\ (t^2 + 1)x^2 + 2t^2x + t^2 - 1 &= 0 & &\text{factored out } x^2 \end{aligned}$$

"Nice," I said. "We know that $t^2 + 1 \neq 0$, so it's a quadratic equation now. We can just solve it using the quadratic formula."

"We could, but we already know that $x = -1$ is a solution, since it's the x-coordinate of the point $P(-1, 0)$, so what's the point? Let's factor out that solution, an $x + 1$, instead:"

$$(x + 1) \cdot \left((t^2 + 1)x + (t^2 - 1)\right) = 0$$

"In other words, we have this:"

$$x + 1 = 0 \quad \text{or} \quad (t^2 + 1)x + (t^2 - 1) = 0$$

"Now we've got x in terms of t:"

$$x = -1, \quad \frac{1 - t^2}{1 + t^2}$$

"We can also write y in terms of t, using the equation for a line. We know $(x, y) = (-1, 0)$ isn't Q, so we only need to pay attention to $x = \frac{1-t^2}{1+t^2}$:"

$$y = tx + t$$
$$= t\left(\frac{1-t^2}{1+t^2}\right) + t$$
$$= \frac{t(1-t^2)}{1+t^2} + t$$
$$= \frac{t(1-t^2)}{1+t^2} + \frac{t(1+t^2)}{1+t^2}$$
$$= \frac{t(1-t^2) + t(1+t^2)}{1+t^2}$$
$$= \frac{2t}{1+t^2}$$

"So now we have the coordinates of Q:"

$$\left(\frac{1-t^2}{1+t^2}, \frac{2t}{1+t^2}\right)$$

"Here's where the cool trick comes. Ready?"

"Fire away."

"Remember this point T on the y-axis? How its y-coordinate is t?"

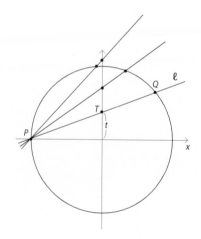

"Sure."

"See how Q's coordinates are just combinations of basic arithmetic operations on t?"

"Yeah. So?"

" 'So?' If you perform basic arithmetic on a rational number, you're going to get another rational number back. Which means—?"

"—that if you make t a rational number, Q will be a rational point. Right."

"Since there are an infinite number of rational numbers we can let t be, and since every one will result in a different point Q, we have our answer."

Answer 2-2

There are infinitely many rational points on the unit circle.

"Huh, pretty slick," I said.

Miruka looked at me, plainly expecting something.

"What?"

"You still don't see it?"

"See what?"

"Wow, you're dense today. *Tetra's card.* Divide the Pythagorean theorem through by c^2. What do you get?"

$$\left(\frac{a}{c}\right)^2 + \left(\frac{b}{c}\right)^2 = 1$$

"Oh, cool! $(x, y) = (\frac{a}{c}, \frac{b}{c})$ is a solution to $x^2 + y^2 = 1$. You can squeeze a unit circle out of the Pythagorean theorem with this!"

"The rational points on a unit circle, at least. So there's a different rational point $(\frac{a}{c}, \frac{b}{c})$ for each primitive Pythagorean triple. Saying there are an infinite number of primitive Pythagorean triples and that there are an infinite number of rational points on the unit circle is basically the same thing. The two cards are basically *the same problem!*"

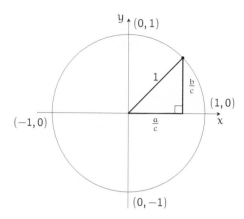

**The relation between the unit circle and Pythagorean
triples**

My jaw dropped.

Miruka shook her head. "You're slipping."

I had seen both cards, but Tetra's card had been all about integers, and Miruka's about rational points. Apparently that's all it took to throw me off—it never occurred to me that the problems might be related.

"Yeah, I shoulda caught that."

"Certainly not the first time Muraki's had something up his sleeve. Finding solutions to an equation is pure algebra. Playing with circles is straight out of geometry." She looked up at me for a long moment before concluding, "I guess he wanted to show us a bridge between the two."

CHAPTER 3

Relatively Prime

Hear us, O Mathematicians of the
World! Let us not wait any longer! We
can make many formulas clearer by
adopting a new notation now! Let us
agree to write '$m \perp n$' and to say "m is
prime to n," if m and n are relatively
prime.

GRAHAM, KNUTH, AND PATASHNIK
Concrete Mathematics

3.1 HIDDEN DEPTHS

"Hey, what's up!" Yuri shouted as she came hobbling in on her crutches. Saturday morning sunshine flooded my room.

"Not much. How's the foot?"

"The operation was over before I knew it. Yay, anesthesia. Just a little cut and a lot of bone grinding. The vibration was the worst part—I can still feel the shaking. Got a cool X-ray as a souvenir, at least."

Yuri propped her crutches against the wall and sat in a chair.

"Sure you should be walking around so soon?"

"That's what crutches are for. Besides, I wanted to talk to you about something. I've decided I really do want you to teach me math."

"Why the sudden interest?"

"Remember the other day, when we were talking about the clock stuff? Greatest common divisors, all that? I should have seen that answer sooner. I mean, I know I might not be as good at math as some people, but I've studied *that*. And I thought I understood it. But after talking, I realize I don't. I want to get to where I *really* understand this stuff."

"Huh, that's funny."

"I'm not trying to be funny. I'm serious."

"No, I just meant Tetra, the girl who came with me to the hospital, told me the same thing once."

"Oh, her. Right."

"Anyway, I know how you feel. Take multiples, for example, or divisors. Anyone your age probably knows the multiples of two are $2, 4, 6, 8, 10...$ And just a little bit of thought would get you the divisors of 12. So on the surface that stuff seems really simple, but there's a lot more to it."

"You're telling me."

"Multiples, divisors, prime numbers... All those things have simple definitions, but the math that pops out is deep. I mean, *really* deep. Number theorists are still doing cutting-edge research with prime numbers."

"Seriously? That stuff isn't all figured out already?"

"Not everything. You could start with what you learned about the primes in school, then follow the implications all the way up to the latest research. Of course, there'd be a lot to learn on the way."

3.2 FRACTIONS

I took out a notebook, and Yuri scooted over to my desk. She pulled her glasses out of her pocket and put them on. Her ponytail flashed gold in the sunlight.

"How are you with fractions?" I asked.

"Okay, I guess."

"Can you show me how to add two fractions? Something like this?"

$$\frac{1}{6} + \frac{1}{10}$$

"Sure, no prob:"

$$\frac{1}{6} + \frac{1}{10} = \frac{1 \times 5}{6 \times 5} + \frac{1 \times 3}{10 \times 3} \qquad \text{find common denominators}$$

$$= \frac{5}{30} + \frac{3}{30} \qquad \text{common denominators}$$

$$= \frac{5 + 3}{30} \qquad \text{combine}$$

$$= \frac{8}{30} \qquad \text{add}$$

$$= \frac{4}{15} \qquad \text{reduce}$$

"Did I get it?"

"Perfect," I said. "You find common denominators, add the numerators, then reduce. See how you used the least common multiple to get like denominators, and the greatest common divisor when you reduced?"

"I did?"

"Sure. If you wrote out the multiples of 6 and 10, then looked for the first number that's in both lists, that's the least common multiple:"

multiples of 6	6	12	18	24	(30)	36	⋯
multiples of 10	10	20	(30)	40	50	60	⋯

"If you listed the divisors of 8 and 30, then looked for the biggest number that's in both lists, that's the greatest common divisor—2, in this case:"

divisors of 8	1	(2)	4	8				
divisors of 30	1	(2)	3	5	6	10	15	30

"That's why you divided the numerator and the denominator by 2 to reduce:"

$$\frac{1}{6} + \frac{1}{10} = \frac{5}{30} + \frac{3}{30} \qquad \text{common denominator} = \text{LCM}$$

$$= \frac{8}{30}$$

$$= \frac{4}{15} \qquad \text{divide both by GCD to reduce}$$

"Pop quiz: What's the relationship between 4 and 15 in the $\frac{4}{15}$ there?"

"No clue."

"Don't strain yourself thinking too hard."

"But I never learned that!"

"You have. We did it together."

"We did? When?"

"When we talked about relatively prime numbers. Numbers like 4 and 15. You reduced to that fraction by dividing 8 and 30 by their greatest common factor, 2. Once you've done that, the greatest common factor of the resulting numbers is 1. Remember how we talked about numbers like that? How we call them relatively prime?"

"So reducing a fraction means to make its numerator and denominator relatively prime?"

"It does. A reduced fraction is said to be in 'lowest terms' because the numerator and the denominator can't go any lower and still be the same fraction. Dividing two numbers by their greatest common divisor to put them in lowest terms is a pretty common trick, so you'll want to get used to it."

"Cool. I'm learning even when I don't know I'm learning."

3.3   GCDs and LCMs

"Let's do some work with greatest common divisors and least common multiples," I said.

I wrote a problem in the notebook:

Problem 3-1

For positive integers a, b with greatest common divisor G and least common multiple L, describe $a \times b$ in terms of G and L.

"Too hard," Yuri said.

"If you want me to teach you, you're going to have to do better than that. At least give it a shot."

"But I've never done anything like this!"

"Sounds like a maximum learning opportunity to me. Let's walk through this one together. When you're faced with a complex problem like this, it's a good idea to try plugging some numbers in to get a feel for things. Why don't you try setting a and b to something and see what happens?"

"Okay," Yuri sighed. "I'll let $a = 1$ and $b = 1$, then. So $1 \times 1 = 1$, and their greatest common divisor is 1, so $G = 1$. Their least common multiple is 1, too, so $L = 1$. Next, uh... I'm not sure. Too many 1s."

"Well, first off you'll never work out a problem like this in your head. You need to write stuff down. Something like this:"

a	b	$a \times b$	G	L
1	1	1	1	1

"Too much work," Yuri said.

"Less work than trying to juggle everything in your head. And about those numbers—you aren't going to learn much from $a = 1$, $b = 1$. Choosing the smallest integer—especially for both variables—isn't going to make things easier for you. The opposite, actually. If you want to get anywhere, you should choose two different, slightly larger numbers. Maybe something like $a = 18$ and $b = 24$."

"Alright, fine. Let's see..."

$$a = 18 = 2 \times 3 \times 3$$
$$b = 24 = 2 \times 2 \times 2 \times 3$$

"Prime factorization," I said. "I'm impressed."

"This is how we did it in school. If you're looking for the greatest common divisor then you want the numbers that are in both, right? They both have a 2, and they both have a 3, so the greatest common divisor is $2 \times 3 = 6$."

"So we know $G = 6$, then. What about the least common multiple?"

"You want the numbers that are in at least one of them, three 2s and two 3s. So the least common multiple is $2 \times 2 \times 2 \times 3 \times 3$, which is, uh..." Yuri jotted down a calculation in the margin. "72."

"Right. So L = 72. Let's add that to our table:"

a	b	a × b	G	L
1	1	1	1	1
18	24	432	6	72

"Do you see how to make a 432 out of 6 and 72?" I asked.

"Multiply them, maybe? So $a \times b$ is the same as $G \times L$?"

"Probably worth trying the multiplication to make sure."

$$a \times b = 18 \times 24 = 432$$
$$G \times L = \ \ 6 \times 72 = 432$$

"Told ya so," she said.

"Still worth making sure."

Yuri shrugged. "Whatever you say, Teach."

"Anyway, it looks like $a \times b = G \times L$ is the answer we were after. Wanna see a better explanation of why?"

"Sure."

"Then let's write out the prime factorizations of 18 and 24 one more time, but with the formatting a little different:"

$$a \ = \qquad\qquad\quad 2 \ \times \ 3 \ \times \ 3$$
$$b \ = \ 2 \ \times \ 2 \ \times \ 2 \ \times \ 3$$

"Now let's do the same thing for G and L, which were 6 and 72:"

$$G \ = \qquad\qquad\quad 2 \ \times \ 3$$
$$L \ = \ 2 \ \times \ 2 \ \times \ 2 \ \times \ 3 \ \times \ 3$$

"See?" I said. "Obvious why they're the same, right?"

"Nope."

"C'mon. You said it yourself—when you want the greatest common divisor you look for the numbers in both, and when you want the least common multiple you look for the numbers in at least one of them. Which 'numbers' did you mean when you said that?"

"The 2s and the 3s."

"Right. The prime factors, in other words. Go ahead and say it—'the prime factors.'"

"'The prime factors.'" Yuri folded her arms. "Um, why did I just say that?"

"Because when you learn something new, it's easier to remember if you say it out loud."

"So what's with the tables?"

"If you line them up like this, you can see that when you multiply $a \times b$ and $G \times L$, all you're doing is changing how you group things. The prime factors getting multiplied are the same in each."

$$
\begin{array}{rcccccccc}
a & = & & & 2 & \times & 3 & \times & 3 \\
b & = & 2 & \times & 2 & \times & 2 & \times & 3 \\
\hline
a \times b & = & 2 & \times & 2 & \times & 2^2 & \times & 3^2 & \times & 3 \\
\\
G & = & & & 2 & \times & 3 \\
L & = & 2 & \times & 2 & \times & 2 & \times & 3 & \times & 3 \\
\hline
G \times L & = & 2 & \times & 2 & \times & 2^2 & \times & 3^2 & \times & 3
\end{array}
$$

"Okay, sure, I guess that makes sense. It's just a difference in the order you multiply the numbers by."

"The *numbers*?"

"Excuse me—the *prime factors*."

"Better. Don't forget, prime factorization means factoring a positive integer into primes. A friend of mine said it 'reveals the integers,' and she's right—this is important stuff."

"*Now* you tell me. Where were you when I was ignoring this in school?"

"As long as you're not ignoring it now."

"Yes, ma'am."

I rolled my eyes. "So you're sure you're good with the relationship between $a \times b$ and $G \times L$ now, right? For $a \times b$, you're multiplying together each prime factor of a and b. For $G \times L$, G is 'the product of all the prime factors that appear in both a and b', and L is 'the product of all the prime factors in both a and b, getting rid of duplicates.'"

Answer 3-1

For positive integers a, b with greatest common divisor G and least common multiple L, $a \times b = G \times L$.

"Another pop quiz," I said. "Say the prime factorization of two numbers a and b looked like this:"

$$a = 2 \times 3^4 \qquad\qquad \times\ 11$$
$$b = \qquad\qquad 5^2 \times 7^2$$

"Tell me what the relationship is between a and b."

Yuri thought for a moment. "They don't have any in common."

"Any *what* in common?"

"Prime factors! Sheesh!"

"If only there were a name for numbers like that..."

"Yeah, yeah, a and b are relatively prime. Are you happy?"

"Only if you learned something."

3.4 MAKING SURE

"All this brain work requires sugar." Yuri pointed at the jar of candy I kept on my desk. "Gimme."

I pulled out a candy and offered it to her. She wrinkled her nose.

"Mint. Yuck. I want lemon." I passed her the jar, and Yuri went on as she unwrapped a candy in a neon-yellow wrapper. "You're pretty good at making sure I'm keeping up before you move ahead. I mean, teachers always ask if everyone's getting stuff, but you can tell they just want to plow on through. You'd think the blank stares would be a clue.

"Which is why I want you to teach me," she continued. "You don't get mad when I don't understand something, even when I thought I did. You just let me bang my head against stuff until I get it. That's pretty cool."

"Whatever it takes. Ready for the next one?"

"Bio break first."

"Sure. You know where it is."

"I do, but I'm gonna need some help getting there." She gestured towards her crutches.

"Ah, right. Sorry."

I offered my hand and pulled her to her feet. She grabbed on to my shoulder for support.

"You're heavier than you look."

She shot me a scathing look. "You may be good at math, but you've got a lot to learn about girls."

As we stumbled into the hallway, we almost ran into Miruka.

3.5 THE POP-IN

"Miruka?" I said. "This is...different."

"I'm here for the three-legged race tryouts," Miruka said. "Am I late?"

"The...? Oh, right." Yuri's hand dropped from my shoulder.

"Your friend Miruka is here!" my mother called from downstairs.

"Thanks, Mom," I shouted back.

* * *

Miruka. In my room. 'Weird' did not begin to describe the feeling.

"So...what brings you by?" I asked.

"Your report card wandered into my bag," Miruka said, digging it out and handing it to me.

"It could've waited 'til Monday."

Yuri's elbow jabbed me in the ribs.

"Oh, sorry. This is my cousin Yuri. Yuri, this is Miruka. She's my...uh...classmate."

Miruka's eyes bored into Yuri. Yuri made a valiant attempt to return the gaze, but she was outclassed. Yuri retreated to the safety of her notebook.

"You two look a lot alike," Miruka concluded.

"That's what everybody says, but I don't see it," I replied. "Actually, we were just working on some math."

Yuri read from the notebook. "For positive integers a, b with greatest common divisor G and least common multiple L—"

"—$a \times b = G \times L$," Miruka said, not missing a beat. She closed her eyes, twirled a finger a few times, then opened her eyes again.

"Let's talk about sequences of prime exponents," she said.

3.6 SEQUENCES OF PRIME EXPONENTS

3.6.1 An Example

"Take the prime factorization of a number and look at the exponents on the prime factors. Use 280 as an example."

Miruka snagged the notebook out of Yuri's hand and the pencil off my desk and began to write:

$$\begin{aligned}
280 &= 2 \cdot 2 \cdot 2 \cdot 5 \cdot 7 && \text{prime factorization of 280} \\
&= 2^3 \cdot 3^0 \cdot 5^1 \cdot 7^1 \cdot 11^0 \cdots && \text{note the exponents} \\
&= \langle 3, 0, 1, 1, 0, \cdots \rangle && \text{the exponents as a sequence}
\end{aligned}$$

"Call the $\langle 3, 0, 1, 1, 0, \cdots \rangle$ in that last line 'a sequence of prime exponents,'" she said. "A number in the sequence is called a 'component.' I'm writing these as infinite sequences, but they all end up with an infinite string of zeros at the end, so in practical terms they're finite.

"A 3^0 means 3 is included in the prime factorization 0 times—in other words, it's not there. Since $3^0 = 1$, it's no stretch to think of that factor as just multiplying by 1.

"Here's the general form of a sequence of prime exponents for a positive integer n:"

$$\begin{aligned}
n &= 2^{n_2} \cdot 3^{n_3} \cdot 5^{n_5} \cdot 7^{n_7} \cdot 11^{n_{11}} \cdots \\
&= \langle n_2, n_3, n_5, n_7, n_{11}, \cdots \rangle
\end{aligned}$$

"So each n_p is the number of times the prime p appears in the prime factorization of n. For $n = 280$, you get $n_2 = 3, n_3 = 0, n_5 = 1, n_7 = 1$, then everything else is 0. The uniqueness of prime factorization guarantees a one-to-one correspondence between the positive integers and these sequences. In other words, there's a sequence of prime exponents for every positive integer, and a positive integer for every sequence of prime exponents."

Miruka turned to Yuri.

"A problem for you," she said. She wrote in the notebook:

$$\langle 1, 0, 0, 0, 0, \cdots \rangle$$

"This is a sequence of prime exponents. What number does it represent?"

"...2?" Yuri squeaked.

"Right." Miruka expanded the sequence:

$$\langle 1, 0, 0, 0, 0, \cdots \rangle = 2^1 \cdot 3^0 \cdot 5^0 \cdot 7^0 \cdot 11^0 \cdots$$
$$= 2$$

Yuri gave a cautious nod.

"What about this one?" Miruka wrote:

$$\langle 0, 1, 0, 0, 0, \cdots \rangle$$

"3?"

"Good."

$$\langle 0, 1, 0, 0, 0, \cdots \rangle = 2^0 \cdot 3^1 \cdot 5^0 \cdot 7^0 \cdot 11^0 \cdots$$
$$= 3$$

"Try this one:"

$$\langle 1, 0, 2, 0, 0, \cdots \rangle$$

"I don't know," Yuri said.

"*Think*," Miruka replied, narrowing her eyes. "You haven't even tried."

"But, I don't know wh—"

"It's not about not knowing, it's about being afraid of being wrong." Miruka's face moved to within inches of Yuri's. "It's about preferring not to try, so you don't have to risk failing."

Yuri froze, her eyes wide.

"Scaredy cat."

"27!" Yuri cried out, tears welling in her eyes.

"Wrong. We aren't adding here."

"Oh, right. Multiply. It's 50. The answer is 50."

"That's right."

$$\langle 1, 0, 2, 0, 0, \cdots \rangle = 2^1 \cdot 3^0 \cdot 5^2 \cdot 7^0 \cdot 11^0 \cdots$$
$$= 2 \cdot 25$$
$$= 50$$

"Okay, I get it now," Yuri sniffled.

"One more, then:"

$$\langle 0, 0, 0, 0, 0, \cdots \rangle$$

"I don't know."

"Yuri..." Miruka's voice rose in a sharp hook.

"0?"

"No. How did you calculate that?"

"Well, it's all 0s, so..."

"*How did you calculate that?*"

"I just... Oh, wait. These are exponents. It should be 1."

$$\langle 0, 0, 0, 0, 0, \cdots \rangle = 2^0 \cdot 3^0 \cdot 5^0 \cdot 7^0 \cdot 11^0 \cdots$$
$$= 1 \cdot 1 \cdot 1 \cdot 1 \cdot 1 \cdots$$
$$= 1$$

"Well done." Miruka smiled, and to my surprise, Yuri smiled back.

3.6.2   Taking It Up a Notch

Miruka took a sip of tea. Her finger began swaying back and forth, like a metronome. She turned to Yuri again.

"You have a sequence of prime exponents. One of the components is 1, the rest are 0. What kind of number is that?"

"...A prime?"

"Right. What if every component is even?"

"I don't... No, hang on. Let me think."

Yuri took the notebook and pencil from Miruka. She began writing, pausing occasionally to think. I'd never seen her like this before.

"Maybe this is wrong," she said, "but is it a number that you can take the root of?"

"Examples," Miruka said.

"Like, 4 and 9 and 16?"

"Good. Those are called square numbers."

Yuri nodded.

"Is 1 a square number?" Miruka asked.

"Yes."

"If you wrote 1 as a sequence of prime exponents, would all the components be even?"

"Um, is 0 even?"

"It is."

"Then they're all even! It works!"

3.6.3 Multiplication

Miruka continued her lecture. The cup of tea my mother had brought up for her sat untouched.

"Okay, let's try multiplying these things. Say you've got two positive integers, a and b, with sequences of prime exponents like this:"

$$a = \langle a_2, a_3, a_5, a_7, \cdots \rangle$$
$$b = \langle b_2, b_3, b_5, b_7, \cdots \rangle$$

"You multiply those together this way:"

$$a \cdot b = \langle a_2 + b_2, a_3 + b_3, a_5 + b_5, a_7 + b_7, \cdots \rangle$$

"It's just the exponent rules at work, but still kinda interesting. Multiplication is supposed to be more complex than addition, but adding components gets the job done. Compare the way we usually do multiplication with the prime exponents method:"

Normal multiplication		Prime exponent multiplication
12×30	$\xrightarrow{\text{prime factorization}}$	$\langle 2, 1, 0, 0, \ldots \rangle \times \langle 1, 1, 1, 0, \ldots \rangle$
$\downarrow$ multiply		$\downarrow$ add
360		$\langle 3, 2, 1, 0, \ldots \rangle$

"Things get easy because we did all the heavy lifting during the prime factorization. This sequence of prime exponents shows us the structure behind the numbers."

Miruka looked at the bandage wrapped around Yuri's foot.

"Kind of like an X-ray of an integer."

3.6.4 Greatest Common Divisors

"All right, time for greatest common divisors," Miruka said. "Yuri, think you can show me how to write a GCD as a sequence of prime exponents?"

$$a = \langle a_2, a_3, a_5, a_7, \cdots \rangle$$
$$b = \langle b_2, b_3, b_5, b_7, \cdots \rangle$$

"I can try," Yuri said, biting her lip. "Does it have to be in math? I don't know how to write what I want to say with symbols."

"What do you want to say?"

"Something like, 'the smallest number out of two.'"

"How about, 'the lesser of two numbers'?"

"Right!"

"When you come across something you don't know how to write in symbols, just define it. Like this:"

$$\min(x, y) = (\text{the lesser of } x \text{ or } y)$$

"What do you mean, define it?"

"Just write it out so people know what you mean."

"Like, make up your own stuff? You can do that?"

"Sure. How else are you going to create something new? Here's another way to do it:"

$$\min(x, y) = \begin{cases} x & \text{if } x < y \\ y & \text{if } x \geqslant y \end{cases}$$

"Okay, so something like this, maybe?"

GCD of a and $b =$

$$\langle \min(a_2, b_2), \min(a_3, b_3), \min(a_5, b_5), \min(a_7, b_7), \cdots \rangle$$

Miruka smiled and nodded.

"Define your own stuff, huh?" Yuri said.

3.6.5 On to Infinite Dimensions

"Now for some real fun: vectors," Miruka said, turning to a new page in the notebook.

"You can look at a sequence of prime exponents like $\langle n_2, n_3, n_5, n_7, \cdots \rangle$ as a vector with infinite dimensions. Since it has infinite dimensions, there are infinitely many axes, one for each prime number. Every positive integer will be a point in that infinite-dimensional space. Finding the prime factorization of a number is like finding the shadows of its prime factors on the axes.

"So now that we're thinking geometrically, what does it mean to say two numbers are relatively prime? Well, if two numbers are relatively prime, then their greatest common divisor is 1. We've already said the sequence of prime exponents for 1 is $\langle 0, 0, 0, 0, \cdots \rangle$, and finding the greatest common divisor of a number means finding $\min(a_p, b_p)$ for each component in the sequence. That means if a and b are relatively prime, then $\min(a_p, b_p) = 0$ for every prime p.

$$a \text{ and } b \text{ are relatively prime}$$
$$\Updownarrow$$
$$\min(a_p, b_p) = 0 \text{ for every prime } p$$

"In other words, for any prime p, at least one of a_p or b_p is 0. And that means these two vectors will never cast a shadow on the same axis. Another way to say that is that the two vectors are orthogonal. The math symbol for 'orthogonal' is $\perp$, so some people write 'a and b are relatively prime' as $a \perp b$."

$$a \text{ and } b \text{ are relatively prime} \quad \Longleftrightarrow \quad a \perp b$$

"'Relatively prime' comes from number theory. 'Orthogonal' is from geometry. Isn't it lovely how they come together?"

Yuri's mouth hung open, awestruck.

I tested my own jaw. Maybe I was a little awestruck, too.

3.7 In Awe of Miruka

I walked Miruka back to the train station. Yuri was still in my room when I got back. When I entered, she grabbed my sleeve.

"She's the one who wrote those quizzes in your notebook, isn't she."

"How'd you know?"

"Her handwriting, dummy. Oh, *wow*. Maybe I should grow my hair out. But, ugh, this brown. That is just so *unfair*, to be so smart and beautiful, too. I mean...*wow*."

"Yeah, well—"

"The way she *talks*! How does she do that? Hey, she mentioned Tetra when she left, didn't she? Is Tetra a genius, too?"

"Speaking of Tetra... What was that stuff back in the hospital? What did you tell her when you called her back to your room?"

"Oh, that," Yuri said, pulling on her ponytail. "Nothing much. I just told her not to even *think* about trying to steal my math teacher."

CHAPTER 4

Proof by Contradiction

Another common practice in
mathematics for proving a theorem P is
to assume P is *false* and derive a
contradiction (that is, derive *false* or
something equivalent to *false*). ... A
shortcut is often taken: instead of
proving *false* directly, prove something
that is obviously equivalent to false, like
$Q \wedge \neg Q$.

GRIES & SCHNEIDER
A Logical Approach to Discrete Math

4.1 WRITING PROOFS

4.1.1 The Definition

It was another lazy Saturday in my room. Yuri sat sprawled on the
floor with a book.

Without warning, she flopped over and kicked my leg.

"I'm bored. Entertain me."

"Glad to see the foot is all healed up."

"Gimme a math problem to work on."

"I live to serve. Okay, here's a classic:"

> ### Problem 4-1
>
> Show that $\sqrt{2}$ is not a rational number.

"I don't know how to— No, wait. We did this at school. How did it go...? You assume $\sqrt{2}$ is a rational number. Then you say that if $\sqrt{2}$ is a rational number, then $\sqrt{2}$ can't *really* be a rational number. Something like that."

"I think you missed a bit in the middle there. Let's go through it together."

"I second that."

* * *

"The first step in solving a problem," I said, "is to read it carefully."

"Well, duh. How can you work a problem if you don't read it?"

"Let me rephrase that: The first step in solving a problem is *understanding* the problem. Lots of people start to work a problem before they're sure what it's really about."

"How can you read a math problem and not understand it?"

"By not knowing the definitions of the parts of the problem, for one thing."

"Definitions... That's where you make up your own stuff, right?"

"There's more to it than that. A definition is a very precise statement of what something means. If you're going to work on a problem like showing that $\sqrt{2}$ isn't a rational number, you need to be sure you know exactly what '$\sqrt{2}$' and 'rational number' mean."

"What, I have to do that for every math problem?" Yuri shook her ponytail. "No way. Too much work."

"Not if you're working on a problem you understand."

"Well, I know what $\sqrt{2}$ means, at least."

"Let's hear it."

"Easy. It's the number that equals 2 when you square it. The positive one, at least. You also get 2 if you square $-\sqrt{2}$."

Yuri crossed her arms and gave a satisfied nod.

"Not bad," I said, returning her nod. "Could use a little polish, though. A mathematician would probably say something like '$\sqrt{2}$ is a positive number whose square equals 2.'"

"Details, details."

"Okay, how about a definition of the rational numbers, then."

"Numbers that can be written as fractions."

"Mmmm... Close."

"Whaddaya mean, 'close'? Rational numbers are things like $\frac{1}{2}$ and $-\frac{2}{3}$, right?"

"Well, what about something like $\frac{\sqrt{2}}{1}$, then?"

"That's what we call 'cheating.' Okay, fine. How about 'a fraction made from two integers,' then?"

"Closer. But you also have to say the denominator can't be 0. And if you're going to use the word 'integer,' go ahead and define that, too."

I wrote a summary in Yuri's notebook:

- The integers are the numbers $\cdots, -3, -2, -1, 0, 1, 2, 3, \cdots$.

- The rationals are those number that can be written as $\frac{\text{integer}}{\text{integer other than 0}}$.

"I'm already exhausted and we haven't even started on the real problem," Yuri said.

"You'll get used to it. The point is, don't move on until you're sure what everything means. That's especially important when you start working on unfamiliar material, like a new math book."

"What if I come across a word I don't know?"

"Try looking it up in the index."

"That's the one in the front?"

"That's the table of contents. The index is in back, and it's a great place to start when you hit a word you don't know."

"Duly noted. In the meantime, I need food. Okay to grab a snack before we actually do the problem?"

My mother called up the stairs: "Hey kids! I made a batch of pancakes. Anybody hungry?"

"Okay, that's scary." Yuri said. "Is your mother psychic or something?"

"I think she has an innate sensitivity to hunger waves," I said.

4.1.2   The Proposition

Two plates of steaming pancakes were waiting for us downstairs in the kitchen.

"Okay," I said, "let's prove $\sqrt{2}$ isn't a rational number."

"Not while you're eating," Mother said.

"Wow, real maple syrup?" Yuri asked, reading the label on the bottle.

"Straight from Canada."

Yuri ran her finger across the plate and licked it. "Yummy."

"Aren't you cute." Mother grinned as she washed a frying pan. "Tea's ready in a minute."

"So how do you start?" Yuri asked me.

"By stating the proposition you're going to prove," I said.

"What's a proposition?"

"A mathematical statement that can be proved or disproved, like '$\sqrt{2}$ is a not a rational number,' or 'there are infinitely many primes.' Propositions can be even simpler than that, though. $1 + 1 = 2$ is a proposition."

"Propositions. Got it. Pass the butter."

"Pop quiz. Is '$1 + 1 = 3$' a proposition?"

"No, because $1 + 1 = 2$."

"Bzzzt. It's a perfectly fine proposition. A false one, but still a proposition. Remember what I said? A proposition is a mathematical statement that can be proven *or disproven*."

"Well then what kind of statement *wouldn't* be a proposition? Can't you prove or disprove pretty much anything?"

"Try proving maple syrup is delicious. Now you might like drowning your pancake in the stuff, but there are going to be other people who don't care for it, and their opinion is just as good as yours. So 'maple syrup is delicious' isn't a valid proposition. You can't mathematically prove it true or false."

"My taste buds disagree with you, but okay."

"So what's the proposition we're trying to prove?"

"That $\sqrt{2}$ is not a rational number."

"Right. When you start to write a proof, you have to be sure your proposition is rock solid. No cutting corners. Once you've got that, trying to write it in mathematical notation is usually a good next step."

I stuffed my mouth with pancake as I opened my notebook to a fresh page.

"No math with your mouth full!" my mother chided me as she placed a pot of tea on the table.

4.1.3 The Equation

"Mathematical notation is the most powerful tool in mathematics. You're shooting yourself in the foot if you don't use it."

Yuri knitted her eyebrows. "How do you write something like 'the square root of two is not a rational number' in math?"

"Well, we've already said a rational number is written as a fraction with an integer numerator and a non-zero integer denominator. So we can write all rational numbers as a fraction like this:"

$$\frac{b}{a}$$

"Okay."

"Not okay yet. We still have to say exactly what a and b are. The fact that they're both integers and a isn't 0 is important. Never use a variable when you aren't exactly sure what it is."

"So b is an integer, and a is also an integer that isn't 0."

"Good. Now we want to use this to rewrite our proposition as something like this:"

There exist no integers a, b such that $\sqrt{2} = \frac{b}{a}$.

"Hmmm. Sure, I see that."

"Now comes the tricky part. Let's assume something like this is true:"

There exist integers a, b such that $\sqrt{2} = \frac{b}{a}$.

"But that's the exact opposite of what we want to prove!"

"It is, but you don't usually use the word 'opposite' in logic. You call that a 'negation' instead. It's a statement that *negates* the proposition we want to prove."

"A negation," Yuri said. "Got it."

"Now, one detail we'd like to work around is the fact that there are an infinite number of ways to write a fraction and end up with the same number. Like, $\frac{1}{2}$ and $\frac{2}{4}$ and $\frac{100}{200}$ are all equivalent, we've just multiplied the numerator and the denominator by the same number to change their form. So we'll sidestep the issue by saying that $\frac{b}{a}$ is the fraction in reduced form.

"So our assumption that there *are* integers a and b such that $\sqrt{2} = \frac{b}{a}$ would mean $\sqrt{2} = \frac{b}{a}$ is a true statement, right?"

"Right," Yuri nodded. "And a and b are integers."

"*And* $\frac{b}{a}$ is in reduced form. That means the relationship between a and b is...?"

"They're relatively prime."

"Nice. Right off the bat."

"I have *mastered* relatively prime."

"We'll see... Now let's square the equation and watch what happens: "

$$\sqrt{2} = \frac{b}{a} \qquad \text{negation of the proposition}$$

$$2 = \left(\frac{b}{a}\right)^2 \qquad \text{square both sides}$$

$$2 = \frac{b^2}{a^2} \qquad \text{expand the right}$$

$$2a^2 = b^2 \qquad \text{multiply both sides by } a^2$$

Yuri held up a hand. "Master, your unworthy student requests enlightenment."

"Enlightenment is unobtainable without seeking. Speak."

"What on earth made you want to square the equation?"

"What was your definition of $\sqrt{2}$?"

"A number that equals 2 when you square it."

"An important property—which is why I gave it a whirl. Doing that got us $2a^2 = b^2$. Remind me what a and b are again."

"Relatively prime integers."

"And don't forget, $a \neq 0$. Sometimes it's good to stop and make sure you haven't forgotten what everything is. Or isn't."

"We're never going to get anywhere with all this stopping," Yuri sighed.

"We're getting there, I promise. Since we're dealing with integers, checking their parity—whether they're even or odd—is usually a good idea. Tell me about that $2a^2$ on the left. Even or odd?"

"Dunno. No, wait, I do. Even."

"Yep. Has to be, since the a^2 is being multiplied by a 2, right? And since we have $2a^2 = b^2$, the b^2 has to be even, too. If the thing on the left is even, the thing on the right is too."

Yuri nodded. "Makes sense."

"Okay, so what kind of number is even when it's squared?"

"...An even one?"

"Bingo. So we know that b is even, which means we can write it like this:"

$$b = 2B$$

"Wait, where'd the big B come from?"

"Glad you asked; it's an integer."

"What integer?"

"*Some* integer. Since b is even, there has to be some integer out there that makes this a true statement."

"But it's easier to just say 'b is even,' not this 'some integer' stuff. Why gunk things up with a new variable?"

"To keep everything as equations, not words. 'Even' and '2B' mean the same thing here."

"What's the big deal about keeping it as an equation? I don't see the point."

"Equations are the best way to keep mathematical concepts straight."

"If you say so..."

"I do. Now, since we know $b = 2B$, we can rewrite $2a^2 = b^2$:"

$$2a^2 = b^2$$
$$2a^2 = (2B)^2 \qquad \text{replace } b = 2B$$
$$2a^2 = 2B \times 2B \qquad \text{expand right side}$$
$$2a^2 = 4B^2 \qquad \text{calculate right side}$$
$$a^2 = 2B^2 \qquad \text{divide both sides by 2}$$

"So now we have $a^2 = 2B^2$. And what are a and B?"

"*Integers.*" Yuri rolled her eyes. "How many times are we going to do this?"

"As many times as it takes. And don't forget, $a \neq 0$. Now, what do we like to do when we look at integers?"

"Um, what was it...? Oh, I know. Even or odd."

"Check their parity, exactly. The right side of $a^2 = 2B^2$ is even:"

$$2B^2 \text{ is even}$$

"So the the left side must be even too:"

$$a^2 \text{ is even}$$

"And what kind of a number is even when you square it?"

"An *even one.*" Another eye roll.

"Right. If a^2 is even, then a must be, too. That means we can write this:"

$$a = 2A$$

"Where A is some integer," I said.

"This all sounds *really* familiar..."

"It should. We did pretty much the same thing to find $b = 2B$. Doesn't that seem strange?"

"It seems repetitive."

"Then you're on the right track. What does it mean to say a and b are both even?"

"I dunno... That they're both multiples of 2?"

"And why is that a problem?"

"It's a problem? Wait—it is a problem! They're supposed to be relatively prime!"

"Yes they are." I smiled.

"But that means their greatest common divisor should be 1. So how can they both be multiples of 2?"

"That's the contradiction we were looking for. We started out with the proposition that a and b are relatively prime. From that, we derived the fact that a and b are *not* relatively prime."

"So this 'contradiction' we found. Is that something like a paradox? One of those 'this statement is a lie' kinda things?"

"Not quite. In math, a contradiction is when you have a statement P, and you've shown that P is both true and not true. Here's a formal definition:"

Definition of contradiction

Let P be a proposition. A contradiction occurs when both "P" and "not P" are held to be true.

"We started out saying a and b are relatively prime, and that $\sqrt{2} = \frac{b}{a}$, right?" I asked.

"Yup."

"When we made that proposition, we didn't know if it was true or false, just that it was one or the other. But when we reached the logical conclusions it led to, we ended up getting a contradiction. One reason that might happen would be because we made a mistake in the stuff we did."

"Well, if we made a mistake, I sure didn't notice it."

"I don't think we did. Not in the math, at least. But there's one place where we could have messed up: assuming the negation of the proposition, that integers a and b exist that make the statement $\sqrt{2} = \frac{b}{a}$ true."

"So the negation has to be false?"

"Assuming we haven't made any other mistakes, then yes, the negation must be false. Put another way, there are *no* integers a and b that make the statement $\sqrt{2} = \frac{b}{a}$ true."

"And that's all it takes to show that $\sqrt{2}$ isn't a rational number?"

"That's all. The definition says a number is rational if it can be written as an integer divided by a non-zero integer, right? And it isn't rational otherwise. So did that give you a feeling for what it's like to develop a proof by starting with a definition?"

"I guess. Proofs look like a lot of work, though."

"They can be. This one used a method called 'proof by contradiction.' Basically, you start from the negation of the thing you want to prove, and show that leads to a contradiction. It's one of the most basic methods of mathematical proof."

Definition of proof by contradiction

Proof by contradiction is a method of mathematical proof by which the negation of a proposition is shown to lead to a contradiction.

Answer 4-1 ($\sqrt{2}$ is not a rational number)

Use proof by contradiction.

1. Suppose $\sqrt{2}$ is a rational number.

2. Then there exist integers a and b ($a \neq 0$) such that:

   · a and b are relatively prime, and
   · $\sqrt{2} = \frac{b}{a}$.

3. Square both sides and multiply by a^2 to get $2a^2 = b^2$.

4. $2a^2$ is even, so b^2 is also even.

5. b^2 is even, so b is also even.

6. Therefore, there exists an integer B such that $b = 2B$.

7. Insert $b = 2B$ into $2a^2 = b^2$ to get $a^2 = 2B^2$.

8. $2B^2$ is even, so a^2 is also even.

9. a^2 is even, so a is also even.

10. a, b are both even, so a, b are not relatively prime.

11. This contradicts the assertion that a and b are relatively prime.

12. Therefore, $\sqrt{2}$ is not a rational number.

"Okay, last things last. Let's sum up what we did today:"

· Read problems carefully.

· Be sure you know how everything is defined.

· Know how to define things yourself.

· Express words in mathematical notation.

· When dealing with integers, try checking parity.

· When dealing with variables, be sure you know what they represent.

"Oh," I said, "and on top of all that, we learned how to do a proof by contradiction. Not bad for a day's work."

"But exhausting," Yuri said. "At least I got a taste of this proof stuff, and how important definitions and equations are. I'm a long way from being able to memorize this one, though."

"No, don't memorize anything. You need to go home, sit down with pencil and paper, and try working through it."

"By myself?"

"Yes, by yourself. You probably won't be able to at first, but that's not the point—in fact, that's the way it works, even when you're pretty sure you understand what you have to do. If you get stuck, look for hints in a book, or look back at your notes. Just keep practicing until it all spills out. It's not about memorizing, it's about thinking. It's about understanding mathematical structures, and learning how to follow the flow of logic. It's about developing the ability to bend the power of math to your own goals."

4.1.4 Proofs are Eternal

We headed back upstairs to my room.

"Candy time," Yuri announced, grabbing the jar off my desk and rooting through it. "Did you eat all my lemons?"

"*Your* lemons?"

"Oh well, guess it's you and me, melon." Yuri unwrapped a green candy and popped it in her mouth. "So proofs are a Big Deal in math, huh?"

"Proofs are the foundation mathematics is built on. Coming up with a new proof is how you make your contribution."

"So becoming a mathematician is like becoming a professional proof writer."

"I guess you could say that. Some people have devoted their lives to developing a single proof."

"We did something we called proofs in geometry class, but they didn't feel like such a big deal—just more of a pain than the regular problems." Yuri snickered. "Hard to imagine someone spending their whole life on something like that."

"Well, maybe saying they devoted their lives to it is going a bit far—it's not like they chained themselves to a desk and did math until they dropped dead. But carving out a new chunk of mathematics was important enough for them to spend a good bit of their limited time here on Earth doing it."

"Sounds crazy to me."

"Well, think about it. If you can make a new statement that begins 'For all integers n...,' you've discovered a truth that holds for an infinite number of things, and wrapped it up in this tiny little n. That's, I dunno...*awesome*, in the truest sense of the word."

"Huh," Yuri said. "Yeah...yeah, I guess it is." She paused to consider this. "You math people have this thing for infinity, don't you?"

"Maybe we do. By the way, what do you think the negation of 'For all n, something-or-other is true' would be?"

" 'Something-or-other is false,' I guess."

"So, 'For all n, something-or-other is false,' then?"

"Yeah, that sounds negative enough."

"Too negative, actually. A better negation would be 'For *some* n, something-or-other is false,' or maybe, 'There exists some n for which something-or-other is false.' " I picked up the candy jar. "So the negation of 'All of these candies are lemon-flavored' would be 'There exists a candy that is not lemon-flavored.' It only takes one melon candy to prove they aren't *all* lemon."

"Because a single non-lemon breaks the allness part?"

"Exactly. The first step in doing a proof by contradiction is negating the statement you want to prove. If you want to prove something is true for every candy, you assume the existence of a candy for which that something isn't true, and show that a contradiction would result. That lets you focus your attention on that one special candy, and go from there."

"I'm happy to use anything involving the existence of candy."

"Cute. But seriously, writing a proof is like touching infinity. Mathematical theorems stick around forever, long after the mathematicians who proved them are dead and gone. They're eternal, a monument that never degrades with time. They're our best chance for immortality."

"I swear, you're like, the ultimate math nerd," Yuri laughed.

I laughed with her. "Not yet, but I'm working on it."

4.2 ANOTHER APPROACH

4.2.1 Parity

The next day after school we were all hanging out in the music room—me, Miruka, Tetra, and Ay-Ay.

Ay-Ay was the president of "Fortissimo," the school piano club, and she spent most of her time here practicing. Today she was largely ignoring us in favor of a two-voice Bach invention.

I was telling Tetra and Miruka about what Yuri and I had worked on the day before—the proof that $\sqrt{2}$ isn't a rational number. Actually, I was mostly telling Tetra; Miruka's eyes were glued to Ay-Ay's fingers as she played.

"I think I've seen that proof," Tetra said, "but I'd love to hear you explain it. I'm sure I'd understand it better coming from you."

"Show her the other proof," Miruka said, turning towards us.

So she was listening...

"What other proof?" I asked.

"The other proof by contradiction. You start out the same—assume $\sqrt{2}$ is rational, so there exist integers a and b such that $\sqrt{2} = \frac{b}{a}$. Then square both sides and multiply by a^2 to get $2a^2 = b^2$. But that's where the paths diverge. You ask, if we were to find the prime factorization of $2a^2$, how many factors of 2 would there be?"

"Huh? How can you figure that out?"

"You can't, really. But you *do* know that the number of factors will be an integer."

"Of course it'll be an integer. What does that have to do with—"

"What was it you should check when dealing with integers?"

Tetra joined in. "Parity, right?"

"Right," Miruka said.

"Wait a minute," I said. "Not the parity of $2a^2$, but the parity of the number of 2s in its prime factorization?"

"Sure. What should it be?"

"I don't—no, wait, it should be odd!" I nearly shouted.

"Where'd you get that from?" Tetra asked.

"Because a^2 is a square number. That means it will have an even number of each of its prime factors, including 2s. But with $2a^2$ we're multiplying by one more 2, so there has to be an odd number of 2s in the factorization. Huh..."

"Very good. And what about the right side? The b^2?"

"No extra 2 tacked on, so it has to have an *even* number of 2s in its prime factorization."

"Meaning...?" Miruka purred.

"An even number of 2s on one side, and an odd number on the other," I said. "A contradiction."

"And so, proof by contradiction shows that $\sqrt{2}$ cannot be a rational number." Miruka raised a finger. "*Quod erat demonstrandum.*"

"Wow, that's slick," I said. "You don't even need to use the fact that a and b are relatively prime."

Answer 4-1a ($\sqrt{2}$ is not a rational number)

Use proof by contradiction.

1. Suppose $\sqrt{2}$ is a rational number.

2. Then there exist integers a, b ($a \neq 0$) such that $\sqrt{2} = \frac{b}{a}$.

3. Square both sides and multiply by a^2 to get $2a^2 = b^2$.

4. The prime factorization of $2a^2$ has an odd number of 2s.

5. The prime factorization of b^2 has an even number of 2s.

6. This is a contradiction.

7. Therefore, $\sqrt{2}$ is not a rational number.

Tetra looked perplexed.

"What's wrong?" Miruka asked.

"I'm not sure, really. It's just...in that proof you used the equation $2a^2 = b^2$, right?" Tetra said. "That's a statement that the right and left sides are equivalent. But what you did after that didn't really seem to have anything to do with them being the same value. It just seems, I don't know, like you changed the rules."

"Hmm. Interesting point." Miruka turned to me. "What do you say to that?"

"Huh? Well, you did compare the number of 2s in the prime factorization, but I guess Tetra's right—that's not the same thing as comparing their actual values. But I don't see anything wrong with the proof. Equal is equal, and that includes things like the number of factors when you break the two sides down into primes. The structure on the left and the right—"

Miruka cut me off with a waggling finger.

"Too many words," she said. "All you have to say is that the uniqueness of prime factorization guarantees the same factorization for both."

"Oh, right. That makes sense," Tetra said.

And it did. That one phrase, "the uniqueness of prime factorization," says everything that needs to be said. *Why don't I come up with things like that? Do I understand this stuff even less than I thought?*

"That's a really cool proof, Miruka," I said. "Thanks."

Miruka shrugged and turned away, refocusing her attention on Ay-Ay, who was still banging out Bach.

Miruka might have a red-hot stare when she's pouring out the math, but a word of praise is enough to shut her down.

The brilliant Miruka couldn't take a compliment.

4.2.2   Contradictions

Miruka and Ay-Ay began playing a piece for four hands. More Bach. Tetra moved to the chair next to mine.

"Proof by contradiction sure gets used a lot," she said. "I need more practice. I've gotten to where I'm okay with the whole 'prove the opposite of what you want to prove' thing, but it still doesn't come easy. I get all confused with what's supposed to be true, and what isn't."

"Yeah, I can see that," I said. "When you're using proper logic on an incorrect premise to demonstrate the correctness of something else, it's easy to get mixed up as to what's what. But the hardest thing for me is finding the contradiction."

"Totally!" Tetra gave an emphatic nod. "I feel like I'm, I don't know, breaking the rules or something."

"No worries there. Deriving a contradiction just means showing both 'P' and 'not P.' Oh, let me show you how to write that."

I went to the music room whiteboard.

"In logic notation, you write 'P and not P' like this:"

$$P \land \neg P$$

"Some textbooks also write the negation of P like $\overline{P}$. Anyway, a proof by contradiction doesn't always mean finding both P and $\neg P$.

The P can be *any* proposition, like something you've already proven, or an existing theorem. In cases like that, you can just derive a ¬P in your proof, then say you've found a contradiction since ¬P can't be right."

"Oh, okay. Cool!" Tetra said, looking up at me with those wide eyes.

"In Miruka's proof, she got a result that said both 'the prime factorization has an odd number of 2s' and 'the prime factorization does not have an odd number of 2s.' That's an example of finding a P and a ¬P. Like this:"

P   the prime factorization has an odd number of 2s

¬P   the prime factorization does not have an odd number of 2s

"Okay, I like that P and not P thing better," Tetra said. "Maybe I just have a hangup about the word 'contradiction.' It sounds so...harsh."

Tetra bit on a fingernail as she continued. "So the P and not P you use...that can be pretty much anything? Like, even if you're doing a proof from number theory, you can pull in stuff from algebra or geometry or whatever?"

"Sure," I said. "As long as the logic is solid, it doesn't really matter what area of math you use it in."

"But some proposition, right? I guess I need to make sure I understand exactly what the definition of a proposition is..."

"Anything you, or someone else, has proved. Like in Miruka's proof, it doesn't have to be some grandiose thing."

"Gotcha!" Tetra said. Her voice dropped, and she turned a bit so that only I would hear her speak. "Um, there's this thing I wanted to ask—"

The music stopped. "Show's over," announced Ay-Ay.

The lid over the keys and Tetra's mouth snapped shut in unison.

CHAPTER 5

Broken Primes

When we expand our world of numbers from $\mathbb{Z}$ to $\mathbb{Z}[i]$, prime decomposition becomes reliant on remainders after division by 4.

KATO, KUROKAWA, AND SAITO
Number Theory, Vol. I

5.1 IMAGINING NUMBERS

5.1.1 A Quiz for Tetra

"Here I am," said Tetra as she walked into our classroom. It was lunchtime, and I'd just gotten back from buying a muffin at the cafeteria.

"This is a first," I said. It was rare to see a student brave a higher grade's territory.

"I invited her," Miruka explained.

"Okay if I sit here?" Tetra dragged a desk over and spun it around to face Miruka. They both pulled out lunches, a bento box for Tetra and a chocolate bar for Miruka. I eyed them as I munched on my muffin.

"Do you always just have a candy bar for lunch?" Tetra asked.

"Chocolate truffles, sometimes."

"Never anything a little...healthier?"

"Chocolate is health food for the soul," Miruka replied. "Anybody have any good math problems?" she asked, changing the subject.

"I have a good one for Tetra," I said.

Tetra's eyes widened. "What is it?"

"What can you square to get −1?"

Problem 5-1

What can you square to get −1?

"That's easy," Tetra said. "The square root of −1, a.k.a. the imaginary unit, i."

"Not quite," I said. Miruka shook her head from side to side.

"What? I'm wrong?"

"Want to show her the error of her ways, Miruka?"

"You rushed. The right answer's ±i," Miruka said.

"Oh, right. I guess −i squared gives −1, too, doesn't it."

Answer 5-1

$(\pm i)^2 = -1$

Tetra frowned. "No fair. You tricked me."

"Nothing unfair about it," I said. "It's a serious question, with an important answer."

"He's right," Miruka chimed in. "You're dealing with a quadratic equation, $x^2 = -1$. A second degree equation, so you should be looking for two answers, like the fundamental theorem of algebra tells you to. He wins this one."

Miruka took another bite of her candy bar. Tetra frowned and turned back to her Salisbury steak.

We ate in silence for a while. Miruka finished eating first and began a careful inspection of Tetra's fancy chopstick case. Tetra finally summoned the nerve to speak again.

"Don't you think there's something weird about i?" she asked. "I mean, squaring something and getting a negative number? It just doesn't make sense. It's...*unnatural*."

"Does -1 seem unnatural to you?" Miruka asked.

"Not really," Tetra said. "Should it?"

Miruka extended an open hand in my direction, an all too familiar gesture. With a sigh, I parted with my notebook and pencil.

5.1.2 Defining Numbers

"Look at the solution to this simple first-degree equation," Miruka said.

$$x + 1 = 0 \qquad \text{a first-degree equation in } x$$
$$x = -1 \qquad \text{move the 1 to the right}$$

"The solution is $x = -1$, of course. Nothing tricky here. But what if you were only interested in nonnegative values of x?"

$$x + 1 = 0 \qquad \text{for } x \geqslant 0$$

"Even better, say you'd never even *heard* of negative numbers. You'd think this was a pretty bizarre equation, right?"

"I'd probably tell you it didn't make any sense," Tetra said. "You can't add 1 to something and end up with nothing."

"Exactly. And if I insisted there *was* a solution to this equation, you'd say it must be a weird solution. An *unnatural* one, even."

"Sure, why not?" Tetra nodded.

"But this isn't unnatural to you, and that's all because of when you were born," Miruka said. "Blaise Pascal was one of the top mathematicians of the seventeenth century, but he thought that if you subtracted something from 0, you just got 0. It wasn't until Euler in the eighteenth century that we finally had number lines with integers stretching off into the positive and negative directions. So considering the thousands of years we've been doing math, negative numbers are a pretty recent invention."

"Wow, that's pretty cool," Tetra said.

"Say you traveled back in time to Pascal's day, and wanted to tell him about negative numbers. You might try saying, 'Let's define a number m as the solution to the equation $x + 1 = 0$.' To which he would no doubt reply, 'Silly girl, there is no such number.' But maybe you could pacify him by saying, 'Humor me. It's just a formal definition,' laughing in your head the whole time because you know it's just -1 that you're talking about."

"Me, giving math lessons to a famous mathematician," Tetra said. "Now *that's* funny."

"Could happen," Miruka said. "Point is, you're using the equation $x + 1 = 0$ to define a new kind of number. Or, looking at it another way, you're establishing a new axiom, using an equation to show what you mean. Of course now we don't see any need to do all that for something like -1, because we're used to negative numbers. They feel natural."

5.1.3 On to Quadratics

"So let's do something similar, but using a quadratic equation this time," Miruka said. "Like this one:"

$$x^2 + 1 = 0$$

"You're fine with negative numbers, but this looks strange because any nonzero real number, even a negative one, is positive when you square it. You wonder, 'How can I add 1 to a nonnegative number and end up with 0?' Well, you can't...if you only know about the real numbers."

Miruka paused to let this sink in.

"So I end up defining a new kind of number?" Tetra asked.

"You do," Miruka said. "A new kind of number that's the solution—well, one of the solutions, at least—to $x^2 + 1 = 0$. Let's call it i. You hesitate at first, asking yourself, 'Can I really do that? There's no such number!' But you reassure yourself, saying, 'It's okay. This is just a formal definition. I'm just using the equation $x^2 + 1 = 0$ to define a new kind of number, a new axiom.'"

"Okay, I get the similarity," Tetra said. "But this still feels different from the jump from positive to negative numbers. I just can't *see* it."

"Most people couldn't 'see' negative numbers until Euler extended the number line in both directions. Let's try doing the same thing for complex numbers. Start with the real number line you already know:"

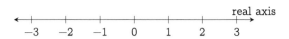

"Call this the 'real' axis. Then add a second line, the 'imaginary' axis, to represent the imaginary part of these numbers:"

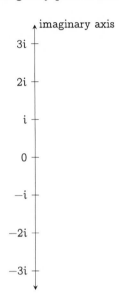

"Together, these two axes form what's called the complex number plane. This is where all the complex numbers live:"

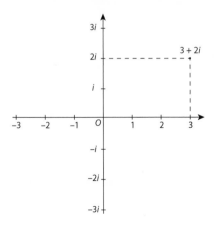

"All we've done here is extend the number line into two dimensions."

Tetra's hand shot up, still clutching her chopsticks.

"Question!" she said. Just then, the warning bell rang. Lunch was over. "Awh, we were just getting to the good stuff!" Tetra gathered up her things and flipped a $1, 1, 2, 3$ Fibonacci sign to us. As she scurried off for class, she shouted over her shoulder, "You better be in the library after school!"

5.2   SUMS AND PRODUCTS OF COMPLEX NUMBERS

5.2.1   Adding Complex Numbers

I rushed to the library as soon as the last bell rang, but Miruka and Tetra were already there.

"I still don't get how you can represent a number with a point, though," Tetra was saying. "I mean, I understand that a complex number like $3 + 2i$ is plotted on the plane as $(3, 2)$, but... Numbers are numbers, and points are points. Aren't they?"

"Numbers are about how you calculate with them, not how you represent them. Let's try some addition and multiplication to get a feel for these things."

Tetra clenched her fists, mentally rolling up her sleeves.

"You can represent both operations geometrically, using shapes on the complex plane. We'll start with addition, representing it as the diagonal of a parallelogram. All you do is add the x and y values, so there's nothing hard or mysterious about it—it's just a sum of vectors."

Miruka wrote in Tetra's notebook:

$$\begin{array}{ccc} \text{Addition of complex} & \longleftrightarrow & \text{Diagonal of a} \\ \text{numbers} & & \text{parallelogram} \end{array}$$

"Of course, that isn't going to make any sense without looking at an example. Let's take $1 + 2i$ and $3 + i$. Their sum would be $4 + 3i$, right? See how that makes a parallelogram?"

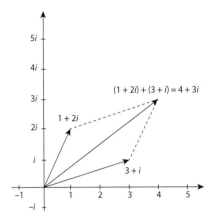

5.2.2 Multiplying Complex Numbers

"Let's try multiplication now," Miruka continued. "We'll use α and β, defined like this:"

$$\begin{cases} \alpha & = 2 + 2i \\ \beta & = 1 + 3i \end{cases}$$

"First, straightforward multiplication:"

$$\begin{aligned}
\alpha\beta &= (2 + 2i)(1 + 3i) & \text{from } \alpha = 2 + 2i, \beta = 1 + 3i \\
&= 2 + 6i + 2i + 6i^2 & \text{expand} \\
&= 2 + 6i + 2i - 6 & \text{use } i^2 = -1 \\
&= -4 + 8i & \text{combine real and imaginary parts}
\end{aligned}$$

"Now, look at α, β and their product as vectors in the complex plane:"

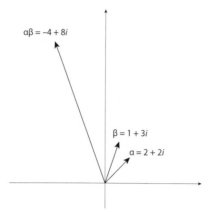

"I'm looking," Tetra said, "but I'm not sure what I'm seeing."

"Their geometric relationship isn't exactly obvious, is it," Miruka said. "Let's add the point $(1, 0)$ and connect a few dots. See the similar triangles that appear?"

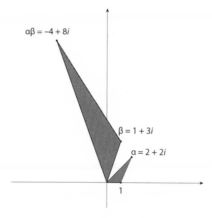

Tetra put a hand to her forehead. "Similar triangles were, uh..."

"Triangles whose sides might have different lengths, but the same proportion. And they can be rotated, like these."

"Right, right! Now I remember."

"You can calculate the side lengths and confirm that the proportions are the same for homework. For now, trust me that multiplication of complex numbers can be represented using similar triangles like this. The more interesting question is: Why?"

Tetra leaned forward, enthralled.

"To answer that, we need to represent complex numbers in polar form. We don't want to use their x- and y-coordinates; instead we'll use their distance from the origin, and their argument."

"Distance from the origin I get, but what's an argument?"

"It's just the angle of a vector with respect to the positive x-axis."

"And where do you get those?"

"Let's try it with $2 + 2i$ and see: "

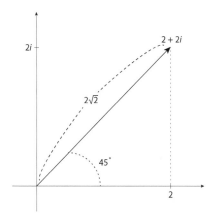

"For $2 + 2i$ the argument is $45°$, and you can use the Pythagorean theorem to find the distance from the origin—see how to make a right triangle to do that?—which for $2 + 2i$ is $2\sqrt{2}$. That distance is also the absolute value of a complex number, by the way. I'm going to write the absolute value of this number as $|2 + 2i|$ and the argument as $\arg(2 + 2i)$: "

$$\begin{cases} \text{x-coord: } 2 \\ \text{y-coord: } 2i \end{cases} \quad \longleftrightarrow \quad 2 + 2i \quad \longleftrightarrow \quad \begin{cases} |2 + 2i| = 2\sqrt{2} \\ \arg(2 + 2i) = 45° \end{cases}$$

"Now let's look at the absolute value of $\alpha\beta$: "

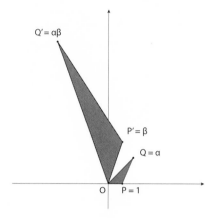

"$\triangle$OPQ and $\triangle$OP'Q' are similar, so the lengths of corresponding sides are proportional:"

$$\frac{\overline{OQ'}}{\overline{OP'}} = \frac{\overline{OQ}}{\overline{OP}}$$

"Multiply through by denominators to get this:"

$$\overline{OQ'} \times \overline{OP} = \overline{OQ} \times \overline{OP'}$$

"Since we know $Q' = \alpha\beta, P = 1, Q = \alpha$, and $P' = \beta$, we can say that $\overline{OQ'} = |\alpha\beta|, \overline{OP} = 1, \overline{OQ} = |\alpha|$, and $\overline{OP'} = |\beta|$, which gives us:"

$$|\alpha\beta| = |\alpha| \times |\beta|$$

"In other words, the absolute value of a product of complex numbers is the product of the absolute values of its factors."

Miruka stopped and looked at Tetra. "You good so far?"

Tetra nodded, her face a mask of determination.

"Okay, on to the argument for $\alpha\beta$. From the diagram you can see this:"

$$\angle POQ' = \angle P'OQ' + \angle POP'$$

"But since $\triangle$OPQ and $\triangle$OP'Q' are similar, we can also say:"

$$\angle POQ = \angle P'OQ'$$

"From that, we get: "

$$\angle POQ' = \angle P'OQ' + \angle POP'$$
$$= \angle POQ + \angle POP'$$

"Since $\angle POQ' = \arg(\alpha\beta)$, $\angle POQ = \arg(\alpha)$, and $\angle POP' = \arg(\beta)$, we can write: "

$$\arg(\alpha\beta) = \arg(\alpha) + \arg(\beta)$$

"In other words, the argument of a product of complex numbers is the sum of the arguments of its factors. Here's a summary of all this polar notation stuff: "

Products of complex numbers	$\longleftrightarrow$	Products for absolute values and sums for arguments

$$\begin{cases} |\alpha\beta| & = |\alpha| \times |\beta| \\ \arg(\alpha\beta) & = \arg(\alpha) + \arg(\beta) \end{cases}$$

"It's no big surprise that absolute values become products, but it's interesting that arguments are sums. It's like the arguments are following the logarithm rules..."

Miruka paused to consider this.

"Anyway, now that we have a good geometric sense for what's going on when we multiply complex numbers, we can extend it to squares. Let's take another look at the complex plane to see how you can square something to get a negative."

5.2.3 ±i in the Complex Plane

"So tell me," Miruka said, looking straight at Tetra, "just what *is* this thing called '-1' we're looking for when we try to solve $x^2 = -1$?"

"What's -1?" Tetra asked. "Not...the number before 0?"

Miruka shook her head. "You're still thinking number lines. Sure, if you look at this as an algebra problem, you're asking, 'What numbers can I square to get -1?' But that didn't get you very far. Look at it as a *geometry* problem, though, and you're asking, 'What kind of scaling or rotation can I perform twice to get to -1?' Don't think of -1 as a step back from 0. Think of it as the point with an absolute value of 1 and an argument of $180°$."

"Whoa." Tetra's breath caught with the realization.

"We talked about how you can calculate complex numbers using products of absolute values and sums of arguments, right? Well, if I want a complex number that equals -1 when it's squared, then its absolute value has to still be 1 after the squaring. So what absolute value did I start with?"

"Just 1."

"Right. Also, the argument has to be something that becomes $180°$ when it gets doubled. So it must be...?"

"$90°$."

"And look what we get when we plot the point with absolute value 1 and a $90°$ argument:"

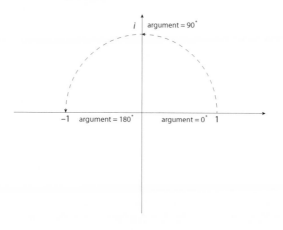

"Of course, i," Tetra said. She bit her lip and squinted at Miruka's diagram. "But hang on, you said I got the $x^2 = -1$ problem wrong because I only gave one solution. Where's the other one?"

"I was hoping you'd ask," Miruka said with a smile. "There's more than one way to get to an argument of $180°$, isn't there? Just go the other way around. Move $-90°$ twice and you end up at the same place as going in the $+90°$ direction, but this time passing through $-i$ on the way:"

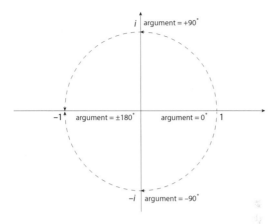

"±i are the complex numbers with an absolute value of 1, and an argument of ±90°, so squaring ±i are the two ways to get to −1. The only difference is the direction you take to get there."

It all makes sense when you put it on a graph. Numbers as points... That's just awesome."

Tetra picked up the notebook for a closer look. I took advantage of the lull to speak up.

"Since real numbers are included in the complex numbers, it seems like you should be able to do the same thing with those, too."

Miruka nodded.

"And thinking in terms of revolutions in the complex plane explains why multiplying two negative numbers gives you a positive," I continued. "Like, if you multiply −1 and −1 you're doing two rotations by the argument of −1, which is 180°. You end up at 360°, or 0°, depending on how you look at it. In either case you're back where you started, at 1."

"Did you follow that, Tetra?" Miruka asked.

"Sure did!"

"Good. The takeaway is that multiplying two negatives and getting a positive is just as natural as doing an about-face twice and ending up facing the same way as when you started out."

The conversation stirred memories of an earlier discussion Miruka and I had about the omega waltz. If you think only in terms of the real numbers, it's hard to explain how a product of negatives gives you a positive—in any kind of way that makes sense, at least. But once you free yourself from the restrictions of the real number line, once you make your way out into the world of complex numbers, everything becomes clear. Looking down at the reals from this higher dimension exposes things that were once hidden.

"I really like this," Tetra said. "Turning numbers into points bothered me at first, not to mention treating operations on numbers as moving those points around, but now that I see it this way, I really *get* it."

"And you should," Miruka said. "Associating numbers and points brings algebra and geometry together."

Algebra		Geometry
The set of all complex numbers	$\longleftrightarrow$	The complex plane
The complex number $a + bi$	$\longleftrightarrow$	The point (a, b) in the complex plane
A set of complex numbers	$\longleftrightarrow$	A shape in the complex plane
A sum of complex numbers	$\longleftrightarrow$	Diagonal of a parallelogram
A product of complex numbers	$\longleftrightarrow$	Products of absolute values, sums of arguments

"The complex plane is the ballroom where algebra and geometry dance," Miruka placed a finger to her lips, "and kiss."

5.3 FIVE LATTICE POINTS

5.3.1 A New Card

The next day after school, I headed home alone. As usual, I'd spent the afternoon in the library working on math, but Miruka had gone home early and Tetra never showed up. Thanks to the lack of intrusion I'd gotten a lot done, but I have to admit it was kind of lonely.

Partway along my shortcut to the station, a familiar voice stopped me.

"Wait up! Wait up!" Tetra gasped and wheezed as she ran.

"Oh, hey," I said. "I thought you already went home."

"No, I was... I was just..." Tetra doubled over, panting to catch her breath. "Just running a little late."

"You need to sit down?"

"I'll be fine in a sec." She took a deep breath. "Anyway, I went by the teachers' lounge this morning. I told Mr. Muraki about the stuff we were doing with the complex plane, and he gave us a new problem."

Tetra pulled a card out of her bag.

Problem 5-2 (Five lattice points)

Let a and b be integers, and call the point in the complex plane corresponding to a complex number $a+bi$ a 'lattice point.'

Given five distinct lattice points, show that regardless of where they lie you can select two of those lattice points as P, Q such that the midpoint M of the line segment PQ lies on a lattice point. (Note that M does not have to be one of the five original lattice points.)

"Think you can do it?" Tetra asked with a sly smile.

"Just five random points to work with? Dunno, could be tricky."

I read the card once more as I continued walking and let the problem bounce around in my skull. Tetra had gotten a second wind, and she was bounding about, sneaking glances at my expression like a puppy that was up to no good.

The midpoint of a line segment PQ would be the point that evenly divides it into two—a geometric construction. But I'm starting with two points (x, y) and (x', y'), which means I'm going to have to get to the geometry by way of algebra. No trouble representing the midpoints, at least. That would just be $\left(\frac{x+x'}{2}, \frac{y+y'}{2}\right)$. *Hmmm...*

"Maybe if I set aside a full day to work on it," I began. "But if I still don't have it after that, I dunno."

"So, sounds like a pretty hard problem, huh?" Tetra's smile was so big it looked painful.

"All right, what's going on?"

"Nothing. Just that—" Tetra raised a fist in a victory pose, *"I already solved it!"*

"Solved what?"

"The problem!"

"Who did?"

"I did!"

"Did what?"

"Solved the— Ha ha, very funny. Seriously though, there was something about this that made me think I could figure it out, and I *did*! And it only took a few hours!"

"Of class time not paying attention, I suppose?"

Tetra dismissed my gibe with a wave.

"Totally worth it. So, wanna hear?"

"Hear what?"

"My solution to the problem, derf! You do wanna hear it...don't you?"

Tetra clutched her hands to her chest and looked up at me with pleading eyes.

She knew I couldn't say no to that...

"Of course."

Tetra thrust her arm forward, index finger outstretched. "To Beans!"

5.3.2   Pigeonholing

We walked into the coffee shop, ordered enough to justify our presence, and sat down side-by-side at a table near the window. *Easier to share the notebook that way*, I told myself.

"Okay," Tetra began, "let's start with an example. Those are—"

"—the key to understanding. Yeah, yeah."

"And we'll use these as our random points:"

$$A(4,1), \quad B(7,3), \quad C(4,6), \quad D(2,5), \quad E(1,2)$$

"Sure enough, if you calculate the midpoints, one lands right on a lattice point. In this case, let A and D be your P and Q, and the midpoint M is at $(3, 3)$."

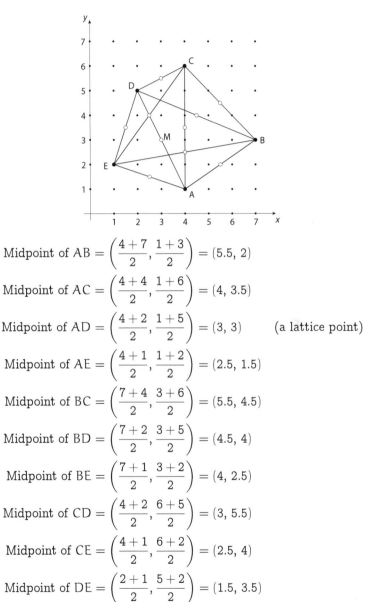

Midpoint of AB $= \left(\dfrac{4+7}{2}, \dfrac{1+3}{2}\right) = (5.5, 2)$

Midpoint of AC $= \left(\dfrac{4+4}{2}, \dfrac{1+6}{2}\right) = (4, 3.5)$

Midpoint of AD $= \left(\dfrac{4+2}{2}, \dfrac{1+5}{2}\right) = (3, 3)$ (a lattice point)

Midpoint of AE $= \left(\dfrac{4+1}{2}, \dfrac{1+2}{2}\right) = (2.5, 1.5)$

Midpoint of BC $= \left(\dfrac{7+4}{2}, \dfrac{3+6}{2}\right) = (5.5, 4.5)$

Midpoint of BD $= \left(\dfrac{7+2}{2}, \dfrac{3+5}{2}\right) = (4.5, 4)$

Midpoint of BE $= \left(\dfrac{7+1}{2}, \dfrac{3+2}{2}\right) = (4, 2.5)$

Midpoint of CD $= \left(\dfrac{4+2}{2}, \dfrac{6+5}{2}\right) = (3, 5.5)$

Midpoint of CE $= \left(\dfrac{4+1}{2}, \dfrac{6+2}{2}\right) = (2.5, 4)$

Midpoint of DE $= \left(\dfrac{2+1}{2}, \dfrac{5+2}{2}\right) = (1.5, 3.5)$

Tetra held up a clenched fist.

"Here's where I used my secret weapon!" she announced, eyes gleaming.

"Hypnosis?" I guessed. "X-ray vision?"

"Parity! I thought of the coordinates as complex numbers $x + yi$ and looked at the parity of x and y. When you do that, you get four possible patterns:"

	x	y
Pattern 1	even	even
Pattern 2	even	odd
Pattern 3	odd	even
Pattern 4	odd	odd

"We're given five points. Since there are only four patterns they can be, the xs and ys will both have the same parity in at least one pair. Whatever pair that is, let them be P and Q. Say we got $P(\text{even}, \text{odd})$ and $Q(\text{even}, \text{odd})$. When we calculate the midpoint M, it looks something like this:"

$$\left(\frac{\text{even} + \text{even}}{2}, \frac{\text{odd} + \text{odd}}{2} \right)$$

"Whether you're adding two even numbers or two odd numbers, the result will be an even number:"

$$\begin{cases} \text{even} + \text{even} & = \text{even} \\ \text{odd} + \text{odd} & = \text{even} \end{cases}$$

"That means when you divide them by two, the result will be an integer. And since you end up with a coordinate with two integers, it's a lattice point!"

Answer 5-2 (Five lattice points)

Regardless of how the five initial lattice points are chosen, the coordinates of at least one pair will have respectively the same parity. Let that pair be P and Q.

Tetra leaned back and folded her arms.

"Done and done."

"Don't let Miruka find out you're stealing her material," I said.

Tetra glanced around.

"Don't worry, you're safe. Good job, Tetra. A classic case of the pigeonhole principle."

"What's that?" Tetra asked.

"It says that if you have a pigeon roost with n holes and $n + 1$ birds, somebody's gonna have a roommate."

The Pigeonhole Principle

If $n + 1$ pigeons are put into n pigeonholes, at least one hole will contain more than one pigeon. Please use only an integer number of pigeons when doing this.

"Doesn't sound like super advanced math," Tetra said.

"No, but that doesn't mean it isn't useful."

"Still not seeing the pigeons in this problem, though."

"Your parity patterns are the nests, and the five lattice points are the birds. Four patterns, five points to squeeze into them, right?"

Tetra pulled a pen out of her pencil case.

"Kinda funny that something so obvious has its own name and all," Tetra said as she copied the definition into her notebook.

"Hey, can I see that?"

"What, my notes? They're a mess."

I flipped back and saw Tetra had filled at least five pages with lattices, points, and connecting lines. She had obviously tested every pattern of lines she could think of.

"Very thorough," I commented.

"Well, I wanted to make sure I tried it on enough examples. Of course, it always worked, no matter what I tried. When I went back to the definition of a lattice point, both coordinates being an integer looked like the thing to focus on. I figured you had to be able to divide the sum of the coordinates by 2, and that led me to the parity patterns, and everything just sort of fell into place from there. I never would have figured it out if it wasn't for the stuff you told me about the other day, though."

Tetra looked at me with a huge grin.

"Pays off to work hard on something, doesn't it?"

As Tetra replaced her pen into the case, I noticed two charms hanging from it. One was a thin silver wire twisted into the shape of a fish. The other was a metallic blue 'M'—not a 'T' for 'Tetra.'

So who's 'M'?

5.4 BREAKABLE PRIMES

The next day after class, I found myself alone with Miruka in our homeroom.

"How's that little cousin of yours?" she asked.

"Yuri? Much better, thanks. Her foot healed up fine."

"You two are pretty close, huh?"

"Yeah, we were practically raised together."

"She looks just like you."

"Well, we are related."

"She's tough, too."

"I think she really got into the grilling you gave her the other day."

"You have the same ears."

"The same *ears*? How could you remember what her ears look like?"

"Inflection points," Miruka said, reaching out and touching my left ear. "You both have an inflection point right here."

"Oh...yeah?" I managed.

Miruka cocked her head. "You're blushing."

"No I'm not."

"Trust me, you're blushing."

"I can see myself in your glasses. See?"

I moved my face closer to Miruka's. Maybe a little closer than necessary.

"Not helpful. I can only see myself in yours," Miruka said.

She reached out and grabbed both of my ears, pulling my face still closer to hers. Then—

"You guys in here?" a voice echoed from the hall. Miruka let go of my ears, and I stumbled backwards.

Tetra appeared in the doorway.

"Oh, there you are! You weren't in the library, so I came looking."

"And here we are," I said, doing my best to act nonchalant.

"I found the *coolest thing*," Tetra said, waving her notebook over her head and walking toward us. "When you use 'the product of a sum and a difference is a difference of squares' on complex numbers, you can factor primes!"

I shook my head. "That doesn't make any sense."

"Like this," she said, showing us a page in her notebook:

$$2 = 1 + 1 \qquad \text{split 2 into a sum}$$
$$= 1^2 + 1 \qquad \text{write 1 as } 1^2$$
$$= 1^2 - (-1) \qquad \text{write 1 as } -(-1)$$
$$= 1^2 - i^2 \qquad \text{from } -1 = i^2$$
$$= (1 + i)(1 - i) \qquad \text{rewrite the difference of squares}$$

"In other words, you get this:"

$$2 = (1 + i)(1 - i)$$

"See?" Tetra said. "A factored prime!"

"Ah, okay," I said. "I see what you're trying to say. Nice try, but no. You didn't factor a prime, you just wrote it as a product of complex numbers. Prime factorization means breaking a number down into a product of *integers*."

"Oh," Tetra said. Her eyes dropped to the notebook, and her shoulders seemed to wilt.

"I know you like prime factorization, but you have to—*ouch!*"

"That's no way to teach somebody," Miruka said, glaring.

"I'm no teacher. And you don't have to kick me!"

"Let's take a broader perspective on things," Miruka said, ignoring me. "He's right that $2 = (1 + i)(1 - i)$ isn't a product of integers. So how about if we loosen up, and call complex numbers with integer parts, like $3 + 2i$ or $-4 + 8i$, a *kind* of integer. In fact, numbers like that already have a name—Gaussian integers. Of course, 0 is an integer, too, so that means numbers where the i is multiplied by 0—a 'normal' integer, in other words—are also Gaussian integers."

Miruka walked to the blackboard and wrote a single symbol:

$$\mathbb{Z}$$

"This means the set of all integers," she said.

She wrote another:

$$\mathbb{Z}[i]$$

"This means the set of all Gaussian integers. Think of it as 'the integers with i' to remember it."

$\mathbb{Z}$ and $\mathbb{Z}[i]$

A number $a + bi$ where a, b are integers is called a 'Gaussian integer.'

$\mathbb{Z} = \{\cdots, -2, -1, 0, 1, 2, \cdots\}$ the set of all integers

$\mathbb{Z}[i] = \{a + bi \mid a \in \mathbb{Z}, b \in \mathbb{Z}\}$ the set of all Gaussian integers

(Here, $\{a + bi \mid a \in \mathbb{Z}, b \in \mathbb{Z}\}$ means 'all numbers in the form $a + bi$ where $a \in \mathbb{Z}$ and $b \in \mathbb{Z}$.')

"Just like the integers are dots on the number line, the Gaussian integers form an array of dots in the complex plane. The Gaussian integers are like a 2D version of the 1D vanilla integers."

"I've seen those," Tetra said. "They're lattice points!"

"That's right," said Miruka. "The lattice points in the complex plane correspond to the Gaussian integers."

Tetra grinned.

"The other thing you've noticed is that while the regular integer 2 is a prime, the Gaussian integer 2 isn't. More precisely, some integers are prime in $\mathbb{Z}$, but not in $\mathbb{Z}[i]$ because they can be broken down into a product."

"Cool," I said. "Kinda feels like splitting the atom or something."

"An interesting way to put it," Miruka said. There was still ice in her voice.

"So none of the primes we're used to are prime in $\mathbb{Z}[i]$?" asked Tetra.

"I never said 'none.' The regular integers fall into two types: those that can be factored into a product when you bring them into the world of $\mathbb{Z}[i]$—let's call those breakable primes—and those that still can't be split up after the journey. Unbreakable primes, I guess." Miruka noticed Tetra writing in her notebook. "Be careful," Miruka said. "Those are just my names for them. They aren't real math terms."

"No worries," Tetra said. "Doubt I'll be talking about them with a mathematician any time soon."

"While you're at it, write down that ± 1 aren't composite numbers *or* primes. They're units. Here, let me break it all down for you." Miruka took Tetra's pencil and wrote in her notebook:

$$\text{The integers } \mathbb{Z} \begin{cases} \text{Zero} & (0) \\ \text{Units} & (\pm 1) \\ \text{Composites} & (\pm 4, \pm 6, \pm 8, \pm 9, \pm 10, \dots) \\ \text{Primes} & \begin{cases} \text{"Breakable" primes} \\ \text{"Unbreakable" primes} \end{cases} \end{cases}$$

Miruka looked at our faces in turn before walking back to the blackboard. She picked up a piece of chalk and stood with her eyes closed for several seconds.

"Let's break some primes," she said. "Maybe we can find a pattern." The chalk clacked across the board:

$2 = (1+i)(1-i)$	breakable
$3 = 3$	not breakable
$5 = (1+2i)(1-2i)$	breakable
$7 = 7$	not breakable
$11 = 11$	not breakable
$13 = (2+3i)(2-3i)$	breakable
$17 = (4+i)(4-i)$	breakable

"No pattern yet," she said. "Let's circle the unbreakable ones."

She wrote a series of primes, then circled some:

$$2 \quad \textcircled{3} \quad 5 \quad \textcircled{7} \quad \textcircled{11} \quad 13 \quad 17 \quad \cdots$$

"Still nothing jumping at me," she said. "Let's try all the integers, from 2 to 17. That should get us closer:"

$$2 \quad \textcircled{3} \quad 4 \quad 5 \quad 6 \quad \textcircled{7} \quad 8 \quad 9 \quad 10 \quad \textcircled{11} \quad 12 \quad 13 \quad 14 \quad 15 \quad 16 \quad 17 \quad \cdots$$

"Now we just rearrange things:

$$
\begin{array}{cccc}
 & & 2 & \textcircled{3} \\
4 & 5 & 6 & \textcircled{7} \\
8 & 9 & 10 & \textcircled{11} \\
12 & 13 & 14 & 15 \\
16 & 17 & \cdots &
\end{array}
$$

"This is *so cool*." Tetra's cheeks were flushed with excitement. "I can't wait to see how it turns out!"

"Things are getting interesting, aren't they," Miruka said. "Let's try some primes beyond 17."

Miruka tapped out a long list of primes in a staccato of chalky squeaks:

$19 = 19$	not breakable
$23 = 23$	not breakable
$29 = (5 + 2i)(5 - 2i)$	breakable
$31 = 31$	not breakable
$37 = (6 + i)(6 - i)$	breakable
$41 = (5 + 4i)(5 - 4i)$	breakable
$43 = 43$	not breakable
$47 = 47$	not breakable
$53 = (7 + 2i)(7 - 2i)$	breakable
$59 = 59$	not breakable
$61 = (6 + 5i)(6 - 5i)$	breakable
$67 = 67$	not breakable

$$71 = 71 \qquad\qquad\qquad\text{not breakable}$$
$$73 = (8 + 3i)(8 - 3i) \qquad \text{breakable}$$
$$79 = 79 \qquad\qquad\qquad\text{not breakable}$$
$$83 = 83 \qquad\qquad\qquad\text{not breakable}$$
$$89 = (8 + 5i)(8 - 5i) \qquad \text{breakable}$$
$$97 = (9 + 4i)(9 - 4i) \qquad \text{breakable}$$

"Okay, time to make our table. This time, I'm just going to draw a dot in place of non-primes:"

		2	③
·	5	·	⑦
·	·	·	⑪
·	13	·	·
·	17	·	⑲
·	·	·	㉓
·	·	·	·
·	29	·	㉛
·	·	·	·
·	37	·	·
·	41	·	㊸
·	·	·	㊼
·	·	·	·
·	53	·	·
·	·	·	(59)
·	61	·	·
·	·	·	(67)
·	·	·	(71)
·	73	·	·
·	·	·	(79)
·	·	·	(83)
·	·	·	·
·	89	·	·
·	·	·	·
·	97	·	·

"Wow," I said. "That's just...wow. All the circled ones are on the right."

"Meaning?" Miruka said.

"Well, from the way you've lined them up, it would mean that when you divide an unbreakable prime by 4 the remainder is 3. But...I don't get it. What's so special about the remainder when you divide by 4?"

"Before we talk about that, we need to be sure that's always the case:"

Problem 5-3 (Breakable primes)

Given a prime p and integers a, b such that $p = (a + bi)(a - bi)$, show that the remainder when dividing p by 4 cannot be 3.

"The proof's not as hard as you might think," Miruka said. "There are only four possibilities for the remainder after dividing by 4: $0, 1, 2$, or 3. So we can write any integer in terms of another integer q like this:"

$$\begin{cases} 4q + 0 \\ 4q + 1 \\ 4q + 2 \\ 4q + 3 \end{cases}$$

"Square each of those, and factor out a 4:"

$$\begin{cases} (4q + 0)^2 = 16q^2 & = 4(4q^2) + 0 \\ (4q + 1)^2 = 16q^2 + 8q + 1 & = 4(4q^2 + 2q) + 1 \\ (4q + 2)^2 = 16q^2 + 16q + 4 & = 4(4q^2 + 4q + 1) + 0 \\ (4q + 3)^2 = 16q^2 + 24q + 9 & = 4(4q^2 + 6q + 2) + 1 \end{cases}$$

"So if you divide a square number by 4, the remainder can only be 0 or 1. If you divide a sum of squares like $a^2 + b^2$, then the remainder can only be $0 + 0 = 0$, $0 + 1 = 1$, or $1 + 1 = 2$. Never 3. Since $(a + bi)(a - bi) = a^2 + b^2$, the remainder can never be 3 here, either."

Answer 5-3 (Breakable primes)

1. The remainder when dividing a^2 by 4 is 0 or 1.

2. The remainder when dividing b^2 by 4 is 0 or 1.

3. The remainder when dividing the sum of squares $a^2 + b^2$ by 4 must be 0, 1, or 2.

4. Therefore, the remainder when dividing $a^2 + b^2 = (a + bi)(a - bi) = p$ by 4 cannot be 3.

"We can go a little further, in fact, and say that if p is an odd prime, this is always true:"

$$p = (a + bi)(a - bi) \iff \text{dividing } p \text{ by 4 leaves a remainder of 1}$$

"Remember that odd-one-out quiz I gave you? The one where 257 was the answer?" Miruka asked me. "That was because 257 was the only breakable prime of the bunch. It was the only one with a remainder 1 when divided by 4:"

$239 = 239$	not breakable
$251 = 251$	not breakable
$257 = (16 + i)(16 - i)$	breakable
$263 = 263$	not breakable
$271 = 271$	not breakable
$283 = 283$	not breakable

"Primes leaving a remainder of 3 when divided by 4 can't be factored into *any* form, not just $(a + bi)(a - bi)$, so those primes in $\mathbb{Z}$ also act like primes in $\mathbb{Z}[i]$."

I was blown away. I could deal with the fact that using Gaussian integers could "break" numbers that were prime in $\mathbb{Z}$. What got me was that something like remainders told you when that happened. I mean, *remainders*? How could something so basic be related to all this? I'd learned about remainders in *elementary school*.

"This is great," Tetra enthused. "I never thought of calculations as being something that changed, but things are different depending on where you do them, aren't they? Whether it's in the complex plane, or in $\mathbb{Z}[i]$, or in $\mathbb{Z}$..."

"The nature of calculations is fascinating," Miruka said. "Thinking about calculations in general terms leads to something called groups. Very cool stuff. But it's getting late—we'll save group theory for tomorrow."

"I can't wait!" Tetra said.

Neither could I.

It's funny how we assume a kind of momentum to our lives, how we expect each day to be like the one before. Gaussian integers today, group theory tomorrow. Another afternoon with Miruka in the library.

I'd lost sight of something she'd once told me: You never know what's going to come next. Predictions fail.

A proof that $\triangle OPQ$ and $\triangle OP'Q'$ are similar

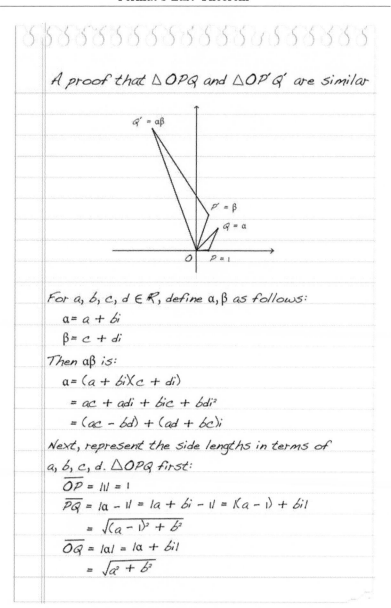

For $a, b, c, d \in \mathbb{R}$, define α, β as follows:

$\alpha = a + bi$

$\beta = c + di$

Then $\alpha\beta$ is:

$\alpha = (a + bi)(c + di)$

$\quad = ac + adi + bic + bdi^2$

$\quad = (ac - bd) + (ad + bc)i$

Next, represent the side lengths in terms of a, b, c, d. $\triangle OPQ$ first:

$\overline{OP} = |1| = 1$

$\overline{PQ} = |\alpha - 1| = |a + bi - 1| = |(a - 1) + bi|$

$\quad = \sqrt{(a - 1)^2 + b^2}$

$\overline{OQ} = |\alpha| = |a + bi|$

$\quad = \sqrt{a^2 + b^2}$

Next, the lengths of the sides of $\triangle OP'Q'$:

$$\overline{OP'} = |\beta| = |c + di| = \sqrt{c^2 + d^2} = 1 \times \sqrt{c^2 + d^2}$$

$$= \overline{OP} \times |\beta|$$

$$\overline{P'Q'} = |\alpha\beta - \beta|$$

$$= |(\alpha - 1)\beta|$$

$$= |((\alpha - 1) + bi) \times (c + di)|$$

$$= |((\alpha - 1)c - bd) + ((\alpha - 1)d + bc)i|$$

$$= \sqrt{((\alpha - 1)c - bd)^2 + ((\alpha - 1)d + bc)^2}$$

$$= \sqrt{((\alpha - 1)^2 + b^2)(c^2 + d^2)}$$

$$= \sqrt{((\alpha - 1)^2 + b^2)} \times \sqrt{(c^2 + d^2)}$$

$$= \overline{PQ} \times |\beta|$$

$$\overline{OQ'} = |\alpha\beta|$$

$$= |(ac - bd) + (ad + bc)i|$$

$$= \sqrt{(ac - bd)^2 + (ad + bc)^2}$$

$$= \sqrt{a^2c^2 - 2abcd + b^2d^2 + a^2d^2 + 2abcd + b^2c^2}$$

$$= \sqrt{a^2c^2 + b^2d^2 + a^2d^2 + b^2c^2}$$

$$= \sqrt{(a^2 + b^2)(c^2 + d^2)}$$

$$= \sqrt{(a^2 + b^2)} \times \sqrt{(c^2 + d^2)}$$

$$= \overline{OQ} \times |\beta|$$

In the end, we have:

$$\overline{OP'} = \overline{OP} \times |\beta|$$

$$\overline{P'Q'} = \overline{PQ} \times |\beta|$$

$$\overline{OQ'} = \overline{OQ} \times |\beta|$$

and thus corresponding sides are in proportion:

$$\overline{OP} : \overline{PQ} : \overline{OQ} = \overline{OP'} : \overline{P'Q'} : \overline{OQ'}$$

CHAPTER **6**

Abelian Groups

When I look back on my life and think
about the times I was the most creative,
I realize that those were the times when
I worked under the harshest conditions.

DONALD KNUTH
*Things a Computer Scientist Rarely
Talks About*

6.1 THE ACCIDENT

I had just sat down in homeroom when Tetra burst in.

"It's Miruka!" she shouted. Tears streaked her face. "She was in an accident!"

I sprang from my seat, my body on autopilot.

"Just now, near the station—a truck..."

"*A truck?*" I was already moving toward the door. "What happened!"

"She was standing at the intersection waiting for the light. A truck came out of nowhere, I heard its brakes screech... An ambulance came, but I was just frozen there, and..." Sobs swallowed the rest of her words.

I bolted out of the room, and in a heartbeat I was down the stairs and through the school gate. I cut through alleys and empty lots towards where I knew it must have happened—the only big intersection between the station and school.

A crowd had gathered in front of the truck, which was half wrapped around a telephone pole. Shattered glass was everywhere. There was a lone police car, but no ambulance, and no Miruka.

I took off again, sprinting towards the hospital.

* * *

I'd never run so hard in my life. I ignored crossing lights, jumped rails—it's a miracle I didn't get hit by a car myself.

Please be okay!

I stumbled into the hospital, too breathless to speak. The receptionist stared at me, then picked up the phone and made a call.

I stared at the whiteboard behind the desk, but none of the marks made sense to me. I had the sensation time around me was slowing, as if in a dream. "I think you're looking for Examination Room A," the receptionist finally said.

I sprinted down the hall, and a moment later I stood in front of her door. I froze, suddenly unsure of myself.

I nudged the door open. A nurse stood with her back to me, washing something. There was a long curtain in the middle of the room, drawn to conceal a bed.

My feet carried me into the room of their own accord, and I pushed the door shut behind me. The nurse turned around.

"Can I help you?"

"My friend—Miruka. She was in an accident. Is she...?"

"She's sleeping right now. You'll have to—"

"I'm awake," came a voice from behind the curtain.

* * *

The nurse pulled the curtain back. Miruka was lying on the bed wearing a blue hospital gown. Her glasses rested on a nearby table; they were bent at odd angles. I realized I'd never seen her without them on.

"Miruka..." I said, but no other words formed.

She answered with a sigh.

I collapsed into the chair next to her bed.

"Are you okay?" I finally managed.

"You'd be surprised how a big truck like that can just come out of nowhere. I was crossing the street—I tried to get out of the way, but I lost my balance and fell. Slammed my arm into something. Hurts pretty bad."

She held up her left arm. It was wrapped in bandages.

"So...it didn't hit you?" I asked.

"That's the funny thing; I'm not sure. Can't remember. My leg got messed up somehow, too. See?"

She started to lift the sheet covering her legs. I saw another flash of beige bandaging.

"That's okay," I said, holding up a hand.

"I guess my head got a pretty strong whack. I remember trying to stand up, but everything was kinda fuzzy. When I finally figured out what was going on, I was already in the ambulance."

"You need anything?" I asked. "Juice? Water?"

"I'm good."

"I'll let you rest then. I'll be outside. Let me know if you need me."

I stood, and she held out her right hand.

"I can't see your face," she said.

I leaned down over her. She rested her hand on my cheek.

I sat back down in the chair and took her hand in both of mine, feeling its warmth. She closed her eyes.

We stayed that way for a while, saying nothing. Eventually her grip loosened as she slipped into sleep. I just sat there, holding her hand as I gazed at her face. Her long lashes. The soft curve of her mouth. Her chest rising and falling as she breathed.

Thank God you didn't leave me, I thought as I let go of her hand to wipe the tears from my eyes.

6.2 DAY ONE

6.2.1 Introducing Operations into Sets

A summons to court came the next day from the queen herself:

```
100 tests & nothing wrong but stuck here for 3 days.
Bored 2 tears. Need math. Bring T.
```

Which is how Tetra and I ended up enrolled in Group Theory 101, held daily in hospital room 112.

"We start with sets," Miruka began.

Her hair was tied back, and she had raised her bed to a semi-inclined position. My notebook was in front of her on the rolling table she used for meals.

"We already know several," she continued, writing as she spoke:

- $\mathbb{N}$: the set $\{1, 2, 3, \cdots\}$ of all natural numbers

- $\mathbb{Z}$: the set $\{\cdots, -3, -2, -1, 0, 1, 2, 3, \cdots\}$ of all integers

- $\mathbb{Q}$: the set of all rational numbers

- $\mathbb{R}$: the set of all real numbers

- $\mathbb{C}$: the set of all complex numbers

"We've been learning about these since elementary school, and we've learned how to use various operations to calculate with these numbers."

A knowing smile spread across Miruka's face.

"But the real fun comes when we create our own sets, and our own operations."

6.2.2 Operations

"Say we have a set G, and an operation we'll call $\star$ defined on it."

"What's that mean?" Tetra asked.

"That for any a and b in G, we can say this:"

$$a \star b \in G$$

"When this is true, we say G is 'closed' under the operation $\star$."

Tetra raised her hand.

"But what does that star operation *do*?"

"Doesn't matter. It just does *something*."

Tetra pursed her lips.

"If you absolutely have to think in specifics," Miruka said, "think of it as a plus sign, or a multiplication symbol. But what you really need to do is think of it as a variable standing for some operation over G, the same way that a and b stand for elements in G."

"One more question," Tetra said. "Remind me what the symbol that looks like an 'E' stands for?"

"Element," Miruka said. "It shows membership in a set. So when you want to say 'a is an element of G,' you write this:"

$$a \in G$$

"You'll also hear people say 'a belongs to G,' or even just 'a is in G.'"

"Got it. But here, you're saying the starred stuff is in G?"

"Right. We don't know what the result of $a \star b$ is, and we don't care. All we care about is that whatever the result is, it'd better be in G. Here, let me draw a picture of it..." Miruka's hand hesitated. "On second thought, you do it. I can't see well enough without my glasses."

Miruka shoved the notebook in my direction. I did as she asked, of course, and drew a diagram showing a, b, and $a \star b$:

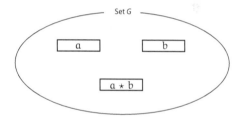

"Okay, I'm good now," Tetra said. "No, wait, I'm not! Why did you name it G, even though we're talking about sets? Shouldn't it be S...?"

"Because this is just our starting point. We want to build up to talking about groups."

"Gotcha. I'll shut up now."

"Don't shut up yet. I'm going to test you to make sure you're getting all this. So tell me, if $\mathbb{N}$ is the set of all natural numbers—the positive integers—is this true?" Miruka took the notebook back and wrote in it:

$$1 \in \mathbb{N}$$

"Yes, because 1 is a natural number."

"Good. How about this one?"

$$2 + 3 \in \mathbb{N}$$

"2 + 3 is 5, which is a natural number, so yes, that's a true statement."

"Right. I'm going to be picky, though, and tell you to say $2 + 3$ *is equal to* 5, not $2 + 3$ *is* 5."

"Fine, $2 + 3$ *is equal to* 5."

"Okay, here comes the bonus round." Miruka stared straight into Tetra's eyes. "Is the set of all natural numbers $\mathbb{N}$ closed under the + operation?"

"Um, yes? At least, I think so."

"Why?"

"I dunno, it just seems... I can't explain it."

"Go back to the definition," I said.

"You be quiet," Miruka said with a glare at me. "Go back to the definition, Tetra. For any elements a and b in the natural numbers, $a + b$ will give you a natural number, right? That means the set of natural numbers $\mathbb{N}$ is closed under the + operation."

"So the only important thing is that adding two natural numbers gives me a natural number?"

"That's it," Miruka said. "That's exactly what it means to say that a set G is closed under an operation $\star$."

"Got it!" Tetra glowed with satisfaction.

Set closure under an operation

A set G is said to be closed under an operation $\star$ when, for any elements a, b in G, $a \star b$ is in G.

6.2.3 Associativity

Miruka raced ahead.

"Now we need to talk about associativity. The associative property says it doesn't matter what order you do the operation in, as long as you don't change the sequence of the operands:"

$$(a \star b) \star c = a \star (b \star c)$$

Tetra raised her hand again.

"I understand the associative property, like, how $(2 + 3) + 4 = 2 + (3 + 4)$ and all, but do we really need to *prove* that?"

"Nobody said we're going to prove it," Miruka said. "For now, I just want you to know that something called the associative property exists, and this is what it means. I'm going to bring up several properties, and in the end we'll say that all of them are needed to create a group. Think of all this as prep work."

"How am I supposed to know when I'm supposed to prove something like this, and when to just move on?"

"It never hurts to ask," I said.

The associative property

The operation $\star$ is associative on the set G if for all a, b, c in G,

$$(a \star b) \star c = a \star (b \star c).$$

6.2.4   The Identity Element

"Next is the identity element. When you add 0 to a number, or multiply it by 1, nothing happens, right? The identity element is a mathematical representation of that—an element in the set that doesn't change other elements, like 0 under addition or 1 under multiplication. It's often written as e. So if you use the operation to combine any element a with e, the result will just be a."

The identity element e

An element e of a set G is called "an identity element with respect to $\star$" if the following holds for all elements a in G:

$$a \star e = e \star a = a$$

"I'm starting to feel like I was the one who got hit by a truck," Tetra said, rubbing her head. "So this identity element thing. Which one is it, 0 or 1?"

"In the set of all integers $\mathbb{Z}$, the identity element under addition is 0. But under multiplication it's 1," Miruka said.

"Huh?"

"The value of the identity changes, depending on the set and the operation. But it doesn't matter what its value is, so long as $a \star e = e \star a = a$ holds for all a in G. Whatever element makes that a true statement is called e. Specific values are fine if it helps you wrap your head around it, but when you start doing proofs you need to rely on these axioms."

"I am so confused..." Tetra sighed.

"Let me put it this way. The only thing that determines if an element is an identity or not is if it satisfies these equations. The definition comes from the math."

"Okay. I'm not sure I understand all this yet, but I'm getting there."

I listened to their back-and-forth without comment, but once again I felt scales falling from my eyes. I'd always thought of a definition as a very precise use of words. I wasn't completely wrong there, but I'd never thought of *equations* as being "words" in that sense.

The definition comes from the math.

For all my talk of how much I loved mathematics, it surprised me that I'd never thought of using mathematical statements themselves as definitions. And this wasn't even the first time we'd done this; when we talked about i, we had defined that number as the solution to the equation $x^2 + 1 = 0$. The definition had come from the math.

6.2.5   The Inverse Element

"Next one's quick," Miruka said. "It's the inverse element, which we define like this:"

The inverse element

Let a be some element of a set G, and e an identity element. Then b is called an inverse of a for an operation $\star$ if the following holds:

$$a \star b = b \star a = e$$

"For the reals, the inverse of 3 under addition would be -3. Under multiplication it would be $\frac{1}{3}$."

6.2.6 Defining Groups

Miruka stretched, spreading her arms wide. I winced at the sight of her bandaged arm, but somehow she pulled the motion off gracefully.

"Okay, so we have operations, associativity, identities, and inverses. Now we can finally define what a group is:"

Definition of a group

A set G with an operation $\star$ is called a group if it meets the following conditions:

· G is closed under $\star$.

· The associative property holds for all elements in G.

· An identity element exists in G.

· The inverse of each element in G also exists in G.

"So there's our recipe: closure, associativity, an identity, and inverses. Bring them all together, and you've got yourself a group."

6.2.7 Example Groups

"So, Tetra," Miruka said. "What do you do when you get slammed with a definition like that?"

"Read it carefully," Tetra said.

"Goes without saying. What else?"

"Then I, uh..." Tetra stole a glance at me.

"Don't look at him. What do you do?"

"Make some examples?"

"Right. Creating examples exercises your understanding and creativity. Here's one for you to start with:"

> Does the set of all integers $\mathbb{Z}$ form a group under the $+$ operation?

"All integers $\mathbb{Z}$," Tetra said. "Yeah, I think that's a group."

"*Why* do you think that?"

"Because it...seems like it should be?"

"*Wrong*," Miruka bellowed, the word ringing in the air like a bell. "Check the axioms. If they're all met, it's a group. If they aren't, it isn't. The *math* defines the thing, not your intuition. So which is it?"

"Oh, uh... Let's see."

"Is $\mathbb{Z}$ closed under addition?"

"...Yes? Yes, because if you add two integers you get an inte—"

"Does the associative property hold?"

"Yes."

"Is there an identity element?"

"An identity... Yes."

"What is it?"

"The number you can add without changing things would be...0."

"Okay, if you have an integer a, does it have an integer inverse?"

"I'm not so sure about that one. How do I—"

"What's the definition of an inverse element?"

"Refresh my memory?"

"If e is the identity, then the inverse of a is the element b where $a \star b = b \star a = e$," said Miruka.

"Okay, so we need $a + b = b + a = 0$. So, uh..."

"What do you have to add to a to get 0?"

"Uh... $-a$?"

"Exactly. That means $-a$ is the inverse of a for the $+$ operation on the set of integers $\mathbb{Z}$. And given any integer a, its inverse $-a$ is also an element of the set $\mathbb{Z}$."

"Right."

"Well?" Miruka asked impatiently.

"Well what?"

"That was the last axiom. We've checked them all, and they all hold. That means the set of all integers $\mathbb{Z}$ forms a group under the $+$ operation."

"Oh, we're done?"

"We're done."

Miruka closed her eyes briefly, but she didn't let up for long. "Next problem:"

> Does the set of odd integers form a group under the $+$ operation?

"Let me run through the axioms," Tetra said, but she looked up from the notebook almost immediately. "No, it doesn't. If you add 1 and 3 you get 4, but 4 isn't odd."

"That's right," Miruka said. "The odd numbers aren't even closed under addition, so that can't be a group. Okay, next one:"

> Does the set of even integers form a group under the $+$ operation?

"Well the odd numbers didn't, so I'd think the even numbers won't, either..."

Miruka closed her eyes, frowned, and shook her head.

"Oh, wait! The sum of two evens is even! And associativity, the identity, and the inverse all work out, too! This one *is* a group!"

"Good. Next one:"

> Does the set of all integers $\mathbb{Z}$ form a group under the $\times$ operation?

"We just did that one. It formed a group," Tetra said.

"No, before we looked at addition. This time it's multiplication, and in this case it doesn't form a group. Why not?"

Tetra grew quiet and chewed on a nail, muttering to herself as she did.

"If you multiply two integers you get an integer, so it's closed. Associativity holds, of course. The identity would be, uh, 1. And...oh!"

"Got it, huh?" Miruka smiled.

"I did! It's the inverse! Like, 3 doesn't have an inverse, for example."

"Sure it does. $\frac{1}{3}$," Miruka said.

"Yeah, but that's not an integer! It's not in $\mathbb{Z}$!"

"Good job." Miruka let herself sink back into the bed. "Getting a feel for this now?"

"I think so. Definitely better than before."

6.2.8 The Smallest Group of All

"Here's one for you, Tetra," Miruka said. "What do you think the smallest group is?"

Problem 6-1

What is the group with the fewest elements?

"A group made from a set with nothing in it?" Tetra said.

"Yeah, the empty set," I added.

"No," Miruka said.

"No?" I said. "You can't have fewer than nothing. That has to be it."

"Okay, let's go through the axioms, then. What's your identity element?"

"Uh... Oh. Right."

"According to the axioms, the group will have to have at least one element, the identity."

"But it has to have an inverse, too," Tetra said. "So don't you need at least two elements?"

"Not if the identity is its own inverse," Miruka said.

"Oh. Hadn't thought of that."

Answer 6-1

The group with the fewest elements is $\{e\}$, with operation $\star$ defined as $e \star e = e$ (in other words, e is its own inverse).

"Sometimes it helps to make a table showing the operation working on all the elements of a group. Not very interesting for a group with just an identity in it, but here's what it would look like:"

$$
\begin{array}{c|c}
\star & e \\
\hline
e & e
\end{array}
$$

"Oh, cool. Sort of like a multiplication table for $\star$," I said. "I guess you could use these to define your own operations, too."

"Careful, though. A normal multiplication table isn't closed," Miruka said.

6.2.9 A Group with Two Elements

"Let's make this at least a little bit bigger," Miruka said. "How about adding an element?"

> ### Problem 6-2
>
> Construct a group with two elements.

"We'll use e as the identity element, as usual, and add a new element a. Let's start with an empty operation table and fill it in:"

$$
\begin{array}{c|cc}
\star & e & a \\
\hline
e & & \\
a & & \\
\end{array}
$$

"The definition of the identity element gives us some freebie answers. Do you see which ones, Tetra?"

"Well, the identity element doesn't change anything, so this row I guess? $e \star e$ and $e \star a$."

Tetra filled in the top row:

$$
\begin{array}{c|cc}
\star & e & a \\
\hline
e & e & a \\
a & & \\
\end{array}
$$

"You can do the column, too," Miruka said, filling in the spot for $a \star e = a$:

$\star$	e	a
e	e	a
a	a	

"Just one more left, $a \star a$. That one would be e:"

$\star$	e	a
e	e	a
a	a	e

Tetra's hand shot up.

"Why does it have to be e? Seems like we could make a different group where $a \star a = a$, like this."

Tetra drew a table for her proposed group:

$\star$	e	a
e	e	a
a	a	a

"Nope," Miruka said.

"If you try that—," I began.

Miruka shushed me. "She can do this." Miruka turned back to Tetra. "Why doesn't this work? Check the group axioms."

"Okay, let's see what goes wrong. There's only e and a in the table, so I guess it's closed. We said the identity is e... The inverse is... Oh, that's it—a doesn't have an inverse!"

"How did you find that?" Miruka asked.

"Because there's no e in the row or column for a, so neither $a \star e$ nor $a \star a$ equals e. That means there's no inverse for a, so one of the group axioms fails!"

"See, nothing to it," Miruka said.

Answer 6-2

A group with two elements can be created from an identity element e, another element a, and an operation $\star$ defined as follows:

$$e \star e = e$$
$$e \star a = a$$
$$a \star e = a$$
$$a \star a = e$$

The group operation table is as follows:

$\star$	e	a
e	e	a
a	a	e

6.2.10 Isomorphism

"Of course, you don't have to represent a group with two elements as $\{e, a\}$," Miruka said. "For example, if we use the $\times$ operator, we can make a group from $\{+1, -1\}$, with identity $+1$:"

$\times$	$+1$	-1
$+1$	$+1$	-1
-1	-1	$+1$

"Or we could make a group for the sums of even and odd numbers. Just let the elements be 'even' and 'odd,' and use $+$ for the operation. 'Even' is the identity:"

$+$	even	odd
even	even	odd
odd	odd	even

"We can even get totally abstract, and use new symbols for the elements and the operator. How about stars and circles?"

"Still a perfectly good group," Miruka said. "The white star is the identity."

"In a sense, they're all the same group," I said. "Numbers, words, stars... You're just replacing one thing with another in the same pattern."

"An excellent point. Actually, *any* group with just two elements will be the 'same' like this. You call groups like that 'isomorphic,' from the Greek *isos* meaning 'equal,' and *morphe* meaning 'form.'"

"Isomorphic..." Tetra muttered as she wrote the word down in her notebook.

"When you abstract things out to isomorphism, there's really only one group with two elements, and that's all there ever will be. The only changes you can make are cosmetic—when you get down to fundamentals, you're still just talking about the same thing."

Miruka paused and cocked her head. When she spoke again her words came slower than before. "It's interesting, though, that there's no axiom anywhere that says 'there is only a single group with two elements.' It's just a side effect of the group axioms. An implicit constraint that's a result of where we started."

She stopped to massage her arm through her bandages. Her voice dropped to a near whisper, and she gazed into the distance.

"A constraint that ties the elements of a group together, but doesn't just bind them. It creates order, builds form. The axioms are limits that give birth to structure."

6.3 DAY TWO

6.3.1 The Commutative Property

Tetra and I returned to the hospital the next day. Miruka wasted no time in quashing any attempts at small talk.

"Today we start with abelian groups," she announced as we entered the room. "Those are groups where the commutative property holds for all elements."

"And the commutative property is...?" Tetra asked.

"It says that you can apply an operation forwards or backwards," I said. "Here, let me write it down."

The commutative property

The operation $\star$ is commutative on the set G if for all a, b in G,

$$a \star b = b \star a.$$

"Isn't that the same as the associative property?" Tetra asked, hastily finding a chair. "They both say it doesn't matter what order you do things in, right?"

"Look closely," Miruka said. "The associative property is about which pair of elements you apply the operation to first; the commutative property is about the order of the elements when you apply it."

$$\begin{array}{ll} (a \star b) \star c = a \star (b \star c) & \text{the associative law} \\ a \star b = b \star a & \text{the commutative law} \end{array}$$

"The integers, rationals, and reals all form abelian groups under addition, so it's easy to confuse yourself if that's what you're thinking of."

"But not under the difference operation," I said. "Subtraction."

"Right. See how $a - b = b - a$ doesn't always hold, Tetra?"

"Oh, sure. I guess multiplying matrices would be the same, huh? We just learned about those."

"Another classic example," Miruka said. "The results you get depend on the order you do things in."

"How about the group with two elements we talked about yesterday? The commutative property works there, I think..."

$\star$	e	a
e	e	a
a	a	e

"Tell me why you can say that," Miruka said.

"Because $e \star a = a \star e$, right?"

"Right, the commutative property holds for this group. That means you've just proved the hypothesis that this group is abelian."

Definition of abelian group

A set G with an operation $\star$ is called an 'abelian group' if it meets the following conditions:

· G is closed under $\star$.

· The associative property holds for all elements in G.

· An identity element exists in G.

· The inverse of each element in G also exists in G.

· The commutative property holds for all elements in G.

(Note: The last condition is the only difference with the definition of a general group.)

6.3.2 Regular Polygons

"Speaking of the group of two elements," Miruka said, "that reminds me of the set $\{-1, +1\}$ we mentioned yesterday:"

$\times$	$+1$	-1
$+1$	$+1$	-1
-1	-1	$+1$

"We talked about multiplication then, but $x = -1, +1$ are also the solutions to this, aren't they:"

$$x^2 = 1$$

"So the solutions of that equation form a group—another example of a group springing forth from constraints. The constraints of an equation, in this case. Let's see what happens with a cubic:"

$$x^3 = 1$$

"The solutions here are the three cube roots of 1:"

$$x = 1, \omega, \omega^2 \quad \text{where } \omega = \frac{-1 + \sqrt{3}\, i}{2}$$

"It turns out that $\{1, \omega, \omega^2\}$ under multiplication is also an abelian group. Here's the operation table, with ω^3 written as 1, since $x = \omega$ is a solution to $x^3 = 1$:"

$\times$	1	ω	ω^2
1	1	ω	ω^2
ω	ω	ω^2	1
ω^2	ω^2	1	ω

"On second thought, maybe it's easier to see what's going on if we write all the exponents. You can see how this meets all the criteria for being an abelian group, right?"

$\times$	ω^0	ω^1	ω^2
ω^0	ω^0	ω^1	ω^2
ω^1	ω^1	ω^2	ω^0
ω^2	ω^2	ω^0	ω^1

"Sorry, getting off track here. Anyway, you can write the n solutions to $x^n = 1$ as a set, like this:"

$$\{\alpha_0, \alpha_1, \alpha_2, \cdots, \alpha_{n-1}\}$$

"When you do that, the elements of the set form an abelian group under multiplication."

"Whoa," I said, holding up a hand. "Abstraction comprehension limits exceeded. Details?"

"Even better, let's take this to the complex plane and look at it geometrically. The absolute value of a complex number on the unit circle will be 1, so products will just be sums of arguments. In other words, the nth roots of 1 will be points that evenly divide the circumference of the unit circle into n equal parts.

"For $n = 1$ you have $\{1\}$, which is isomorphic to the group containing just the identity.

"For $n = 2$ you have $\{1, -1\}$, which is isomorphic to the group containing two elements.

"For $n = 3$ you have $\{1, \omega, \omega^2\}$, which you can associate with the three vertices of an equilateral triangle.

"For $n = 4$ you have $\{1, i, -1, -i\}$, four vertices that form a square: "

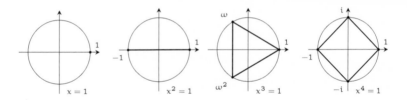

"Since the 360° argument gets sliced into n equal divisions, you can write the solution of $x^n = 1$ like this, using $k = 0, 1, \cdots, n - 1$: "

$$\alpha_k = \cos \frac{2\pi k}{n} + i \sin \frac{2\pi k}{n}$$

"So the vertices of the regular n-gons that we know and love are solutions to the nth root of 1, if you look at them as equations. Look at them as groups, and they're examples of abelian groups with n elements.

"More dancing on the unit circle."

6.3.3 Interpreting Mathematical Statements

"A riddle for you, Tetra. What does this mean?" Miruka closed her eyes and half recited, half sang, "An elliptic curve has the structure of an abelian group."

"I have...no idea," Tetra said. "Should I?"

"Give it a shot," Miruka said. "Don't be afraid of unfamiliar words. They've been waiting for you for hundreds of years. Reach out and embrace them."

Tetra nodded and slipped into deep-thought mode. After a time, she looked up.

"Well, I think I know—no, I know—what it means to have the structure of an abelian group. I know what the commutative property is, and I know what a group is, and I know when you combine them you get an abelian group. That's just from the definition. I'm not sure what an 'elliptic curve' is, but I guess it's some kind of set? Oh, and I guess there has to be some operation defined..."

"The definition of a group says—" I began.

Tetra waved me to silence.

"No, hang on. I've almost got it. A group has to have a set, and an operation defined on that set, and since the statement is 'an elliptic curve has the structure of an abelian group,' the operation defined on this 'elliptic curve' set has to obey the axioms of an abelian group. That means it's closed for the operation, and has the associative property, and an identity element, and all of the elements have an inverse, and, uh, one more... Oh, the commutative property."

Miruka gave a satisfied nod.

"I'm impressed," I said. "You've got the definition down cold. Even if you don't know what an elliptic curve is yet, you nailed everything else. Good job."

But Tetra wasn't done.

"So I guess if you were studying elliptic curves, knowing they're a kind of abelian group would be pretty big. It would let you use your whole toolbox of abelian group stuff on it."

"Tetra," Miruka said, her tone serious. Tetra froze.

"Y-Yes?"

"I love it when you talk nerdy."

"Huh?"

Without warning, Miruka grabbed Tetra by the neck, yanked her down, and planted a kiss on her cheek.

6.3.4 Braided Axioms

Once Tetra had sufficiently recovered, she stumbled off to make tea. Miruka was fighting with her hair, a battle made more difficult by her bandaged arm.

"Can I help?" Tetra asked, bringing tea for us all.

"Sure. Looks like I need it."

"Okay if I braid it?"

"Suit yourself."

Tetra set to braiding Miruka's hair, still clearly elated by Miruka's praise.

"Is there a mathematical representation of braids?" she asked.

"As long as no axioms are violated, sure. Consistency implies existence," Miruka replied.

I wondered what kind of axioms those could possibly be, but I figured holding my tongue was the wiser course.

"I wore my hair long when I was younger," Tetra said. My mom used to braid it every morning, humming 'Greensleeves' while she did it. It was my favorite time of the day."

I made a gagging sound. "Girly girl."

"This from a guy whose friends are all girls," Tetra said.

"I have guy friends. Well, sorta. And Yuri doesn't count—she's more like a sister."

"What about you, Miruka? Any brothers or sisters?"

"I had an older brother."

"*Had?*"

"He died when I was in third grade," she said.

"Sorry...I didn't know."

Miruka shook her head and changed the subject. "I get out tomorrow," she said. "No need to come."

6.4 TRUE FORMS

6.4.1 Essence and Abstraction

Tetra and I met in the library after school the next day. We didn't have any problems we were working on, and we didn't really feel motivated enough to start something new, so we just hung out and talked. Miruka was home from the hospital, but it would be a little while longer before she was back at school.

"Learning about groups got me thinking," Tetra said. "Just what *are* numbers? I've always thought of them as the things you use to calculate, but it's all kind of fuzzy now. We've been doing calculations using elements of sets, points in the complex plane, and I guess I'm okay with that, but..."

Tetra chewed on her lip.

"It's like, where have the numbers gone?" she continued. "What are numbers, *really*? Do they, I dunno, *exist*?"

"Can any of you tell me what these things *really* are?" I muttered.

"What?"

"Nothing," I said. "I was thinking pretty much the same thing when we were talking with Miruka in the hospital. Like, how we have this word 'imaginary numbers,' but in a sense, aren't *all* numbers imaginary? What was it Miruka said? 'Consistency implies existence'? Not sure I entirely follow that, but my take on it is that when you get too deep into specifics, you tend to lose sight of true forms."

"Meaning?"

"Well, like how when you get down to isomorphisms, all groups with two elements are essentially the same. That's something that naturally falls out of the group axioms, but it's hard to get there when you're pushing actual numbers around. The true nature of the operation is uncovered when you strip away the trappings."

"Colored stars instead of numbers," Tetra said.

"Exactly. If you think about it, using 0 and 1 as identity elements, treating them essentially alike, is a pretty crazy idea. Same with $+$ and $\times$. Once you start chipping away at the assumptions you carry around in your head, all the stuff that isn't essential to a thing, the true forms that emerge are...surprising."

"Like how making abstractions—generalizations of things—then proving them, lets you apply them to a wider scope of problems."

"Sure, I think it's hard to get to true forms without abstracting specifics. That's the process of carving away the unessential. That's how you pull out what's important, and throw away the rest."

6.4.2 The Essence of a Heart

"The other day," Tetra began, "when Miruka had her accident." She wrapped her arms tightly around herself, as though to stave off a shiver. "When you ran out of the room..."

"Yeah, I kinda lost it there. I ran all the way to the hospital. I didn't know I could run that far. Paid for it hard, though—my legs still hurt."

Tetra sat there, holding herself.

"Miruka's something, isn't she?" I went on. "Hit by a truck in the morning, and by afternoon she's already giving math lectures again."

I looked at my watch. "Almost time for Ms. Mizutani to make her appearance," I said. "You ready to head home?"

Ms. Mizutani was the school librarian. Every day when it was time to lock up she would emerge from her office, march to the center of the room, and announce that the library was closed. You could set your watch by her.

"What do you think would happen if the library was empty?" Tetra said. "Think she would still make her announcement?"

"Interesting question," I said. "I have no idea."

"Wanna find out?" Tetra grinned and looked around the room. "We can hide over there," she said, pointing at the literature shelves. We knew Ms. Mizutani's patrol route almost as well as she did. The shelves would keep us hidden.

I crouched behind the shelf. Tetra scrunched behind me.

"This is fun!" Tetra whispered. "Like playing hide and seek!"

"Shhh!"

I heard Ms. Mizutani's footsteps as she entered the room.

"The library is *closed*!"

There were more footsteps as she returned to her office, and then the quiet click of the door shutting.

"Mystery solved," I said.

As I began to turn around, I felt Tetra press against my back.

"Tetra—?"

"Don't turn around," she said.

My heart began to pound.

"I know I'm not the one," she said. "It's okay, I understand. I can't compete with Miruka. She's just...beyond me."

I didn't know what to say. My eyes scanned the books on the shelf, just inches from my face. *The True Story of Ah Q. The Dancing Girl of Izu. Rashomon.*

"You don't have to say anything. Just...don't turn around. Not yet. When you do, I'll be the Tetra you've always known. Let me be like this...just a little longer."

I could feel her shaking. She rested her forehead on my shoulder.

The moment seemed like it would never end—until she pounded my back and burst into laughter. I caught my balance just in time to keep from tumbling face first into the shelf.

"Had you going there, didn't I!"

She sprang up and flipped a half-hearted Fibonacci sign.

"I'm gonna head on home," she said, bounding towards the door. "See you tomorrow!"

CHAPTER 7

Modular Arithmetic

> The difference between study and research? You *study* in math class, which means reading the textbook, learning some formulas, solving some problems, checking the answers, and that's about it. But *research* should be plowing ahead even though you're not sure what you're looking for. It's finding those answers on your own that fascinates me.
>
> HIROKO YAMAMOTO
> *Math Starts at 11*

7.1 CLOCKS

7.1.1 Defining Remainders

"Whaddaya think?" Yuri asked me, spinning around.

"About what?"

"This, doofus," she said, pointing at her ponytail. She had tied it up with a moss-green ribbon.

"Nice."

"You really don't know anything about girls, do you?"

"What? I said it was nice."

"You're supposed to say, 'It looks good on you.'"

"What's the difference?"

Yuri sighed.

"Okay, fine. 'It looks good on you.'"

Another sigh. "At least you're good at math..."

* * *

"So what're we doing today?" Yuri asked.

"The definition of remainders."

"Easy—that's what's left over after you divide."

"Not a very mathematical definition. Try starting with, 'A remainder is...'"

"Okay. A remainder is what's left over after you divide."

"Keep going. You have to say what's being divided by what, and what the remainder is. And be specific; don't leave any room for confusion."

"Sorry, my brain doesn't work that way."

"Let's work it out together, then," I said, opening my notebook.

"I'll second that." Yuri pulled up a chair and put on her glasses.

"To do this right, you need to use equations," I began. "Something like this:"

$$a = bq + r \quad (0 \leqslant r < b)$$

"In this equation, the remainder when you divide a by b is r. Also, a and b are positive integers, and q and r are either positive integers or 0."

"How can that be a definition of remainders? You aren't even dividing anything!"

"You don't need division to define remainders. Division is just a multiplication problem in disguise, and you end up with remainders when there's no integer solution. But don't rush ahead, just look at this equation closely. Be sure you understand what all those letters stand for."

"Alright, alright. So there's four variables, a, b, q, and r. a is the number being divided. b is the number it's being divided by. r is the remainder. ...Not sure what q is."

"What do you think it is?"

"Well, when you multiply b and q, then add r, you get a. So q is the answer to the division problem?"

"Right. q is the quotient when you divide a by b."

"Okay, so $a = bq + r$ means that a divided by b gives you q with a remainder of r. So what's the $0 \leqslant r < b$ on the right?"

"Glad you asked—these conditions are important. But take some time and work through it yourself. What do *you* think it's there for?"

"You sound just like my teacher. Fine, gimme a minute. Let's see... Since r is a remainder, I guess the $0 \leqslant r$ part makes sense—can't have a remainder less than 0. That $r < b$, though..."

Yuri pushed the bridge of her glasses up her nose and crossed her arms.

"I can do this. r is the remainder, b is the number you're dividing by... Oh, it's just saying the remainder has to be smaller than the number you're dividing by. Like, if you divide 7 by 3, you get 2 with a remainder of 1. And of course the remainder can't be 3 or anything bigger. If it is, you're doing it wrong."

"Exactly. Working it through with actual numbers makes things a lot clearer, right? Don't rush math, and don't try to just memorize it. Read stuff slowly, write it out, and think through anything that doesn't make sense. Always write out examples, too. That's part of rolling up your sleeves and digging in. After a while, it'll all feel natural."

I wrote out a formal definition in Yuri's notebook:

The division algorithm (for natural numbers)

When dividing a by b, the quotient q and remainder r are given by:

$$a = bq + r \quad (0 \leqslant r < b)$$

Here, a, b are positive integers and q, r are positive integers or 0.

"To do this right we should really prove that the q and r are unique, but we'll skip that for now."

Yuri put the back of her hand to her forehead. "If we must."

"So let's take your example and see how it fits into this equation," I said, ignoring her performance. "Like you said, when you divide

7 by 3, you get a quotient of 2 and a remainder of 1. That means $a = 7$, $b = 3$, $q = 2$, and $r = 1$:"

$$7 = 3 \times 2 + 1 \quad (0 \leqslant 1 < 3)$$

"I totally get that. What I *don't* get is why this is interesting."

"It's interesting because of what you can do once you're able to represent things as mathematical statements. I know you know what remainders *are*. I just want you to learn how to write them, in the language of math."

7.1.2 What Clocks Really Tell Us

I pointed to the clock on my wall.

"When the short hand is pointing at 3, you can't tell if it means 3:00 am or 3:00 pm, right? That's because what it's pointing at is really the remainder when you divide the current military time by 12. At 15:00 it points at 3 because $15 \div 12 = 1$ with remainder 3."

"I can honestly say I never thought of it that way. Let's see, if it was 23:00, then 23 divided by 12 leaves a remainder of 11, so the short hand points at 11. Yeah, it works."

"So clocks are actually something like remainder calculators."

"Hang on, you messed up," Yuri said.

"What? Where?"

"When the remainder is 0. Like, if it's 12, the short hand is pointing at 12, not 0."

"Well for clocks, 12 and 0 are the same thing."

"Oh no, you're not getting off that easy. Check out the definition."

Yuri pointed to the definition of remainders in the notebook:

$$a = bq + r \quad (0 \leqslant r < b)$$

"When you divide by 12 the remainder r has to be $0 \leqslant r < 12$, so 12 can't be the remainder." She grinned. "Gotcha."

I shook my head. "I've created a monster."

7.2 CONGRUENCE

7.2.1 Remainders of the Day

Miruka returned to school the next day, albeit on crutches and sporting bandages on her leg and arm. A different pair of glasses—similar to her old ones but with slightly different curves—completed her new look. Since it was hard for her to get around, we opted for our homeroom over the library after school was out.

Tetra joined us as I was telling Miruka about my attempt to explain clock math to Yuri. After our game of hide-and-seek I was worried things would be awkward between us, but as far as I could tell she was the same old Tetra. Except for one thing.

"Tetra, did you do something to your hair?" I asked.

"I just cut it back a bit. Too much?" Tetra pulled down a lock of hair and rolled her eyes up to peek at it.

"It, uh...looks good on you."

"Yeah? Ya think? Thanks!" Tetra pumped her fists like a cheerleader after a big win at the game. I shook my head, confused.

"That was fun, but can we math?" Miruka was tapping her foot impatiently. "So...Yuri said 12 can't be the remainder. What did you tell her? You couldn't have just left it at that."

"What was I supposed to tell her?"

"You talked about clocks, but you didn't bring up mod?"

"Mod?"

"Residues, etc.?"

Miruka sighed at my blank stare and held out her hand. I pulled out my notebook and pencil and handed them to her.

"Let's start where you left off, defining division for positive integers:"

$$a = bq + r \quad (0 \leqslant r < b)$$

"When you divide a by b you get a nonnegative integer quotient q and remainder r. Fine so far. Now let's drop all those restrictions and broaden things out to all integers, the only exception being that $b \neq 0$, of course. The equation's still pretty much the same, but since b can be negative now, we need to use its absolute value in the inequality:"

$$a = bq + r \quad (0 \leqslant r < |b|)$$

"A given a, b will give you a unique pair of q, r, but you knew that."

'I nodded.

"Then we're ready to define mod:"

---

mod (for integers)

Let a, b, q, r be integers, with $b \neq 0$. Then,

$$a \bmod b = r \quad \Longleftrightarrow \quad a = bq + r \quad (0 \leqslant r < |b|).$$

"Nothing hard about this," Miruka said, "mod is just another operator, like $+$, $-$, $\times$, and $\div$. For example, if you divide 7 by -3, you get a quotient of -2 and a remainder of 1:"

$$7 \bmod (-3) = 1 \quad \Longleftrightarrow \quad 7 = (-3) \times (-2) + 1 \quad (0 \leqslant 1 < |-3|)$$

"The condition that $0 \leqslant r < |-3|$ means the value of $7 \bmod (-3)$ can't be anything other than 1. Combine mod with military time, and you see that h hours after midnight, the hour hand on a clock is pointing at $h \bmod 12$. I guess you'd have to replace the 12 on the clock with a 0 to keep your cousin happy, though."

Miruka shifted on her crutches.

"You can even let h be negative. -1 hours from midnight would be $(-1) \bmod 12$. Sure enough, that's 11:00:"

$$-1 = 12 \times (-1) + 11 \quad (0 \leqslant 11 < |12|)$$

"A quiz for Tetra. Say you have integers a, b like this:"

$$a \bmod b = 0$$

"What's the relationship between a and b?"

"Gimme a sec..." Tetra said. "Well, $a \bmod b$ means you're dividing a by b, right? And when you do that, the remainder is 0."

"Shorter," Miruka said.

"Shorter? Um, well..."

"Time's up. The answer is that a is a multiple of b. Or that b is a divisor of a."

"Or that b divides a evenly," I added.

"Oh, sure." Tetra nodded. "Sure, I see that."

"So mod just looks for remainders, right?" I asked. "I don't see the point. I mean, I can see wanting the quotient *and* the remainder, but *just* the remainder? Who cares?"

"Hmph. Mister 'check the parity' over here, asking something like that."

"What's parity got to... Oh."

"Exactly. 'Checking parity' is just a fancy way of saying 'look at the remainder when you divide by 2.'"

"And ignoring the quotient. I'll just go take my foot out of my mouth now."

"Question," Tetra said. "Why's it called 'mod'?"

"It's short for 'modulo,'" Miruka said.

"Latin," Tetra said. "Figures."

7.2.2 Congruence Relations

"If we're all happy with mod, let's talk about congruence," Miruka continued. "In this case, congruence means equivalence between two numbers that have the same remainders."

"Equivalence?" Tetra asked.

"Looking at two different things as being essentially the same," I said.

"It's easy to see if we stick to clocks a little longer," said Miruka. "3:00 and 15:00 are different times, but they both mean the short hand on a clock will be pointing at 3. So as far as a clock display is concerned, we can treat 3 and 15 as being equivalent, or congruent. Same with any other number whose remainder is 3 when you divide by 12. You show congruence mathematically like this:"

$$3 \equiv 15 \pmod{12}$$

"This is called a congruence relation. Be careful with that symbol; congruence is three lines, not two like an equals sign. The 12 there is called the modulus of the congruence."

"How do you read this?" Tetra asked.

"You say, '3 is congruent to 15, modulo 12.' Or 'mod 12,' if you prefer."

"...modulo 12," Tetra said, writing this in her own notebook.

"Let me give you some more examples of numbers that are congruent mod 12. They're all just pairs of numbers that leave the same remainder after being divided by the modulus, tied together by the congruence sign:"

$$3 \equiv 15 \quad (\text{mod } 12)$$

$$15 \equiv 3 \quad (\text{mod } 12)$$

$$12 \equiv 0 \quad (\text{mod } 12)$$

$$12000 \equiv 0 \quad (\text{mod } 12)$$

$$36 \equiv 12 \quad (\text{mod } 12)$$

$$14 \equiv 2 \quad (\text{mod } 12)$$

$$11 \equiv (-1) \quad (\text{mod } 12)$$

$$7 \equiv (-5) \quad (\text{mod } 12)$$

$$1 \equiv 1 \quad (\text{mod } 12)$$

"Since both numbers leave the same remainder, you can also say this:"

$$a \equiv b \quad (\text{mod } m) \quad \Longleftrightarrow \quad a \bmod m = b \bmod m$$

"You can even use that as the definition of the $\equiv$ symbol."

"Question," Tetra said, raising her hand.

"You have the floor."

"I'm getting confused about what mod means. At first I thought $a \bmod b$ meant 'the remainder when you divide a by b,' but this $(\text{mod } m)$ when m is the modulus is throwing me. Why isn't there a number that's being divided on the left?"

"Yeah, I can see how that might be confusing. You understand this, though, right?"

$$a \bmod m = b \bmod m$$

"Sure. It means you get the same remainder whether you're dividing a or b by m."

"Exactly, you're dividing something by m on both sides. So think of the (mod m) on the right as an abbreviation, a kind of shorthand to make the equation simpler. If you just yanked the (mod m) out and stuck it off to the side, you'd leave an equals sign behind. But a and b aren't equal, just their remainders are. So we replace the $=$ symbol with a $\equiv$ symbol; something similar, but just different enough to show what we mean. In the end, we get this: "

$$a \equiv b \quad (\text{mod } m)$$

"Okay, so we use $a \bmod m$ to calculate remainders, and $a \equiv b$ (mod m) to show that two remainders are the same. That makes sense now."

Miruka's finger traced a circle in the air as she continued:

"Like I said, we can show that the remainder when you divide a by m and b by m are the same by writing this: "

$$a \bmod m = b \bmod m$$

"But here's another way to do it: "

$$(a - b) \bmod m = 0$$

"In other words, the difference between two numbers that are congruent mod m is a multiple of m."

"Hold up, you lost me," said Tetra. She scanned the equation in the notebook for a few seconds. "...Oh, I see. When you calculate $a - b$, you lose the remainders."

"Well put," Miruka said. "For example, using 15 and 3..."

$$(15 - 3) \bmod 12 = 12 \bmod 12$$
$$= 0$$

"Voilà. What's left after the subtraction is a multiple of 12."

---

mod (alternate descriptions)

Let a, b, m be integers, with $m \neq 0$. Then,

$$a \equiv b \quad (\mathrm{mod}\ m) \quad \text{congruent mod } m$$

$$\Updownarrow$$

$$a \bmod m = b \bmod m \qquad \text{equivalent remainders}$$

$$\Updownarrow$$

$$(a - b) \bmod m = 0 \qquad \text{difference is a multiple of } m$$

7.2.3 Different Congruences?

"Actually, I've heard of congruence before," Tetra said. "Not for this stuff though; we learned about it when we studied congruent triangles. Why are they called the same thing?"

Miruka cocked her head and smiled. "Hung up on words again, huh? You're right, there's a congruence in geometry, too. When you say two triangles are congruent, it means they're equivalent—if you ignore differences in position and rotation. You can still match up congruent triangles if you move them around, and maybe flip them, right?"

Tetra nodded.

"Congruent integers are kinda the same, except that what you're ignoring is multiples of the modulus m. You can always match up congruent integers just by adding enough ms."

7.2.4 More or Less Equivalent

"It's kinda weird," Tetra said. "I always thought of math as this super-precise thing. More precise than anything in real life. But these equivalences we've been talking about... Isn't it a stretch to call some of these things 'equivalent'?"

"Example," said Miruka.

"Well, we made numbers equivalent to points in the complex plane, for one thing. When we talked about groups in the hospital, we threw some operations on top of the elements of a set, which we treated as equivalent to numbers. Now we're treating congruent integers as equivalent if we ignore multiples. We even made the word 'congruent' equivalent, even though it's used in different ways for shapes and numbers!"

"I think finding new equivalences is kinda cool," I said. "Noticing two things are similar, then realizing they're basically the same thing—there's a thrill to that, like you've uncovered some kind of hidden structure."

"It all comes down to structure," Miruka said. "Remember when we talked about isomorphic groups? Isomorphisms are a mathematical way of talking about equivalent structures. And isomorphic mappings are the root of meaning. They're how you bridge worlds."

7.2.5 Equalities and Congruences

"But enough philosophy," Miruka said. "It's no coincidence that the signs for equality and congruency are similar. They were chosen to show the similarities between the two. And in fact, they are very similar:"

Equality

Given $a = b$ and integer C, the following are true:

$a + C = b + C$	addition preserves equality
$a - C = b - C$	subtraction preserves equality
$a \times C = b \times C$	multiplication preserves equality

Congruence

Given $a \equiv b \pmod{m}$ and integer C, the following are true:

$a + C \equiv b + C \pmod{m}$	addition preserves congruence
$a - C \equiv b - C \pmod{m}$	subtraction preserves congruence
$a \times C \equiv b \times C \pmod{m}$	multiplication preserves congruence

7.2.6   The Exception

Tetra's hand shot up.

"You wrote rules for addition, subtraction, and multiplication, but not division. Why's that? Can't you divide both sides by the same number?"

"Sharp eye, Tetra. No, the parallel doesn't go that far; things break down for division." Miruka pushed the notebook toward me. "Care to give us an example?"

"Way to put me on the spot," I said. "Hmmm... Let 12 be the modulus, and let's look at the congruence between 3 and 15:"

$$3 \equiv 15 \pmod{12}$$

"This statement works, but not if you divide both sides by 3. That would give you 1 on the left and 5 on the right, which breaks the congruence:"

$$(3 \div 3) \not\equiv (15 \div 3) \pmod{12}$$

"Yeah," Tetra said, "1 and 5 are definitely different places on a clock. Too bad."

$$3 \equiv 15 \pmod{12} \qquad 3 \text{ and } 15 \text{ are congruent}$$
$$(3 \div 3) \not\equiv (15 \div 3) \pmod{12} \quad \text{division by 3 breaks congruence}$$

"That's an example of when it *doesn't* work," Miruka said, "but sometimes it does. Check out 15 and 75:"

$$15 \equiv 75 \pmod{12}$$

"Wow, what time is 75:00..." Tetra said. "Let's see, $75 \div 12$ gives...6 with a remainder of 3, and $15 \div 12$ is 1 with remainder 3. Yep, they're congruent."

"Now see what happens when we divide both by 5:"

$$(15 \div 5) \equiv (75 \div 5) \pmod{12}$$

"Okay. $15 \div 5 = 3$ and $75 \div 5 = 15$, and yeah, 3 and 15 are congruent. What if we try 3 again? $15 \div 3 = 5$ and $75 \div 3 = 25$, so that would be 5:00 and, uh, 1:00. It broke again!"

$$(15 \div 3) \not\equiv (75 \div 3) \pmod{12}$$

That's weird. The congruence is preserved when you divide both sides by some numbers, but not others. Which leads to an interesting—

"Which leads to an interesting question," Miruka said.

Problem 7-1

Given integers a, b, C, and m, what characteristic must C possess for the following to be true?

$$a \times C \equiv b \times C \pmod{m}$$
$$\Downarrow \text{ implies}$$
$$a \equiv b \pmod{m}$$

"In other words," said Tetra, "when can you divide both sides by C, right?"

"Uh huh," answered Miruka.

Tetra and I fell silent, slipping into deep think mode. I played around with the equation we used to define mod and noticed Tetra writing something in her notebook as well. It wasn't long before she threw in the towel, though.

"Sorry guys, but could somebody give me a hint? I'm trying to think this thing through, but I'm not even sure where to start."

"What's the first thing you do when working on a problem?" Miruka asked.

"Make examples," Tetra said. "But we already have some—I'm trying to use the $3 \equiv 15$ and $15 \equiv 75$ we were talking about."

"Using division?"

"Uh, sure. I was looking at when you can divide—"

Miruka raised a hand, cutting her off. "To get to the heart of division, you have to start with multiplication. Let's give the set $\{0, 1, 2, \cdots 11\}$ a new name, $\mathbb{Z}/12\mathbb{Z}$:"

$$\mathbb{Z}/12\mathbb{Z} = \{0, 1, 2, \cdots, 11\}$$

"We also define an operation $\boxtimes$ on $\mathbb{Z}/12\mathbb{Z}$ as 'multiply two numbers, and take the product's remainder after dividing by 12.' Of course, this operation is closed in $\mathbb{Z}/12\mathbb{Z}$, since the remainder r will be $0 \leqslant r < 12$:"

$$a \boxtimes b = (a \times b) \bmod 12 \quad \text{definition of the } \boxtimes \text{operation}$$

"Tetra, why don't you make an operation table for $\boxtimes$, like the ones we did when I was in the hospital. I think it'll help get you started."

"Okay, but first...is this operation what this boxy times symbol always means?"

"No, the symbol isn't important. We could have used a circle or a star or whatever, but I wanted to use something that reminds us of multiplication. Let's work though a couple examples to get a feel for it:"

$$
\begin{aligned}
2 \boxtimes 3 &= (2 \times 3) \bmod 12 && \text{definition of } \boxtimes \\
&= 6 \bmod 12 && \text{calculate } 2 \times 3 \\
&= 6 && \text{remainder of } 6 \div 12 \text{ equals } 6 \\
6 \boxtimes 8 &= (6 \times 8) \bmod 12 && \text{definition of } \boxtimes \\
&= 48 \bmod 12 && \text{calculate } 6 \times 8 \\
&= 0 && \text{remainder of } 48 \div 12 \text{ equals } 0
\end{aligned}
$$

"Okay," Tetra said, "time to plug and chug."

She began work on the table, first plucking the low-hanging fruit by filling in 0s for the 0 row and column, then $1, 2, 3, 4, \cdots, 11$ for the 1 row and column. Then it was time for some actual number crunching:

⊠	0	1	2	3	4	5	6	7	8	9	10	11
0	0	0	0	0	0	0	0	0	0	0	0	0
1	0	1	2	3	4	5	6	7	8	9	10	11
2	0	2	4	6	8	10	0	2	4	6	8	10
3	0	3	6	9	0	3	6	9	0	3	6	9
4	0	4	8	0	4	8	0	4	8	0	4	8
5	0	5	10	3	8	1	6	11	4	9	2	7
6	0	6	0	6								
7	0	7										
8	0	8										
9	0	9										
10	0	10										
11	0	11										

Less than halfway through the 6 row she jerked her head up from the notebook.

"Yikes! I was supposed to be home early today! Sorry guys, gotta run. Let's finish up next time!"

Tetra stuffed the notebook and partially completed operation table into her bag and vanished through the door.

7.2.7 Crutches

The room was pin-drop quiet after Tetra's sudden departure. I glanced at Miruka's bandaged leg.

"Getting used to the crutches?" I asked.

"If you can call it that."

"How long till you can walk without them?"

"Already can. I just wanted to try something out."

Okay, this could be interesting.

"Help me to the restroom?"

Miruka held out her hand.

"What?" I said.

"You gonna make me limp all the way on my own?"

"Oh, sorry."

I took Miruka's crutches in my left hand and wrapped my right arm around her. She put her left arm around my neck. A medicinal smell from the bandage tickled my nose. Under the best of circumstances it would have been a precarious balancing act; with my heart pounding as it was, it's a miracle I didn't fall and break her other leg.

I paused when we reached the hall. We were completely alone. A shaft of amber light fell through the window.

"Left," she whispered in my ear.

"Uh huh."

By the end of the hall we'd fell into a rhythmic trudge that improved our pace.

"Too fast?"

"You're fine."

Miruka must have been putting most of her weight on me, but she felt like a feather. The softness of her waist burned beneath my hand.

"This is good," Miruka said. I looked up and realized we were in front of the girls' room.

"Uh, yeah. I'll wait out here."

Miruka leaned in and whispered again, "Thanks for the three-legged race."

I slumped against the wall with a long sigh and watched the dying glow of the sunset through the window. I wondered if Miruka would want me to help her all the way to the station, and if I'd make it that far if she did.

7.3   THE NATURE OF DIVISION

7.3.1   Math and Hot Chocolate

That night I sat in my room, a cup of hot chocolate cradled in my hands. My mother had brought it up to me as a reward for what she thought was a late-night cram session. I'd told her countless times that I preferred coffee, but I was still a child in her eyes.

My mind wandered, and I began thinking about families. About how a new family materialized when my parents married and had me. About what Tetra's family might be like. About Miruka's family, and how things must have changed when her brother died.

I sighed and opened my notebook, staring at a random page of math within.

Mathematics had always felt so solid to me, but I was starting to see that things were a bit fuzzier around the edges.

When all the pieces come together in math, there's an inherent permanence to it. But an unfinished equation or half-written proof is ephemeral, insubstantial. Open a textbook and you're presented with the finished product, like a building after all the construction scaffolding has been removed. All you see is order and perfection, with no hint of the mess made in the process.

Mathematics is, after all, a human discovery, a human creation. I had thought of it as something created by people with a love of structure, a yearning for eternity, a desire to capture some part of infinity. Now I saw that it was also something created by humans with all their shortcomings and weaknesses.

For the first time I considered the possibility that math wasn't something you obtained, but something you nurtured. You planted the acorns, but they would only grow into mighty oaks through diligence and patience. There were seeds in the form of axioms, waiting to be coaxed into the trunks of theorems and branches of corollaries. Tiny things with the potential to grow into something massive enough to support the heavens, but they needed to be watered with the elegance of a Miruka, the dedication of a Tetra, the alertness of a Yuri.

They changed the way I thought about mathematics in ways more profound than I could have known then.

I took a sip of hot chocolate and let its warmth fill me.

7.3.2 Studying the Operation Table

I set down my cup and turned to a fresh page in my notebook.

I decided to take a shot at the group operation table Tetra had started. I began by writing the definition of the operation:

$$a \boxtimes b = (a \times b) \bmod 12$$

The calculation wasn't terribly hard, just multiplication then a division by 12, so I had a table of remainders pretty quick:

⊠	0	1	2	3	4	5	6	7	8	9	10	11
0	0	0	0	0	0	0	0	0	0	0	0	0
1	0	1	2	3	4	5	6	7	8	9	10	11
2	0	2	4	6	8	10	0	2	4	6	8	10
3	0	3	6	9	0	3	6	9	0	3	6	9
4	0	4	8	0	4	8	0	4	8	0	4	8
5	0	5	10	3	8	1	6	11	4	9	2	7
6	0	6	0	6	0	6	0	6	0	6	0	6
7	0	7	2	9	4	11	6	1	8	3	10	5
8	0	8	4	0	8	4	0	8	4	0	8	4
9	0	9	6	3	0	9	6	3	0	9	6	3
10	0	10	8	6	4	2	0	10	8	6	4	2
11	0	11	10	9	8	7	6	5	4	3	2	1

What had Miruka hoped Tetra would see in those numbers? She had told Tetra to do this when we talked about the conditions for dividing both sides of a congruence equation, and I knew she must have had her reasons. But what? I flipped back to look at my copy of the problem:

Problem 7-1 (Congruences and division)

Given integers $a, b, C,$ and m, what characteristic must C possess for the following to be true?

$$a \times C \equiv b \times C \pmod{m}$$
$$\Downarrow \text{ implies}$$
$$a \equiv b \pmod{m}$$

I recalled something else she had said, a typically cryptic comment about how you should start with multiplication to get to the depths of division.

Okay, then. Let $m = 12$ *and we'll see what falls out.*

The first row was all 0s. A no-brainer, since multiplying anything by 0 gives 0. The second row was the integers 0 through 11 in sequence; no thought required here, either. The third row was a sequence of even integers, $0, 2, 4, 6, 8, 10$, that reset to 0 when it would have hit 12. Again, nothing surprising since we're dividing things by 12 and looking at remainders. The row for 3 was pretty much the same thing, but with multiples of 3.

I realized I could take a congruence equation like this:

$$a \times C \equiv b \times C \pmod{12}$$

and write it using the $\boxtimes$ operator like this:

$$a \boxtimes C = b \boxtimes C$$

Since the $\boxtimes$ operator had a built-in mod calculation, that let me replace the $\equiv$ sign with an $=$ sign.

Maybe I should look for the inverse operation for $\boxtimes$, *then—or not. I don't want the inverse operation for* $\boxtimes$ *in* $\mathbb{Z}/12\mathbb{Z} = \{0, 1, 2, \cdots, 11\}$, *I want the inverse element for* C! *Now how to get that...?*

I started with the obvious, filling in the blank of the inverse element relationship with a variable C':

$$C \boxtimes C' = 1$$

I should be able to do division in $\mathbb{Z}/12\mathbb{Z}$, *if such a* C' *exists*, because then I could multiply both sides of

$$a \boxtimes C = b \boxtimes C,$$

which would give me this:

$$(a \boxtimes C) \boxtimes C' = (b \boxtimes C) \boxtimes C'$$

Associativity should hold for $\mathbb{Z}/12\mathbb{Z}$ under $\boxtimes$, so I could rewrite that:

$$a \boxtimes (C \boxtimes C') = b \boxtimes (C \boxtimes C')$$

Since $C \boxtimes C' = 1$, that would simplify like this:

$$a \boxtimes 1 = b \boxtimes 1$$

Then from the definition of $\boxtimes$, I could rewrite that as follows:

$$(a \times 1) \bmod 12 = (b \times 1) \bmod 12$$

In other words:

$$a \bmod 12 = b \bmod 12$$

Which, as we'd seen, was the same as:

$$a \equiv b \quad (\bmod\ 12)$$

So everything hinged on the existence of C', the inverse element of C; if C' existed, both sides could be divided by C.

I finally had my connection between multiplication and division. Dividing by a number, C, was the same as multiplying by its inverse, $\frac{1}{C}$. *Except I need to keep* mod *in mind...*

To keep this straight, I wondered if it might not be better to think of C' as something more like $\frac{1}{C}$ or C^{-1}. Regardless, I needed to find the exact conditions under which the inverse of C would exist in the first place. That meant searching through $\mathbb{Z}/12\mathbb{Z}$ for combinations where $C \boxtimes C' = 1$.

I sat there trying to figure out how to accomplish that, then facepalmed when I realized the answer was staring right at me.

The group operation table! I just have to find the 1s!

I had finally stumbled across the reason Miruka made Tetra create the table.

I scanned the table and drew circles around all the 1s:

⊠	0	1	2	3	4	5	6	7	8	9	10	11
0	0	0	0	0	0	0	0	0	0	0	0	0
→1	0	(1)	2	3	4	5	6	7	8	9	10	11
2	0	2	4	6	8	10	0	2	4	6	8	10
3	0	3	6	9	0	3	6	9	0	3	6	9
4	0	4	8	0	4	8	0	4	8	0	4	8
→5	0	5	10	3	8	(1)	6	11	4	9	2	7
6	0	6	0	6	0	6	0	6	0	6	0	6
→7	0	7	2	9	4	11	6	(1)	8	3	10	5
8	0	8	4	0	8	4	0	8	4	0	8	4
9	0	9	6	3	0	9	6	3	0	9	6	3
10	0	10	8	6	4	2	0	10	8	6	4	2
→11	0	11	10	9	8	7	6	5	4	3	2	(1)

I was surprised at how few rows had 1s in them—just 1, 5, 7, and 11.

Why do those numbers sound so familiar?

Facepalm number two.

It's clock math! Relative primes!

It had taken an embarassing amount of fumbling about, but I'd finally realized that numbers that are relatively prime with 12 were the numbers for which an inverse element for ⊠ exists.

Which means I can divide by numbers that are relatively prime with the modulus?

I recalled the example Miruka had come up with at school:

$$15 \equiv 75 \quad (\text{mod } 12) \qquad \text{15 and 75 are congruent}$$
$$(15 \div 5) \equiv (75 \div 5) \quad (\text{mod } 12) \qquad \text{division by 5 preserves congruence}$$
$$(15 \div 3) \not\equiv (75 \div 3) \quad (\text{mod } 12) \qquad \text{division by 3 breaks congruence}$$

As I suspected, congruence was preserved when the values were divided by 5, which is relatively prime to 12, but not by 3, which isn't.

7.3.3 The Proof

Confident in my progress, I wrote a formal statement of my prediction:

A prediction

Both sides of a congruence equation can be divided by a number that is relatively prime with the modulus without breaking congruence. Specifically, given

$$a \times C \equiv b \times C \pmod{m},$$

if C and m are relatively prime ($C \perp m$) then the following will also be true:

$$a \equiv b \pmod{m}$$

Now it was time to turn prediction into proof.

I had managed an exhaustive check of $\mathbb{Z}/12\mathbb{Z}$ using a group operation table, but that wasn't possible for the general case, $\mathbb{Z}/m\mathbb{Z}$. Only a general proof would get the job done here.

At least I knew where I had to start:

$$a \times C \equiv b \times C \pmod{m}$$

Simple algebra gave me this:

$$a \times C - b \times C \equiv 0 \pmod{m}$$

Then I could factor out the C:

$$(a - b) \times C \equiv 0 \pmod{m}$$

If $(a-b) \times C$ is congruent to 0 modulo m, that means $(a-b) \times C$ must be a multiple of m. So there would be some integer J out there that made this true:

$$(a - b) \times C = J \times m$$

Now I had everything as an integer, and both sides in multiplicative form. I knew what I needed to do—show there was some integer K that would make this true:

$$a - b = K \times m$$

If I could do that, I'd have

$$a \equiv b \pmod{m},$$

because $a - b$ is a multiple of m and $a - b \equiv 0 \pmod{m}$.

But I already knew that $(a-b) \times C = J \times m$, and thus $(a-b) \times C$ was a multiple of m. If C and m were relatively prime, that would mean $a - b$ contained all the prime factors of m. In other words, $a - b$ was a multiple of m. So sure enough, I could state that as $a - b = K \times m$.

Once again, the fact that relatively prime numbers have no shared factors had saved the day.

Answer 7-1 (Congruences and division)

Given integers a, b, C, and m, the following is true when C and m are relatively prime:

$$a \times C \equiv b \times C \pmod{m}$$

$$\Downarrow \text{ implies}$$

$$a \equiv b \pmod{m}$$

7.4 GROUPS, RINGS, AND FIELDS

7.4.1 Reduced Residue Class Groups

The next day I showed Miruka and Tetra my results.

"So it turns out you can divide both sides of a congruency when you're dividing by a number that's relatively prime with the modulus. Here's my proof."

"A proof, huh?" Miruka said, skimming through what I'd written. "Hmph. You didn't show that associativity holds in $\mathbb{Z}/m\mathbb{Z}$. Oh, and you didn't consider inverses. But I guess I'll let that slide."

Tetra frowned and remained silent.

"What's wrong?" I asked.

"It's nothing. I'm just, I dunno, disappointed I guess."

"About what?"

"Not getting anywhere with this problem. I mean, if it was completely beyond me that would be one thing, y'know?" Tetra fiddled with the corner of her notebook, looking for the right words. "Like, if I could point at some part of this solution and say 'This! This is the part I don't understand,' then I'd be okay with that. There's always going to be math I don't know. But this time I had everything I needed. Remainders, congruences, groups...everything. Miruka even gave me a big hint and I *still* didn't get it. There's nothing hard about looking at division as the inverse of multiplication. I've done it a million times when I divide fractions. But stick this little word 'mod' in there, and I'm lost."

Tetra shook her head.

"What do I have to do to make this stuff *click*? Why do I keep missing these key steps? You even took me as far as making an operation table and I just got stuck there, even though the only thing left to do was find some 1s. I always thought I was pretty good at hammering away at something until I could do it, but this stuff..."

Tetra gripped her notebook until her knuckles whitened.

"Tetra," I began, then shot a glance at Miruka. She nodded, so I continued. "Tetra, sometimes things come together in a math problem, and sometimes they don't. Problems that looked really hard at first can seem to practically solve themselves, and the ones that look the simplest can turn out to be the hardest. Like the five lattice points problem, the one I said I might never figure out. You solved that one all by yourself, and you'd never even heard of the pigeonhole principle."

"Yeah, but..."

"But nothing. This is the same thing. You understand the problem and its solution, and there's a lot to be said for that."

Tetra only sighed. "I'll be fine. Just ignore me for now."

With a look, I passed the baton to Miruka. Little did I know how far she would run with it.

"Does your misery want some company, Tetra? Just watch this guy when we show him everything he missed."

Miruka pointed a finger at me and traced a φ symbol in the air. "For one thing, you didn't pick up on the fact that $\mathbb{Z}/12\mathbb{Z}$ doesn't form a group under the operation."

"Er, no. No I didn't. But now that you mention it..."

All that time spent looking for the conditions under which an inverse element would exist, and I never stopped to consider how the existence of such conditions meant the set $\mathbb{Z}/12\mathbb{Z}$ didn't form a group; the definition of a group calls for an inverse for *all* elements, not just certain ones.

"And I assume you didn't notice that the set $\{1, 5, 7, 11\}$ *does* form a group?"

"It does?" I blurted, but even as the words spilled out I felt the set snap into place, each element bonding with the others. "Hey! It does!"

"Under what operation?" asked Tetra.

"An excellent question," Miruka said. "Never talk about a group unless you're perfectly clear what its set and its operation are. See how the definition is starting to come more naturally?"

"Uh, thanks."

"The set $\{1, 5, 7, 11\}$ forms a group under the $\boxtimes$ operator," Miruka continued. Here's an operation table: "

$\boxtimes$	1	5	7	11
1	1	5	7	11
5	5	1	11	7
7	7	11	1	5
11	11	7	5	1

"Oh, too sweet," I said, running through the group axioms in my head. The result of each pair of elements was 1, 5, 7, or 11, so it was closed. The identity element was 1, of course. There was an inverse for each element, since every element was its own inverse, and associativity checked out.

"If you pull out just the elements of the set $\mathbb{Z}/12\mathbb{Z}$ that have an inverse, then that subset of elements forms a group all its own. Pretty cool," I concluded.

"There's a name for a group like that," Miruka said. "A 'reduced residue class group.' Here's how you write the reduced residue class group created from $\mathbb{Z}/12\mathbb{Z}$:"

$$(\mathbb{Z}/12\mathbb{Z})^{\times}$$

"It's abelian, too, isn't it?" Tetra asked.

"What makes you say that?" Miruka asked, eyes narrowed.

"Because the group operation table is diagonally symmetric. That means it's commutative, right?"

"Good to see someone's paying attention."

Another jab, but seeing Tetra's smile return, even at my expense, was worth it.

7.4.2   From Groups to Rings

"Let's talk rings," Miruka said.

"We only added one operation to a group, but a ring has two. Just like with groups, we don't care what the operations actually do, so long as they fulfill the requirements of the ring axioms.

"We're going to use a $+$ and a $\times$ symbol to represent the two operations, since we're used to them. We'll also call the operations 'addition' and 'multiplication' to keep things simple, but don't forget that when we talk about rings those words may not mean normal adding and multiplying."

"Another case of 'more or less equivalent'?" Tetra said. "We're using a $+$ sign and calling its operation 'addition,' but that may not mean adding. We're using a $\times$ sign and calling its operation 'multiplication,' but that may not mean multiplying."

"Yep," Miruka said. "We aren't done yet, though. We're going to call the identity element for addition 0, and the identity element for multiplication 1. You know what my next warning is going to be, don't you?"

"That those aren't necessarily the integers 0 and 1," I said. "They're just convenient symbols. Mathematical metaphors."

"Exactly. Just one last thing before we get to the ring axioms: the distributive property. Distribution in a ring works just like it does in vanilla algebra. It's a property that binds two operations together, so we didn't need it when we talked about groups."

The distributive property

$$(a + b) \times c = (a \times c) + (b \times c)$$

"Okay, now we have all the pieces to assemble a ring:"

The ring axioms

A set that meets the following axioms is called a ring.

· **The 'addition' operator +...**

  – is closed,

  – has an identity element (called '0'),

  – is associative for all elements,

  – is commutative for all elements, and

  – has an inverse element for all elements.

· **The 'multiplication' operator ×...**

  – is closed,

  – has an identity element (called '1'),

  – is associative for all elements, and

  – is commutative for all elements.

· **The operators + and × together...**

  – are distributative for all elements.

"To be precise, this is called 'a commutative ring with a multiplicative identity.' Well, I guess the terminology can depend on the book you're reading. When in doubt, check the book's definition. Anyway, I thought of another quiz for Tetra."

Tetra sat up straight. "I'm ready."

"Then tell me this: Does a ring form an abelian group under addition?"

"I don't even know what that means."

"Sure you do. We said a ring has two operations, which we named addition and multiplication. What I'm asking is, if you just think about the addition operation, will the ring be an abelian group? And I know you know how to check if something is an abelian group or not."

"Just go through the axioms, right? Lessee, an abelian group is a set that's closed under some operation, and has an identity, and everything is associative and commutative, and—uh, one more—oh, and everything has an inverse! Yeah, that all matches up. So the answer is yes, a ring forms an abelian group for addition."

"How about under multiplication?"

"Sure, it should hold for multiplication too."

"Why?"

"Well, if it works for addition then—"

"Did you go through the axioms?"

"No, but—"

"Why not?" Miruka pointed at the notebook. "They're right here in front of you. What was all that moaning and groaning about missing key steps?"

"My bad. I'll go through them. But the operations are—no, wait. They're *not* the same! The multiplication operation doesn't have an axiom that says an inverse has to exist!"

"Right. Never forget that the rules for the two operations aren't exactly alike. Elements in a ring won't necessarily have an inverse for multiplication, so they won't always form a group. And if they don't even form a group, there's no way they can be an abelian group."

Rings and groups

Every ring is a group with respect to its addition operator.
Rings are not groups with respect to their multiplication operator.

"Doesn't seem very graceful to do it like that, though," Tetra muttered.

"Why not?"

"It just doesn't seem balanced out somehow. Isn't it kinda random to have the operators play by different rules?"

"But you already know a ring that's full of grace and beauty."

Miruka smiled, and I could swear I saw her eyes sparkle.

"I do?" Tetra said.

"Think about it. Where is it that you can add, and since there's always an inverse available, subtract as well? Where can you multiply, too? Where is it that distribution works for the addition and multiplication operator, but you can't always divide because multiplication might not have an inverse? What set would that be?"

"A set where you can't do division? Because there's no $\frac{1}{a}$?"

"Well, one where you can make a $\frac{1}{a}$, but the result might be outside of the set."

Tetra twisted her face in concentration.

"Think about what it means for a set to be closed under an operation. What set wouldn't have $\frac{1}{a}$ in it?"

"Sorry," Tetra said, "I'm drawing a total blank."

"The integers, Tetra. The set of all integers $\mathbb{Z}$ forms a ring with the addition operation $+$ and the multiplication operation $\times$. An integer may or may not have its inverse $\frac{1}{a}$ in the set—in fact, it only will if a is ± 1—but just because division doesn't usually work in $\mathbb{Z}$, that doesn't mean it isn't 'graceful.' The world of integers is a rich and beautiful place."

"Just a thought," I said, "but I wonder if rings aren't just an abstraction of $\mathbb{Z}$?"

"You can think of them that way," said Miruka. "The set $\mathbb{Z}$ with the addition operation $+$ and the multiplication operation $\times$ is called the ring of integers. You can also make a ring out of the set

$\mathbb{Z}/m\mathbb{Z} = \{0, 1, 2, \cdots, m - 1\}$ with $+$ and $\times$, if you think in terms of mod m. That's called a residue ring. Using rings lets you think of $\mathbb{Z}$ and $\mathbb{Z}/m\mathbb{Z}$ as more or less the same thing."

"Why are they called 'rings'?" Tetra asked.

"No idea. Maybe because the residue ring $\mathbb{Z}/m\mathbb{Z}$ acts like a loop?"[1] Miruka shrugged.

"Whatever the reason, the ring of integers $\mathbb{Z}$ and the residue ring $\mathbb{Z}/m\mathbb{Z}$ both fulfill the requirements of the ring axioms, but they're very different beasts. $\mathbb{Z}$ is like a bunch of points on the number line, but $\mathbb{Z}/m\mathbb{Z}$ is more like the numbers on a clock. $\mathbb{Z}$ is an infinite set, while $\mathbb{Z}/m\mathbb{Z}$ is finite and periodic. But despite their differences, since they're both rings, any theorem you can derive from the ring axioms can be applied to either one. That's the power of abstract algebra."

I was awestruck. I didn't know what sort of ring-related theorems were out there, but suddenly I saw them as the stones of a great cathedral, built up by the work of countless mathematicians over centuries. I had only to find a set that I could fit into the framework of a ring, and they would be mine to play with.

7.4.3 From Rings to Fields

"As we've seen, there won't always be an inverse element for multiplication in a ring," Miruka said. "There *might* be, but no guarantees, since the ring axioms don't require them. But what if we want to be sure we can use division?

"A ring where you can always divide by an element other than 0 is called a 'field.'"

Tetra started to ask a question, but Miruka cut her off.

"No, I don't know why it's called that."[2] She continued. "When we made groups, we added an operation to a set. When we made rings, we added a second operation to a group. When we create a field—"

---

[1] 'Ring' is a shortened form of the German *Zahlring*, or 'number ring,' first used by Hilbert to describe a specific type of ring.

[2] The original term, from Dedekind, is the German *Körper* ("body"), and the notion of 'body' is retained in the terminology for this concept in many non-English languages. 'Field' comes from E.H. Moore's translation of Kronecker's *Rationalitaetsbereich* ("domain of rationality"), perhaps because 'field' is one definition for *Bereich* given in many German-English dictionaries.

"We add a *third* operation!" Tetra said.

"No."

"Oops."

"We don't add more operations, we add a new inverse. Just like 'subtraction' becomes possible when you're guaranteed an inverse for the 'addition' operation, 'division' becomes possible when you know there's an inverse for the 'multiplication' operation. The only difference between a field and a ring is that fields require a multiplicative inverse for all elements except 0."

"Except for 0..." Tetra said, speaking aloud as she took notes.

"Right. That condition is the equivalent of excluding division by 0."

The field axioms

A set that meets the following axioms is called a field.

- The 'addition' operator +...

  - is closed,
  - has an identity element (called '0'),
  - is associative for all elements,
  - is commutative for all elements, and
  - has an inverse for all elements.

- The 'multiplication' operator ×...

  - is closed,
  - has an identity element (called '1'),
  - is associative for all elements,
  - is commutative for all elements, and
  - has an inverse for all elements except 0.

- The operators + and × together...

  - are distributive for all elements.

Note: The only difference between rings and fields is the existence of a multiplicative inverse of each nonzero element.

"Okay, let's see if we understand this by creating an example. Go for it, Tetra."

"I'll try..." Tetra said. She mumbled to herself as she scribbled in her notebook. After a minute, her hand shot up.

"How about this? Does the set of all fractions $\frac{a}{b}$ make a field?"

"What are a and b?" Miruka shot back.

"Integers. So I think the set of all integers divided by integers makes a field."

"And what do you think about that?" Miruka asked, lobbing the ball into my court.

"Two problems," I said. "One is that she's forgotten to keep 0s out of her denominators. She should have said 'all integers divided by nonzero integers.' The other problem is that this set already has a name—the set of all rational numbers $\mathbb{Q}$."

"I thought it sounded familiar," Tetra said. "But anyway, the rationals form a field, right?"

Miruka nodded.

"They do. Formally, you should call that 'the field of rational numbers $\mathbb{Q}$.' Actually, we've used this field before, when we proved there are infinitely many primitive Pythagorean triples."

"Hey, we did, didn't we."

"You can think of the field of rational numbers $\mathbb{Q}$ as the ring of integers $\mathbb{Z}$ with division glommed on. So tell me, how would you do the same thing to the residue ring $\mathbb{Z}/m\mathbb{Z}$? Here, let me write that down:"

Problem 7-2 (Rings into fields)

Give the conditions on the modulus m such that $\mathbb{Z}/m\mathbb{Z} = \{0, 1, 2, \cdots, m - 1\}$ is a field.

"I'm gonna need a minute" Tetra said. "This is all still new to me."

"Take as long as you want."

I thought a bit myself, and since Miruka had given us plenty of hints it wasn't long before I came up with what I was pretty sure was the answer. I started whipping up some operation tables to make sure.

"Okay, I think I might have it," Tetra said. "Maybe."

"I'm listening." Miruka said.

"Um, I think that for all integers, no, for all elements in the set—oh, except for 0—the modulus m has to...hang on. No, let's try this: If each of the $m - 1$ integers is relatively prime with m, then $\mathbb{Z}/m\mathbb{Z}$ is a field."

Miruka's reaction was...no reaction at all.

"No?" Tetra ventured. "Because, when we talked about dividing congruences, you could only divide when the numbers were relatively prime with the modulus, so I—"

"But Tetra," I began. "That means—*mrph!*"

Miruka clapped a hand over my mouth. "You talk too much." Her voice took on a musical lilt. "Oh, Tetra, Tetra, my word-loving Tetra," she said, her hand still over my mouth. "Doesn't your heart leap when you think of a sequence of integers $\{1, 2, 3, \cdots, m-1\}$ and a modulus that they are *all* relatively prime with?"

"Should it? Wait, let me work through this... So 1 is relatively prime with m, and 2 is relatively prime with m, and 3 is—"

Tetra's eyes went wide and her mouth hung open.

"So that means...m is prime?"

"It is," Miruka said.

"*Mnph*," I added with a nod.

"So the answer is that the ring $\mathbb{Z}/m\mathbb{Z}$ forms a field when m is prime?"

"Exactly. When m is prime, every nonzero element in $\mathbb{Z}/m\mathbb{Z}$ will have a multiplicative inverse, which means $\mathbb{Z}/m\mathbb{Z}$ will be a field. You can also go at it from the other direction, and say that if $\mathbb{Z}/m\mathbb{Z}$ is a field, then m is prime."

Answer 7-2 (Rings into fields)

The residue ring $\mathbb{Z}/m\mathbb{Z} = \{0, 1, 2, \cdots, m-1\}$ is a field when the modulus m is prime.

Tetra looked close to tears—the happy kind.

"I'm not sure why, but it's just so...*amazing*...to run into the primes here," she said. "I mean, the axioms for rings and fields don't say anything about primes. But when you make a field out of a residue ring, they just show up. It's almost kind of spooky."

Miruka finally took her hand off of my mouth, and I took a deep breath to make up for lost breathing cycles.

"When p is prime," Miruka said, "and you're dealing with a residue ring $\mathbb{Z}/p\mathbb{Z}$, that's called a finite field $\mathbb{F}_p$:"

$$\mathbb{F}_p = \mathbb{Z}/p\mathbb{Z}$$

"If you think of numbers spinning round and round on a clock face as a miniature model of the integers, you can think of a finite field $\mathbb{F}_p$ as a miniature model of the rationals."

Miruka leaned back and relaxed, a satisfied look on her face.

"From clocks to mod," she said, "and from there to groups, rings, and fields. Now *that's* what I call a trip worth taking."

7.5 MOD HAIRSTYLES

"Clocks to fields in one afternoon," I told Yuri. I had just spent another Saturday in my room giving her a rundown of division, congruence, and all the other stuff we had talked about that week.

"Wow, you guys really hit it hard, don't you," she said, leaning back against my bookcase. "I never thought I'd be jealous of someone hanging out with friends in a *library*, but I have to admit it sounds like fun."

"Did you follow all that stuff about congruence?"

"Basically, you can do addition and subtraction with remainders, right? Multiplication, even. And division if everything is relatively prime. And you can generalize stuff until pretty much anything becomes the same as anything else. I get it."

"Close enough, I guess."

"I remember you said something about folding up infinity once. This congruence stuff sounds like that."

"Yeah, you're right. The ring of integers $\mathbb{Z}$ gets folded up into the residue ring $\mathbb{Z}/m\mathbb{Z}$, the field of rational numbers $\mathbb{Q}$ gets folded up into the finite field $\mathbb{F}_p$..."

Yuri tugged on her ponytail and fell silent.

"Oh, your advice came in handy," I said.

"What advice?"

"Your girl advice."

"The 'looks good on you' line? You did *not* use that."

"Tetra got a haircut, so—"

"You idiot! You can't go around dropping bombs like that! No, I'm the idiot for telling you in the first place. Like giving a gun to a baby... Wait, how did she cut her hair?"

"What do you mean? She cut it. It was shorter."

"Just shorter? Details, please."

"Shorter is details."

"Ugh. You know *nothing* about girls."

Couldn't have said it better myself.

CHAPTER 8

Infinite Descent

By repeating this, we could get smaller
and smaller integers that fulfill the
same conditions, and we can continue
this without end. But such a thing is
impossible, because there cannot be an
infinite sequence of decreasing positive
integers.

NORIO ADACHI
Fermat's Great Theorem

8.1   FLT

"Question," Yuri said.

"Shoot," I replied, looking up from my notebook.

It was a Saturday afternoon in November. We'd finished the rice pilaf my mother made us for lunch, and Yuri was stretched out on the floor of my room reading a book, while I wrestled with operation tables for the finite field $\mathbb{F}_p$.

"What's the big deal about Fermat's last theorem?"

I craned my neck to look at the book she was reading. It was opened to a definition:

Fermat's last theorem

There exists no positive integer solution to the following equation for $n \geqslant 3$:

$$x^n + y^n = z^n$$

"It's famous. So simple anyone can understand it, but it took centuries for mathematicians to prove it's true. Fermat left a note saying he'd found a 'truly marvelous proof' for it, but he died before he could show it to anyone."

I picked up the book to admire this beautiful theorem.

"Most of the problems mathematicians are working on today are so complex you need all kinds of specialized knowledge just to understand what they mean, much less solve them. But this..." I shook my head in awe. "A layperson can understand it in a minute, but a professional mathematician couldn't solve it solo in a lifetime."

"But Fermat did?"

"Well, he said he did, but it's kinda hard to believe, even if he was one of the top mathematicians of the seventeenth century."

"A top mathematician? The book says he was an amateur."

"In the sense that he wasn't a career mathematician, yeah, but there weren't many of those back then. Fermat was actually a lawyer; math was just a hobby. Still, calling him an amateur is a little misleading, seeing as how he came up with some of the most advanced mathematics of his time. He left lots of other notes that became a kind of classic set of hard math problems that later generations of mathematicians chiseled away at. They didn't figure out this one for over 350 years."

"And that's how it got its name?" Yuri said. She cocked her head and thought a moment. "I think I would have called it 'Fermat's last boss.'"

I laughed and handed the book back to her.

"Fermat came up with that problem in 1637, but it wasn't really a theorem until Wiles published a definitive proof in 1995."

"What do you mean wasn't *really* a theorem?"

"Technically something isn't a theorem until it's been proven. You could say Fermat asserted that $x^n + y^n = z^n$ doesn't have a solution for $n \geqslant 3$, or that he made a conjecture. But no proof, no theorem. So it probably should have been called 'Fermat's conjecture' or 'Fermat's prediction' or 'Fermat's mighty powerful hunch' or something until it was finally proven once and for all."

"If it wasn't proven until 1995, what's with this table? It looks like there were a whole bunch of proofs..."

She held the book out again and showed me a list of names and dates:

1640	FLT(4)	Proof by Fermat
1753	FLT(3)	Proof by Euler
1825	FLT(5)	Proof by Dirichlet and Legendre
1832	FLT(14)	Proof by Dirichlet
1839	FLT(7)	Proof by Lamé

"That's a list of proofs for specific values," I said. "Fermat's last theorem has that equation $x^n + y^n = z^n$ in it, right?"

"It's practically the whole theorem."

"And the rest says there's no set of values (x, y, z) that will make the equation true for *any* value of n that's 3 or greater. The proofs listed here were for specific values of n. So FLT(3) means a proof of Fermat's last theorem for $n = 3$. In other words, FLT(3) says 'there are no values (x, y, z) that make the equation $x^3 + y^3 = z^3$ true:'"

$$x^3 + y^3 = z^3 \text{ has no solution} \quad \Longleftrightarrow \quad \text{FLT(3)}$$
$$x^4 + y^4 = z^4 \text{ has no solution} \quad \Longleftrightarrow \quad \text{FLT(4)}$$
$$x^5 + y^5 = z^5 \text{ has no solution} \quad \Longleftrightarrow \quad \text{FLT(5)}$$
$$x^6 + y^6 = z^6 \text{ has no solution} \quad \Longleftrightarrow \quad \text{FLT(6)}$$
$$x^7 + y^7 = z^7 \text{ has no solution} \quad \Longleftrightarrow \quad \text{FLT(7)}$$
$$\vdots$$

"How come the book's missing a proof for FLT(6)?"

"Bonus points for noticing. It's not missing, though. Euler proved that one."

"It says here Euler only proved FLT(3)."

"Yeah, but when you prove FLT(3), you've also proved FLT(6)."

"How's that?"

"Because if $x^3 + y^3 = z^3$ doesn't have a solution, then $x^6 + y^6 = z^6$ won't either. Wanna see why?"

"Is this an excuse to show off your mad math skills and leave me confused?"

"Nah, you'll be able to follow along. It's a simple proof by contradiction."

I turned to a new page in my notebook.

"Let's say we already have a proof that $x^3 + y^3 = z^3$ doesn't have a solution," I began, "and we want to prove that $x^6 + y^6 = z^6$ doesn't have a solution either. Since we're using proof by contradiction, we start out with a negation of the thing we want to prove:"

> Proposition:
> There exists a positive integer solution to $x^6 + y^6 = z^6$

"Next, we say our solution for (x, y, z) is (a, b, c). Remember, these numbers don't really exist, we're just pretending they do to see what happens. We're hoping that'll lead to a contradiction, since that would complete the proof. So anyway, from the definition of (a, b, c), we can write this:"

$$a^6 + b^6 = c^6$$

"But we can also write $x^6 + y^6 = z^6$ like this:"

$$(a^2)^3 + (b^2)^3 = (c^2)^3$$

"That all comes from $x^6 = (x^2)^3$. You've seen this before?"

Yuri nodded, her eyes fixed on the page. "The exponent rules, right?"

"Very good," I said. "Okay, three more variables, positive integers again, named (A, B, C). We define them like this:"

$$(A, B, C) = (a^2, b^2, c^2)$$

"But look what happens when we do that:"

$$a^6 + b^6 = c^6 \qquad \text{from the definition of } a, b, c$$
$$(a^2)^3 + (b^2)^3 = (c^2)^3 \qquad \text{exponent rules}$$
$$A^3 + B^3 = C^3 \qquad \text{from the definition of } A, B, C$$

"In other words, we've found that (A, B, C) is a solution to $x^3 + y^3 = z^3$. What's the problem with that?"

"We started out saying $x^3 + y^3 = z^3$ doesn't have a solution."

"Exactly. So this is a contradiction, which means our premise must be wrong, which in turn means we've proven $x^6 + y^6 = z^6$ doesn't have a solution."

"Okay, I think I follow that. If there was a solution to $x^6 + y^6 = z^6$ then you could use it to make a solution for $x^3 + y^3 = z^3$, but Euler's already proved you can't."

"Not just for 6s, though—any multiple of 3. So, more generally, if you want to prove FLT(n) for any $n \geqslant 5$ you don't have to do a proof for every n; just prove FLT(p) for all the primes $p = 5, 7, 11, 13, \cdots$."

"So that Dirichlet guy wasted his time doing 14 instead of 7. Guess he wasn't as smart as he thought he was."

"I'm sure he would've loved to have done 7. He just didn't know how."

"Oh." Yuri shrugged. "Maybe I shouldn't be talkin'. I hit problems I can't figure out every math test."

"Next time, try solving for 14 instead of 7."

Yuri laughed.

8.2 TETRA'S TRIANGLES

8.2.1 In the Zone

The next Friday after school Tetra was already waiting for me when I got to the library. She was hunched over a notebook, writing furiously.

"You're here early," I said.

"Oh, hey," said Tetra. "You just missed Miruka. She's practicing with Ay-Ay today."

"What're you working on? Is that a card from Mr. Muraki?"

"Yeah, another triangle problem."

I picked up the card and read it:

Problem 8-1

Does there exist a right triangle with integer-length sides and square area?

"Huh," I said. "Interesting. Made any progress?"

"I'm still just drawing some examples. No spoilers on this one, please. I want to try it by myself."

Tetra held a finger to her lips in a "silence" gesture.

"Sure, no problem. I have some stuff of my own to work on. Let me know when you're done and I'll walk you to the station."

"Deal," Tetra said with a smile.

I found an empty seat a few tables down. I had every intention of playing around in $\mathbb{F}_p$ some more, but my mind kept wandering back to Tetra's problem. Right triangles with integer sides brought back fond memories of Pythagorean triples. I wondered if I couldn't use them as a springboard to an answer.

Examples first. Examples, not hunches, are the key to understanding.

I decided to use a, b, c as my side lengths, with c as the hypotenuse. I began with the classic Pythagorean triple:

$$(a, b, c) = (3, 4, 5)$$

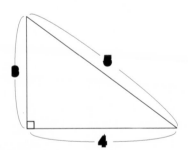

Below that, I wrote:

$$\text{area of a right triangle} = \frac{ab}{2} = \frac{3 \times 4}{2} = 6$$

Definitely not a square area.

I tried again with the next Pythagorean triple that came to mind, $(5, 12, 13)$, but didn't get a square with that, either:

$$\text{area of the right triangle} = \frac{5 \times 12}{2} = 30$$

My math sense was tingling, telling me no such triangle would exist, but I kept plugging along with all the Pythagorean triples I could think of:

(a, b, c)	Area	Square?
$(3, 4, 5)$	$\dfrac{3 \times 4}{2} = 6$	nope
$(5, 12, 13)$	$\dfrac{5 \times 12}{2} = 30$	nope
$(7, 24, 25)$	$\dfrac{7 \times 24}{2} = 84$	nope
$(8, 15, 17)$	$\dfrac{8 \times 15}{2} = 60$	nope
$(9, 40, 41)$	$\dfrac{9 \times 40}{2} = 180$	nope

Verrry interesting.

Interesting or not, in a sea of infinite possibilities five examples wasn't even a drop. I needed proof. I turned to a new page in my notebook, and wrote what I hoped to prove at the top:

> There exists no right triangle with integer-length sides and square area.

The structure of the problem just begged for a proof by contradiction. I would assume such a triangle existed, then see if that didn't make something explode.

I wrote down the negation of the statement I was trying to prove as a starting point:

> There exists a right triangle with integer-length sides and square area.

Okay, let's turn this into some math, starting with what I know about a right triangle.

I had said a, b, c were the side lengths of the triangle, with c as the hypotenuse, so from the Pythagorean theorem I knew this:

$$a^2 + b^2 = c^2$$

To keep things as simple as possible, I wanted to be sure a and b were relatively prime. The easiest way to do that would be to divide them by their greatest common divisor. If I called the GCD g, that would mean somewhere out there were positive integers A and B that made these equations work:

$$a = gA, \quad b = gB, \quad A \perp B$$

Since g would mop up all the prime factors common to a and b, A and B shouldn't have any common prime factors, either. In other words, A and B were relatively prime.

I tried sticking my new equations $a = gA$ and $b = gB$ into the Pythagorean theorem:

$$\begin{aligned}
a^2 + b^2 &= c^2 && \text{the Pythagorean theorem} \\
(gA)^2 + (gB)^2 &= c^2 && \text{substitute } a = gA, b = gB \\
g^2(A^2 + B^2) &= c^2 && \text{factor out a } g^2
\end{aligned}$$

This told me c^2 is a multiple of g^2, which means c is a multiple of g. That in turn meant there would be a C that made this true:

$$c = gC$$

Okay, more crunching:

$$\begin{aligned}
g^2(A^2 + B^2) &= c^2 && \text{what we had} \\
g^2(A^2 + B^2) &= (gC)^2 && \text{substitute } c = gC \\
g^2(A^2 + B^2) &= g^2C^2 && \text{expand the right} \\
A^2 + B^2 &= C^2 && \text{divide both sides by } g^2
\end{aligned}$$

Since I had $A \perp B$ and $A^2 + B^2 = C^2$, I also knew $B \perp C$ and $C \perp A$. I had replaced a, b, and c with A, B, and C, three numbers from which any pair was relatively prime. (A, B, C) was a new Pythagorean triple.

I'd made it this far without any problems, but I wasn't sure how to proceed. I decided to set the lengths aside for the time being, and play with the area part of the problem using A and B.

I could represent the "square area" using some positive integer d:

$$\frac{ab}{2} = d^2$$

Substituting $a = gA$ and $b = gB$ gave me this:

$$\frac{(gA)(gB)}{2} = d^2$$

And after a bit of calculation:

$$g^2 \times \frac{AB}{2} = d^2$$

Since (A, B, C) was a Pythagorean triple, I knew one of A or B had to be even, which meant $\frac{AB}{2}$ would be a positive integer. That meant d^2 must be a multiple of g^2, and I could summon up a positive integer D where $d = gD$:

$$g^2 \times \frac{AB}{2} = (gD)^2$$

Getting rid of the denominator and dividing both sides by g^2 gave me this:

$$AB = 2D^2$$

Taking stock of what I had so far, I realized I could now reword Tetra's problem algebraically, and with the new condition that A and B were relatively prime:

Problem 8-2 (rewording of Prob. 8-1)

Do there exist positive integers A, B, C, D that fulfill these conditions?

$$A^2 + B^2 = C^2, \quad AB = 2D^2, \quad \text{and} \quad A \perp B$$

$(A \perp B$ means A and B are relatively prime.)

So far so good, but I hadn't found anything that looked like a contradiction yet.

Maybe if I—

"The library is now *closed!*"

I leapt in my seat. Ms. Mizutani had struck again.

I looked out the window and saw it was dark out. I'd been so focused I completely lost track of time. I still had one foot in the math world when Tetra walked up.

"Ready to head home?" she asked.

Unable to form a coherent non-mathematical sentence, I sat there staring at her.

"Are you okay?"

"Yeah... Yeah, sorry. Let's go. And, uh, thanks."

"For what?"

"I dunno. Just...thanks."

8.2.2 A Hint from Tetra

We headed toward the train station, winding our way through the neighborhood surrounding our school. Tetra was quiet most of the way, but eventually she spoke up.

"What is it with me? All the progress I've made, but I still keep forgetting conditions. It's like, when I see a new equation it fills up my head, and everything else gets squeezed out."

Tetra waved her hands over her head, apparently miming escaping conditions.

"No worries, you'll get better," I said. "How're you coming along with defining new variables? You said that was giving you trouble, too."

"Well, I'm not quite busting out the 'let this be thats' like you and Miruka do, but I'm working on it."

"It's worth it, believe me. I know it looks harder with more variables floating around, but in the long run it can save a lot of pain."

"Yeah, I'm doing my best with this new problem. I'm using your Pythagorean juicer, by the way."

"My what?"

"Remember? The equation you made where you can drop in an m and an n to squeeze out a primitive Pythagorean triple. I'm using that generalization to work on the problem."

"Oh, sure. Yeah, that might work."

Might even be a good idea, representing A, B, C *in terms of* m *and* n. *I wonder if that's where my contradiction is hiding...?*

"Thanks for the hint," I said.

"What, you're working on it, too? Well, don't cry like a little baby when I beat you to it," Tetra laughed.

8.3 THE JOURNEY

8.3.1 Setting Out

That night at home, I prepared myself for a journey: a quest in search of a contradiction.

I started by surveying my starting point, the relationship between the A, B, C, and D I had found:

My starting point
$A^2 + B^2 = C^2 \quad AB = 2D^2 \quad A \perp B$

From $A^2 + B^2 = C^2$ and $A \perp B$, I knew A, B, C formed a primitive Pythagorean triple. That meant I could use the generalization I'd found before—my Pythagorean juicer—to rewrite A and B in terms of m and n.

Generalized form of primative Pythagorean triples

$$A^2 + B^2 = C^2, A \perp B \quad \Longleftrightarrow \quad \begin{cases} A &= m^2 - n^2 \\ B &= 2mn \\ C &= m^2 + n^2 \end{cases}$$

Conditions on m, n:

· $m > n$

· $m \perp n$

· m, n have differing parity

I took a deep breath, and decided to start by sticking m and n into $AB = 2D^2$, the condition that said the area of the triangle had to be square, and see if I couldn't learn anything about D.

As much as I'd been pressing Tetra to start using more definitions, to be honest, introducing new variables always put me on edge, too. I could never shake the feeling I'd end up drowning in a sea of letters.

But as always, I decided to trust the math, to let it fly free and see where it would go. Once I'd merged primitive Pythagorean triples and the area equation, I could forget about right triangles and the like. I knocked on wood and hoped for the best.

Off we go. First thing to do is rewrite $AB = 2D^2$ *as* m *and* n. *Not sure where this will take me, but there's only one way to find out...*

$$AB = 2D^2 \quad \text{the ``square area'' condition}$$
$$(m^2 - n^2)B = 2D^2 \quad \text{substitute } A = m^2 - n^2$$
$$(m^2 - n^2)(2mn) = 2D^2 \quad \text{substitute } B = 2mn$$
$$mn(m^2 - n^2) = D^2 \quad \text{divide both sides by 2 and clean up}$$
$$mn(m + n)(m - n) = D^2 \quad \text{product of a sum and difference}$$
$$\text{is a difference of squares}$$

I stared at my creation:

$$D^2 = mn(m + n)(m - n)$$

It looked familiar—a square on the left, and a product of relatively prime numbers on the right.

Hang on. Those are all relatively prime, right? Like, $(m+n) \perp (m-n)...right?

...Aren't they?

I sighed and admitted I needed to do this by the book. Knowing $m + n$ and $m - n$ were relatively prime could be a powerful weapon, so I wanted to be sure I could use it.

Time for my millionth proof by contradiction.

I partitioned off part of the page I was working on and had at it.

If $m + n$ and $m - n$ were not relatively prime, then there would be some prime p and positive integers J, K that made these equations work:

$$\begin{cases} pJ & = m+n \\ pK & = m-n \end{cases}$$

The prime number p would be a factor common to $m + n$ and $m - n$. If I could get from this to a contradiction, I'd know $m + n$ and $m - n$ were indeed relatively prime, and I'd be able to keep my weapon. I added the equations together to pull out the relationship between p and m:

$$pJ + pK = (m + n) + (m - n) \qquad \text{add the equations}$$
$$p(J + K) = (m + n) + (m - n) \qquad \text{factor out a p}$$
$$p(J + K) = 2m \qquad \text{clean up the right side}$$

Subtracting the equations gave me the relationship between p and n:

$$pJ - pK = (m + n) - (m - n) \qquad \text{subtract the equations}$$
$$p(J - K) = (m + n) - (m - n) \qquad \text{factor out a p}$$
$$p(J - K) = 2n \qquad \text{clean up the right side}$$

That gave me a new relationship, with everything as products:

$$\begin{cases} p(J + K) & = 2m \\ p(J - K) & = 2n \end{cases}$$

Here it comes...

I knew p couldn't be 2, because m and n had different parity, which meant $pJ = m + n$ was odd. *No even primes allowed here, looks like.*

Then again, $p \geqslant 3$ didn't work either, because m and n both had to be multiples of p. But since $m \perp n$, a $p \geqslant 3$ would violate that.

That settles it, then. $m + n$ and $m - n$ are relatively prime.

I'd come this far, so I figured I might as well show that $m + n$ and m are relatively prime, too.

The proof was similar to what I'd just done—start off by assuming they *aren't* relatively prime, which would imply the existence of a prime p and positive integers J, K that made these equations true:

$$\begin{cases} pJ & = m + n \\ pK & = m \end{cases}$$

A little fiddling turned the equations into this:

$$\begin{cases} pK & = m \\ p(J - K) & = n \end{cases}$$

Now I had m, n both as multiples of p, a contradiction since $m \perp n$.

It would be just as easy to do the same thing with $m - n$ and m, $m + n$ and n, and $m - n$ and n. So now I was sure any pair from among m, n, $m + n$, and $m - n$ would be relatively prime. Secure in my weapons, I was ready to wade back into battle.

Before I'd headed off on this sortie, I'd been wondering what to do with this:

$$D^2 = mn(m + n)(m - n)$$

On the left I had a square, which meant every factor in its prime factorization would be present an even number of times. On the right, I had four factors that were pairwise relatively prime, meaning they couldn't have any prime factors in common.

I imagined the factors from the prime factorization of the D^2 on the left being sprinkled among the four factors on the right. The only way to do that would be to drop an even number of each of D^2's prime factors into the four available slots. And that meant...

m, n, m + n, and m − n are all squares!

I was starting to like this relatively prime business. When you think of it as meaning a greatest common divisor of 1, it doesn't seem like such a big deal. But integers tremble before you when you charge forward shouting, "No common prime factors shall pass!"

8.3.2 Atoms and Elementary Particles

I wanted to represent my new discovery, that m, n, $m + n$, and $m - n$ each had to be squares, as an equation. One step back I had represented A, B, C, and D as m and n. Now I was preparing to write m and n as e, f, s, and t.

At first I had thought of this problem as setting out on an expedition into the great unknown, but now it was starting to feel more like shrinking farther and farther down into the realm of some microcosm. Investigating the molecules A, B, C, D, I had discovered the atoms m, n. Now I was preparing to split those atoms into the elementary particles e, f, s, t.

If this keeps up, I'm going to end up looking for quarks...

Given that m, n, $m + n$, and $m - n$ were squares, there had to be positive integers e, f, s, t that made these equations true:

$$m, n, m + n, m - n \textbf{ as } e, f, s, t$$
(Atoms and particles)

$$\begin{cases} m & = e^2 \\ n & = f^2 \\ m + n & = s^2 \\ m - n & = t^2 \end{cases}$$

Note: e, f, s, t are pairwise relatively prime integers.

More new variables. Four of them, no less.

Trust the math, trust the math.

I flipped back through my notes and considered where to head next. No better ideas coming to mind, I decided to try writing m in terms of e, f, s, and t.

I already had $m = e^2$. I wondered if there wasn't something I could do with this:

$$\begin{cases} m + n & = s^2 \\ m - n & = t^2 \end{cases}$$

Adding and subtracting these equations gave me m, n in terms of s, t, leaving me with a breakdown of the particles in these particular atoms:

$$\begin{cases} 2m & = s^2 + t^2 \\ 2n & = s^2 - t^2 \end{cases}$$

The right side of $2n = s^2 - t^2$ was a difference of squares. I instinctively rewrote that as a product of a sum and a difference, since an integer in multiplicative form often said something about its structure:

$$2n = s^2 - t^2 \qquad \text{from the above}$$
$$2n = (s + t)(s - t) \qquad \text{a difference of squares...}$$
$$2f^2 = (s + t)(s - t) \qquad \text{substitute } n = f^2$$

This had given me the relationship between f and $s + t, s - t$, the relationship between three of my particles.

The relationship between f and $s + t, s - t$
(A relationship between particles)

$$2f^2 = (s + t)(s - t)$$

8.3.3 Into the Particles

I needed to dig deeper into this equation I'd found, $2f^2 = (s+t)(s-t)$.

I started with the product on the right. I knew $s + t$ and $s - t$ had to be integers, so I decided to see if checking their parity would tell me anything.

I didn't know what the parity of s was yet, but I *did* know that $m + n = s^2$ from my atom-particle relationship.

The parity of $m + n$ wasn't hard to find: I knew m and n had differing parity, so I'd be adding an even and an odd number, which meant $m + n$ would be odd. That meant s^2 had to be odd, too, and only an odd number could be squared to get another odd number.

Drop s into the 'odd' box...

Next was t, which followed a similar pattern: I knew $m - n = t^2$, and the differing parity of m and n again meant $m - n$ would be odd, so t^2 was odd, meaning t was odd. With both s and t odd, $s + t$ and $s - t$ both had to be even.

One of my big discoveries of the night was that $(m+n) \perp (m-n)$, and that meant $s^2 \perp t^2$. No common factors between two squares means there couldn't be any common factors in the numbers being squared, and that meant s and t were relatively prime.

I was pretty pleased with myself...until I looked back at my "atoms and particles" relationship and realized I'd already established that s and t would be relatively prime.

Ah, well. At least nobody's watching.

I'd learned a lot about s and t, so I wrote up a list to keep everything organized:

Things I know about s and t

- s is odd

- t is odd

- $s + t$ is even

- $s - t$ is even

- s and t are relatively prime ($s \perp t$)

I flipped back through my notes, looking for a good place to apply what I'd learned about $s + t$ and $s - t$. Of course it was in $2f^2 = (s + t)(s - t)$, the equation that had set me off on this investigation to begin with.

I knew $s + t$ and $s - t$ were even, which meant $\frac{s+t}{2}$ and $\frac{s-t}{2}$ would be integers. That meant I could rewrite the equation as a product of four integers, like this:

$$2f^2 = 2 \cdot \frac{s + t}{2} \cdot 2 \cdot \frac{s - t}{2}$$

Dividing both sides of the equation by 2 left this:

$$f^2 = 2 \cdot \frac{s+t}{2} \cdot \frac{s-t}{2}$$

So now I have a square on the left, and... Hang on, have I already done this, too? Am I running around in circles?

I paused to take stock and realized I was indeed making progress. Here I had the square f^2 on the left, and something with a prime factor 2 on the right. Since the right side would have to be a square, just like the left, there would have to be another prime factor 2 somewhere in either $\frac{s+t}{2}$ or $\frac{s-t}{2}$.

In other words, either $\frac{s+t}{2}$ or $\frac{s-t}{2}$ had to be even.

I sighed, realizing I needed to do another check for relative primeness.

No use putting it off...

If $\frac{s+t}{2}$ and $\frac{s-t}{2}$ were not relatively prime, then they would share a common prime factor p, and there would exist integers J, K that made the following true:

$$\begin{cases} pJ & = \dfrac{s+t}{2} \\[2mm] pK & = \dfrac{s-t}{2} \end{cases}$$

Adding and subtracting these equations gave me this:

$$\begin{cases} p(J+K) & = \dfrac{s+t}{2} + \dfrac{s-t}{2} = s \\[2mm] p(J-K) & = \dfrac{s+t}{2} - \dfrac{s-t}{2} = t \end{cases}$$

Nothing hard about this check, at least...

The equations I'd just gotten said both s and t were multiples of p. That meant s and t shared p as a prime factor, a contradiction since $s \perp t$, and so proof that $\frac{s+t}{2}$ and $\frac{s-t}{2}$ were relatively prime.

That also told me that in $f^2 = 2 \cdot \frac{s+t}{2} \cdot \frac{s-t}{2}$ one of $\frac{s+t}{2}$ and $\frac{s-t}{2}$ was even, and since they were relatively prime the other would have to be odd. So the distribution of primes in the prime factorization would be $2 \times$ [a square] for the even one, and the odd one would be a squared odd number.

This is going to be easier to follow as symbols than words. But to do that...uh oh.

I was left with little choice but to introduce two *more* variables, u and v—the 'quarks' that would show the structure of my elementary particles s, t.

My quarks u, v would be relatively prime positive integers, and would allow me to write the $2 \times$ [a square] number as $2u^2$ and the odd square as v^2. Then one of $\frac{s+t}{2}$ and $\frac{s-t}{2}$ would be $2u^2$, and the other would be v^2.

8.3.4 The Shores of Quantum Foam

I had taken my variables to the edges of known physics. Now it was time to clean up.

I looked back through my notes to summarize what I knew about these quarks.

$$\frac{s+t}{2}, \frac{s-t}{2}$$

(particles s, t and quarks u, v)

- $\frac{s+t}{2}$ and $\frac{s-t}{2}$ are relatively prime.

- One of $\frac{s+t}{2}, \frac{s-t}{2}$ is $2u^2$, the other is v^2.

- u and v are relatively prime ($u \perp v$).

- v is odd.

At this point I thought I was seeing the light at the end of the tunnel, but it turned out to be an oncoming train. With only this, I couldn't tell which of $\frac{s+t}{2}$ and $\frac{s-t}{2}$ was $2u^2$, and which was v^2. The best I could do would be to split things up into cases.

I gritted my teeth and began writing:

Case 1: Where $\frac{s+t}{2} = 2u^2, \frac{s-t}{2} = v^2$—

$$\begin{cases} s & = 2u^2 + v^2 \\ t & = 2u^2 - v^2 \end{cases}$$

Case 2: Where $\frac{s+t}{2} = v^2$, $\frac{s-t}{2} = 2u^2$—

$$\begin{cases} s = 2u^2 + v^2 \\ t = -2u^2 + v^2 \end{cases}$$

Ugly, ugly, ugly...

I stood at this fork in the road, hesitating. The surefire way to hammer through this would be to just walk both paths, but that would be twice the effort, and it was getting late. I *really* wanted to find something a bit more elegant.

I combed through what I'd written so far, looking for some forgotten equation that might be of use. I paused as I re-examined the relationship between my atoms and particles—and I discovered I hadn't used $m = e^2$ anywhere.

I found m in relation to the particles s, t, like so:

$$\begin{cases} m + n = s^2 \\ m - n = t^2 \end{cases}$$

Adding those equations and dividing by 2 gave me this:

$$m = \frac{s^2 + t^2}{2}$$

So now I had e tied to s and t:

$$e^2 = m = \frac{s^2 + t^2}{2}$$

Since s and t were being squared and added, I had a way to combine my two cases into a single equation:

$$e^2 = \frac{s^2 + t^2}{2} \qquad \text{the equation above}$$
$$e^2 = \frac{(2u^2 + v^2)^2 + (2u^2 - v^2)^2}{2} \qquad s, t \text{ as } u, v$$
$$e^2 = 4u^4 + v^4 \qquad \text{simplify}$$

I let out a sigh of relief, both at avoiding my use of cases and at the relatively simple equation I had ended up with to tie together my particle e with quarks u, v.

Unfortunately, my satisfaction was shortlived, as I realized I had lost sight of my goal. I wasn't doing this for the fun of writing equations in new forms, I was trying to find a contradiction. But I had no idea if this new discovery would lead me to one.

I glanced at the clock and was shocked at the time. I jotted down one last note before crashing:

Relation between particle e and quarks u, v

Does this lead to a contradiction?

$$e^2 = 4u^4 + v^4$$

· $u \perp v$

· v is odd

8.4   Yuri's Awakening

8.4.1   *Math, Interrupted*

"Hey, what's up!" Yuri said as she entered my room the next day.

I grunted a response, not even lifting my eyes from my notebook.

"Hello to you, too." She peeked over my shoulder. "Whatcha workin' on?"

"Math."

"You aren't writing anything."

"I'm thinking."

"Well ex*cuse* me. I'll get out of your way."

"Sorry, I didn't mean to be rude."

I turned around and saw Yuri standing with her hands on her hips. Her hair was in her customary ponytail, and she was wearing jeans and a jacket. Her glasses protruded from a shirt pocket.

"You do *way* too much math. Let's go do something that doesn't involve pencils."

"It's cold."

"Yeah, that happens in winter."

I sighed. "How about the bookstore?"

Yuri made a face. "Well, at least we'll get some sun on the way."

8.4.2   The Playground

Yuri and I set off toward town.

"So what was so engrossing you couldn't even say 'hello'?" she asked.

As we walked I gave her a condensed, equation-free description of the problem I was working on, my quest to prove the nonexistence of a triangle with integer sides and a square area.

"—and after all that, I finally got as far as this really promising relationship between the particle e and the quarks u, v. If I can just show it leads to a contradiction, I'll be done. If not... I guess it's back to the drawing board."

We were approaching a footbridge when I felt Yuri tug my sleeve. She was pointing at our old elementary school on the far side of the bridge.

"Let's go play on the playground!"

"What about the bookstore?"

"This'll be way more fun!"

"Whatever."

We crossed the bridge, which took us right to the front gate. It was locked, but we knew a way to get into the playground from the back. There was a small track behind the school, beyond which stood the playground used by the youngest kids. It had swings, a seesaw, a dome like a wireframe dodecahedron, and a slide—everything a kid could want. I forgot the cold for a moment as the fond memories came rushing back.

Yuri spoke, interrupting my reverie.

"That card you got—it just asked you if a triangle like that exists or not?"

"Yeah? So?"

"It didn't say to prove a triangle like that *doesn't* exist, right?"

Yuri made a break for the swings.

"Wait, what do you mean?" I asked, jogging to catch up.

"Wow, were these swings really this small?" she said, jumping up on one and starting to rock back and forth.

I sat in the swing next to her. She was right—they definitely weren't designed for a high-school sized posterior.

"You think I'm trying to prove the wrong thing?"

"Pssh, what do I know?" Yuri said, pumping herself higher.

She was right, of course—the card only asked if triangles like that exist or not. Maybe my hunch was wrong, and such a triangle *did* exist. I'd only tried a few examples, after all, which meant practically nothing.

I shuddered at the possibility that she was right. It would certainly explain why I was having so much trouble finding a contradiction. *Which would mean all that work last night was for nothing...*

Yuri's squeal brought me back to earth. She had moved over to the slide. She waved to me from the top.

"Here I go!"

She skidded to the bottom and came to rest just short of the edge.

She frowned. "I remember that being more fun."

"Well, given the angle of the slide with respect to the horizontal and your potential energy from that height, not to mention the coefficient of kinetic friction between the metal and—"

"Ugh! You are *such* a geek!"

8.4.3 Drinks with Pythagoras

After she'd made her circuit of the playground, Yuri complained she was thirsty. We left the playground and found a bank of vending machines along the road near the school. I bought two hot lemon drinks and took them to the nearby bench where Yuri was waiting.

"Here ya go," I said, handing her one.

"Thanks... Yowch!"

Yuri looked up at me as she rolled the can between her hands while she waited for it to cool.

"Sorry for dragging you out here."

"Nah, it's okay. Probably did me good to get some fresh air, clear my head."

"Tell me more about that relationship with particles or whatever you were talking about. Oh, I guess you don't have your notebook with you."

"I have a little notepad. Oops, no pen, though."

"I have one." She fished around in her purse. "You can really remember it off the top of your head?"

"After how much time I spent on it last night, I better. It looks like this:"

$$e^2 = 4u^4 + v^4$$

"Huh. And what about this looks so promising?"

"I dunno. Not too simple, not too complex...something like that."

"Some sort of math nerd intuition thing?"

"Something like that. I've been pounding away at this thing for a long time, but it's been like beating my head against a wall. I may be heading down a dead end."

"What were you working on this morning?"

"Rewriting it as $e^2 - 4u^4 = v^4$, then as a product like this:"

$$(e + 2u^2)(e - 2u^2) = v^4$$

"Didn't get me anywhere interesting, though." I sighed.

"So you're looking for what it *really* is."

"What do you mean?"

"You know, that line from Night on the Galactic Railroad."

"Oh, that again. Yeah, I guess."

"Give it here," Yuri said, holding out a hand.

"All yours."

I handed her the notepad. Yuri sipped her drink as she stared at it.

"That's funny..." She said.

"What is?"

"This equation, $e^2 = 4u^4 + v^4$. If you switch the left and right sides, it looks kinda like the Pythagorean theorem."

My world froze in place for an eternal heartbeat. In that moment, it was as if Yuri was bathed in a golden light, transformed into my own personal Pythia, delivering wisdom from some other plane.

The Pythagorean theorem...?

I rearranged the equation in my head.

$$4u^4 + v^4 = e^2$$

The Pythagorean theorem!

My hand trembled as I rewrote the equation as a sum of squares:

$$\left(2u^2\right)^2 + \left(v^2\right)^2 = e^2$$

Define a few more variables...

$$A_1 = 2u^2, B_1 = v^2, C_1 = e$$

Then I have...

$$A_1^2 + B_1^2 = C_1^2$$

Wait a minute... Isn't this where I started?

I pressed a fist against my forehead, working backwards from what I'd done the previous night. I made it back to my starting point soon enough:

$$A^2 + B^2 = C^2, \quad AB = 2D^2, \quad A \perp B$$

Maybe I can define a D_1 so that $A_1 B_1 = 2D_1^2$?

Sure enough, since $A_1 = 2u^2, B_1 = v^2$ I could do this:

$$A_1 B_1 = \left(2u^2\right)\left(v^2\right) = 2\left(uv\right)^2$$

Then I define D_1 as

$$D_1 = uv$$

and I end up with this:

$$A_1 B_1 = 2D_1^2$$

Since I know $u \perp v$, and v is odd, I can show that $A_1 \perp B_1$.

The variables were different, but I'd come full circle to a set of equations with the same form as the ones I started with.

Departures and arrivals

$A^2 + B^2 = C^2$	$AB = 2D^2$	$A \perp B$	where I started
$A_1^2 + B_1^2 = C_1^2$	$A_1 B_1 = 2D_1^2$	$A_1 \perp B_1$	where I ended up

---

But what does this mean? Have I been running around in circles?

Half-formed images of circles and periodicity filled my head, spiraling forever downward...

Wait...forever? No, not forever! It can't be!

I started with 'molecules' A, B, C, D. From there, I broke things down into 'atoms' m, n, and 'particles' e, f, s, t, and 'quarks' u, v. I said $C_1 = e$, which put it at the 'particles' level.

So doesn't that mean C_1 should be smaller than the atom-level C?

If it is...

I cursed myself for not bringing my notebook.

"C'mon Yuri, we gotta head back," I said, grabbing her by her sleeve and pulling her up.

"Hey, what's the—wait up!"

"No time! Come on!"

We half-walked, half-ran back to my place. A single thought repeated itself in my mind like a mantra.

Please let $C > C_1$... Please let $C > C_1$... Please let $C > C_1$...

Back home, I rushed to my room, opened my notebook, and flipped through its pages.

Where are you? Where? ...Gotcha!

All the numbers in this problem were positive integers. That gave me two key facts:

· $C = m^2 + n^2$, so $C > m$

· $m = e^2$, so $m \geqslant e$

Combining that with $C_1 = e$, I could say $C > m \geqslant e = C_1$. Cut out the stuff in the middle, and that left:

$$C > C_1$$

Smashing the atoms A, B, C, D had resulted in positive integers A_1, B_1, C_1, D_1. Since all of this showed up in exactly the same form in the equations I started with, I could follow the same atom-smashing process over and over to end up with $C_1, C_2, C_3, \cdots$, as many Cs as I wanted. And those Cs would look like this:

$$C > C_1 > C_2 > C_3 > \cdots > C_k > \cdots$$

If I had enough patience, I could make C_k as small as I wanted, except for one tiny detail: That was impossible.

You can't just keep getting smaller and smaller with positive integers; eventually you're going to hit a wall called '1'. So if there's a chain of positive integers $C > C_1 > C_2 > C_3 > \cdots$, then there would always be some value C_k you could call the minimum value. That means you can always make this proposition:

C_k is the smallest value.

But I'd just shown that any time you had a C_k, you could always create a smaller value C_{k+1}. In other words, this proposition would be possible:

C_k is *not* the smallest value.

You couldn't ask for a clearer contradiction.

And with that, the proof was done. There could be no triangle with integer-length sides and a square area.

I looked up from my notebook, grinning like a fool. Yuri was grimacing with boredom.

"I did it, I did it, I did it!" I shouted, giving her ponytail a bat with my hand.

"Hey, hands off the 'tail!"

Answer 8-2

There exist no positive integers A, B, C, D such that the following hold:

$$A^2 + B^2 = C^2, \quad AB = 2D^2, \quad A \perp B$$

Answer 8-1

There exists no right triangle with integer-length sides and square area.

Roadmap of the proof

Goal: Prove area isn't square

$\downarrow$ Suppose proposition is false

Proposition: Area is square

$\downarrow$ Set up as equations

Forget right triangles, think only a, b, c

$\downarrow$ relatively prime

Think 'molecules' A, B, C

$\downarrow$ General form for PPTs

Write A, B, C, D as m, n (Pythagorean juicer)

$\downarrow$ Prime factorization

Write m, n as e, f, s, t (atoms to particles)

$\downarrow$ Product of a sum and difference...

Write f as $s + t$ and $s - t$ (relation between particles)

$\downarrow$ Prime factorization

Write e as u and v (particles to quarks)

$\downarrow$ Try to derive a contradiction

Similar A_1, B_1, C_1, D_1, with $C > C_1$

$\downarrow$

Contradiction

$\downarrow$

Proposition is false

$\downarrow$

Proof complete: Area is not square

8.5 Miruka's Proof

8.5.1 Wax On, Wax Off

I couldn't wait to see Tetra in the library after school that Monday, but when I showed her my proof, her response was less than enthusiastic.

"It's so...long," she said. "So many variables."

Her eyes glazed over as she flipped through the pages.

She sighed. "This is just like last time. I had all the tools, but I didn't know what to do with them. I made it as far as using the general form for primitive Pythagorean triples, but I didn't get deep enough into the relatively prime stuff to go much beyond that. To be honest, I forgot it was even a condition."

"When you get stuck you need to go back and look for things like that, things you might have overlooked. This is a long proof, but it's only a small part of all the stuff I tried. You have to rewrite equations in different forms, go back and read through what you've done, prove what your intuition tells you—and you make mistakes, lots of them. But that's okay. When you notice a mistake you go back and fix it, and sometimes that leads you in new directions. Just keep at it."

"But how do you know what to try?" Tetra asked.

"You don't. Not always. And definitely not right away. But after you've been messing with stuff for a while you start to see relationships, hints of things to investigate. Equations pop up that seem to point in some direction, so you head that way, one step after another, and see where it leads."

"And that works?"

"Sometimes. Not with this problem, though. Not for me. I'd probably still be stuck if it wasn't for the nudge Yuri gave me. She noticed I had something similar to the Pythagorean theorem. That got me over the final hurdle and let me find the contradiction. And don't forget, you're the one who gave me the hint about the general form of Pythagorean triples."

"I guess I'm getting a little bit more comfortable with changing geometric shapes into equations, but that doesn't get you far if you don't know what to do with the equations afterwards."

"Good point. But you'll only get better with practice. You've got to push that pencil on your own. A *lot*."

Tetra nodded.

"I always thought the math you guys do is a lot different than what I do in class. Like, your math was somehow more *alive*, and schoolwork was just dead, dry, and boring. But I think I might have been wrong about that. It's not that what we're doing in school isn't important, it's just more about the basics. Like practicing serves in tennis, or swinging at balls in a batting cage."

Tetra swung at an imaginary pitch, and I couldn't help but smile.

8.5.2 An Elementary Proof

"Whatcha workin' on?" Miruka asked, appearing from nowhere. Her leg was finally bandage-free.

"Hey, Miruka!" Tetra said. "We were going over a proof that right triangles with integer side length can't have a square area. I think I'll start calling it the 'right triangles with integer-length sides can't have a square area theorem.'"

"Catchy title," I said.

I gave Miruka a rundown of my proof.

She waited for me to finish before making her one and only comment. "Proof by infinite descent."

"It has a name?" I said.

"Sure. It was Fermat's ace in the hole. First you create an equation that uses positive integers. Then you shuffle things around until you get a different equation in the same form, but involving smaller numbers. Keep repeating that and the numbers get smaller and smaller, but since there's a limit to how small a positive integer can get, you can't go on forever. If you can use that to find an inconsistency somewhere, *bang*, proof by contradiction. I guess you could also think of it as a special case of mathematical induction—"

Miruka's eyes winked shut. I felt something building within her, charging the air around us.

Silence.

Miruka reopened her eyes, and we remembered to breathe. She nodded to herself, sending a ripple through her long, black hair and a gleam off of her new glasses.

"I think your 'right triangles with integer side length can't have a square area theorem' might be useful for an elementary proof."

"An elementary proof of what?" I asked.

"Fermat's last theorem," she replied.

"*What?*"

"Well, for the biquadratic version, at least. FLT(4)."

I mentally fastened my seat belt. This was going to be a wild ride.

Miruka pulled out an index card and placed it on the table.

"My latest from Muraki," she said.

Problem 8-3

Show that the following equation has no positive integer solution:

$$x^4 + y^4 = z^4$$

"We'll use proof by contradiction," she began. "We want to prove that $x^4 + y^4 = z^4$ has no solution, so we'll show that the negation of the statement, that $x^4 + y^4 = z^4$ *does* have a solution, leads to a contradiction."

Miruka yanked my notebook out from under my elbow and took the pencil Tetra offered.

"Define the (x, y, z) solution as (a, b, c). You can say those are relatively prime if you want, but there's no need. Here's the equation, rewritten:"

$$a^4 + b^4 = c^4$$

"Next, use a, c to define m, n like this:"

$$\begin{cases} m &= c^2 \\ n &= a^2 \end{cases}$$

"Then turn around and use m, n to define A, B, C like this:"

$$\begin{cases} A &= m^2 - n^2 \\ B &= 2mn \\ C &= m^2 + n^2 \end{cases}$$

"Now use those definitions to write A, B, C in terms of a, b, c:"

$$A = m^2 - n^2 \qquad \text{from the definition of A}$$
$$= (c^2)^2 - (a^2)^2 \qquad \text{from the definition of } m, n$$
$$= c^4 - a^4 \qquad \text{simplify}$$
$$B = 2mn \qquad \text{from the definition of B}$$
$$= 2c^2 a^2 \qquad \text{from the definition of } m, n$$
$$C = m^2 + n^2 \qquad \text{from the definition of C}$$
$$= (c^2)^2 + (a^2)^2 \qquad \text{from the definition of } m, n$$
$$= c^4 + a^4 \qquad \text{simplify}$$

"Now we have $(A, B, C) = (c^4 - a^4, 2c^2 a^2, c^4 + a^4)$. We know a, b, c are positive integers with $c > a$, so A, B, C are positive integers too. Let's see what happens when we add A^2 and B^2:"

$$A^2 + B^2 = \left(c^4 - a^4\right)^2 + \left(2c^2 a^2\right)^2 \qquad \text{substitute}$$
$$= \left(c^8 - 2c^4 a^4 + a^8\right) + \left(2c^2 a^2\right)^2 \qquad \text{expand } \left(c^4 - a^4\right)^2$$
$$= \left(c^8 - 2c^4 a^4 + a^8\right) + 4c^4 a^4 \qquad \text{expand } \left(2c^2 a^2\right)^2$$
$$= c^8 + 2c^4 a^4 + a^8 \qquad \text{simplify}$$
$$= \left(c^4 + a^4\right)^2 \qquad \text{factor}$$
$$= C^2 \qquad \text{from } C = c^4 + a^4$$

"So we've learned that $A^2 + B^2 = C^2$, meaning A, B, C are positive integer lengths of a right triangle, with C the hypotenuse."

Miruka paused to make eye contact and gauge whether we were keeping up. We both nodded.

"Okay, let's talk areas:"

$$\text{area} = \frac{AB}{2} \qquad \text{area of a right triangle}$$
$$= \frac{(c^4 - a^4)(2c^2 a^2)}{2} \qquad \text{substitute } A = c^4 - a^4, B = 2c^2 a^2$$
$$= (c^4 - a^4)c^2 a^2 \qquad \text{cancel 2s}$$

"From $a^4 + b^4 = c^4$, we know $c^4 - a^4$ is equal to b^4. We'll use that to take this calculation further:"

$\text{area} = \dfrac{AB}{2}$	area of a right triangle
$= (c^4 - a^4)c^2a^2$	what we got before
$= b^4c^2a^2$	replace $c^4 - a^4$ with b^4
$= a^2b^4c^2$	shuffle things around
$= (ab^2c)^2$	rewrite as a square

"Looky, looky. A square area. It's even prettier if we define D as ab^2c:"

$$\frac{AB}{2} = D^2$$

"Now we've proved this proposition:"

> There exists a right triangle with integer-length sides and a square area.

"But your 'right triangles with integer-length sides can't have a square area theorem' has already established something else:"

> There exists no right triangle with integer-length sides and square area.

"That's a contradiction, so the assumed negation must be false, yadda yadda, and I hereby claim the statement that $x^4 + y^4 = z^4$ has no positive integer solution...proven!"

Miruka tossed the pencil onto the table and smiled.

"That was fun."

Answer 8-3 (FLT(4))

Use proof by contradiction:

1. Suppose $x^4 + y^4 = z^4$ does have a positive integer solution.

2. Let that solution be $(x, y, z) = (a, b, c)$.

3. Define $m = c^2, n = a^2$.

4. Define $A = m^2 - n^2, B = 2mn, C = m^2 + n^2$.

5. Define $D = ab^2c$.

6. Then $A^2 + B^2 = C^2$ and $\frac{AB}{2} = D^2$.

7. This contradicts Answer 8-1.

8. By proof by contradiction, $x^4 + y^4 = z^4$ has no positive integer solution.

8.5.3   Final Pieces

"Wow," I said. "It's so short."

"Only because of your proof," Miruka replied. "I just dropped the final piece into place."

"That's pretty neat," said Tetra. "I never thought of pitting one hunk of our own math against another. But I guess proof by contradiction lets you do that, huh."

Tetra pulled the notebook over and started going through Miruka's proof line by line.

"You got the problem from Mr. Muraki?"

"Yeah, just now when I dropped by the teacher's lounge."

I was truly impressed by the subtlety with which he'd tied the cards together this time. On the surface, Tetra's card didn't look like anything more than an amusing problem about the area of triangles. Never in a million years would I have thought it might be the key to solving a special case of Fermat's last theorem, or that FLT(4) was a bridge from equations to geometric shapes. Another illustration that mathematical equations aren't like individual stars; they're tied to each other, forming beautiful constellations.

"Oh, almost forgot," Miruka said. "Muraki was asking if we're going to the winter open seminar."

Tetra looked up from the notebook.

"What's an open seminar?"

"Sometimes the math department at the university has seminars open to the general public," I said. "It's a lecture, basically. Mr. Muraki's always telling us we should go. Miruka and Kaito and I went last year. It's going to be in December again?"

Miruka nodded.

"I want to go!" Tetra shouted, raising both hands.

Her hands dropped almost as quickly as they had shot up. "Um...you don't have to, like, take a test to get in or anything, do you?"

"No, no, nothing like that," I said, laughing. "Don't worry, all are welcome."

I turned to Miruka.

"Did he say what it's about this year?"

Miruka's mouth curved in a mischievous grin.

"Fermat's last theorem."

CHAPTER 9

Euler's Identity

$e^{i\pi} = -1$ is the most famous equation in mathematics. It is the link that binds e and π with the complex numbers, a truly amazing feat. Some have called it "a gem," but its value is far greater than that of any mere diamond or ruby.

TAKESHI YOSHIDA
The Moods of Complex Numbers

9.1 THE MOST BEAUTIFUL EQUATION

9.1.1 Components of the Identity

A bitter winter wind blew outside the window, making the warmth of my room all the more comforting. Yuri was there, her nose buried in a book. I sat hunched over my notebook, absorbed in math.

Yuri rose from the floor, jolting me back to reality. "Here's one for you," she said, removing her glasses and grinning. "What's the most beautiful equation in mathematics?"

I answered without hesitation. "Euler's identity, $e^{i\pi} = -1$."

"Already knew that one, huh."

"Anybody into math knows it."

"Okay, then, Mr. Smartypants. Tell me what it means."

"Whaddaya mean, 'what it means'?"

"Like how the Pythagorean theorem is about the sides of a triangle. What does Euler's identity mean?"

"Hmmm... Kinda hard to sum up in a few words."

"Use a bunch, then. Start with the e. What's that?"

"The base of the natural logarithms."

"You're gonna need more words."

"Just think of it as a famous number. It's about 2.71828, but irrational and infinitely long."

"I guess I'll get there when I get there. I think I know the i in $e^{i\pi}$. It's the i that equals -1 when you square it, right?"

"Right. The imaginary unit."

"And π is just plain old pi? The one from geometry that's 3.14?"

"The one that's *approximately* 3.14. It's another infinitely long irrational number."

"Yeah, yeah. So I sorta know all the parts, but what does it mean to say e to the $i\pi$?"

"That's where it gets tricky."

"Does it even make sense?" Yuri asked, crossing her arms. "I mean, 2^3 I can understand—multiply three 2s together. But how can you multiply something by itself $i\pi$ times? If there's something beautiful about this, I'm missing it."

I was ecstatic to see Yuri so upset about this.

"You're smarter than you look," I said, reaching out to rub her head. She knocked my hand aside.

"You have *got* to learn that a girls' hair is *not* to be messed with."

"Look, I know when you see an exponent like 2^3 you want to think of it as meaning 'multiply three 2s,' but to really understand Euler's identity you have to go beyond that. Actually, Euler's identity is just a special case of Euler's formula, so that's probably the best place to start."

"And once I hear about that, raising e to the $i\pi$ will suddenly make sense?"

"I think so. If we skip over some of the technical stuff, you should at least get the gist."

"All right, let's see what happens."

I knelt in front of the low table in the middle of my room and opened my notebook. Yuri sat on the floor next to me.

Just as I was about to begin, my mother knocked on my door. She grinned as she poked her head in.

"Sorry to interrupt, but a friend of yours is here...I think," she said.

"You *think*?"

"She hasn't rung the bell; she's just been pacing in front of the house."

I peeked through my blinds to see who could be crazy enough to linger outside in this cold, even though I had a pretty good idea.

Tetra.

9.1.2   Euler's Formula

Tetra, Yuri, and I sat around the small table in my room. My mother brought up green tea and cakes.

"You must be frozen through," she said. "Have some hot tea to take the chill off."

"Th-th-thank you," Tetra said. I wasn't sure if the stutter was the cold or nerves. "Sorry to barge in on you. I just happened to be p-p-passing by, and..."

"Not a problem," I said. "Yuri and I were just about to do some math. The more the merrier."

I realized Yuri and Tetra hadn't seen each other since the incident at the hospital. I was worried what might happen, but after an awkward moment, they bowed to each other. A little stiff for a greeting, but not antagonistic.

Then again, in karate they bow before the punches start flying...

"What were you working on?" Tetra asked.

"I was explaining Euler's formula. It looks like this:"

Euler's formula (Exponential and trigonometric functions)

$$e^{i\theta} = \cos\theta + i\sin\theta$$

"Let's forget about the imaginary unit i for now," I said, "and just look at the formula."

I underlined the left and right sides.

"This part on the left is an exponential function, so it's kind of strange that the right side uses trig functions."

"Why's that?" Yuri asked.

"Because exponential functions usually get really big, really fast, like this:"

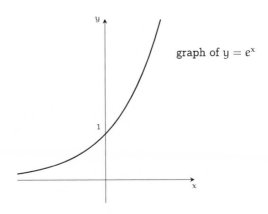

graph of $y = e^x$

"Trig functions, on the other hand, usually look like waves:"

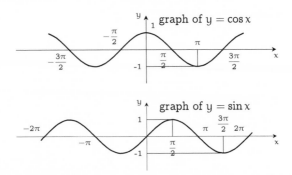

graph of $y = \cos x$

graph of $y = \sin x$

"But this equation says they're the same?" Yuri asked.

"Well, that they're related at least. But before we dive deeper into that, let me show you how Euler's *identity* is something that pops out of Euler's *formula*:"

$$e^{i\theta} = \cos\theta + i\sin\theta$$

"That's Euler's formula. Let's plug π in as the value of θ: "

$$e^{i\pi} = \cos \pi + i \sin \pi$$

"You can read the value for $\cos \pi$ off that graph of $\cos x$ I just drew. $y = -1$ when $x = \pi$, so $\cos \pi = -1$, right?"

Yuri nodded.

"That means we can rewrite the equation like this: "

$$e^{i\pi} = -1 + i \sin \pi$$

"Same thing for the value of $\sin \pi$. Look at the $\sin x$ graph; when $x = \pi$, $y = 0$, so $\sin \pi = 0$: "

$$e^{i\pi} = -1 + i \times 0$$

"The only thing left is to multiply i by 0, and voilà: "

$$e^{i\pi} = -1$$

"So this 'most beautiful equation' we're talking about is the special case of Euler's formula where $\theta = \pi$."

"Okay, hold up," Yuri said. "I get how Euler's identity pops out of Euler's equation, but I still don't know what exponential functions and trigonometric functions and all that are. I'm in eighth grade, remember?"

"Yeah, I guess that's still a few years off."

"Take that $\sin x$ thing," Yuri said. "It doesn't mean you're multiplying sin and x, it looks like."

"No, $\sin x$ isn't multiplication, it's a function. It's probably easier to understand if you write it $\sin(x)$. When you have a value for x, you can plug it into sin and get some other number back. That's what a function does. For example, the value of $\sin 0$ is 0. That means when $x = 0$, plugging it into sin gets you a 0 back. See how that works on the graph? How it passes through the point $(0, 0)$ where $x = 0$?"

"Sure."

"You can do the same thing with other values of x. So $\sin x = 1$ when $x = \frac{\pi}{2}$, and $\sin x = 0$ again when $x = \pi$. You can just read all that off the graph."

"I've seen this graph before, I think. This is called a sine curve, right?"

"Right. When you plot out all of the points where $y = \sin x$, you get a sine curve."

"Got it."

"Okay, then what's the value of $\cos \pi$?"

"Dunno."

"C'mon, Yuri. Just look at the other graph."

"Oh, right. This one. Uh, when x is π, the curve goes down here. I guess that's -1? Yeah, okay, so $\cos \pi = -1$."

"Good job. Not so hard, right?"

"But what's all this got to do with $e^{i\pi}$?"

"Don't worry, we're getting there."

During my back-and-forth with Yuri, Tetra had been quietly sipping her tea and watching us, smiling. I took it as a sign that her nervousness was dissipating. Either that or she was starting to thaw out.

9.1.3 Exponent Rules

"Before we get back to Euler's formula," I said, "we want to be sure we have all the basics covered. Stop me if there's anything you aren't getting, Yuri. You, too, Tetra."

Both nodded.

"Okay, let's talk about exponents then. When you first learned about exponents, your teacher probably told you to think of the small, raised number as the number of times to multiply the bigger number by itself. Like, if you see 2^3, you're supposed to think of three 2s being multiplied together:"

$$2^3 = \underbrace{2 \times 2 \times 2}_{\text{multiply 2 by itself 3 times}}$$

"That's wrong?" Yuri asked.

"No, it's not wrong at all. As long as you have a positive integer exponent, at least. Well, I guess things get a little weird if the exponent is 1, since there isn't really any multiplication going on:"

$$2^1 = \underbrace{2}_{\text{multiply 2 by itself 1 time?}}$$

"A little weird, yeah," Yuri said.

"And what about when the exponent is 0?" I asked. "What do you think you get then?"

"A 0, of course," Yuri said.

"No, 0 exponents give you a 1," said Tetra.

"Tetra wins this one," I said. "2^0 is 1:"

$$2^0 = 1$$

"No way!" Yuri protested. "If you're multiplying zero things together, how can that not give you 0?"

"Do you know the answer, Tetra?"

"Uh, I don't think so, no..."

"Try looking at it this way," I said. "Check out what happens when you start with 2^4, then let the exponent get smaller:"

$$2^4 = 2 \times 2 \times 2 \times 2 = 16$$
$$2^3 = 2 \times 2 \times 2 = 8$$
$$2^2 = 2 \times 2 = 4$$
$$2^1 = 2 = 2$$
$$2^0 = ?$$

"See what's happening to the answers?" I asked.

"They get halved each time," Yuri said.

"Right. To put it in mathematical terms, each time you reduce the exponent n in 2^n by 1, the value of 2^n becomes half of its previous value. So if you reduce the exponent of 2^1 by one, and you want to keep up the pattern, what does the value of 2^0 have to be?"

"It'd be half of 2," Yuri said, "which is...oh, 1. Huh."

"That's right. That's why we define 2^0 as 1."

"Something still doesn't feel right, though."

"I'm with Yuri," Tetra said. "I still can't get over multiplying zero things and getting 1. It feels...*forced.*"

"That's because you're sticking to this idea of exponents being about multiplication. As long as you do that, you're limiting yourself to positive integers. You even have to 'force' the idea of 1 exponents being about multiplication. And things just get worse when you go beyond that, to exponents like 0 or -1."

"I know what 0 means, though," Yuri said. "It means 'nothing.' "

"So what does it mean to multiply zero somethings?"

"Uh, well—"

"And how about multiplying -1 somethings?"

"I'd say -1 means borrowing something, I guess..."

I nodded.

"Yeah, that'd work in some cases. But you'd still be limiting yourself. You still aren't able to deal with things like 0.5, much less what it means to multiply $i\pi$ somethings together."

"Which is what got us into this mess in the first place."

"Exactly. So you can think of exponents as being something about multiplication, but only when you're dealing with positive integers. When other kinds of numbers pop up, you need to use equations to define what you mean."

"Equations?" Tetra asked.

"Right. We want to define what it means to say 2^x. To do it, we define exponents as things that follow these rules, the exponent rules: "

Exponent rules

$$\begin{cases} 2^1 & = 2 \\ 2^s \times 2^t & = 2^{s+t} \\ \left(2^s\right)^t & = 2^{st} \end{cases}$$

"We could do this for any positive integer, but things are clearer if we stick to a specific number, so we'll just use 2 for now."

"Before that," Tetra said, raising her hand, "what do you call the number the exponent sits on? The 2 in 2^3."

"The 'base,' " I said.

"Who cares what it's called?" Yuri said.

"Well, I do," Tetra replied. "It's an important part of the number, so I want to know how to say it. Doesn't it bother you when you don't know what to call something?"

"Nope, can't say it does."

I'd always thought of Tetra as being a bit flighty, but paired up with someone younger, the contrast made her seem downright adult.

"On with the show," Yuri said. "Get to it. Show me how to define exponents!"

"Okay, let's look at the value of 2^0. The exponent has to follow this rule:"

$$2^s \times 2^t = 2^{s+t}$$

"So when we replace the s with a 1 and the t with a 0, we get this:"

$$2^1 \times 2^0 = 2^{1+0}$$

"Makes sense. What's next?"

"When we add the 1 and the 0 in the exponent on the right we get 1, so now the equation looks like this:"

$$2^1 \times 2^0 = 2^1$$

"We know what 2^1 equals, from the exponent rules. It's just 2, so we get this equation:"

$$2 \times 2^0 = 2$$

"Divide both sides by 2, and there's your definition of 2^0:"

$$2^0 = 1$$

"Okay, let me make sure I have this straight," Yuri said. "So there's no more multiplying anywhere, everything is just based on the exponent rules?"

"Exactly."

"I get it now," Tetra said. "Using the exponent rules as your starting point lets you work things out so you can decide what 2^0 should be, based on what 2^1 is."

"That's right," I said. "There's no more multiplying things by themselves going on anywhere. It all falls out of the rules."

"Wait a minute," Tetra said. "We've done something like this before, haven't we? When you taught me how $2^{\frac{1}{2}}$ and $\sqrt{2}$ are equal. We're just making sure everything stays consistent."

Tetra seemed convinced, but the look on Yuri's face made it plain that she wasn't quite there yet.

"I get what Tetra's saying," Yuri said, "but how do you know something else doesn't break? I mean, we only did this using $s = 1$ and $t = 0$. Is it really okay to define stuff like this using some random numbers you pulled out of thin air? If s and t are different, couldn't, uh... Wow, I'm not sure how to explain what I'm trying to say."

I held up a hand to stop her.

"Don't worry, I know exactly what you're trying to say, and it's an excellent point. You're asking if the exponent rules themselves make sense. You're saying it's fine to define exponents so that they obey the exponent rules, but we need to make sure the exponent rules will work with all exponents, right? In mathematics, that's called being 'well-defined.'

"When you define something new in mathematics, it's really important to show your definition is well-defined. If you could make up new concepts and rules on a whim, then everything would just fall apart. Formally proving that the exponent rules are well-defined would be a bit much for today, though, so for now just trust me—they are."

This conversation brought to mind something Miruka had once said: *Consistency implies existence.*

I'd just said the exponent rules "make sense," but I realized it was really consistency I was talking about. If the same rules could give you either 1 or 0 when talking about 2^0 in different situations, then that inconsistency, that contradiction, would imply the non-existence of the concept of 0 exponents.

"Is the term 'well-defined' well-defined?" Tetra asked.

"Huh?" The question took me by surprise.

"I was just wondering if the concept of being 'well-defined' was itself truly well-defined."

"Tetra, I'm not getting into a deep discussion of semantics with you. You're too far out of my league."

9.1.4 Negative and Rational Exponents

"Now that we have 0, can we keep going and define negative exponents the same way?" Yuri asked.

"Let's give it a shot and see," I said, picking up the pencil. "For example, if we let $s = 1$ and $t = -1$, then—"

"Bup bup bup," she said. "I'm doing this one. Let's see, something like this?"

$$2^s \times 2^t = 2^{s+t} \qquad \text{exponent rule}$$
$$2^1 \times 2^{-1} = 2^{1+(-1)} \qquad \text{let } s = 1, t = -1$$
$$2^1 \times 2^{-1} = 2^0 \qquad 1 + (-1) = 0$$
$$2 \times 2^{-1} = 1 \qquad \text{from } 2^1 = 2, 2^0 = 1$$
$$2^{-1} = \frac{1}{2} \qquad \text{divide both sides by 2}$$

"Oh, cool. So $2^{-1} = \frac{1}{2}$?"

"It does indeed," I said.

"And that solves 2^n for any integer n, right?" Tetra asked.

"How's that?" asked Yuri.

"Because the exponent rules also say that if you multiply a 2^1 then you're adding 1 to the exponent, and if you multiply a 2^{-1} you're subtracting an exponent."

"Oh, right. So you just have to repeat enough times to get to whatever your n is."

"That's right," I said, "but you can go beyond the integers and expand this to rationals. Here's how you do it for $2^{\frac{1}{2}}$:"

$$(2^s)^t = 2^{st} \qquad \text{exponent rule}$$
$$\left(2^{\frac{1}{2}}\right)^2 = 2^{\frac{1}{2} \cdot 2} \qquad \text{let } s = \frac{1}{2}, t = 2$$
$$\left(2^{\frac{1}{2}}\right)^2 = 2^1 \qquad \frac{1}{2} \cdot 2 = 1$$
$$\left(2^{\frac{1}{2}}\right)^2 = 2 \qquad \text{because } 2^1 = 2$$
$$2^{\frac{1}{2}} = \sqrt{2} \qquad \text{take the root of both sides}$$

"Yeah! That's how we did this before!" Tetra said. "So a $\frac{1}{2}$ power is a square root!"

"Isn't there something funny about that last line?" Yuri said.

"Yeah, it's a little bit of a shortcut," I said.

"What is? Where?" Tetra asked.

"When you take the root," Yuri said.

"She's right," I said. "To be precise, I have to state somewhere that $2^{\frac{1}{2}} > 0$, because there are two values that give you 2 when you square them, $+\sqrt{2}$ and $-\sqrt{2}$."

Tetra put her hands to her temples. "And another condition flies right by me..."

9.1.5 The Exponential Function

"We better get moving if we're going to reveal the mysteries of Euler's identity," I said, "but we still need to define the exponential function, using the derivative of e^x."

"What's a derivative?" Yuri asked.

"Good question, but hold off for now. You don't really need to know what a derivative is for what I'm going to do, just the form is important here. We're going to define the exponential function as the function that doesn't change when you take its derivative—whatever that means:"

Derivative of e^x

$$\begin{cases} e^0 & = 1 \\ (e^x)' & = e^x \quad \text{unchanged by derivation} \end{cases}$$

"Also, to nail down the form of the exponential function, let's say that it can be written as a power series like this:"

$$e^x = a_0 + a_1 x + a_2 x^2 + a_3 x^3 + \cdots$$

"There you go again," Yuri said. "What's a power series?"

"Doesn't matter. Just look at the form of the equation. There's a first-degree x term, and a second-degree one, and a third-degree one, and so on. Oh, and a constant at the beginning, which you can think of as a zero-degree x term. A power series is just an infinitely long sum of all that stuff."

"And you can write e^x like that?" Yuri asked, obviously suspicious.

"That's a better question than you might think, but once again the answer is yes. You're just going to have to trust me on this one, too."

"Okay, but you're running out of 'just trust me' cards here pretty fast."

"Duly noted. To get back to your other question, about what a derivative is, just think of it as a way of changing one function into another one. The 'prime' mark shows we've done that."

"This little apostrophe here, right?" Yuri said, pointing to the $(e^x)'$ I'd written.

"Right. You'll learn plenty about derivatives someday, but for now just keep two rules in mind: One is that when you take the derivative of a constant, it becomes 0. The other is that when you take the derivative of something in the form x^k, you get kx^{k-1}. Here's a summary of those rules as math statements:"

$$\begin{cases} (a)' & = 0 \\ \left(x^k\right)' & = kx^{k-1} \end{cases}$$

"Okay, let's apply these rules to the power series for the exponential function we were just talking about. Technically we should also demonstrate the linearity of the differential operator and its applicability to the power series, I guess, but—"

Yuri leaned over and whispered to Tetra. "You following this?"

"Yeah, been here before."

"Urgh."

"—anyway, here's what we get:"

$$e^x = a_0 + a_1 x + a_2 x^2 + a_3 x^3 + \cdots \qquad \text{function as power series}$$

$$(e^x)' = \left(a_0 + a_1 x + a_2 x^2 + a_3 x^3 + \cdots\right)' \qquad \text{derivative of both sides}$$

$$(e^x)' = 0 + 1a_1 + 2a_2 x + 3a_3 x^2 + \cdots \qquad \text{rewrite right side}$$

"We said the exponential function remains unchanged after differentiation, which means the equation $(e^x)' = e^x$ is true. Start by setting the power series equal to its derivative:"

$$(e^x)' = e^x$$
$$1a_1 + 2a_2 x + 3a_3 x^2 + \cdots = a_0 + a_1 x + a_2 x^2 + a_3 x^3 + \cdots$$

"When we compare the coefficients between the two, we get a bunch of relationships like this:"

$$\begin{cases} 1a_1 & = a_0 \\ 2a_2 & = a_1 \\ 3a_3 & = a_2 \\ & \vdots \\ ka_k & = a_{k-1} \\ & \vdots \end{cases}$$

"A tiny bit of manipulation turns those into this:"

$$\begin{cases} a_1 & = \frac{a_0}{1} \\ a_2 & = \frac{a_1}{2} \\ a_3 & = \frac{a_2}{3} \\ & \vdots \\ a_k & = \frac{a_{k-1}}{k} \\ & \vdots \end{cases}$$

"See how knowing what a_0 is tells us what a_1 is? And if we know what a_1 is, we can find a_2, and so on down the line, like falling dominos."

"So what *is* a_0?" Tetra asked.

"We can find out pretty easily with e^x written as a power series:"

$$e^x = a_0 + a_1 x + a_2 x^2 + a_3 x^3 + \cdots$$

"If we let $x = 0$, then $a_1 x$, $a_2 x^2$, and all the other terms with an x in it disappear. Combine that with $e^0 = 1$, which we got from the derivative, and we have this:"

$$e^0 = a_0 + a_1 \cdot 0 + a_2 \cdot 0^2 + a_3 \cdot 0^3 + \cdots$$
$$1 = a_0$$

"In other words, $a_0 = 1$. And now that we know what a_0 is, the rest falls into place:"

$$\begin{cases} a_1 & = \frac{a_0}{1} = \frac{1}{1} \\ a_2 & = \frac{a_1}{2} = \frac{1}{2 \cdot 1} \\ a_3 & = \frac{a_2}{3} = \frac{1}{3 \cdot 2 \cdot 1} \\ & \vdots \\ a_k & = \frac{a_{k-1}}{k} = \frac{1}{k \cdots 3 \cdot 2 \cdot 1} \\ & \vdots \end{cases}$$

$$e^x = 1 + \frac{x}{1} + \frac{x^2}{2 \cdot 1} + \frac{x^3}{3 \cdot 2 \cdot 1} + \cdots$$

"We can write $k \cdots 3 \cdot 2 \cdot 1$ as a factorial $k!$, giving us a power series, the Taylor series expansion of the exponential function e^x:"

$$e^x = +\frac{x^0}{0!} + \frac{x^1}{1!} + \frac{x^2}{2!} + \frac{x^3}{3!} + \cdots$$

"Aren't you dividing by 0 in the first one there?" Yuri asked.

"No, $0! = 1$, just like x^0, so you could write that first term as 1. I'm only writing it like this to make the pattern more obvious."

"$0! = 1$, huh? I'm going to pretend I already knew that, so you don't try to explain why."

Taylor expansion of the exponential function e^x

$$e^x = \frac{x^0}{0!} + \frac{x^1}{1!} + \frac{x^2}{2!} + \frac{x^3}{3!} + \cdots$$

9.1.6 Staying True to the Equations

"We're coming to the climax of our discussion of exponential functions," I said, "so hold on to your seats."

"I can barely contain myself," Yuri said. Snark or not, I could see she was enjoying this.

"So we've gone beyond thinking of exponents as being about multiplication, and now we're just making sure everything plays out according to the exponent rules. Being sure to maintain the consistency of the equations is what let us broaden our use of exponents."

Tetra and Yuri nodded.

"We want to do the same kinda thing one more time, letting equations define what the exponential function is. Specifically, we're going to let the Taylor expansion—the equation we just got—be its definition:"

$$e^x = +\frac{x^0}{0!} + \frac{x^1}{1!} + \frac{x^2}{2!} + \frac{x^3}{3!} + \cdots$$

Yuri raised a palm to stop me.

"You're confusing me. I thought we started with e^x, and got that Taylor thing from it. Now you're saying the Taylor thing is the *definition* of e^x? Aren't there some chicken and egg issues here?"

"Well, not really, since I want to hatch a new-and-improved chicken. When we started out, the x in e^x could only be a real number. What I want to do is level up so we can use complex numbers, too. The power series we got from the Taylor expansion is the perfect way to do it."

"Okay, fine. I'll assume you know what you're doing, then. Proceed."

"So you remember the left side of Euler's formula?"

$$e^{i\theta}$$

"To get there, we let $x = i\theta$ in the power series. Kind of an audacious substitution, in a way, but we'll trust the math to see us through:"

$$e^x = +\frac{x^0}{0!} + \frac{x^1}{1!} + \frac{x^2}{2!} + \frac{x^3}{3!} + \cdots$$
$$e^{i\theta} = +\frac{(i\theta)^0}{0!} + \frac{(i\theta)^1}{1!} + \frac{(i\theta)^2}{2!} + \frac{(i\theta)^3}{3!} + \cdots$$

"When we substitute $x = i\theta$ and use $i^2 = -1$, then we get this nice cycle $1 \to i \to -1 \to -i$, and..."

I let the sentence hang there, waiting for Tetra's response. I didn't have to wait long.

"Aaaah!" she screamed.

"What? What'd I miss?" Yuri asked.

"What are you kids doing up there?" my mother shouted from downstairs.

"Sorry," called Tetra. "Overreaction. Everything's under control."

9.1.7 A Bridge to Trig

"So what was that all about?" Yuri asked.

"The Taylor expansion of $\cos\theta$ and $\sin\theta$," Tetra said.

"More high school math?"

"No, not from school. We did this one together, on another problem."

"What does it have to do with this one?"

"Take a look: "

Taylor expansion of $\cos\theta$

$$\cos\theta = +\frac{\theta^0}{0!} - \frac{\theta^2}{2!} + \frac{\theta^4}{4!} - \frac{\theta^6}{6!} + \cdots$$

Taylor expansion of $\sin\theta$

$$\sin\theta = +\frac{\theta^1}{1!} - \frac{\theta^3}{3!} + \frac{\theta^5}{5!} - \frac{\theta^7}{7!} + \cdots$$

"And?" Yuri said.

"Isn't that kind of...interesting?"

"Uh...no? Should it be?"

"When you combine them, you get Euler's formula!"

"Combine them how?"

"Look, the $\cos\theta$ one has all the even numbers, and the $\sin\theta$ one has all the odd numbers. See?"

Yuri looked at the equations, but didn't seem to be picking up on Tetra's discovery.

"What she's trying to say is, when you combine the Taylor expansions of $\sin\theta$ and $\cos\theta$, you end up with Euler's formula."

"Combine them how?" Yuri said. "I think you need to write this out for me."

"No problem. Watch. First, start with the Taylor expansion of e^x:"

$$e^x = +\frac{x^0}{0!} + \frac{x^1}{1!} + \frac{x^2}{2!} + \frac{x^3}{3!} + \frac{x^4}{4!} + \frac{x^5}{5!} + \cdots$$

"Then, substitute $x = i\theta$..."

$$e^{i\theta} = +\frac{(i\theta)^0}{0!} + \frac{(i\theta)^1}{1!} + \frac{(i\theta)^2}{2!} + \frac{(i\theta)^3}{3!} + \frac{(i\theta)^4}{4!} + \frac{(i\theta)^5}{5!} + \cdots$$

"Expand the $(i\theta)^k$s into $i^k\theta^k$..."

$$e^{i\theta} = +\frac{i^0\theta^0}{0!} + \frac{i^1\theta^1}{1!} + \frac{i^2\theta^2}{2!} + \frac{i^3\theta^3}{3!} + \frac{i^4\theta^4}{4!} + \frac{i^5\theta^5}{5!} + \cdots$$

"Then when you use $i^2 = -1$, the i's on the terms with even powers go away. See what's happening to the signs?"

$$e^{i\theta} = +\frac{\theta^0}{0!} + \frac{i\theta^1}{1!} - \frac{\theta^2}{2!} - \frac{i\theta^3}{3!} + \frac{\theta^4}{4!} + \frac{i\theta^5}{5!} - \cdots$$

"So now let's separate out the even and odd powers of θ:"

$$\begin{cases} \text{even powers of } \theta \;\; = +\dfrac{\theta^0}{0!} - \dfrac{\theta^2}{2!} + \dfrac{\theta^4}{4!} - \cdots \\[2mm] \text{odd powers of } \theta \;\; = +\dfrac{i\theta^1}{1!} - \dfrac{i\theta^3}{3!} + \dfrac{i\theta^5}{5!} - \cdots \end{cases}$$

"See what's happening? What I just wrote is the power series of the exponential function e^x with $x = i\theta$, but with the even and odd powers split up. Compare that with Tetra's Taylor expansions of the sin and cos functions. All the even powers of θ are in the Taylor expansion of $\cos\theta$, and all the odd powers are in the expansion of $\sin\theta$, with an i on each. If you combine the two, you get Euler's formula:"

$$e^{i\theta} = +\frac{\theta^0}{0!} + \frac{i\theta^1}{1!} - \frac{\theta^2}{2!} - \frac{i\theta^3}{3!} + \frac{\theta^4}{4!} + \frac{i\theta^5}{5!} - \cdots$$

$$= \left(+\frac{\theta^0}{0!} - \frac{\theta^2}{2!} + \frac{\theta^4}{4!} - \cdots \right) \qquad \cos\theta \text{ in parentheses}$$

$$+ i\left(+\frac{\theta^1}{1!} - \frac{\theta^3}{3!} + \frac{\theta^5}{5!} - \cdots \right) \qquad \sin\theta \text{ in parentheses}$$

$$= \cos\theta + i\sin\theta$$

"I skipped over some of the details, but that's the heart of it. Make sense?"

"Mmm, maybe." Yuri thought for a moment. "All this stuff about exponential functions and trig functions and derivatives and everything is too much to take in at once, but I did get one thing—what $e^{i\pi}$ means. You're right, I'd only ever thought about exponents as a shortcut for writing multiplication, so raising something to the $i\pi$ power didn't make any sense. But now I know exponents aren't really about multiplication, they're their own thing, with their own rules."

"Pretty good for one day, I'd say."

"I'm getting a lot out of this too," Tetra said. "I always thought of definitions being about words, but this way of doing it with exponent rules and power series is pretty neat. The power series one, especially. I had no idea the exponential function and trig functions could be tied together so neatly like that. Another abstraction into similar forms?"

"I hadn't thought of that, but you're right, it is," I said.

"It's cool to think about i, too," I continued. "I love how you can start with this..."

$$i^0, i^1, i^2, i^3, i^4, i^5, i^6, i^7, \cdots$$

"...and rewrite it like this:"

$$1, i, -1, -i, 1, i, -1, -i, \cdots$$

"There's so much to read from the repetition. Continuous revolutions by $90°$, the solutions to x^4, the derivatives of trig functions... It's just all over the place."

I turned to a new page in the notebook.

"Let's look at this thing geometrically, on a unit circle in the complex plane:"

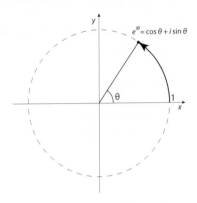

Euler's formula in the complex plane

"Points on this circle are all complex numbers $\cos\theta + i\sin\theta$, with θ as their argument. Euler's formula says $e^{i\theta} = \cos\theta + i\sin\theta$, so another way to look at it is points on the circle being associated with the complex number $e^{i\theta}$. So when Euler's identity says $e^{i\pi} = -1$, it means that in the complex plane a number with argument π takes you to -1 on the unit circle:"

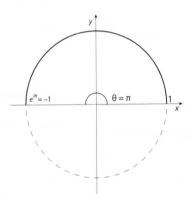

Euler's identity in the complex plane

"I think that answers your question about what Euler's identity means, Yuri."

"Oooh, so Euler's identity is another about-face!" Tetra said, spinning away from us. "Just one this time, though."

"Uh, sure," I said.

My mother appeared at the door.

"You kids ready to take a break and come down for a snack?"

"Sure, mom. We'll be right there."

"Okay, I'll go whip something up."

I returned to the unit circle.

"Of course, you can keep increasing θ to move the point associated with $e^{i\theta}$ around the circle. Every time you increase the angle θ by $360°$, or 2π radians, you end up back where you started. So there's a kind of periodicity here. Let's make sure we can see it when we stick to equations:"

$$
\begin{aligned}
e^{i(\theta+2\pi)} &= e^{i\theta+2\pi i} && \text{expand } i\,(\theta + 2\pi) \\
&= e^{i\theta} \cdot e^{2\pi i} && \text{exponent rules} \\
&= e^{i\theta} \cdot (\cos 2\pi + i \sin 2\pi) && \text{from Euler's formula} \\
&= e^{i\theta} \cdot (1 + i \times 0) && \text{from } \cos 2\pi = 1, \sin 2\pi = 0 \\
&= e^{i\theta} && \text{from } 1 + i \times 0 = 1
\end{aligned}
$$

"Back where we started from, right? An argument of $\theta + 2\pi$ and an argument of θ take you to the same place."

"Around and around and around," Tetra muttered. I could see her eyes tracing laps around the circle.

Yuri frowned and said, "Maybe I'm still missing something, but I think I like Euler's formula better than his identity."

She tapped it in the notebook:

$$
e^{i\theta} = \cos \theta + i \sin \theta
$$

"Why's that?" I asked.

"I dunno, it just seems like there's so much more to it. Lots of neat things tucked away in there; the identity is just one of them. That Euler guy must have been pretty smart."

"You're not the first person to say that."

"Pretty cool. Thanks for showing me all that."

"Yeah," Tetra added. "Thanks!"

My mother called up the stairs: "Snacks are ready, kids! Come and get it!"

A blink of an eye later, Yuri was halfway down the hall.

9.2   Party Preparations

9.2.1   Solve M for Mystery

The following week, I found Miruka, Tetra, and Ay-Ay hanging out in the music room after school.

"We're having a party at your place, to celebrate the end of finals," Ay-Ay announced.

"At *my* place?"

"Don't worry, Miruka and I'll do all the planning. Nothing fancy, just some snacks and drinks. It'll be fun."

"But why does it have to be at my place?" I asked.

"Because you have a piano. I hear your mom's nice, too. Think of it as a chance to show her you actually have friends. Cute ones at that. You can come, can't you, Tetra?"

"A piano? Why do you need—?"

"I don't do parties that don't have a piano. What else is there to do, if parents are going to be around?"

"It's settled then," Miruka concluded.

I sighed, giving in to the inevitability of the situation.

"Fine, fine. I'll make sure it's okay with my parents. So, just the four of us?"

"What about Yuri?" Tetra asked.

"Wouldn't she feel kinda weird at a party with a bunch of high schoolers?" I said.

"Then tell her to bring a date, doofus," said Ay-Ay.

"Since when does Yuri date?"

"Don't ask me. If you talked to her about anything besides math, maybe you'd know."

Tetra pulled out an elegant schedule book and her pencil case— the one with the 'M' on it.

"Sorry, don't think I can make it on Sunday."

"No prob, Saturday works," Miruka said.

"Tetra, that 'M'—," I began.

She followed my gaze to her pencil case. "Oh, this," she laughed. "You'll find out."

9.2.2 Mom

My mother's reaction was not what I had expected.

"A party? Sounds like fun! What should I make? Is this a formal thing? I bet you're going to say you want pizza. Like you don't eat enough junk food as it is—"

"Mom... Mom! You don't have to make anything, we just need a place to—"

"Oh, I know! I'll just get all the ingredients for sushi rolls, and everybody can roll their own! Or if everyone wants to chip in, we can order from that nice place down the street."

"Mom, are you listening? Everybody is bringing stuff to eat. You don't have to do anything."

"Your piano-playing friend is coming, right? I can't wait to hear her play! Oh, I should get the piano tuned... This is going to be so much fun!"

I left the room, shaking my head and hoping my mother realized the party was for us, not her.

CHAPTER 10

Fermat's Last Theorem

> If you want to capture the hearts of your students, let them refashion what they've learned into something their own. Give them the freedom to think for themselves, to craft new ideas. Don't make them study, allow them to do research.
>
> YUTAKA TANIYAMA
> *The Complete Writings of Yutaka Taniyama*

10.1 THE SEMINAR

"I have *no* idea what we just listened to," Yuri said.

"Don't worry," Tetra commiserated, "I'm right there with you."

"What'd you think, Miruka?" I asked.

"It was *wonderful*," she sighed.

We spilled out of the lecture hall and onto the university campus. The seminar on Fermat's last theorem that Mr. Muraki had urged us to attend was over. I had been surprised by the turnout—easily several hundred people. A professor from the school's math department delivered the lecture, though I doubt I could have picked him out in a crowd; he'd addressed most of the talk to his notes on the podium.

I had warned Yuri the talk would be over her head, but when she heard Miruka and Tetra were going, her heart was set. She insisted she wanted to hear the math, but I think she was more interested in a chance to hang out with Miruka. I'd hoped she'd be able to understand at least a few bits and pieces, but the lecture ended up being a wild ride through Wiles' proof that even left me in the dust. I couldn't help but wonder how many in the audience were able to keep up. Still, the event was a powerful reminder of my long-term goal—to someday walk the wild frontier of modern mathematical research.

We'd decided to grab lunch at the university cafeteria. There weren't many students around, it being a cold December Saturday, but we did see a couple of other groups that looked like they'd come from nearby high schools. I had visited the campus once before during a school festival; the place had been a chaotic mess then, a stark contrast from the calm today. Peering through windows at the labs and classrooms, lined wall-to-wall with overflowing bookshelves and computer workstations, I couldn't wait to become a college student myself.

* * *

"The only words I understood in that whole thing," Yuri said, twirling a forkload of spaghetti, "were Taniyama, Shimura, and Iwasawa. At least I got the Japanese names!"

"Yeah, I felt like I was drowning in a flood of vocabulary," Tetra said. She poked at her omelette. "By the time I got a handle on one word, two more would pop up. I should have read up on this stuff before coming."

"I was trying to keep up with the equations," I said between bites of rice pilaf, "but no way. They just flew by on the screen. You're right, Tetra—we should have studied before we came."

Miruka sank her fork into a piece of tiramisu.

"A pre-seminar crash course wouldn't cut it," she said. "The vocabulary and equations aren't the problem. What we need is a deeper understanding of the topic. Wiles' proof is too technical to follow as a lecture. But one thing was crystal clear: the two worlds that Wiles brought together."

10.2 SOME HISTORY

10.2.1 The Problem

"So can you help us get at least some idea of what that lecture was all about?" Yuri asked Miruka when we'd finished eating.

"Maybe," Miruka replied, "but a bit of history may be in order first."

I reached for my notebook, knowing it would soon be called on, and was surprised to see Yuri already holding hers out. Miruka took it, opened to a blank page, and wrote Fermat's last theorem at the top:

Fermat's last theorem

There exists no positive integer solution to the following equation for $n \geqslant 3$:
$$x^n + y^n = z^n$$

"The problem at hand. Fermat jotted down a version of this in the margin of a book he was reading, along with a famous note: 'I have discovered a truly marvelous proof of this, which this margin is too narrow to contain.' Nobody ever found his proof, but that note challenged generations of mathematicians to try."

"If it was just something he jotted down in a book, how did people find out about it?" Tetra asked.

"We have his son Samuel to thank. The book was *Arithmetica* by Diophantus, a mathematician from the third century. Bachet reprinted it in the seventeenth century, and that's the version Fermat owned and wrote his cryptic message in, next to a related problem. Samuel republished an edition of *Arithmetica* with all his father's margin notes included. If he hadn't, Fermat's last theorem may never have been found."

"Wow," I said. "From Diophantus in the third century to Fermat via Bachet in the seventeenth. Then from Samuel to us. Now *that's* math transcending time."

10.2.2   The Era of Elementary Number Theory

"The true battle," Miruka continued, "one that would last for more than three and a half centuries, began with the discovery of Fermat's note.

"The problem as posed was for all values of n. But proving that was turning out to be too much of a challenge, so various mathematicians tried to approach it piecemeal, proving it for specific values. Fermat himself was the first, giving a proof for FLT(4). We did that one ourselves not too long ago, using your 'right triangles with integer side length can't have a square area theorem.'"

"Oh, yeah! That was fun!" Tetra said.

"The next proof came in the eighteenth century, when Euler proved FLT(3). Then Dirichlet got FLT(5) in the nineteenth century, and Legendre improved it. Lamé bagged FLT(7), but after that...silence. The proofs had just gotten too hairy to handle with the tools of the day—multiples, factors, GCDs, prime numbers, co-primes, and proof by infinite descent."

"It's cool when you think about it," I said. "They started with specific examples and worked toward generalizations, just like we do."

10.2.3   The Era of Algebraic Number Theory

"A new era dawned in the nineteenth century, with Sophie Germain and the development of algebraic number theory. Sophie made some real progress toward proving the theorem around 1825, when she showed there were no positive integer solutions to $x^p + y^p = z^p$ where p and $2p + 1$ were both odd primes. There was one more condition, though, that $xyz \not\equiv 0 \pmod p$.

"In 1847, Lamé and Cauchy led the vanguard against Fermat's last theorem. Their attack used prime factorization into complex numbers to 'break up' $x^p + y^p = z^p$, like this:"

$$x^p + y^p = (x + \alpha^0 y)(x + \alpha^1 y)(x + \alpha^2 y) \cdots (x + \alpha^{p-1} y) = z^p$$

"The α here is a complex number equal to $e^{\frac{2\pi i}{p}}$. Since Euler's formula says $\alpha = \cos \frac{2\pi}{p} + i \sin \frac{2\pi}{p}$, the absolute value of α is 1, and the argument is $\frac{2\pi}{p}$. In other words, α is a pth root of 1. The ring

$\mathbb{Z}[\alpha]$ created from α is a type of algebraic ring of integers using the natural addition and multiplication operations:"

$$\mathbb{Z}[\alpha] = \{a_0\alpha^0 + a_1\alpha^1 + a_2\alpha^2 + \cdots + a_{p-1}\alpha^{p-1} \mid a_k \in \mathbb{Z}, \alpha = e^{\frac{2\pi i}{p}}\}$$

"Lamé and Cauchy attempted to perform a prime factorization of $x^p + y^p$ in the algebraic ring of integers $\mathbb{Z}[\alpha]$, and then coax each of the $(x + \alpha^k y)$ factors into being relatively prime, show each factor was a pth root, and finally use infinite descent to put a nail in Fermat's last theorem once and for all."

Miruka pushed her glasses back on her nose, and smiled.

"Didn't work, though. They'd overlooked the fact that the uniqueness of prime factorization doesn't necessarily hold in algebraic integer rings. So even if each pth root factor was relatively prime, not every factor would necessarily be a pth root. When Kummer pointed that out, it was back to the drawing board.

"Kummer himself took a different approach by creating something called ideal numbers, and Dedekind figured out how to gather them up into a kind of ring called an ideal. Ideals have their own set of axioms, and number-like calculations with them are defined. But most importantly, they guarantee unique prime factorizations.

"Ideals breathed new life into things, and Kummer managed to prove Fermat's last theorem for a kind of number called regular primes, but things died down for a while after that."

"Everybody just gave up?" asked Tetra.

"No," Miruka said, shaking her head. "Kummer's algebraic number theory gave birth to lots of cool math, and Wiles' proof even uses it as a fundamental tool, but it still wasn't enough to prove Fermat's last theorem. The next major advances didn't come until the twentieth century, here in Japan, with the birth of *geometric* number theory."

10.2.4   The Era of Arithmetic Geometry

Miruka fortified herself with another dose of tiramisu and continued her history lesson.

"Just ten years after the end of World War II, the 1955 International Symposium on Algebraic Number Theory was held in Tokyo, and that's where the Taniyama-Shimura conjecture was introduced to the world.

"Turning this 'conjecture' into a full-blown theorem would bridge two important worlds—elliptic curves and automorphic forms, if you're curious—so for a while, that became a hot topic in number theory. Wasn't long before everyone saw how hard it would be, though. Like, *really* hard. So it was more-or-less shelved. A real treasure, the key to solving Fermat's last theorem, lying there forgotten.

"Then, in 1985, Frey realized something wonderful: if Fermat's last theorem *wasn't* true, you could create a counterexample to the Taniyama-Shimura conjecture. Of course, that just meant cracking one impossibly hard nut would split open another, so it's not like mathematicians were rushing for their chalkboards—except for a professor named Wiles, that is.

"Wanna talk dedication? Wiles spent his next *seven years* working on the problem. He was still teaching classes, but all that time nobody knew he was working on a solution to one of the most famous problems in mathematics.

"He stunned the world when he announced a proof in 1993, but unfortunately somebody found an error. He went right back to work though, and in 1995 published a correction along with Taylor, one of his former students."

There was a gleam in Miruka's eye.

"Fermat's last theorem had finally been proven."

10.3   How It Was Done

10.3.1   Back in Time

"Enough history," Miruka said. "Let's do some math."

Yuri held her hands up in surrender.

"I think I'm gonna head home. I could barely even follow the history lesson."

Miruka fixed her gaze on Yuri. "We'll start with a problem for you."

Miruka began making a list in the notebook, talking as she wrote.

"We're going to step a few years back in time to 1986. *Top Gun* is rockin' the box office, *The Legend of Zelda* is wowing gamers, and nobody has a proof for Fermat's last theorem. Yuri, you're going to play the role of Wiles, and you're looking for something juicy to work on."

Miruka finished her list, and spun the notebook to face Yuri. "Here's the lay of the mathematical land:"

The state of mathematics in 1986

The Taniyama-Shimura conjecture

[UNPROVEN] All elliptic curves are modular.

$\mathbf{FLT(3), FLT(4), FLT(5), FLT(7)}$

[PROVEN] There exists no x, y, z such that $x^k + y^k = z^k$ for $k = 3, 4, 5, 7$.

Frey curves

[PROVEN] If there exists p, x, y, z (where x, y, z are positive integers, and $p \geqslant 3$ is a prime) such that $x^p + y^p = z^p$, then an associated Frey curve also exists.

The relation between Frey curves and elliptic curves

[PROVEN] Frey curves are a type of elliptic curve.

The relation between Frey curves and modular forms

[PROVEN] Frey curves are not modular.

"Okay, Yuri, you're up," Miruka said.

Yuri eyed the notebook doubtfully.

"You're allowed to use anything that's labeled 'proven.' I know you can solve this problem, even if you don't understand all the words in the list:"

Problem 10-1 (A problem from 1986)

As of 1986, what do you have to do to prove Fermat's last theorem?

10.3.2   Getting to the Problem

Yuri's usual bravado vanished beneath the glare of Miruka's spotlight. For a moment I thought she might crumble under the pressure, but she pulled herself together and turned to face Miruka's problem head-on. Her lips worked as she examined the list, jotting down notes as she did.

I knew the answer, but only because of all the hints Miruka had dropped. Still, this meta-level approach to mathematics came as a surprise.

Perhaps I've said this before, but I *love* equations. I love their specificity, their consistency. I love how decoding them lets me see the structure of things, and I love the discoveries I make when I rewrite them in new forms. When I can write something as an equation, I know I understand it. When I can't, I know I don't.

But this stuff...

The proof of Fermat's last theorem we'd seen at the seminar was *way* beyond me. And though I would never have admitted it, the equations the lecturer had shown us filled me with dread. It was as though I was seeing advanced mathematics for the first time.

But I didn't have trouble following Miruka's overview of the state of things in 1986. There were no equations to decipher, only a clear path of logic to trace. It was wonderful, like gazing at a constellation and grasping its pattern, even if the stars themselves were out of reach.

In school I was often given problems that said "prove this," but never a problem that said "what do you need to prove?" Of course, knowing how to prove things is important, but no more than knowing *what* to prove. That's how you find the paths leading out of the forest.

"Got it," Yuri said. "You have to prove the Taniyama-Shimura conjecture, that all elliptic curves are modular. If you can do that, you've proven Fermat's last theorem."

"How?" Miruka asked.

"It would let you use proof by contradiction."

Yuri pointed to a line she'd written in the notebook:

Fermat's last theorem does not hold.

"That's the opposite—no, the *negation*—of what you want to prove."

Yuri continued, "If that's the case, then there's numbers n, x, y, z where $x^n + y^n = z^n$. Then— Oops, no, this doesn't work; p has to be prime... Oh, wait, that's okay, FLT(4) is already proven, so you can assume n isn't 4. Okay, so anyway, you can write n as $n = mp$. That's multiplying a positive integer with a prime factor $p \geqslant 3$. Then if there's an n, x, y, z that works for $x^n + y^n = z^n$, you can use the exponent rules like this:"

$$(x^m)^p + (y^m)^p = (z^m)^p$$

"Rename x^m, y^m, z^m as x, y, z, and there's a p, x, y, z that works with $x^p + y^p = z^p$."

Yuri glanced at me for moral support. I nodded encouragement.

"Go on," Miruka said.

The confidence in Yuri's voice grew as she spoke.

"Well, according to this list of what we know in 1986, if there's p, x, y, z that make $x^p + y^p = z^p$ true, then there's also a Frey curve for it, a kind of elliptic curve that isn't modular. So now you can say this:"

There exists an elliptic curve that is not modular.

"At least, that's what the logic says. I have no idea what a 'Frey curve' or an 'elliptic curve' is, or what 'modular' means."

Yuri bit her lip as she ran her finger down the list.

"It looks like all this is okay using only the stuff that's been proven. But proving the Taniyama-Shimura conjecture would change everything. If you did, then you could say this:"

All elliptic curves are modular.

"That contradicts what you got when you assumed Fermat's last theorem doesn't hold, so your assumption must be wrong. Then proof by contradiction says Fermat's last theorem must be true."

Yuri looked up at Miruka, her face filled with expectation and trepidation.

"So, that's my answer. If you prove the Taniyama-Shimura conjecture, you've proven Fermat's last theorem."

Miruka smiled and winked.

"Perfect."

Answer 10-1 (A problem from 1986)

Proving the Taniyama-Shimura conjecture simultaneously proves Fermat's last theorem.

Miruka continued, her voice soft.

"Frey came up with Frey curves, and Serre formulated a conjecture as to how the existence of Frey curves would be a counterexample to Fermat's last theorem. Ribet proved Serre's conjecture was true. You can imagine how excited Wiles must have been when he heard—Fermat's last theorem, a jigsaw puzzle mathematicians had been trying to put together for over 350 years, had just one piece missing.

"Proving the Taniyama-Shimura conjecture would slide it into place."

10.3.3 Semistable Elliptic Curves

"So Wiles proved the Taniyama-Shimura conjecture, and that was it!" Tetra gushed.

"Not quite," Miruka said.

"But, I thought—"

"Like Yuri said, proving the Taniyama-Shimura conjecture would also prove Fermat's last theorem. That much is true. But that's not quite what Wiles did."

"What happened?" Tetra asked.

"He proved that all *semistable* elliptic curves are modular." Miruka stood and walked around the table as she spoke. "It was just too hard to prove the Taniyama-Shimura conjecture without the 'semistable' condition on it."

Miruka stopped behind Tetra and placed a hand on her shoulder.

"But why do you think that didn't matter, Tetra?"

"Huh? I...I don't know."

"What about you, Yuri?" Miruka asked.

Yuri knitted her eyebrows. She thought for a moment, then realization lit her eyes.

"Because Frey curves are semistable too!"

"Exactly."

Miruka pushed her glasses back on her nose.

"Wiles wanted to find some way to show Frey curves couldn't exist. One of the properties Frey curves would have, if they did exist, would be that they're semistable. So proving the Taniyama-Shimura conjecture for semistable elliptic curves would be enough, and that's exactly what he did. That meant all semistable elliptic curves were modular, so Frey curves disappeared in a puff of logic, and Fermat's last theorem became a true theorem at last."

Overview of the proof of Fermat's last theorem

1. Assume that Fermat's last theorem does not hold.

2. From the assumption, a Frey curve can be created.

3. A Frey curve is a semistable elliptic curve that is not modular.

4. Therefore, a semistable elliptic curve that is not modular exists.

5. Wiles' theorem: All semistable elliptic curves are modular.

6. Therefore, no semistable elliptic curve that is not modular exists.

7. 4 and 6 contradict.

8. Using proof by contradiction, Fermat's last theorem holds.

10.3.4 Whetting Our Appetite

Miruka scanned our faces before continuing.

"That's the highlights at least, the logical flow of the thing. But it should leave you hungry for more. I hope you're asking yourself, what's this Taniyama-Shimura conjecture all about? What's an elliptic curve, and a Frey curve? What's it mean to be 'modular'? Even if we can't understand the details of Wiles' proof, can we get a little closer in? Get a taste of what the actual *math* is like?"

I felt myself nod involuntarily.

Miruka grinned and said, "Well let's dive in." Then she added, "But somewhere else. We've drawn a crowd."

I looked up and realized the tables around ours were full of other students. They'd been hanging on Miruka's every word...just like us.

10.4   The World of Elliptic Curves

10.4.1   Elliptic Curves 101

We moved to the café upstairs and sat down at a large table. Yuri had a hot chocolate, the rest of us coffee.

"Still want to head home early?" Miruka asked Yuri.

"Maybe I'll stick around a little more," she replied.

"Good for you." Miruka opened my notebook. "We'll start with the definition of an elliptic curve:"

$$y^2 = x^3 + ax^2 + bx + c$$

"An elliptic curve is a curve that can be represented with an equation like this, where a, b, c are rational numbers. Oh, and one more condition: when $x^3 + ax^2 + bx + c = 0$, there can't be any repeated roots."

Miruka cocked her head and looked at what she'd written.

"Technically, this is the definition of an elliptic curve over the rational number field $\mathbb{Q}$. In other words, x and y are elements of $\mathbb{Q}$. Here's an example of an elliptic curve:"

$$y^2 = x^3 - x$$

"All I did to get this was start with $y^2 = x^3 + ax^2 + bx + c$, and let $(a, b, c) = (0, -1, 0)$. We can factor the $x^3 - x$ on the right like this:"

$$x^3 - x = (x - 0)(x - 1)(x + 1)$$

"The solutions to $x^3 - x = 0$ are $x = 0, 1$, and -1. No repeated roots, so this satisfies the conditions for an elliptic curve. Here's a graph of it:"

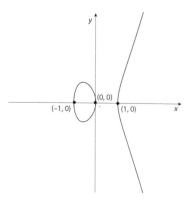

Graph of the elliptic curve $y^2 = x^3 - x$

Tetra raised a hand. "That round thing on the left looks kinda stretched. Is that supposed to be an ellipse?"

"No," Miruka said. "Don't let the word 'elliptic' fool you. It's there for historical reasons, but elliptic curves don't really have anything to do with ellipses."

10.4.2 Rational Number Fields to Finite Fields

"Let's take an algebraic look at $y^2 = x^3 - x$." Miruka held up a hand to stop herself.

"Actually, before that, let's talk about some of the major areas of mathematics. First there's *algebra*, which is about things like groups, rings, and fields. Also, equations and their solutions. Next there's *geometry*, which covers points, lines, surfaces, solids, intersections, tangents, all that. Then there's *analysis*, which is about limits, differentials, derivatives, integrals...all that calculusey stuff.

"Of course, they're all connected. Like, 'repeated roots' is an algebraic concept, but 'tangent curves' is a similar geometric thing, and setting a derivative to 0 is a parallel from analysis."

"Do we need to know all those areas to understand this Taniyama-Shimura conjecture?" Yuri asked.

"Thankfully no," Miruka replied. "The recipe just calls for a heap of modular arithmetic, a dash of perseverance, and a pinch of imagination.

"To start, there's only one rational number field $\mathbb{Q}$, but that field contains infinitely many elements, since there are infinitely many rational numbers. Let's turn that on its head—we want to say there's an infinite number of fields, but each of them have only a finite number of elements."

"How would you construct something like that?" I asked.

"Forget already?" Miruka grinned. "We've done this before."

"Must have slipped my mind..."

"The finite field $\mathbb{F}_p$. It has p elements, a finite number, but since there are infinitely many primes, there are also infinitely many $\mathbb{F}_p$s."

"Oh, of course. Never thought of it that way, but yeah, that works."

"And it's a good place to do what I want to do, so let's jump from the world of the rational number field $\mathbb{Q}$ to the world of finite fields $\mathbb{F}_p$, and look for (x, y) solution points to the equation for our elliptic curve:"

$$y^2 = x^3 - x \qquad (x, y \in \mathbb{F}_p)$$

"We started out playing with the elliptic curve $y^2 = x^3 - x$, and got three rational points $(0,0)$, $(1,0)$, and $(-1,0)$ by factoring out the $x^3 - x$ and setting it to 0. So if you want to look at this equation another way, you can think of it as being a congruence equation, like this:"

$$y^2 \equiv x^3 - x \pmod{p}$$

"Hold up," Tetra said. "Can you give me a quick refresher on finite fields? It's been a while."

"Sure," Miruka said. "The finite field $\mathbb{F}_p$ was a set with p elements, and we could perform addition, subtraction, multiplication, and division on it using mod p:"

$$\mathbb{F}_p = \{0, 1, 2, \ldots, p-1\}$$

"We made p a prime to be sure we could do division by any

nonzero element. There's an infinite number of them, like this:"

$$\mathbb{F}_2 = \{0, 1\}$$
$$\mathbb{F}_3 = \{0, 1, 2\}$$
$$\mathbb{F}_5 = \{0, 1, 2, 3, 4\}$$
$$\mathbb{F}_7 = \{0, 1, 2, 3, 4, 5, 6\}$$
$$\mathbb{F}_{11} = \{0, 1, 2, 3, 4, 5, 6, 7, 8, 9, 10\}$$
$$\vdots$$

"Why's it so important that they have a finite number of elements?" Tetra asked.

"So we can comb through them," Miruka said. "If there's only p elements to check, we can plug every one into x and y and see what happens. If p isn't too big, we can even do it by hand, looking at every possible point (x, y) for solutions to the elliptic equation."

"I guess that's where the dash of perseverance comes in," Yuri said.

10.4.3 The Finite Field $\mathbb{F}_2$

"The simplest finite field is $\mathbb{F}_2 = \{0, 1\}$. Since it's a field, addition and multiplication are defined for it. Just perform those operations as usual, then divide the result by 2 and take the remainder as your answer. Here's an operation table:"

+	0	1		×	0	1
0	0	1		0	0	0
1	1	0		1	0	1

"So there are four possible (x, y) combinations that might work:"

$$(x, y) = (0, 0), (0, 1), (1, 0), (1, 1)$$

"What we have to do is plug each of those into the equation $y^2 = x^3 - x$ and see if the equation holds. But don't forget—we've gotta use the operation tables to do the arithmetic. You can subtract using the inverse element of the addition operator, but that's kind of a pain, so let's move the x in the equation to the other side of the equals sign to make things easier:"

$$y^2 + x = x^3 \qquad \text{move the x to get rid of subtraction}$$

"Can we do an example?" Tetra asked.

"Don't worry, we'll do plenty. Take $(x, y) = (0, 0)$ to start with. Plug that into $y^2 + x = x^3$ and you get $0^2 + 0 = 0^3$. When we use the operation table to work those values out, we end up with 0 on the left and 0 on the right, so the equation is a true one, meaning $y^2 = x^3 - x$ holds for the point $(0, 0)$ in $\mathbb{F}_2$. One down, three to go."

Miruka worked out the remaining calculations and added them to the table:

(x, y)	$y^2 + x = x^3$	holds?
$(0, 0)$	$0^2 + 0 = 0^3$	holds
$(1, 0)$	$0^2 + 1 = 1^3$	holds
$(0, 1)$	$1^2 + 0 = 0^3$	doesn't hold
$(1, 1)$	$1^2 + 1 = 1^3$	doesn't hold

"So now we know the equation $y^2 = x^3 - x$ has two solutions in $\mathbb{F}_2$:"

$$(x, y) = (0, 0), (1, 0)$$

"Hang on, Miruka," Yuri said. "That condition about no multiple roots... Does that not stick around after we make the jump?"

"Oh, nice catch!" I said.

"Yuri, I love you," said Miruka.

"Wait, what am I missing?" Tetra said.

Miruka gestured at Yuri. "You have the floor."

"Um, sure. Well, before we made the jump into $\mathbb{F}_p$ we said $x^3 + ax^2 + bx + c = 0$ can't have multiple roots. So I was just wondering if we didn't have to check that again after we entered the world of finite fields."

"And we do," said Miruka. "There's a chance it's not an elliptic curve after the move."

"What about this case?" I asked.

"It fails the check. $y^2 = x^3 - x$ is *not* an elliptic curve in $\mathbb{F}_2$. Look what happens when we factor out $x^3 - x$:"

$$x^3 - x = (x - 0)(x - 1)^2 \qquad \text{factorization in } \mathbb{F}_2$$

"The $(x - 1)^2$ means multiple roots."

"Wait, is that the right factorization?" Tetra asked.

"It is. Look at how we factored it out in the finite number field:"

$$x^3 - x = (x - 0)(x - 1)(x + 1) \qquad \text{factorization in } \mathbb{Q}$$

"In $\mathbb{F}_2$, 1 is its own inverse for the addition operation, so 'adding 1' and 'subtracting 1' gives you the same value. In other words, $x + 1$ and $x - 1$ are essentially the same thing."

$$
\begin{aligned}
x^3 - x &= (x - 0)(x - 1)(x + 1) &&\text{factor} \\
&= (x - 0)(x - 1)(x - 1) &&\text{replace } x + 1 \text{ with } x - 1 \text{ (in } \mathbb{F}_2) \\
&= (x - 0)(x - 1)^2 &&\text{gather the } (x - 1) \text{ factors}
\end{aligned}
$$

"Great," said Tetra. "Something else to keep track of—what field we're performing the operations in!"

10.4.4 The Finite Field $\mathbb{F}_3$

"Let's take things up a notch to $\mathbb{F}_3 = \{0, 1, 2\}$," Miruka said. "Here's the operation table:"

+	0	1	2		×	0	1	2
0	0	1	2		0	0	0	0
1	1	2	0		1	0	1	2
2	2	0	1		2	0	2	1

"There are nine possible (x, y) combinations. Let's see if they make the equation true:"

(x, y)	$y^2 + x = x^3$	holds?
$(0, 0)$	$0^2 + 0 = 0^3$	holds
$(1, 0)$	$0^2 + 1 = 1^3$	holds
$(2, 0)$	$0^2 + 2 = 2^3$	holds
$(0, 1)$	$1^2 + 0 = 0^3$	doesn't hold
$(1, 1)$	$1^2 + 1 = 1^3$	doesn't hold
$(2, 1)$	$1^2 + 2 = 2^3$	doesn't hold
$(0, 2)$	$2^2 + 0 = 0^3$	doesn't hold
$(1, 2)$	$2^2 + 1 = 1^3$	doesn't hold
$(2, 2)$	$2^2 + 2 = 2^3$	doesn't hold

"So we have three solutions to the equation $y^2 = x^3 - x$ in $\mathbb{F}_3$. Namely, these:"

$$(x, y) = (0, 0), (1, 0), (2, 0)$$

"Is the equation still an elliptic curve in $\mathbb{F}_3$?" Yuri asked.

"It is. In fact, the only time it won't stay an elliptic curve is when we drop it into $\mathbb{F}_2$, but I'm going to skip proving that if you don't mind."

Yuri wiped imaginary sweat from her brow.

"Is it really called 'dropping' the equation into a finite field?" Tetra asked.

"The technical term is 'reduction,'" Miruka said. "When you move an elliptic curve from the rational number field to a finite field, you say you've reduced it. If you reduce an elliptic curve into $\mathbb{F}_p$ and no multiple roots pop up, you call that a 'good reduction at p.'"

"And if you *do* get multiple roots, it's a bad reduction at p?" Tetra asked.

"Right. So the elliptic curve $y^2 = x^3 - x$ has a bad reduction at 2, since we got multiple roots in $\mathbb{F}_2$."

"Bad reductions sounds like a failed chemistry experiment." Tetra said.

"Or a decent band name," I suggested.

"There are different kinds of bad reduction," Miruka said, ignoring our banter. "If you reduce to p and only get a double root, you say the curve has a multiplicative reduction at p. If you get a triple root, you say it has an additive reduction at p—"

"Please, no more..." Yuri groaned.

"—and if you only get good reductions or multiplicative reductions no matter what prime you reduce to, you say the elliptic curve is semistable."

"Whoa!" I said, sitting up straight. "Semistable, as in...?"

"As in Wiles' theorem," Miruka said. " 'All semistable elliptic curves are modular.' So a semistable elliptic curve is one that will have at most a double root when you reduce it modulo any prime number."

10.4.5 The Finite Field $\mathbb{F}_5$

"$\mathbb{F}_5$ is up to bat," Miruka said. "Here's the operation table: "

+	0	1	2	3	4
0	0	1	2	3	4
1	1	2	3	4	0
2	2	3	4	0	1
3	3	4	0	1	2
4	4	0	1	2	3

×	0	1	2	3	4
0	0	0	0	0	0
1	0	1	2	3	4
2	0	2	4	1	3
3	0	3	1	4	2
4	0	4	3	2	1

"There are 25 (x, y) pairs to get through this time. Let's get cranking:"

(x, y)	$y^2 + x = x^3$	holds?
$(0, 0)$	$0^2 + 0 = 0^3$	holds
$(1, 0)$	$0^2 + 1 = 1^3$	holds
$(2, 0)$	$0^2 + 2 = 2^3$	doesn't hold
$(3, 0)$	$0^2 + 3 = 3^3$	doesn't hold
$(4, 0)$	$0^2 + 4 = 4^3$	holds
$(0, 1)$	$1^2 + 0 = 0^3$	doesn't hold
$(1, 1)$	$1^2 + 1 = 1^3$	doesn't hold
$(2, 1)$	$1^2 + 2 = 2^3$	holds
$(3, 1)$	$1^2 + 3 = 3^3$	doesn't hold
$(4, 1)$	$1^2 + 4 = 4^3$	doesn't hold
$(0, 2)$	$2^2 + 0 = 0^3$	doesn't hold
$(1, 2)$	$2^2 + 1 = 1^3$	doesn't hold
$(2, 2)$	$2^2 + 2 = 2^3$	doesn't hold
$(3, 2)$	$2^2 + 3 = 3^3$	holds
$(4, 2)$	$2^2 + 4 = 4^3$	doesn't hold
$(0, 3)$	$3^2 + 0 = 0^3$	doesn't hold
$(1, 3)$	$3^2 + 1 = 1^3$	doesn't hold
$(2, 3)$	$3^2 + 2 = 2^3$	doesn't hold
$(3, 3)$	$3^2 + 3 = 3^3$	holds
$(4, 3)$	$3^2 + 4 = 4^3$	doesn't hold
$(0, 4)$	$4^2 + 0 = 0^3$	doesn't hold
$(1, 4)$	$4^2 + 1 = 1^3$	doesn't hold
$(2, 4)$	$4^2 + 2 = 2^3$	holds
$(3, 4)$	$4^2 + 3 = 3^3$	doesn't hold
$(4, 4)$	$4^2 + 4 = 4^3$	doesn't hold

"So here are the seven solutions to $y^2 = x^3 - x$ in $\mathbb{F}_5$:"

$$(x, y) = (0, 0), (1, 0), (4, 0), (2, 1), (3, 2), (3, 3), (2, 4)$$

10.4.6 How Many Points?

"New function," Miruka announced. "Let $s(p)$ be the number of solutions to $y^2 = x^3 - x$ over the finite field $\mathbb{F}_p$:"

$$s(p) = \text{the number of solutions to } y^2 = x^3 - x \text{ over } \mathbb{F}_p$$

"We've already found $s(2)$, $s(3)$, and $s(5)$:"

$\mathbb{F}_p$	$\mathbb{F}_2$	$\mathbb{F}_3$	$\mathbb{F}_5$	$\mathbb{F}_7$	$\mathbb{F}_{11}$	$\mathbb{F}_{13}$	$\mathbb{F}_{17}$	$\mathbb{F}_{19}$	$\mathbb{F}_{23}$	$\cdots$
$s(p)$	2	3	7							

"Maybe something interesting will show up if we fill in the rest of the table. But I don't want to steal all the fun, so I'll let you guys do some too. Yuri, you take $\mathbb{F}_7$ and $\mathbb{F}_{11}$. Tetra, you get $\mathbb{F}_{13}$ and $\mathbb{F}_{17}$." Miruka pointed at me. "You get $\mathbb{F}_{19}$ and $\mathbb{F}_{23}$."

"What are you going to do?" Yuri asked.

"Take a nap," she replied. "Wake me when you're done." Miruka leaned back and closed her eyes.

The rest of us shrugged and set to work.

We crunched numbers in silence. Bigger values of p meant a lot more work, but at least the calculations weren't difficult. I stole glances at Miruka as I wrote. Soon her chin was resting on her chest; she was sound asleep.

Tetra poked me with her pencil.

"Eyes down, hands busy," she said with mock seriousness.

Once we had finished, we swapped papers and checked each other's work. I'd made one mistake, Tetra three, and Yuri none at all.

"Wow, Yuri, you're amazing," Tetra said.

"Busy work is my specialty."

"Shall we awaken the queen from her slumber, then?" I said.

10.4.7 Prisms

Miruka raised her head. "We're done," I told her.

Miruka stretched as she looked over the table we'd created.

$\mathbb{F}_p$	$\mathbb{F}_2$	$\mathbb{F}_3$	$\mathbb{F}_5$	$\mathbb{F}_7$	$\mathbb{F}_{11}$	$\mathbb{F}_{13}$	$\mathbb{F}_{17}$	$\mathbb{F}_{19}$	$\mathbb{F}_{23}$	$\cdots$
$s(p)$	2	3	7	7	11	7	15	19	23	$\cdots$

"Good job."

"Awful lot of prime number action going on here," Yuri noted.

"So what does $s(p)$ mean?" Tetra asked.

"Think of the numbers you got from $s(p)$ as facets of the elliptic curve $y^2 = x^3 - x$," Miruka said. "Each of the infinitely many finite fields presents a new angle to look at it from."

"Like a prism!" Tetra said. "When you shine sunlight through a prism, it gets split up into an infinite number of colors. But when you recombine the colors, you get back the original beam of light. This is just like that. The rational number field $\mathbb{Q}$ is the sunlight, and each p is a new color!"

"Not a bad analogy," Miruka said. "Now we're going to leave elliptic curves for a bit and go on a brief tour of the world of automorphic forms."

Miruka cocked her head.

"But to do that, there's something I need..."

"Graph paper?" I asked.

"Magic markers?" Tetra offered.

"Chocolate pudding," Miruka said.

Yuri jumped up.

"I'm on it!"

Miruka handed her some money, and Yuri darted toward the dessert counter, ponytail bouncing.

10.5 Automorphic Forms

10.5.1 Staying True to Form

Pudding in hand, Miruka was ready to move on. "Let me introduce you to a very curious function named 'phi.'"

$$\Phi(z) = e^{2\pi i z} \prod_{k=1}^{\infty} \left(1 - e^{8k\pi i z}\right)^2 \left(1 - e^{16k\pi i z}\right)^2$$

"The z parameter is going to be a complex number, and— Yuri, what's wrong?"

"I have *no* idea what that means," Yuri said, the corners of her mouth turned down.

"I'm sure your cousin would be happy to explain." Miruka turned her attention back to her pudding.

"Uh, yeah, sure..." I hesitated for a moment, gathering my thoughts.

"Well, first off, when you see a complex equation like this, don't just throw your hands up and decide you can't understand it."

"I didn't!" Yuri protested. She tapped the Π symbol on the page. "I just don't know what this means."

"Oh, the capitol pi. It's like a shorthand for repeated multiplication. See the $k = 1$ at the bottom, and the infinity sign up top? That means you're going to start with $k = 1$, then increment it up through $2, 3, 4, \cdots$. While you do that, you plug each value of k into the stuff on the right here, and that becomes another factor to multiply. Make sense?"

"Not in the slightest. Put it on paper," Yuri said.

"Okay, here's what the equation would look like without the Π symbol. It's an infinite product, like this:"

$$\Phi(z) = e^{2\pi i z} \prod_{k=1}^{\infty} \left(1 - e^{8k\pi i z}\right)^2 \left(1 - e^{16k\pi i z}\right)^2$$

$$= e^{2\pi i z} \times \left(1 - e^{8 \times 1\pi i z}\right)^2 \times \left(1 - e^{16 \times 1\pi i z}\right)^2$$

$$\times \left(1 - e^{8 \times 2\pi i z}\right)^2 \times \left(1 - e^{16 \times 2\pi i z}\right)^2$$

$$\times \left(1 - e^{8 \times 3\pi i z}\right)^2 \times \left(1 - e^{16 \times 3\pi i z}\right)^2$$

$$\times \cdots$$

"Okay, I think I get it. But wow, what a mess."

"That's why you use the Π, to clean things up."

"This $\Phi(z)$ function is a kind of automorphic form," Miruka continued. "Specifically, it's a kind of automorphic form called a modular form.

"A few conditions: Let a, b, c, d be integers where $ad - bc = 1$, and c is a multiple of 32. Also, z is a complex number, so $z = u + vi$

with $v > 0$. If you put all those conditions together, and pop $\frac{az+b}{cz+d}$ into the Φ function, here's what you get:"

$$\Phi\left(\frac{az+b}{cz+d}\right) = (cz+d)^2\,\Phi(z)$$

"When you look at them through the lens of Φ, both z and $\frac{az+b}{cz+d}$ appear to be the same; the original form is retained, even after the transformation $z \to \frac{az+b}{cz+d}$. Well, I guess it's off by $(cz+d)^2$, but close enough."

Miruka shrugged.

"Oh, and the exponent 2 there on $(cz+d)^2$ is called the 'weight,' so you'd say $\Phi(z)$ is an automorphic form of weight 2. Everybody with me so far?"

Tetra held her head in her hands. "I am *so* lost," she said.

"Hmmm... Okay, let's try a simple example. Remember our conditions: a, b, c, d are integers, $ad - bc = 1$, and c is a multiple of 32. Now let's look at $\left(\begin{smallmatrix} a & b \\ c & d \end{smallmatrix}\right) = \left(\begin{smallmatrix} 1 & 1 \\ 0 & 1 \end{smallmatrix}\right)$:"

$$\Phi\left(\frac{az+b}{cz+d}\right) = (cz+d)^2\,\Phi(z) \qquad \text{equation for } \Phi(z)$$

$$\Phi\left(\frac{1z+1}{0z+1}\right) = (0z+1)^2\,\Phi(z) \qquad \text{substitute } \begin{pmatrix} a & b \\ c & d \end{pmatrix} = \begin{pmatrix} 1 & 1 \\ 0 & 1 \end{pmatrix}$$

$$\Phi(z+1) = \Phi(z) \qquad\qquad \text{simplify}$$

"See? When you pass them through Φ, you can think of $z+1$ and z as being the same. It becomes a function with periodicity 1 in the direction of the real axis."

"I don't think I got all that, but it sounds cool," Tetra said.

"My brain hurts," Yuri groaned.

"Alright, alright. Let's make $\Phi(z)$ a little prettier, then." Miruka smiled and placed a hand on Yuri's head.

10.5.2   q-*Expansions*

Miruka pointed to the top of the page we were working on.

"Look carefully at the definition of $\Phi(z)$:"

$$\Phi(z) = e^{2\pi i z} \prod_{k=1}^{\infty} \left(1 - e^{8k\pi i z}\right)^2 \left(1 - e^{16k\pi i z}\right)^2$$

"Lots of $e^{2\pi i z}$s scattered all over the place. Infinitely many, in fact. Let's define q like this:"

$$q = e^{2\pi i z} \qquad \text{definition of q}$$

"Now I want to rewrite $\Phi(z)$ in terms of q... No, on second thought, I want Tetra to do it."

Miruka slid the notebook towards Tetra and held out a pencil. Tetra didn't seem thrilled to be chosen, but she took the pencil anyway.

"Oh, I have an idea," she mumbled and began writing. "Something like this?"

$$\Phi(z) = q \prod_{k=1}^{\infty} \left(1 - q^{4k}\right)^2 \left(1 - q^{8k}\right)^2$$

"Turns out it isn't so hard after all. I just had to apply the exponent rules like this."

She pointed at a block of equations she'd written off to the side:

$$\begin{cases} e^{2\pi i z} &= q \\ e^{8k\pi i z} &= \left(e^{2\pi i z}\right)^{4k} = q^{4k} \\ e^{16k\pi i z} &= \left(e^{2\pi i z}\right)^{8k} = q^{8k} \end{cases}$$

"Well done," Miruka said. "Using a $q = e^{2\pi i z}$ like this to clean things up is called a 'q-expansion.'"

10.5.3 From F(q) to a(k)

"Let's talk some more about this q," Miruka said. "To help us forget about $\Phi(z)$ and focus on q, we're going to rename the q-expanded version $F(q)$:"

$$\begin{aligned} F(q) &= q \prod_{k=1}^{\infty} \left(1 - q^{4k}\right)^2 \left(1 - q^{8k}\right)^2 \\ &= q \left(1 - q^4\right)^2 \left(1 - q^8\right)^2 \\ &\quad \left(1 - q^8\right)^2 \left(1 - q^{16}\right)^2 \\ &\quad \left(1 - q^{12}\right)^2 \left(1 - q^{24}\right)^2 \\ &\quad \cdots \end{aligned}$$

"Right now $F(q)$ is a product, but I want to rewrite it as a sum. Remember what that's called, Yuri?"

"Hmmm, 'expanding,' maybe?"

"Right. And it just so happens there's someone in our midst who loves nothing more than expanding equations..."

"Expand this?" I protested. "$F(q)$ is an infinite product."

"Just worry about q^1 through q^{29} for now. No need to create a function out of it either; a formal power series will do."

I wasn't any happier to have been picked than Tetra had been. No slick shortcuts came to mind, so I decided to brute force it.

Miruka had said I didn't need to worry about the q^{30} terms and beyond, so I decided to summarize all that mess as Q_{30}.

Here goes nothing...

$$F(q) = q \prod_{k=1}^{\infty} \left(1 - q^{4k}\right)^2 \left(1 - q^{8k}\right)^2$$

Start by pulling the factors where $k = 1$ out in front of the $\prod$...

$$= q \left(1 - q^4\right)^2 \left(1 - q^8\right)^2 \prod_{k=2}^{\infty} \left(1 - q^{4k}\right)^2 \left(1 - q^{8k}\right)^2$$

Expand the squares...

$$= q \left(1 - 2q^4 + q^8\right) \left(1 - 2q^8 + q^{16}\right) \prod_{k=2}^{\infty} \left(1 - q^{4k}\right)^2 \left(1 - q^{8k}\right)^2$$

Let's stick that q inside the first set of parentheses...

$$= \left(q - 2q^5 + q^9\right) \left(1 - 2q^8 + q^{16}\right) \prod_{k=2}^{\infty} \left(1 - q^{4k}\right)^2 \left(1 - q^{8k}\right)^2$$

Multiply those first two factors...

$$= \left(q - 2q^5 - q^9 + 4q^{13} - q^{17} - 2q^{21} + q^{25}\right)$$
$$\times \prod_{k=2}^{\infty} \left(1 - q^{4k}\right)^2 \left(1 - q^{8k}\right)^2$$

I checked over my work, but it was just a stalling tactic to put off what I knew would come next—doing the same thing over and over until I stopped changing the terms of degree less than 30.

This isn't going to expand itself...

$$F(q) = \left(q - 2q^5 - q^9 + 4q^{13} - q^{17} - 2q^{21} + q^{25}\right)$$

$$\times \left(1 - q^8\right)^2 \left(1 - q^{16}\right)^2 \prod_{k=3}^{\infty} \left(1 - q^{4k}\right)^2 \left(1 - q^{8k}\right)^2$$

$$= \left(q - 2q^5 - 3q^9 + 8q^{13} - 8q^{21} + 8q^{25} - 8q^{29} + Q_{30}\right)$$

$$\times \prod_{k=3}^{\infty} \left(1 - q^{4k}\right)^2 \left(1 - q^{8k}\right)^2$$

$$= \left(q - 2q^5 - 3q^9 + 6q^{13} + 4q^{17} - 2q^{21} - 9q^{25} - 6q^{29} + Q_{30}\right)$$

$$\times \prod_{k=4}^{\infty} \left(1 - q^{4k}\right)^2 \left(1 - q^{8k}\right)^2$$

$$= \left(q - 2q^5 - 3q^9 + 6q^{13} + 2q^{17} + 2q^{21} - 3q^{25} - 18q^{29} + Q_{30}\right)$$

$$\times \prod_{k=5}^{\infty} \left(1 - q^{4k}\right)^2 \left(1 - q^{8k}\right)^2$$

$$= \left(q - 2q^5 - 3q^9 + 6q^{13} + 2q^{17} + q^{25} - 12q^{29} + Q_{30}\right)$$

$$\times \prod_{k=6}^{\infty} \left(1 - q^{4k}\right)^2 \left(1 - q^{8k}\right)^2$$

$$= \left(q - 2q^5 - 3q^9 + 6q^{13} + 2q^{17} - q^{25} - 8q^{29} + Q_{30}\right)$$

$$\times \prod_{k=7}^{\infty} \left(1 - q^{4k}\right)^2 \left(1 - q^{8k}\right)^2$$

$$= \left(q - 2q^5 - 3q^9 + 6q^{13} + 2q^{17} - q^{25} - 8q^{29} + Q_{30}\right)$$

$$\times \left(1 - q^{28}\right)^2 \left(1 - q^{56}\right)^2 \prod_{k=8}^{\infty} \left(1 - q^{4k}\right)^2 \left(1 - q^{8k}\right)^2$$

$$= \left(q - 2q^5 - 3q^9 + 6q^{13} + 2q^{17} - q^{25} - 10q^{29} + Q_{30}\right)$$

$$\times \prod_{k=8}^{\infty} \left(1 - q^{4k}\right)^2 \left(1 - q^{8k}\right)^2$$

$\prod_{k=8}^{\infty} \left(1 - q^{4k}\right)^2 \left(1 - q^{8k}\right)^2$ would only spit out 30th or higher degree terms, so I didn't need to expand anything beyond $k = 7$.

"Okay, I think I've got it:"

$$F(q) = q - 2q^5 - 3q^9 + 6q^{13} + 2q^{17} - q^{25} - 10q^{29} + \cdots$$

"Excellent," Miruka said, nodding. "Let's use $a(k)$ to represent the coefficient for q^k . Then we can take $F(q)$ as the generating function for the sequence $a(k)$. Here's a summary of what we get:"

k	1	5	9	13	17	25	29	$\cdots$
$a(k)$	1	-2	-3	6	2	-1	-10	$\cdots$

"Think of the sequence $a(k)$ as a DNA sample of $F(q)$—it contains everything we need to clone a new copy."

10.6   THE MODULARITY THEOREM

10.6.1   Two Worlds

"We've talked about two very different worlds today," Miruka said. She held up a finger. "First, the world of elliptic curves, where we used $y^2 = x^3 - x$ to create the sequence $s(p)$." Miruka held up a finger on her other hand. "Then we talked about the world of automorphic forms, where we used $\Phi(z)$ to create $F(q)$, and from that, the sequence $a(k)$. The Taniyama-Shimura conjecture—which is now called the 'modularity theorem,' since it's been proven and isn't just a conjecture any more—says there's a correspondence between these two very different worlds." Miruka touched the tips of her fingers together.

An elliptic curve   An automorphic form

$$y^2 = x^3 - x \quad \rightarrow \quad s(p) \quad (?) \quad a(k) \quad \leftarrow \quad q\prod_{k=1}^{\infty}\left(1 - q^{4k}\right)^2\left(1 - q^{8k}\right)^2$$

"Here's a summary of the functions we got today:"

$\mathbb{F}_p$	$\mathbb{F}_2$	$\mathbb{F}_3$	$\mathbb{F}_5$	$\mathbb{F}_7$	$\mathbb{F}_{11}$	$\mathbb{F}_{13}$	$\mathbb{F}_{17}$	$\mathbb{F}_{19}$	$\mathbb{F}_{23}$	$\cdots$
$s(p)$	2	3	7	7	11	7	15	19	23	$\cdots$

k	1	5	9	13	17	25	29	⋯
a(k)	1	−2	−3	6	2	−1	−10	⋯

"If you pay attention to the primes, I think you'll see the connection:"

Problem 10-2 (Bridging elliptic curves and automorphic forms)

Find the relation between sequences $s(p)$ and $a(p)$.

p	2	3	5	7	11	13	17	19	23	⋯
s(p)	2	3	7	7	11	7	15	19	23	⋯
a(p)	0	0	−2	0	0	6	2	0	0	⋯

"Oh! Oh! I see it!" Tetra said.

Yuri laughed. "Heck, even *I* see it."

I sat there in silence.

Mind...blown.

Just as I thought I was recovering, a realization ricocheted in my skull: I'd spent the afternoon playing with elliptic curves and automorphic forms, finite fields and q-expansions. I had touched these exotic mathematical objects *with my own hands.*

A wave of dizziness passed over me, and I placed my hands on the table to steady myself.

"Well, Yuri, what are you waiting for?" Miruka said. "Spit it out!"

"Uh, okay. The relationship is $s(p) + a(p) = p$. But, I don't know... It seems too simple."

Answer 10-2 (Bridging elliptic curves and automorphic forms)

$$s(p) + a(p) = p$$

Blueprint for the bridge between elliptic curves and automorphic forms

Elliptic curves	Automorphic forms

$$y^2 = x^3 - x \text{ over } \mathbb{Q}$$

$$q \prod_{k=1}^{\infty} \left(1 - q^{4k}\right)^2 \left(1 - q^{8k}\right)^2$$

$$\downarrow \qquad\qquad\qquad\qquad\qquad \downarrow$$

$$y^2 = x^3 - x \text{ over } \mathbb{F}_p$$

$$\sum_{k=1}^{\infty} a(k)q^k$$

$$\downarrow \qquad\qquad\qquad\qquad\qquad \downarrow$$

$$s(p) \qquad \to s(p) + a(p) = p \leftarrow \qquad a(p)$$

(# solutions over $\mathbb{F}_p$)   (coefficients of q^p)

"Isn't it glorious?" Miruka said. "Elliptic curves and automorphic forms come from very different places, but they're deeply related. We only looked at their connection with one example, but the modularity theorem tells us the relation is there for *every* semistable elliptic curve. The bridge between them has a name, by the way: '*zeta*.'"

"What's that?" I asked.

"A topic for another day. There's still something important we haven't covered yet."

10.6.2 Frey Curves and Semistability

Miruka moved straight into the next topic.

"A mathematician named Gerhard Frey noticed something interesting: If you assume Fermat's last theorem doesn't hold, then you can construct a certain type of elliptic curve. Since they're his invention, they're called Frey curves.

"Getting rid of Fermat's last theorem means you can find a prime $p \geqslant 3$ that works with relatively prime positive integers a, b, c like this:"

$$a^p + b^p = c^p$$

"Then you construct a Frey curve using the a and b:"

$$y^2 = x(x + a^p)(x - b^p) \qquad \text{a Frey curve}$$

"Let's show that a Frey curve is semistable. I'm going to start writing the primes we're using in reductions as ℓ, so we don't get them confused with the primes p in the Frey curve.

"An elliptic curve is called semistable when reducing it by ℓ results in a good reduction or a multiplicative reduction."

"Sorry, can you remind me what that means?" Tetra asked.

"When you squeeze the elliptic curve $y^2 = x^3 + ax^2 + bx + c$ into the finite field $\mathbb{F}_\ell$, it either has no repeated roots—that's a good reduction—or a doubled root, a multiplicative reduction."

"Cool, thanks."

"When a Frey curve is reduced over ℓ, it will never have a triple root. If it did, that would mean the three solutions $x = 0, -a^p, b^p$ would be congruent modulo the prime ℓ. That, in turn, would mean $-a^p$ and b^p are both multiples of ℓ, but since we know $a \perp b$, that can't be the case. Either way, Frey curves can't have more than two repeated roots, so they're all semistable.

"Wiles proved all semistable elliptic curves are modular, so they can be classified as modular forms, a kind of automorphic form. Wiles' proof provided a bridge between semistable elliptic curves and automorphic forms, so that can be used to associate semistable *Frey* curves with automorphic forms, too.

"There's something called a 'level' defined for automorphic forms, and Serre and Ribet showed that Frey curves were automorphic forms with weight 2 and level 2. But—and this is a big 'but'—automorphic form theory had already shown there *can't be* an automorphic form with weight 2 and level 2."

"A classic contradiction," I said.

Miruka nodded and leaned back in her chair.

"So to sum up," she continued, "if you assume Fermat's last theorem doesn't hold, you can create a Frey curve in the world of elliptic curves. Then you can use Wiles' theorem as your bridge to the world of automorphic forms, taking your Frey curve along to pair it up with the automorphic form it should correspond with. But when you get there, you'll be faced with the reality that no such corresponding automorphic form exists. Tracing back, the only thing that could have gone wrong would be your assumption that Fermat's last theorem doesn't hold."

Tetra slowly raised a hand. "Sorry if this is a weird question, but why can't there be an automorphic form with weight 2 and level 2?"

"That's a wonderful question, and I'm glad you asked," Miruka said. "Unfortunately, it isn't one with a simple answer. To do the job right, we'd have to start with elliptic curves and automorphic forms, then follow Ariadne's thread deep into the wilds of the forest of mathematics. Something I'd love to do, but it's a little late to start today."

As if on cue, one of the café staff appeared and told us they were closing up. I glanced around—we were the last ones there.

"Guess we should get going," I said, collecting the many sheets of paper that covered the table.

"Thank you, Miruka," Tetra said. "That was wonderful."

"Yeah, I'm glad I stayed!" Yuri added.

"That was cool, Miruka," I said. "Thanks."

Miruka's eyes went to the door. "Don't mention it," she said.

"Guess I'll see you at the party?" Yuri asked.

"Oh, that's this Saturday, isn't it," I said.

"Which means finals this week!" Tetra said. "I know I'll need a party!"

10.7 MATH PARTY

10.7.1 *Everyone Arrives*

Somehow we made it through finals, and as planned we gathered at my house to celebrate.

"Thanks for letting us do this here," Miruka said to my mother when she and the others arrived.

"Don't be silly," my mother replied. "This will be fun."

Miruka stared intently at my mother.

"Something wrong?"

"He has your ears," Miruka said.

"H-H-Hi again!" Tetra stuttered, the cold once again obscuring the cause of her stammer.

"Here, let me get your coats," my mother said, taking the girls' coats one by one and hanging them in the small closet in our foyer.

"Yeah, thanks for having us over," Ay-Ay said.

"Not at all! I've been looking forward to hearing you play."

Yuri arrived as my mother was hanging the last coat. "Hey, everybody!"

"What, no boyfriend?" Ay-Ay teased.

"No time," Yuri said, dismissing the notion with a wave of her hand.

"Let's all head into the living room," my mother said, taking charge. "The pizza's already here."

"Pizza? Mom, I told you—"

"Everyone have a drink? Well then, cheers!"

"Mom, I think I'm supposed to—"

My protests went unheeded. Mom was too involved in a conversation with the girls. I sighed and grabbed a slice of pizza.

10.7.2 A Zeta Variation

Ay-Ay rolled her shoulders and flexed her fingers as she sat down at the piano. "Prepare yourselves for a treat," she said.

She hit a single key, then another. The notes came haltingly, from keys seemingly chosen at random. At first I wondered if this was some weird technique she had for checking the piano's tuning, but her pace slowly built and the trickled chaos of notes began to bump into one another, creating subtle harmonies.

Fractured motifs emerged, only to fall back into the foam of their genesis. Gradually, however, an overarching structure took shape and held. The multitude of patterns merged into one, and the discrete become continuous.

I found myself cast upon a churning sea as Ay-Ay pounded out a torrent of sound that swept me through the maelstrom; I could only sit back and let it take me where it would. The storm finally washed me onto a darkened shore where I lay stunned beneath an infinite canopy of stars. The tempest receded, first into crashing waves, then to the white sound of rustling surf, and finally silence.

Slowly the stars faded. Had I been counting them, or searching for constellations?

The room remained quiet for several seconds, and then we burst into applause. I clapped so hard my hands hurt. I didn't know sounds like that could come out of our old piano.

"Amazing, Ay-Ay! What's that piece called?" Tetra asked.

" 'A Zeta Variation,' by none other than our own Miruka."

"You wrote that, Miruka?" Tetra gasped. "What's a zeta variation?"

"It's named after the many zeta functions found throughout mathematics," Miruka replied. "Riemann's zeta function isn't the only one, you know. Zetas are all over the place."

"Didn't you mention one the other day when we were talking about the modularity theorem?"

"I did. Want a quick overview?"

"Sure!" Tetra exclaimed.

"Oh, no. They're slipping into math mode," Ay-Ay said, striking a minor chord as her head sagged forward.

Miruka grabbed a napkin and a nearby pen.

"We start by defining a function $L_E(s)$ that multiplies together a term for each prime that results in a 'good reduction' of an elliptic curve E:"

$$L_E(s) = \prod_{\text{'good reduction' prime } p} \frac{1}{1 - \frac{a(p)}{p^s} + \frac{p}{p^{2s}}}$$

"Let's represent this product as a formal power series like this:"

$$L_F(s) = \sum_{k=1}^{\infty} \frac{a(k)}{k^s}$$

"Next, use the $a(k)$ sequence to create a q-expansion:"

$$F(q) = \sum_{k=1}^{\infty} a(k)q^k$$

"When we do this, $F(q)$ is an automorphic form with weight 2. $L_E(s)$ is a zeta function associated with the algebraic elliptic curve. $L_F(s)$ is a zeta function associated with the analytic automorphic form. The modularity theorem says all elliptic curves can be associated with an automorphic form, via a zeta function:"

Algebraic zeta = Analytic zeta

$$\prod_{\text{'good reduction' prime } p} \frac{1}{1 - \frac{a(p)}{p^s} + \frac{p}{p^{2s}}} = \sum_{\text{positive integer } k} \frac{a(k)}{k^s}$$

"Now look at the Euler product of the Riemann zeta function, which says that this product over the primes and this sum over the natural numbers is the same thing:"

Euler product = Riemann zeta function

$$\prod_{\text{prime } p} \frac{1}{1 - \frac{1}{p^s}} = \sum_{\text{positive integer } k} \frac{1}{k^s}$$

"Pretty similar, right?"

Tetra squinted at the equations. "Yeah, I guess you can say they're similar. Calling them both zeta functions seems like a stretch, though."

"Yuri," my mother whispered, "are you following any of this?"

"Not a word," Yuri whispered back.

"What is all this weird math for?" my mother asked her.

"No clue. But isn't it *cool*?"

* * *

"Anybody care if I scarf the last piece?" I said, reaching for the pizza.

"Hey, I was gonna eat that!" Yuri complained.

"All yours, then."

"Such a gentleman," Yuri said, picking off pepperonis.

"Oh, Miruka, I'd been meaning to tell you," Tetra said. "I think I finally understand your solution to the primitive Pythagorean triples problem!"

Yuri perked up. "Primitive Pythagorean triples? What're those?"

What can I say? We knew how to party.

10.7.3   The Fruits of Solitude

At some point someone had dimmed the lights. Ay-Ay was playing a moody jazz rendition of some Bach piece.

Tetra drifted into her usual half-to-herself lilt. "I read that Wiles basically locked himself in his study for seven years while he worked on his proof. Seven years! I can't even imagine... You'd think he'd have gotten the answer a lot faster if he'd worked on it with some friends."

"There's something to be said for realizing a dream on your own," Miruka said. "Of course, he didn't really do it alone. Mathematics is built up layer by layer. No one's smart enough to come up with the whole thing on their own."

"Maybe," I said, "but most great ideas come from a single head, so solitude is important, too. I know Yuri likes to work by herself, but sometimes you have to— Uh, where'd Yuri go?"

I looked around the room and found her huddled in a corner, writing something.

My mother came in with a tray of tea. "Sounds like giving birth," she said. "Your husband is there, you're surrounded by doctors and nurses, but in the end it's all up to you."

"Mathematicians write papers like lonely people write letters, I guess," Miruka said. "But letters to the future, and to persons unknown."

"That doesn't sound so lonely to me," Tetra said. "I think giving gifts like that, to people you don't even know, sounds pretty wonderful."

"Sure," I agreed. "We wouldn't have Fermat's last theorem if his son hadn't passed on his father's words."

"History is a chain of miracles," Tetra concluded.

10.7.4 Yuri's Realization

"I got it! I got it!" Yuri shouted from her corner. She leapt up and dashed to where I was sitting.

"All you have to do is line up the squares!"

"What are you talking about?"

Yuri pointed at the paper clutched in her hand.

"The problem you guys told me about! Finding if there are an infinite number of primitive Pythagorean triples! All you have to do is line up the squares and subtract!"

1		4		9		16		25		36	$\cdots$	squares
	3		5		7		9		11		$\cdots$	subtract

"You get a bunch of odd numbers, right?"

"Sure. That's called a sequence of differences."

"Brilliantly done, Yuri," Miruka said.

"What is?" I asked.

Yuri gave Miruka a sly smile.

"Already see what I'm doing, huh?"

"I don't," I said. "What is this?"

"These subtractions—what did you call them, a sequence of differences?—they have all the odd numbers, right? That means they also have all the *square* odd numbers. Like the 9 here."

Yuri pointed at the 9 in the upper sequence she'd written.

"That's a square of an odd number—3^2, right? So when you add an odd square to a square, you get the next square. Won't that give you infinite primitive Pythagorean triples?"

"Yuri, I still don't see what you're trying to say."

Yuri rolled her eyes and shoved the paper at me.

"Look:"

1		4		9		<u>16</u>		<u>25</u>		36	$\cdots$
	3		5		7		<u>9</u>		11		$\cdots$

$$9 = 25 - 16 \qquad \text{from the sequence of differences}$$
$$3^2 = 5^2 - 4^2 \qquad \text{represent as a square}$$
$$3^2 + 4^2 = 5^2 \qquad \text{add } 4^2 \text{ to both sides}$$

"That's how you find the primitive Pythagorean triple $(3, 4, 5)$. It's not just a coincidence it shows up, either. It has to, because every odd square shows up in the sequence of differences. And that means you can find an infinite number of (a, b, c)s like you want!"

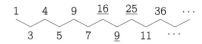

"Argh! I don't know how to say it in the right mathy way..."

"No, I get it now," I said. "You're using infinitely many odd squares to make sure you're covering infinitely many primitive Pythagorean triples."

"A weak formulation," Miruka said, "and you've ignored the requirement that the elements are relatively prime. But you hit the high points."

Yuri turned to Miruka. "Will you finish this for me?"

"I'm sure your cousin would love to."

"Sure," I said, and began explaining.

"Start off with a sequence of squares:"

$$\cdots, (2k)^2, (2k+1)^2, \cdots$$

"You can write your sequence of differences as $(2k+1)^2 - (2k)^2$:"

$$\begin{aligned}
(2k+1)^2 - (2k)^2 &= (4k^2 + 4k + 1) - (2k)^2 &&\text{expand } (2k+1)^2 \\
&= (4k^2 + 4k + 1) - 4k^2 &&\text{expand } (2k)^2 \\
&= 4k + 1 &&4k^2\text{s cancel}
\end{aligned}$$

"Here's how you were showing that before:"

$$\underbrace{(2k)^2 \quad (2k+1)^2}_{4k+1} \quad \cdots$$

"When you replace the k in $4k + 1$ with an appropriate number, you get an odd square back. Let's use $4k + 1 = (2j - 1)^2$, in other words $b = 2j - 1$, as an example:"

$$\begin{aligned}
4k + 1 &= (2j - 1)^2 &&\text{represent as an odd square} \\
&= 4j^2 - 4j + 1 &&\text{expand} \\
&= 4j(j - 1) + 1 &&\text{factor out a } 4j
\end{aligned}$$

"So if you let $k = j(j - 1)$, then $4k + 1$ will be an odd square. If $j = 2$ then $k = 2$, so in that case $4k + 1 = 9 = 3^2$. That means with $j = 2$ we get the Pythagorean triple $(a, b, c) = (4, 3, 5)$. When $j = 3$ you get $k = 6$, so $(a, b, c) = (12, 5, 13)$. When $j = 4$, $k = 12$, giving you $(a, b, c) = (24, 7, 25)$, and so on. Every time you increase j, you get a new Pythagorean triple."

"But not a *primitive* Pythagorean triple?" Yuri asked.

"Well, they are, but we haven't proven it yet. To do that, we have to show that any pair from among (a, b, c) are relatively prime."

"Show me how to do that."

"Sure. First, we know $c \perp a$, because $c = a + 1$."

"How's that?"

"Because if c and a had a common prime factor p, then $c - a$ would be a multiple of p. But $c - a = 1$, so they must be relatively prime."

"Okay, didn't know that. How about b and c?"

"First, let's use g as the greatest common divisor of b and c. Then we could say $b = gB$ and $c = gC$, and do this:"

$$a^2 + b^2 = c^2 \qquad \text{because } a, b, c \text{ is a Pythagorean triple}$$
$$a^2 = c^2 - b^2 \qquad \text{move the } b^2$$
$$a^2 = (gC)^2 - (gB)^2 \qquad \text{substitute } b = gB, c = gC$$
$$a^2 = g^2C^2 - g^2B^2 \qquad \text{simplify}$$
$$a^2 = g^2 (C^2 - B^2) \qquad \text{factor out a } g^2$$

"The last line here says that a^2 is a multiple of g^2, which means a is a multiple of g. But since $c = gC$, c is a multiple of g, too."

"So g is a divisor of both a and c," Yuri said.

"Right. But don't forget, we already know $c \perp a$, so their common divisor g is 1. That means the common divisor g between b and c is 1, so $b \perp c$. You can also do basically the same thing to show $a \perp b$."

"So everything is relatively prime with everything else, which means this Pythagorean triple *is* primitive."

"Hey," Tetra said. "All of these are right triangles where the difference in the length of two of the legs is 1! I *told* you that looked like some kind of clue."

"Looks like you were right. Huh... And I thought it was just because of how you were searching for them."

"Yuri,," Miruka said. "Get over here."

"Um...okay." Yuri started toward Miruka.

I held up a hand to stop her.

"You might not want to do that," I said.

10.7.5 No Coincidence

Ay-Ay played a few more songs while the rest of us talked and did math. A tame party by any standard, but we were having fun.

I stepped out to use the restroom, but instead of going back I stopped in the hallway. I leaned back against the wall and sank to the floor.

I couldn't shake the feeling I'd made a fool of myself trying to teach Yuri. I took the lead when we told her about primitive Pythagorean triples, showing her how to get the general form, and even how to parameterize them using t. I didn't think she'd gotten much from it, but a few minutes alone in the corner and she'd come up with a solution I'd never even considered. Not only that, but it was something Tetra might have discovered too, if I hadn't shut her down when she mentioned the clue she'd found.

That's no way to teach somebody.

Tetra came out of the living room to find me sitting there, head between my hands.

"You okay?" she asked.

"I'm fine. Just doing a little soul searching."

"Hmmm... If you say so."

Her frown melted into a sly smile.

"You ever figure out the mystery of my 'M'?"

"Huh? Oh, the charm on your pencil case. No, I didn't follow up on it, but I'm sure he's a very nice guy."

Tetra laughed.

"It's not a *guy*, it's a sigma. Or at least it's supposed to be—I looked everywhere for a real one, but I finally settled on an 'M' instead."

"I'd love to see the store that sold sigma charms."

"Maybe I'll go to Greece someday. They're bound to have them there."

I looked up at her. "I'm sorry I never said anything about that day in the library. I just—"

Tetra waved both hands to stop me.

"Don't." She swallowed and continued. "I used to think that the people we meet, the friends we make, all that was just random chance.

But now I know it isn't. Getting to know you was...it was a kind of miracle."

With that, she turned and continued down the hallway, hands pressed to her cheeks.

10.7.6 Silent Night

"Hey, it's almost Christmas!" my mother half shouted. "We should close with a Christmas carol! Ay-Ay, do you know Silent Night?"

"Do I know Silent Night, she asks."

As we stumbled through the song, enough of us remembering the lyrics to avoid everyone humming through the same section, I reflected back on the year. The events of a single life may be trivial in the grand scheme, but all in all it had been quite a year. I couldn't wait to see what the next one would bring.

The song came to an end, and we gave each other a hearty round of applause.

"Clean up time!" my mother announced. "Then I'll send our only knight to escort the ladies to the station. And if you girls can keep his mouth shut, he'll be a silent knight!" She tittered at her own joke.

"Mom..."

10.8   THEY'RE DOING MATH IN ANDROMEDA

We finished cleaning and trooped off to the train station. The sun had set, but I was disappointed to see an overcast sky concealing the stars. We walked in darkness, white puffs of breath trailing our heads.

"That was a really cool proof, Yuri," Tetra said.

"Heh, thanks. Come to think of it, I guess it was my first ever."

"And one I missed," I said. "But not the first."

"Awww," said Yuri. "I'll let you rub my head if it'll make you feel better."

I laughed, but I took her up on the offer anyway.

"I wonder if there's an alternate proof to Fermat's last theorem?" Tetra asked.

"No elementary one," Miruka said, turning back to look at us. "At least, that's what mathematicians think today, and they're probably right. But who knows what the future holds? Maybe the mathematics of the future will lead to a simpler solution."

"You never know," I said. "Somebody had to discover negative numbers, and complex numbers. Who can say what's out there, waiting to be found?"

"What, whole new kinds of math?" Tetra said.

"Sure," Miruka said. "At one point, using the Pythagorean theorem to create right triangles was cutting edge mathematics, but today we learn it in grade school. The solutions to second degree equations, complex numbers, matrices, differentiation... All that was deep stuff not so long ago, and now it's homework for teenagers. Maybe someday Fermat's last theorem will be an exercise for fifth graders."

"I hope they don't ask me for help with their homework," said Tetra.

"We have to live in the present," Miruka continued, "so we can only develop the math that's projected onto our 'now.' But there's lots more out there, scattered along the timeline of history."

Something about her words resonated deep inside me. My feet stopped. A beam of light from the past pierced my mind and swept through me into the future. For an instant, I realized the scale of time and space.

The millions of stars that form the Milky Way are no tiny things. Each is a colossal object, separated from its neighbor by hundreds, even thousands of light years. The smallness, the closeness—it's all a trick of projection. The photons that hit my retina when I look up at the night sky have traveled unimaginable distances for inconceivable eons, just to play tricks in my brain. Somewhere out there, the residents of another world look up at a completely different field of stars and teach their young about constellations we can only imagine.

But are they teaching a completely different math? If aliens count, won't they stumble across prime numbers? Won't they attach a special significance to even divisions? And won't that lead them to relative primes? Won't they see how to use congruence to fold up infinities?

Fermat's last theorem burns bright in our mathematical firmament. Fertile worlds orbit it, carrying the seas and jungles of entirely new branches of mathematics, awaiting further exploration. We've sent our first tentative probes there, but our search has only just begun. Might we someday be joined by travelers from other worlds, drawn to this shining beacon as we were?

Is mathematics the language of the cosmos, transcending distance, impervious to time?

Realizing I'd fallen behind, the others turned to look at me.

"Drop something?" Yuri asked.

"I had a vision of what math's like in Andromeda," I said.

"Do they do it in libraries there too?" Tetra asked.

"I'll bet we're pretty much the same, modulo the planet we live on," Miruka said, looking up at the blanket of clouds overhead.

The others followed her gaze.

"Look!" Tetra shouted.

"Nice timing," said Ay-Ay. She began whistling.

I looked up to see that the heavens were having their own math party, dropping an infinitude of hexagonal crystals down on us.

"Snow!" squealed Yuri.

* * *

We had found mathematics, and through mathematics we had found each other. There were things we could do, and things we couldn't. Things we knew, and things we didn't. All was as it should be.

Another year stretched ahead. A year of counting stars and connecting them into constellations. Another timeless year with my friends and the mathematics that bound us together.

Epilogue

The silver of the Milky Way... The warmth of a hand... A soft, wavering voice... Sunlight shining in her hair, one moment gold, the next chestnut brown... She turns, smiling, and says...

"Are you asleep?"

"Hrumph?"

"You *were* asleep. Right there at your desk. Admit it."

"I was just...thinking. Deeply. You have an answer already?"

"I do. There *are* an infinite number of rational points on the circle $x^2 + y^2 = 1$."

"Good. And the other problem?"

"There are *no* rational points on the circle $x^2 + y^2 = 3$."

"Very nice."

"I never knew circles could be so deep."

"Anything that involves infinities usually is. It's hard to pin down the true form of things like that. Like when they thought they had a proof of Fermat's last theorem back in the twentieth century. It was infinities that tripped them up then, too."

The girl eyed the teacher with suspicion.

"What do you mean, *thought* they had a proof?"

"Didn't you hear? They found a counterexample."

"No way..."

The teacher handed her a card.

A counterexample to Fermat's last theorem (?)

$$951413^7 + 853562^7 = 1005025^7$$

705640613575942055661379802908637985206717
$+$330099986418375923201140352082288543214208
$=$1035740599994317978862520154990926528420925

"Something doesn't feel right," she said. "Hang on, let me do some test calculations from the ones units."

She went to the whiteboard and started writing:

$$951413^7 \equiv 3^7 \equiv 2187 \equiv 7 \qquad (\text{mod } 10)$$
$$853562^7 \equiv 2^7 \equiv 128 \equiv 8 \qquad (\text{mod } 10)$$
$$1005025^7 \equiv 5^7 \equiv 78125 \equiv 5 \qquad (\text{mod } 10)$$

"And $7+8 \equiv 5$ (mod 10), so that checks out..." she said, frowning as she wrote:

$$951413^7 + 853562^7 \equiv 1005025^7 \quad (\text{mod } 10)$$

"Convinced yet?"

"No, you're up to something. What's the catch?"

She furrowed her brow, then laughed.

"951413, huh? And I suppose it's just a coincidence that's the first six digits of pi?"

"Foiled again," he said, pulling a second card out of his desk:

$951413^7 + 853562^7 = 10357405999943179788625201549909265284209\underline{25}$

$1005025^7 = 10357097264618589680992322822351135253906\underline{25}$

"I'll bet you spent hours on this."

"Not *hours*. Well, not many, at least."

Her eyes moved to a poster on the wall next to the whiteboard.

"Hey, that's new. What is it?"

"Those are the points on the elliptic curve $y^2 = x^3 - x$ after reduction modulo 23."

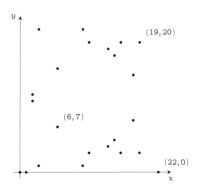

Points on $y^2 = x^3 - x$ **over** $\mathbb{F}_{23}$

She chuckled at some unspoken joke.

"Is there a pattern to this?"

The teacher shrugged.

"I don't know. Maybe you should plot the points yourself and try connecting them. Who knows what you'll find?"

"Maybe I will...but not today. See ya tomorrow!" She shouldered her backpack.

"Oh, I heard it's going to snow tonight."

"Thanks for the warning."

"Later!"

She flicked her fingers one-one-two-three, and he waved five in response as she ran out the door.

"Snow," he muttered.

He leaned back in his chair, his mind dancing with snow, stars, infinity, and friends from long ago.

> Nor do I hesitate to proclaim that within this book there are contained many things which are clearly new, but also some sources have been uncovered from which many significant further discoveries can be drawn.

LEONHARD EULER
Introduction to Analysis of the Infinite

Afterword

Thank you for reading *Math Girls 2: Fermat's Last Theorem*.
This book is the sequel to *Math Girls*, which I wrote in 2007, the
300th anniversary of Euler's birth. Writing these books allowed me to
enjoy through its characters the thrill of discovery that mathematics
provides, and to once again marvel at what a wonderful thing it is. I
hope that you have experienced something similar.

As with the previous book, this is a story about youth and
mathematics. Lots and lots of mathematics. So much, in fact, that
my publisher and I were quite surprised at the reception the first
book had. It is only because of the support from my readers that this
sequel became possible, so please allow me to express my sincerest
gratitude.

As before, this book was created using LaTeX 2_ε and the AMS
Euler font. Also as before, Haruhiko Okumura's book *Introduction
to Creating Beautiful Documents with LaTeX 2_ε* was an invaluable
aid during layout, and I thank him for it. I would also like to thank
Kazuhiro Okuma (a.k.a. tDB) for his elementary mathematics hand-
out macro, emath, which I used to create the diagrams. I would also

like to thank the following persons for proofreading and giving me invaluable feedback.

"ayko," Hiroaki Hanada, Tatsuya Igarashi, Tetsuya Ishiu, Toshiki Kawashima, Masahide Maehara, Kohei Matsuoka, Kiyoshi Miyake, Kenta Murata (mrkn), Shunichi Shinohara, Tamami Soma, Shohei Takeuchi, Hal Tasaki, Ryuhei Uehara, Kenji Yamaguchi, Tsutomu Yano, Yuko Yoshida, Kanaya Yasoo (Gascon Labs)

I would like to thank my readers and the visitors to my website, and my friends for their constant prayers.

I would like to thank my editor, Kimio Nozawa, for his continuous support during the long process of creating this book.

I thank the many readers of *Math Girls* for their support and comments, many of which have made me happy to the point of tears.

I thank my dearest wife and my two sons. Special thanks to my oldest son for his comments while reading the manuscript.

I dedicate this book to Pierre de Fermat for the wonderful problem he left us, to Andrew Wiles for his dedication and solution, and to all mathematicians, everywhere.

Finally, thank *you* for reading my book. I hope that someday, somewhere, our paths shall cross again.

Hiroshi Yuki

2008

http://www.hyuki.com/girl/

Recommended Reading

"Here's a key to the study. If that
doesn't suffice, go to the library. Half
the answers you seek lie in books."
"Only half? Where are the others?"
"Waiting to be discovered."

YASUKO SAKATA
Basil's Elegant Life

This section is divided up as follows:

· General reading

· Recommended for high school students

· Recommended for college students

· Recommended for graduate students and beyond

· Web pages

These classifications are meant only as a guideline. Some texts may
be more or less challenging depending on the level of the reader.

[Note: The following references include all items
that were listed in the original Japanese version of
Math Girls 2: Fermat's Last Theorem. Most of
those references were to Japanese sources. Where
an English version of a reference exists, it is included in the entry.]

292 Fermat's Last Theorem

GENERAL READING

[1] Yuki, H. (2011). *Math Girls*. Bento Books. Published in Japan as *Sūgaku gāru* (Softbank Creative, 2007)

> The story of two girls and a boy who meet in high school and work together after school on mathematics unlike anything they find in class.

[2] Singh, S. (1998). *Fermat's Enigma: The Epic Quest to Solve the World's Greatest Mathematical Problem*. Anchor. Translated by Kaoru Aoki as *Ferumā no saishū teiri: Pyutagorasu ni hajimari, wairuzu ga shōmei suru made* (Shinchosha, 2000).

> A dramatic presentation of how Fermat's last theorem came about and its history through Wiles' proof. Especially moving was the section related to the discovery of the error in Wiles' intial attempt at a proof and his struggle to overcome that setback.

[3] Takagi, T. (1995). *Kinsei sūgaku shidan* [Historical Tales from Modern Mathematics]. Iwanami Shoten.

> An interesting treatment of the lives and accomplishments of many modern mathematicians, including Gauss, Cauchy, Dirichlet, Galois, and Abel.

RECOMMENDED FOR HIGH SCHOOL STUDENTS

[4] Matsuda, S. and the Tsuyama National College of Technology Math Club. (2008). *Jū-ichi kara hajimaru sūgaku: k-pasukaru sankakkei, k-fibonacchi sūretsu, cho-ōgonkinsū* [Math Starts at Eleven: k-Pascal Triangles, k-Fibonacci Numbers, and Ultra-Golden Numbers]. Tokyo Shuppan.

> A book that summarizes the research of four real-life math girls and math boys who formed

a mathematics circle at their school. Topics include Pascal's triangle and the Fibonacci numbers. A great starting point for students and educators interested in forming a club of their own. The quote at the end of Chapter 7 came from this book.

[5] Serizawa, S. (2002). *Sosū nyūmon: Keisan shinagara rikai dekiru* [An Introduction to Primes: Understanding Through Calculations]. Kodansha.

This book contains many example problems from elementary number theory. A great book to work through while working out the problems and proofs yourself. I used this book as a reference for the definitions of groups, rings, and fields in Chapter 7.

[6] Kurokawa, N. (2006). *Oirā, Rīman, Ramanujan* [Euler, Riemann, and Ramanujan]. Iwatani Shoten.

A book about the mysterious world of the zeta function, focusing on the work of Euler, Riemann, and Ramanujan. This book gave me the prism metaphor in Chapter 10, and the comparison between algebraic and analytic zetas.

[7] Kobayashi, S. (2003). *Nattoku suru Oirā to Ferumā* [Understanding Euler and Fermat]. Kodansha.

A collection of interesting topics from number theory. I referenced this book for the proof of FLT(4) in Chapter 8.

[8] Adachi, N. (1995). *Ferumā no daiteiri ga toketa!: Oirā kara wairuzu no shōmei made* [Fermat's Great Theorem, Proved!: From Euler to Wiles' Proof]. Kodansha.

Fermat's last theorem from the perspective of elliptic curves. This is an equation-heavy book, but it's written so that you can skip over the equations and still get the gist of things. I used this book as a reference for the relation between the unit circle and Pythagorean triples in Chapter 2.

[9] Adachi, N. (2006). *Ferumā no daiteiri: Seisūron no genryū* [Fermat's Great Theorem: The Headwaters of Integer Number Theory]. Chikuma Gakugei Bunko.

Biographical sketches, the historical background, and research areas of several mathematicians, and a multi-dimensional treatment of Fermat's last theorem. The balance between text and math is superb, making this a good read for those interested in the mathematical details. I used this book as a reference for the historical background of Fermat's last theorem in Chapter 10.

[10] Adachi, N. (1986). *Ferumā wo yomu* [Reading Fermat]. Nippon Hyoronsha.

An explanation of page 48 of Diophantus' *Arithmetica*, the page on which Fermat wrote his famous last theorem. I used this book as a reference for the descrption of *Arithmetica* in Chapter 10.

[11] Shiga, K. (1994). *Sūgaku ga sodatte iku monogatari (dai-ni shū): Kaisetsusei, jissū kara fukusosū e* [The Stories that Mathematics Tells (Week 2): Analyticity, From Real to Complex Numbers]. Iwanami Shoten.

This book explains mathematical topics using dialogues between a student and a teacher. Also touches on the personality of mathematicians. A relaxed, fun read. I used this book as a reference for the discussion of complex numbers in Chapter 5.

[12] Yano, K. and Takahashi, M. (1990). *Kaitei-ban fukusosū (Monogurafu 9)* [Complex Numbers, Revised Edition (Monograph 9)]. Kagaku Shinkō Shinsha.

A textbook for high school students. The *Monograph* series is a good resource for high school students wanting to go deeper into specific topics. I used this book as a reference for the discussion of products of complex numbers in Chapter 5.

[13] Fukuda, K. and Ishii, T. (2001). *Sūgaku wo kimeru ronshōryoku* [It's the Proofs That Make Math]. Tokyo Shuppan.

A book that helps readers develop proof-writing skills. Proof by contradiction and mathematical induction are of course covered, as are a number of common pitfalls. I used this book as a reference for the alternate proof that $\sqrt{2}$ is irrational in Chapter 4.

[14] Kurita, K. and Fukuda, K. (1998). *Masutā obu seisū* [Master of Integers]. Tokyo Shuppan.

This textbook covers a number of topics related to integers, including prime factorization, greatest common divisors, Euler's totient function, relative primeness, and Pythagorean triples. I referenced this book for the alternate proof that $\sqrt{2}$ is irrational in Chapter 4, and for the lattice point problem in Chapter 5.

[15] Yoshida, T. (2000). *Kyosū no jōcho—Chūgakusei kara no zenpōi dokugaku-hō* [The Moods of Imaginary Numbers—All About Self-Study From Middle School and Beyond]. Tokai University Press.

A massive volume on becoming self-motivated in "learning by doing" from the very basics, with a special emphasis on math and physics. A wonderfully interesting book.

RECOMMENDED FOR COLLEGE STUDENTS

[16] *Iwanami sūgaku nyūmon jiten* [The Iwanami Dictionary of Elementary Mathematics]. Iwanami Shoten.

A dictionary with easy-to-understand definitions of mathematical terms.

[17] Takagi, T. (1971). *Shotō seisūron kōgi, dai-ni-ban* [Lectures on Elementary Number Theory, Second Edition]. Kyoritsu Shuppan.

A classic book on number theory.

[18] Kato, K. (1995). *Kaiketsu! Ferumā no saishū teiri: Gendai sūron no kiseki* [Fermat's Last Theorem, Solved!: The Path to Modern Number Theory]. Nippon Hyoronsha.

A book about Fermat's last theorem and related mathematical topics. This book is a collection of a series of articles that appeared in the magazine *Mathematics Seminar Monthly*. A fantastical description of advanced mathematics that uses numerous metaphors and even fables to explain its topics.

[19] Fujisaki, G., Morita, Y., and Yamamoto Y. (2004). *Sūron e no shuppatsu, zōho-ban* [Heading for Number Theory, Expanded Edition]. Nippon Hyoronsha.

A compact treatment of topics from elementary number theory to Fermat's last theorem. I used this book as a reference when writing Chapter 10.

[20] Graham, R., Knuth, D., and Patashnik, O. (1994). *Concrete Mathematics: A Foundation for Computer Science (2nd Edition)*. Addison-Wesley Professional. Translated by Arisawa, M., Yasumura, M., Akino, T., and Ishihata, K. as *Konpyūtā no sūgaku* (Kyoritsu Shuppan, 1993).

> A textbook on discrete mathematics, with finding sums as its theme. I referenced this book for the representation of prime exponents in Chapter 3, and for the a ⊥ b notation for relatively prime numbers.

[21] Gries, D. and Schneider, F. (1993). *A Logical Approach to Discrete Math.* Springer. Translated by Shibagaki, W., Shimizu, K., and Tanaka, Y. as *Konpyūtā no tame no sūgaku: Ronriteki apurōchi* (Nippon Hyoronsha, 2001).

> A book on discrete mathematics with the goal of learning to use logic as a tool for thought.

[22] Davis, P. and Hersh, R. (1999). *The Mathematical Experience.* Mariner Books. Translated by Shibagaki, W., Shimizu, K., and Tanaka, Y. as *Sūgakuteki keiken* (Morikita Shuppan, 1986).

> A book that examines mathematics itself from a number of angles. At times the topics become so broad that things become hard to follow, but a very thought-provoking title nonetheless.

[23] Silverman, J. and Tate, J. (2010). *Rational Points on Elliptic Curves.* Springer. Translated by Adachi, N. *et al* as *Daenkyokusen Nyūmon* (Springer Fairlark Tokyo, 1995).

> An introduction to elliptic curves, focusing on aspects related to number theory.

[24] Euler, L. (translation by Blanton, J.) (1988). *Introduction to Analysis of the Infinite: Book I*. Springer. Translated by Takase, M. as *Oirā no mugen kaiseki* (Kaimeisha, 2001).

[25] Euler, L. (translation by Blanton, J.) (1989). *Introduction to Analysis of the Infinite: Book II*. Springer. Translated by Takase, M. as *Oirā no kaiseki kika* (Kaimeisha, 2005).

> A book about infinite series (Vol. 1) and coordinates, curves, and functions (Vol. 2), written by Euler himself. Euler gives many concrete examples, showing the importance he placed in them.

RECOMMENDED FOR GRADUATE STUDENTS AND BEYOND

[26] Kato, K., Kurokawa, N., and Saito, T. (2005). *Sūron I: Fermat no yume to ruitairon* [Number Theory I: Fermat's Dream and Class Field Theory]. Iwanami Shoten.

> A textbook on number theory. Written such that you get a solid education on the topics covered, while still experiencing the mystery and thrills that number theory can provide. A huge help when writing this book, I referenced it when writing Chapters 2–4, 7, and 10.

[27] Kurokawa, N., Kurihara, M. and Saito, T. (2005). *Sūron II: Iwasawa riron to hokei keishiki* [Number Theory II: Iwasawa Theory and Automorphic Forms]. Iwanami Shoten.

> The continuation of *Number Theory I*. I referenced it when writing Chapters 2–4, 7, and 10.

[28] Taniyama, Y. (1994). *Taniyama Yutaka zenshū, zōho-ban* [The Complete Writings of Yutaka Taniyama, Expanded Edition]. Nippon Hyoronsha.

> The collected writings of Yutaka Taniyama, co-creator of the Taniyama-Shimura conjecture (now the modularity theorem). Contains his papers, reviews, essays, correspondences, and the Taniyama problem that was later formulated as the modularity theorem.

[29] Andrew Wiles, "Modular Elliptic Curves and Fermat's Last Theorem", *The Annals of Mathematics*, 2nd Ser., Vol. 141, No. 3 (May, 1995), pp. 443–551.

> The paper in which Wiles proved Fermat's last theorem. Given that the proof spans 5 chapters over 109 pages, if Fermat did indeed have a proof it's no surprise he couldn't fit it in the margins of a book!

WEBSITES

[30] Frey, G.: "The Way to the Proof of Fermat's Last Theorem". http://citeseerx.ist.psu.edu/viewdoc/summary?doi=10.1.1.27.6567.

> A history of the solution to Fermat's last theorem written by Gerhard Frey, inventor of Frey curves. I referenced this paper when planning the structure of Chapter 10.

[31] Yuki, H.: *Math Girls* http://www.hyuki.com/girl/en.html.

> The English version of the author's *Math Girls* web site.

"Wait, the *hard* books are the ones you read for *fun*?"
"Learning isn't fun if you don't test your limits."

HIROSHI YUKI
Math Girls: Fermat's Last Theorem

Index

≡, 151

A
abelian group, 134
absolute value, 95
algebra, 253
algebraic ring of integers, 245
analysis, 253
argument, 95
associativity, 124
automorphic form, 263
axiom, 90

B
Bachet, 243
base, 224

C
Cauchy, Augustin-Louis, 244
clock math, 9
closure, 124
commutative property, 134
complex number plane, 91
component, 62

congruence, 151
contradiction, 35
coprime, 20

D
Dedekind, Richard, 245
Diophantus, 243
Dirichlet, Johann, 183
Dirichlet, Peter, 244

E
e, 218
equivalence, 151
Euler, Leonhard, 89, 183
Euler's formula, 219
Euler's identity, 217
exponent rules, 65, 184, 224
exponents, 222

F
factor, 46
field, 174
finite field, 178
formal power series, 266

Frey curve, 270
Frey, Gerhard, 246
fundamental theorem of algebra, 88

G
Gaussian integer, 107
generating function, 268
geometry, 253
Germain, Sophie, 244
greatest common divisor, 19, 55
group, 127
group operation table, 130

I
i, 218
ideal (ring), 245
ideal number, 245
identity element, 125
imaginary axis, 91
induction, 16
inverse element, 126
isomorphism, 134

K
Kronecker, 3
Kummer, Ernst, 245

L
Lamé, Gabriel, 183, 244
lattice point, 101
lattice points, 108
least common multiple, 55
Legendre, Adrien-Marie, 183, 244

M
mod, 150, 154

modular, 271
modular form, 263
modulus, 151
multiplicative form, 46

N
negation, 73
negative numbers, 89
number theory, 21

O
operation, 122, 124
orthogonal, 67

P
parity, 35, 45
Pascal, Blaise, 89
pigeonhole principal, 105
polar form, 95
power series, 228
prime factorization, 46, 59, 62
prime factors, 59
prime number, 8
primitive Pythagorean triple, 27
proof by contradiction, 39, 77
Proof by infinite descent, 210
proposition, 72
Pythagorean theorem, 26
Pythagorean triple, 27

Q
q-expansion, 265
quotient, 146

R
rational point, 29
real axis, 91

reduced residue class group,
        170
reduction, 258
regular prime, 245
relatively prime, 20, 46, 56
remainder, 147
residue ring, 174
Ribet, Kenneth, 250, 271
ring, 170
ring axioms, 171
ring of integers, 173

S
sequence of prime exponents,
        62
Serre, Jean-Pierre, 250, 271
set, 122
similar triangles, 94
sine curve, 222
square number, 8

T
table, 16
Taniyama-Shimura conjecture,
        245
Taylor, Richard, 246

U
uniqueness of prime factoriza-
        tion, 41, 62, 245
unit, 109
unit circle, 29

W
well-defined, 226
Wiles, Andrew, 182, 246

Other works by Hiroshi Yuki

(in Japanese)

- *The Essence of C Programming*, Softbank, 1993 (revised 1996)

- *C Programming Lessons, Introduction*, Softbank, 1994 (Second edition, 1998)

- *C Programming Lessons, Grammar*, Softbank, 1995

- *An Introduction to CGI with Perl, Basics*, Softbank Publishing, 1998

- *An Introduction to CGI with Perl, Applications*, Softbank Publishing, 1998

- *Java Programming Lessons (Vols. I & II)*, Softbank Publishing, 1999 (revised 2003)

- *Perl Programming Lessons, Basics*, Softbank Publishing, 2001

- *Learning Design Patterns with Java*, Softbank Publishing, 2001 (revised and expanded, 2004)

- *Learning Design Patterns with Java, Multithreading Edition*, Softbank Publishing, 2002

- *Hiroshi Yuki's Perl Quizzes*, Softbank Publishing, 2002

- *Introduction to Cryptography Technology*, Softbank Publishing, 2003

- *Hiroshi Yuki's Introduction to Wikis*, Impress, 2004

- *Math for Programmers*, Softbank Publishing, 2005

- *Java Programming Lessons, Revised and Expanded (Vols. I & II)*, Softbank Creative, 2005

- *Learning Design Patterns with Java, Multithreading Edition, Revised Second Edition*, Softbank Creative, 2006

- *Revised C Programming Lessons, Introduction*, Softbank Creative, 2006

- *Revised C Programming Lessons, Grammar*, Softbank Creative, 2006

- *Revised Perl Programming Lessons, Basics*, Softbank Creative, 2006

- *Introduction to Refactoring with Java*, Softbank Creative, 2007

- *Math Girls*, Softbank Creative, 2007

- *Math Girls / Fermat's Last Theorem*, Softbank Creative, 2008

- *Revised Introduction to Cryptography Technology*, Softbank Creative, 2008

- *Math Girls Comic (Vols. I & II)*, Media Factory, 2009

- *Math Girls / Gödel's Incompleteness Theorems*, Softbank Creative, 2009

- *Math Girls / Randomized Algorithms*, Softbank Creative, 2011

- *Math Girls / Galois Theory*, Softbank Creative, 2012

510 -FIC
9|21

Made in the USA
Monee, IL
05 March 2020